DOUBLE REVENGE IN YELLOWSTONE

ALL PROCEEDS FROM
THE SALE OF THIS NOVEL
ARE SHARED EQUALLY
BETWEEN TWO
CHARITABLE ORGANIZATIONS:

HABITAT FOR HUMANITY
&
COMPASSION INTERNATIONAL.

ON BEHALF OF THESE CHARITABLE
ORGANIZATIONS, THANK-YOU FOR
YOUR PURCHASE OF THIS NOVEL.

Raymond N. Kieft

DOUBLE REVENGE IN YELLOWSTONE

Yellowstone Mystery Series
A Parker Williams Novel

Raymond N. Kieft

authorHOUSE®

AuthorHouse™
1663 Liberty Drive
Bloomington, IN 47403
www.authorhouse.com
Phone: 1-800-839-8640

First published by AuthorHouse   10/12/2011

ISBN: 978-1-4670-4372-4 (sc)
ISBN: 978-1-4670-4371-7 (hc)
ISBN: 978-1-4670-4370-0 (ebk)

Library of Congress Control Number: 2011917969

Printed in the United States of America

OTHER NOVELS IN THE YELLOWSTONE MYSTERY SERIES

. . . . Firehole River Murder

. . . . Old Faithful Murder

Comments from readers:

". . . the book sweeps up the reader into the mystery. The fishing scenes are good and accurate. I won't give away the ending but it seems to come quickly. I enjoyed this book and look forward to more fly-fishing mysteries by the author." D. McQuickly

"This murder mystery is in the Hillerman vein . . . treats the reader as an intelligent person, not spoon feeding everything, and with emphasis on current detective science . . . It is an easy read, with just enough false leads to make the mystery realistic . . ." A. Marks

Firehole River Murder & *Old Faithful Murder* may be purchased from Authorhouse or Amazon

ACKNOWLEDGMENTS

I know no author who writes a novel, especially a fictional novel, without the encouragement, advice, and assistance of numerous individuals. At the top of my list of those individuals is my wife, Sandy. She has practiced understanding and exhibited patience with me for forty-seven years through all types and kinds of change. I love her more today than when each of us said, "I do", not having a clue as to what we were getting ourselves into together.

Each of the novels I have written, including *Double Revenge in Yellowstone,* would not have been written without the encouragement from several readers who kindly and directly asked, "When can we expect to read your next book?" While they are too numerous to list and if I tried to do so, I would invariably forget to include someone, I am grateful for their encouragement to write this third novel in the *Yellowstone Mystery Series.*

Raymond N. Kieft

AUTHOR'S NOTE

This is a work of fiction. I ask you to keep that in mind. Readers of my other two novels in the Yellowstone Mystery Series, *Firehole River Murder* and *Old Faithful Murder,* know I use real places in the Yellowstone region whenever possible. I see no reason to create fictitious cities, towns, hotels, rivers, lakes, businesses, shops, housing areas, or attractions within Yellowstone National Park when the existing ones make the novel come more alive, especially for readers who have visited the Yellowstone region and have memories of these real places. However, from time-to-time, I do deviate from the practice of using real places. I ask the reader's indulgence for such fabrications. For readers intimately familiar with the Yellowstone region, please be advised that occasionally I use my literary license and tweak geography in favor of storytelling.

Because certain characters in this novel are decidedly unsavory and professionally bankrupt, I'm sure law enforcement agencies, the administration of Yellowstone National Park, and the Montana State government would not appreciate having such individuals portrayed as their employees. More to the point, neither the Park County Sheriff's Department, Park County Commissioners, United States Department of the Interior, National Park Service, Yellowstone National Park, Federal Bureau of Investigation, nor any people associated with them played any part in inspiring the characters I've imagined for this novel or the story I've told. All the misdeeds, overt and covert lies, cover-ups, crimes, and depictions of felonious deeds and conspiratorial individuals in *Double Revenge in Yellowstone* are my responsibility and mine alone. Any similarity to the reality that comprises the Yellowstone region and the wonderful people who inhabit it is purely coincidental.

Readers may come across misspelled words, grammatically incorrect phrases, or typographical errors. Excuses are never satisfactory, but here is mine. The less money devoted to the word and grammar editing of this novel means more money for *Habitat for Humanity* and *Compassion*

International, the two charities which share equally in 100% of the royalties earned from the sale of this novel. Rather than employing a skilled editor to carefully review every word and phrase, and check for mistakes prior to giving the o.k. to publish the novel, I chose to employ an unskilled, non-editor; namely yours truly. My excuse is I tried to eliminate all mistakes, as any author would desire. Failing to eliminate all mistakes, I ask for your indulgence.

I welcome any and all comments, suggestions, criticisms, and I would much appreciate knowing your reaction to the novel. Send me an e-mail at ray@raykieft.com. Also, check out my website: www.raykieft.com. Happy reading.

Raymond N. Kieft

MAIN CHARACTERS

(in alphabetical order of last name)

Barrozo, Victor................... Owner of Barrozo, Inc. and Former Partner of Michael Valentine

Belgrade, Ryan .... Administrative Assistant for Beth Richardson

Black, Karen....................... Owner of the Black Real Estate Agency, West Yellowstone

Black, Laurie .... Employee in the Gold Medal Fly-Fishing Shop and Daughter of Karen Black

Bostick, Kurt...................... Regional Ranger, Yellowstone National Park

Caruth, Sid .... Part-time Employee in the Gold Medal Fly-Fishing Shop

Cortez, Vanessa .... Employee in Yellowstone National Park and Contestant in the Miss Illinois Pageant

Dickson, Bruce................... Director of Law Enforcement and Security, Yellowstone National Park

Dirkse, Leo........................ FBI Special Agent-in-Charge, Cheyenne Office, Cheyenne, Wyoming

Evenhouse, Marilyn............ Sheriff of Park County, Wyoming

Farrington, Marcia .... Defense Lawyer

Greenbrier, Becky.............Assistant Director of Visitor Services, Yellowstone National Park

Henderson, Byron.............Coroner and Chief Medical Examiner for Gallatin County, Montana

Hill, Jim...........................Employee and Fly-Fishing Guide for the Gold Medal Fly-Fishing Shop

Jackson, Cynthia...............Administrative Assistant for Janet VanKampen

Lopez, Sophia...................Receptionist in the Roosevelt Lodge, Yellowstone National Park

Mancuso, Kevin...............Fly-Fishing Guide for the Gold Medal Fly-Fishing Shop

Marsman, Cathy...............Librarian for the West Yellowstone Public Library

McFarlin, Elizabeth..........Junior Administrative Assistant for Bruce Dickson

Medina, Carlos.................Deputy Sheriff of Park County, Wyoming

Mendez, Yolanda..............Pseudo Name of Vanessa Cortez

Myerson, Nancy...............Administrative Assistant in the Law Enforcement and Security Office, Yellowstone National Park

Nesbitt, Susan..................Owner of the Book Peddler Store, West Yellowstone

Newberry, Gretchen.........Assistant Deputy Ranger, Yellowstone National Park

Poole, Blake........................ Fly-Fishing Guide for the Gold Medal Fly-Fishing Shop

Richardson, Beth................ Associate Superintendent, Yellowstone National Park and Contestant in the Miss Illinois Pageant

Richardson, Mary............... Mother of Beth Richardson

Samuels, Jessica .... Assistant Director of Law Enforcement and Security, Yellowstone National Park

Tompkins, Brenda.............. Seasonal Ranger, Yellowstone National Park

Valentine, Michael .... Former Co-Owner and Partner of Media Promotions, Inc and Former Judge for the Miss Illinois Pageant

VanHousen, Rick .... Deputy Ranger, Yellowstone National Park

VanKampen, Janet.............. FBI Special Agent-in-Charge, Billings Office, Billings, Montana

Vogelzang, Ann .... Assistant Deputy Sheriff of Park County, Wyoming

Voss, Karen .... Administrative Assistant for Kurt Bostick

Wainwright, Maria............. Senior Administrative Assistant in the Law Enforcement and Security Office, Yellowstone National Park

Wells, Dick........................ Manager, Fly-Fishing Guide, and Fly-Tier for the Gold Medal Fly-Fishing Shop

Williams, Parker................. Owner of the Gold Medal Fly-Fishing Shop, West Yellowstone

PROLOGUE

Sunday Evening
10:15 p.m.
South Parking Lot, Buffalo Bill Historical Center, Cody, Wyoming
Behind the Sylvan Lake Picnic Area, Yellowstone National Park, Wyoming

Revenge. Tis so sweet. Double revenge. Sweeter still. All the planning. All the waiting. Over and over again evaluating the various scenarios and running them through the mind. The time for fulfillment was at hand. Everything had been checked and double checked. Inconsistencies or potential pitfalls had been identified and eliminated. Should there have been more planning? Had something been overlooked? No chance. No more second-guessing. The plan decided upon was good. No, not just good. Perfect. It was now time for action. Action that would kill two birds with one stone. Absolute ecstasy. Both going down. One now; one later. No backing away now. Just do it.

So far, so good. The most nerve racking few seconds had been when the dirtbag opened the driver's side door and slid behind the steering wheel. Had he turned to look through the rear passenger's side window or the rear-view mirror on the passenger side of the car, his peripheral vision may have alerted him to what was behind his seat. If that had happened, all would have been lost. Being a creature of habit, he hadn't looked toward the floor behind the driver's seat. He hadn't given the slightest attention to anything other than sliding behind the steering wheel, putting the key into the ignition, and starting the car. He must have been in a hurry as he seemed to accelerate quite quickly from the parking lot and merged rapidly onto U.S. highway 20 heading west out of Cody.

It had been easier than expected. It was a definite advantage to be short. Easier to stay hidden behind the driver's seat. Only one feeling of panic. A brief hesitation which was quickly replaced with a realization that there was no turning back. Not now. Not after so much waiting. Sticking the syringe into the beefy backside portion of his upper arm and pushing the plunger had been almost too easy. The stuff acted quickly, just as it was supposed to act. Probably because it was meant to bring down bears, bison, and elk, not humans. What made it so perfect was when the body was discovered and an autopsy performed, it would easily pinpoint it. When the stuff was discovered, it would point to someone within the National Park Service or a major zoo, since only the National Park Service and zoos dealt with big animals on a routine basis. With no major zoos in the area, investigators would first look to national park employees as the source of the stuff. That would begin the ball rolling in the planned direction.

Being able to keep a hand on the steering wheel and easing the car to the shoulder of the road proved not to be difficult thanks to the times it had been practiced over the past several weeks. Quickly moving from the back seat floor to between the front bucket seats and then driving the car had also worked well. Thankfully, no other cars had passed on either side. There would be no drivers of other cars that might remember seeing two heads close to one another on the driver's side of the car.

The most anxious time had been entering Yellowstone National Park through its east entrance. Given the budget problems of Yellowstone, the east entrance did not have any employees working the entrance booth after 8 p.m. If there had been someone at the entrance booth, an alternative plan would have been required. However, there were security cameras recording every vehicle that entered and exited after 8 p.m., making it essential that the body be sitting in the driver's seat, with the head up, and at least one hand on the steering wheel when the camera took its picture. It had to look like he was alive and driving. Otherwise, all might be lost. Don't they say practice makes perfect? It sure did this time. Practicing with a dummy had shown that winding a thin, transparent nylon line around the neck and tying it to the headrest kept the head in an upright position looking ahead. Placing the left hand on the steering wheel and tying the wrist to the steering wheel also worked. Since the area captured by the camera was the front license plate and the driver's side of the front seat, the car needed only to travel in a straight line a few feet with no one, other than the driver, being in the lens of the camera. Practice had solved this problem as well. Sitting on the floor on the passenger side and reaching across with one hand to gently push the accelerator, while the other hand rested on the bottom of the steering wheel to keep it from turning, had proven to be the ticket.

What had turned out to be more difficult than anticipated was moving the dead weight body from behind the steering wheel. The body was heavier than anticipated. Scoping out various areas a few miles into Yellowstone had resulted in discovering a flat area, about twenty-five yards from the highway, totally concealed by trees and brush between it and the highway. Fortunately, the trees were spaced somewhat apart in several clumps making it possible to maneuver a car through them. Parking the car, it had taken quite a bit of time of pulling and pushing to move the body to the passenger side. The guy must have weighed two hundred lbs. The adrenaline had worn off, making the task that much more difficult. Whatever the reason, it had taken more time and effort than anticipated. The body was finally positioned in the passenger seat with the neck tied to the headrest. Pulling back onto the highway, anyone in a car behind them or one passing on the other side of the road would see a driver and a passenger. That was the plan. If any drivers were questioned by the cops, they would remember two people in the car.

Continuing over Sylvan Pass, a sense of accomplishment helped to offset the anguish associated with taking another person's life. Don't think about it. He had it coming. All these years of living with the hurt and humiliation he caused. Besides, there was still more to be done. Another person had to fall before double revenge would be completed. Mile marker 17 passed on the right. About hundred yards more. There. A popular picnic area across from Sylvan Lake. Behind the picnic area was a little known clearing which could be accessed by driving around the back of the picnic area and following the tire tracks.

Planning ahead had been so smart. Tangible evidence for the investigators to find would point to a specific individual as the killer. That was the plan. Not too much evidence. Otherwise, it would look staged. That had to be avoided. It hadn't taken too much coercion to obtain the evidence. Blackmail had worked well. However, involving more than two people had been a concern from the beginning. That might become a problem which would require more planning and probable elimination of the problem. Don't worry about that now. For now, placing the evidence properly was critical.

Wearing latex gloves and shoe booties to eliminate fingerprints and shoe prints, one shoe was taken from the backpack, which had been placed on the floor of the car behind the passenger's front seat. The shoe was pushed into various places in the loose soil outside the driver's side door and occasionally in places around the car, making it look like the killer had gotten out of the car on the driver's side and walked around the car. Next the button. Taken from the sleeve of the uniform jacket, it was placed under the leg of the body. There. Perfect. Next the strands of hair. They were pushed into a few places on the clothes with a few strands also placed on the driver and passenger headrests.

The checklist was reviewed to make sure nothing was overlooked. Content that all had been accomplished as planned, the interior of the car was wiped as well as the exterior door handles. Leaving the keys in the ignition, the walk to the pick-up spot went without a hitch. Revenge. So sweet. Double revenge would be sweeter still.

CHAPTER 1

Sunday Evening
9:45 p.m.
Buffalo Bill Historical Center, Cody, Wyoming

Another rubber chicken banquet. Thank goodness it was over. How many did that make over the past year? Too many. The Superintendent had warned her about the social and community obligations she would be expected to fulfill when she accepted the promotion, but she hadn't paid much attention. The satisfaction of reaching the second highest position with the nation's most famous national park, coupled with the surety of eventually achieving a Superintendent's appointment in the not too distant future, had overshadowed any negative thoughts of more meetings, more personnel problems, and more community and social obligations.

This one had been especially boring, although the cause was one she believed in and supported with her own time and money. The Yellowstone Foundation was a non-profit organization, independent of Yellowstone National Park, which worked hand-in-glove with Yellowstone's administration to provide funds to support particular needs which Yellowstone's general operating funds couldn't address. It was no secret that Federal funds for the national parks had declined significantly over the past several years as part of the budget problems in Washington, D.C. Support from organizations like the Yellowstone Foundation was critical in maintaining a half-way decent level of service for the millions of visitors to Yellowstone each year. For example, improvements to the much used self-guided trails throughout the lower geyser basin, which included the world famous Old Faithful Geyser, had been a big ticket priority project which the Foundation had helped fund.

Tonight's event had been a fund-raising banquet featuring, as the speaker, the Department of Interior's Assistant Secretary for Western National Parks. He had been recently appointed by the Secretary of the

Interior even though he had spent his entire professional career in banking and had no understanding or appreciation of the complex workings of a national park. Some middle management job with Chase banks and now overseeing all the national parks west of the Mississippi River. Go figure how that made sense. Add that neither the Secretary nor Assistant Secretary had any background or experience in the issues and matters involving the environment, public land usage, wildlife and forestry management, oil and gas exploration, wilderness oversight, stewardship of the national parks, or any of the myriad of responsibilities of the large and diversified Department of the Interior, and it became totally mystifying how such appointments were made. She knew the answer, of course, which she didn't like at all. Both the Secretary and Assistant Secretary were political appointees, having been supporters of the President, whom had only been in office a short time. Due to the shortcomings of leadership in D.C., it was critical to the wellbeing of the national park system that every opportunity to smooze the new Secretary or any of the Secretary's inner circle be milked for everything it could. When the opportunity presented itself in your own backyard, it was doubly important. Hence, her presence at the banquet.

She had smiled, laughed, applauded, shook her head up and down when appropriate—all intended to make a positive impression on the Assistant Secretary and others from the Secretary's Washington D.C. office. She was doing it for the sake of the National Park Service and, in particular, Yellowstone. It also wouldn't hurt her personal agenda to have the Assistant Secretary aware of her. While the Assistant Secretary had been cordial and friendly to her and his speech supportive of Yellowstone and its premiere role among the national parks, his chief-of-staff had been a royal pain. Arrogant, pompous, and into himself, he had been too aggressive and overly demonstrative with her. He stood too closely, touched her too often, and went so far to suggest they get together after the banquet in his suite at the Erma Hotel, using the guise of discussing how the Secretary and he might help her while helping Yellowstone. She had been propositioned in so many ways over the years that she saw immediately through this bozo. In as friendly a tone of voice as she could muster, she told him she would like to meet with him but reluctantly had to decline since the drive back to Yellowstone's headquarters at Mammoth Hot Springs would take her a few hours and she needed some sleep before chairing a meeting of a wolf management task force in the morning. All this had been thought up on the spot. She neither intended to drive to Mammoth Hot Springs tonight nor did she have to chair a meeting in the morning. She had other plans. She had told her administrative assistant she wouldn't be into the office tomorrow until late morning. She hadn't told anyone her real plans and she wasn't going to allow this bozo to mess them up.

During the Assistant Secretary's speech, she had noticed a man seated among the media in the back of the hall staring at her. She would look away, and then steal a quick glimpse at him. His eyes never seemed to move from staring at her. She had become hardened to men looking her over with lusting eyes but this guy was different, causing her discomfort. To heighten her discomfort, she knew she had seen him before. Not recently. Not locally. In a different setting. Different place. Different time. Where? She couldn't place it. When had she seen him? Why was he staring at her? Maybe she was overreacting. After all, this wasn't the first time a man had stared at her. It happened all the time. When she entered a room or walked across a restaurant or conference room, she felt the eyes of men on her. She knew she was considered attractive—a 10 is what the promotional literature had given her back when she won the Miss Illinois pageant and moved on as one of the ten finalists for Miss America. The looks by men were common and harmless. Let them look, she had concluded. But this guy's stare was something else. There was something predatorial about his look. She debated whether to alert security. But that would mean a scene and she didn't want anything to detract from the Assistant Secretary having a positive experience. She would make sure she avoided the guy if he tried to approach her after the banquet.

She intended to leave Cody and drive into Yellowstone through the Cooke City/SilverGate northeast entrance. She had her sleeping bag and she knew the exact spot in the Lamar Valley near Soda Butte Creek where she would sleep under the stars and be ready at dawn to listen and watch the Slough Creek wolf pack in its early morning activities, including, she hoped, a hunt. She needed times like these to recharge her batteries, get away from all the petty nonsense which seemed to control her life at times, and get back to why she had devoted her career to the National Park Service in the first place. The only thing that could spoil her plan was an emergency in Yellowstone which demanded her attention. Highly unlikely, but one never knew. She was fairly confident she wouldn't be contacted. There were excellent regional rangers, she realized, that could handle anything in her absence. Tonight and tomorrow morning were going to be all hers.

Driving the Chief Joseph Highway toward the Cooke City/Silvergate northeast entrance, she felt herself relaxing and thinking about how fortunate she was to be living and working in a place she loved. Glancing at the passenger seat where she had placed her uniform jacket with her name badge, "Beth Richardson, Associate Superintendent, Yellowstone National Park", she felt deep satisfaction and contentment. She was living out her dream in the place she had hoped her work might take her someday. All was well. Even the budget constraints, internal politics, incompetent people in Washington, demanding public, bickering among personnel, too few staff, and too many needs and requirements, couldn't detract from her overall sense of satisfaction and accomplishment. Yet, she wasn't being totally honest with herself. There was one area of discontent. Her social life, or more correctly, her love life, left a lot to be desired. It wasn't that she wasn't interested in establishing a relationship with a man. To the contrary, she realized the clock was ticking and before not too far down the road, the majority of available men would be second-timers, meaning divorced and usually with commitments to children and former wives. Not that second-timers couldn't be wonderful husbands and fathers, but one couldn't help wondering if the guy was so wonderful, how come his first marriage had gone sour? A bigger problem than second-timers, however, was the immaturity of so many men that, although well into their 30s and even 40s, continued to act like adolescents. Binging, bar hopping, drag racing, and sexual exploitation of vulnerable women constituted their idea of fun. She wanted no part of any of it.

There was an exception to her pessimistic picture of available men. Probably a few more than just one, but she knew one for sure. Parker Williams. He was everything the booze, bar scene, sports cars, and babe's guys were not. Conscientious, kind, goal-oriented, responsible, and yet not a fuddy-duddy or goodie two-shoes. Parker and she had known each other for about four years and had endured some traumatic times together which had brought them closer, or she had thought so at the time. Ever since being involved in solving the murder of a well-known historian by a former male acquaintance of hers, they had become distant. Why? She wasn't sure. Maybe it had nothing to do with anything other than both of them being involved and busy with their work. Plus, the distance between his business, in West Yellowstone, and hers, in Mammoth Hot

Springs,—some sixty miles over winding two-lane roads which often had traffic completely stopped because of herds of bison or elk using the roads as if they owned them—created an obstacle to a spur of the moment get-together. Nevertheless, she knew she enjoyed Parker's company and wanted to nurture a relationship. It had to be a two-way street, however, and she wasn't sure if he felt the same way. They needed to have a heart-to-heart in the near future. Put up or shut up, she told herself. He did light a fire in her being. Their friendship was strong, but that was just it, it was a friendship. They had shared life stories, held each other, and kissed quite passionately. Nothing beyond that had happened. Not because the urge wasn't there. Something held them both back. It was as if they both wouldn't allow themselves to abandon their moral underpinnings. She cared for him and she knew he had felt the same way toward her. He had told her about his first marriage and the unexpected and hurtful departure of his former wife with another man. She did not feel he had yet come to grips with the rejection and was both cautious and suspicious of establishing a committed relationship again with any woman.

As she approached the Cooke City/Silvergate northeast entrance, she glanced at her uniform jacket and noticed that a button was missing from the right arm sleeve. I wonder when that happened? Did it happen this evening or had it been missing for some time? Missing even a small part of her ceremonial uniform jacket, as small a thing as a button, cast a negative picture of the senior employees of Yellowstone. She would have to locate a new button and have it sewed on as soon as possible, after which the jacket should be dry-cleaned and pressed. Even though she wore her ceremonial uniform jacket only on special occasions, she wanted to correct it before she found herself wearing it again. Maybe tomorrow afternoon after she arrived at her office. Driving toward the entrance booth at the Cooke City/Silvergate entrance gate, she looked toward where the security camera was placed under the eve on the roof of the entrance booth. She intended to wave for the camera and give the employee, who might review, in the morning, the photographs of vehicles entering Yellowstone during the night, a chuckle when she or he saw her. She was surprised to see it wasn't there. Since there were no vehicles behind her, she parked her Explorer and walked around the booth, checking other potential places where the camera might have been mounted. Nothing. She saw the mount for the camera and it was empty. The camera was probably in the repair shop correcting some malfunction. Not having a security camera, when an employee was present in the booth, wasn't a big deal since the employee would record the time of entrance, license plate number, and state or Canadian province of registration into a log. Doing so slowed down the progress of vehicles entering Yellowstone, which sometimes caused visitors to complain about the wait, but it was important to have a record of every vehicle entering and exiting Yellowstone in case visitors needed to be contacted sometime down the road, although it was rare to do so. It had only happened twice over the four years she had been with Yellowstone. The information provided by the visitor had proven to be invaluable, so the practice was continued even though it took valuable and scarce resources to do so. But tonight, with no employees on site, there hadn't been and wouldn't be any record of vehicles entering or leaving Yellowstone through this entrance. Not good. She made a mental note to call Byron Newberry, the ranger in charge of this region of Yellowstone, first thing in the morning to alert him about the lack of a security camera. Either a new camera had to be installed as soon as possible or employees had to be assigned to cover the entrance 24/7 until a camera was installed.

She walked back to her Explorer, started it, and headed for Soda Butte Creek and the secluded place she intended to be her bedroom for the night. After fifteen minutes, she passed the sign for Soda Butte Creek, drove over the bridge spanning the Creek, and immediately slowed down. There. Not noticeable to anyone driving by, that didn't know where to look or what to look for, were two tire impressions leading away from the road. She drove slowly, careful to avoid as many rocks and gullies as possible. She had been here several times, so she knew the best way to avoid bottoming out or ruining the underside of the Explorer. Her goal was a stand of lodgepole pine trees close to the bank of the Creek. Unless you had been there, you wouldn't have any idea that a 20 ft. by 15 ft. rock free, grassy area lay between the trees and the Creek. A perfect place to pitch a tent or just roll out a sleeping bag, which she intended to do.

Pulling her Explorer into the area, she parked it in the only open space between the trees, thereby denying easy access by a person or animal. The moonlight provided sufficient light so she turned off the parking lights. Lifting the rear hatchback, she pulled out her sleeping bag, mosquito netting, Coleman lantern, and fleece sweatsuit. Lighting the lantern, she placed it on the bed of the rear compartment of the Explorer while she pulled her Winchester shotgun from behind the front seat and bear spray from under the front seat. Bear spray in every Yellowstone vehicle had become mandatory. No reason not to be prepared should an inquisitive grizzly come along or a drunken poacher. She folded the rest of her uniform as best she could, placing it on the front seat next to her jacket. Pulling on the sweatsuit, she laid the shotgun, bear spray, and her pistol next to the sleeping bag. She could already hear the mosquitoes beginning to swarm. She quickly attached the netting, doused the lantern, and crawled inside the sleeping bag, zipping the netting closed behind her. The sky was a masterpiece of brilliant, diamond-like white lights. Millions of white lights. The Big Dipper looked close enough to touch. Only the gurgling of Soda Butte Creek broke the utter silence of the night.

Staring into the glorious night sky, she thought back to her parents, her childhood and teen years, and the path she had followed to where she was now, the number two person in the administration of America's first and most famous national park. Her father had owned a hardware store in Peoria, Illinois. He had seen the hand writing on the wall of the emergence of the big box stores so he sold all the hardware store's inventory to Home Depot and the building and land to a specialty ice cream manufacturer. He had invested wisely the money from the sales and now occupied himself playing the commodity markets. He knew every soybean, corn, and hog farmer for miles around Peoria and used the information he gleaned from hours spent in the local coffee shop and café in his decisions about commodity futures. Her mother had been a stay-at-home mom, when doing so wasn't thought to be condescending or unfulfilling. She helped with the books, ordering and checking inventory, and performed numerous behind the scenes activities at the hardware store. She had been active in the local PTA, various community organizations, and the Presbyterian church. The aging process had only enhanced her beauty. Townspeople and relatives often commented that Beth owed her porcelain complexion, warm and penetrating blue eyes, thick auburn hair, and classic features to her mother, who still caused men to watch her cross a room and women to glare with jealousy, something Beth knew a whole lot about herself.

Listening to the complete silence surrounding her, she recalled her college days when her path to where she was now had been forged. Academics had come easily for her, even in college. She had graduated with a degree in wildlife management. After her family had taken a trip to Rocky Mountain National Park when she was a sophomore in high school, she realized she wanted to devote her professional life to the National Park

Service. The time in Colorado had sparked a hunger for the mountains of the western U.S. Her employment goal became joining the National Park Service and having a full-time position in one of the national parks in the Rocky Mountain regions of the western U.S. She had achieved her goal much faster than she had imagined.

Enough thinking and reminiscing. Tomorrow would bring its own issues. Time to thank God for the blessings she was experiencing. Mindful of the gurgling of Soda Butte Creek, she drifted off to sleep.

CHAPTER 2

Monday Morning
6:30 a.m.
Ranger Housing, Grant Village, Yellowstone National Park, Wyoming

Kurt Bostick was awakened by the ringing of his satellite phone. The bedside clock showed 6:30 a.m. This must be important, as the satellite phones of Yellowstone officials were used only for emergencies or urgent communication. The cost of calls on the satellite phones was expensive and the Superintendent had reminded all of them to utilize the phone only when absolutely necessary. It was also early. Calls usually weren't made until 7:30 a.m., a full hour from now.

Kurt was the regional ranger in charge of the eastern and south-eastern regions of Yellowstone. His regions included the most isolated and remote areas of Yellowstone and little occurred in the areas requiring a call on his satellite phone. There were quite a few seasonal employees throughout the regions that, for the most part, handled anything short of a fire which threatened human life or an accident with serious injury or possible death. Ninety percent of Kurt's time and energy was devoted to the busy locations within his regions including the historic Fishing Bridge, Lake Yellowstone Lodge and cabins, Lake Yellowstone Hotel, and Grant Village. Every year, more than one-half million visitors stayed in the Lodge or the cabins around the Lodge, an RV, or campsite in his regions of Yellowstone. They either ate at the few eating places run by Transwest, the caterer employed by Yellowstone, or cooked their own meals in their RVs or around their campsites. They hiked the trails, used the few restrooms, which too often ran out of toilet tissue, dropped tons of trash, hopefully in trash receptacles, waited in long lines to purchase fuel, and turned the roads into parking lots by stopping in the middle of the road to take photos of bison, elk, or the occasional bear or wolf. Probably the greatest pain for Kurt and those seasonal employees involved in traffic control was the limited amount of parking. During the peak summer season, finding a parking spot became a hunting contest. The inability to find a parking spot brought out the worst in normally mild-mannered people. Double and triple parking were common. Arguments and even fist-fights erupted when two cars went after the same spot. But none of these visitor issues would prompt a call on his satellite phone unless something drastic had occurred.

"Hello. Kurt speaking."

"Kurt. It's Brenda. Sorry to call so early, but I think you need to know what we have. It isn't good."

"It's o.k., Brenda. I was getting dressed. What's up?" He knew he wasn't going to like what he was about to hear, so he readied himself for the worst. Brenda Tompkins was his lead seasonal employee, actually a seasonal ranger, for the very eastern portion of the east region. She had recently changed her shift to 11 p.m. to 8 a.m. because some vandalism had been occurring during the night at two of the campgrounds in the east region and she wanted to try and apprehend the culprits. She wouldn't be giving him a warning about what she was going to tell him unless she knew it was going to be a difficult situation.

"Rick was doing his early morning patrol along the west side of Sylvan Lake, near the picnic area, and came across a car parked behind the area." Rick VanHousen was the deputy ranger in charge of the east region of Yellowstone. "He thought he should check it out. When he did, he found a body in the car. A male. He said he immediately called Bruce Dickson's office and left a voice mail. He also sent a text message. Rick said he would stay there and keep everyone away from the car, although he didn't expect anyone to be around since it's early. He hoped you or I could get there as soon as we could. I have that meeting this morning with the representatives of the Greater Yellowstone Coalition, so I'm hoping you can get there."

"I'll leave right now. On my way, I'll call Bruce's office again. I have some crime scene tape in my truck so Rick and I will be able to place tape around the scene. I'm not thinking a crime is involved, but you never know. Did Rick say anything about how the guy died?

"No, he didn't and I didn't ask. He sounded pretty frazzled."

"O.k., thanks, Brenda. Do me a favor and contact Beth and tell her what is going on. Tell her I'll be in touch when I knew more. When I get there, we'll see what we can find out about the victim. I'll call Karen and ask her to alert everyone after 8 a.m." Karen Voss was Kurt's administrative assistant that would open the office at 8 a.m. She would contact all the other seasonal rangers and alert them as well as office staff. Brenda would be calling Beth Richardson's office. Beth was Kurt's boss and he knew she would expect to be informed.

Hanging up the phone, Kurt realized this day was going to be much different than most. There weren't many days when a death was involved. Injuries, for sure. Usually broken bones or severe sunburn and dehydration. The few deaths occurring in Yellowstone were almost always from natural causes, with the exception of visitors falling into boiling pools or being gored by a bison or trampled by an elk after provoking the animal. Hikers would fall from a cliff or canyon wall. In his seven years with Yellowstone, he could remember only two homicides. Thankfully, homicides in national parks automatically came under the jurisdiction of the FBI. By chance this death turned out to be a homicide, the FBI would take over.

Brenda said the victim was behind the Sylvan Lake picnic area. That area wasn't known to anyone other than persons very familiar with Yellowstone since it was essentially cut off from the main picnic area. The ground was unstable there due to the proximity of numerous fumaroles and small boiling pools. Consequently, it wasn't shown on any literature provided to visitors nor were there any trails in the vicinity. It was too dangerous for the average visitor to walk around the area.

It would take him about one-half hour to get to the area. As he drove, he called Bruce Dickson's office. His administrative assistant answered. "Kurt, I think I know why you are calling. Bruce is already on his way to Sylvan Lake. He should be there in less than an hour, depending on traffic. He told me if you called to tell you he would meet you there."

"Thanks, Liz. I'll meet Bruce there." Liz was Elizabeth McFarlin, a relatively new employee in the Law Enforcement and Security Office, who was Bruce Dickson's administrative assistant.

He assumed someone had informed the Superintendent. Kurt didn't want to go over his boss' head and notify the Superintendent's office, although Beth wasn't the type of person to care about such things. Nevertheless, there were certain protocols to follow. He would wait to hear from Beth. If she asked him to notify the Superintendent, he would do so. Once the Superintendent knew, the media could be informed. That was a job he didn't want to wade into if he could avoid it. The media could be a royal pain when it came to a death in Yellowstone.

In the distance he could see a green Ford Explorer parked in the small parking lot in front of the Sylvan Lake picnic area. That would be the

SUV Rick VanHousen was using. He parked behind the Explorer. Rick walked up to him.

"Kurt, thanks for coming," said Rick. "I've kept traffic moving. If you walk behind that grove of lodgepole pine, you'll see the car with the body inside." He pointed to small grove of lodgepole pines. Walking together, Kurt spotted a silver Lexus parked next to another grove of lodgepole pines about 30 yards behind the picnic area. "No one has gotten near the car," said Rick, "I've made sure of that."

"Great job, Rick. I guess we better stay here on the road and continue to control traffic. Bruce Dickson will be here shortly and then I'll go with him to check the victim. He is more on top of how to go about doing that without contaminating the scene."

"You mean you think this may be a crime scene?"

"I'm not saying that. Maybe it is or maybe it isn't. What I do know is that we have to be very careful to not contaminate the scene until the cause of death is known. I doubt we have anything other than a normal death, as normal as death can be, that is, but that isn't your or my call. Until we know for sure, we treat the scene as if it is a crime scene."

"I walked to the Lexus to check it out when I first spotted it," said Rick. "I hope I didn't destroy any evidence should this turn out to be worse than we think. I only looked through the windshield. I didn't touch the door or anything around the car."

"You did exactly what procedure calls for," replied Kurt. "I doubt it would make any difference anyway, since I'm thinking the guy felt something strange coming on so he pulled off the road, parked by the trees, and then died. Probably a heart attack. Why he drove as far back as he did is anyone's guess. If he felt something coming on, you would think he would stop in the parking lot. Doesn't make sense to me, but what do I know? We'll have to wait to hear what Bruce wants to do. In the meantime, the car has a Montana license, so call the plate number into the Montana DMV. Let's get a name to go with the car. See to whom it's registered. It's a place to start."

"Will do."

The crunching of gravel announced the arrival of another vehicle. Kurt turned to see a green van, with the seal of the Department of Interior on the side panels, parking next to his Explorer. It should be Bruce Dickson, he thought. Now the work of figuring out what happened would begin.

CHAPTER 3

Monday morning
7:00 a.m.
Home of Parker Williams on Duck Creek, 9 Miles North of West
Yellowstone off U.S. Highway 191, Montana

Parker Williams rolled over and looked at the bedside clock. 7:00 a.m. Time to rise and shine, or at least rise. There were two fly-fishing float trips scheduled for the day and the clients would be arriving at his shop in about an hour, eager to get underway. He should be in the shop when they arrived to assist with last minute details related to hooking the drift boats to pickup trucks, loading any fly-fishing equipment needed by the clients, making sure lunches were packed and drinks in the cooler, and, of course, an ample supply of several different fishing flies so whatever particular insect hatch might occur during the float, flies imitating that particular insect would be available to be fished. The clients for each float would be a whole lot more likely to provide their guides with a generous tip if fish had been caught and landed. All fish would be released as was the policy of his fly-fishing shop, the Gold Medal Fly-Fishing Shop of West Yellowstone, Montana. When potential clients inquired about a guided fly-fishing trip with his shop, they were asked if they would abide by the shop's "catch and release" policy. If there was any reluctance expressed by the client, she or he was encouraged to book her or his trip with one of the other trip providers that didn't practice "catch and release".

Opening the double slider in his great room and stepping onto the deck, he looked on what he considered as his piece of paradise. The snow-capped Spanish mountain peaks sparkled like vanilla ice cream cones in contrast with the dark green hue of the pine tree covered slopes. Several blue jays and magpies were in competition with each other to determine which group would win the prize for the most vocal morning greeting. Several elk were grazing on the long grasses growing on the banks of Duck Creek which gurgled through several twists and turns as it flowed to its meeting with the South Fork of the Madison River only a few miles west of Yellowstone's boundary. He reflected on his good fortune in finding his home on the bank of Duck Creek. At times, he was embarrassed to live in such a large home when his employees and most of the folks working and living in the West Yellowstone area lived in modest homes or cabins. He had first seen the house during an afternoon of evaluating various places with Karen Black. Karen owned the Black Real Estate Agency in West Yellowstone. He had contacted her while he was still in Sturbridge, Massachusetts, after he found her agency during a search of real estate agency web sites. A few months before purchasing the house, it had undergone remodeling and upgrading. New triple-pane thermal wood windows, recessed lighting, and a large mossrock, wood-burning fireplace in the great room brought openness and light into the main living area. One end of the great room housed the kitchen, complete with a wood-plank island, double ovens, built-in microwave, and countertop range. A large master suite, powder room, and an office/study, with satellite internet connection, comprised the remainder of the main floor. The upper level included two bedrooms with a full bath between them, as well as a den with built-in pine bookcases. On the main floor, a floor-to-ceiling picture window framed the forested hillsides and meadows adjacent to Yellowstone National Park. A double slider from the master suite led to a deck from which Duck Creek could be viewed and the gurgling of it heard during the stillness of the early morning and evening. Almost every evening, the rising of trout, breaking the surface of the water in pursuit of flying mayfly insects, could be seen from the deck, a sight which never failed to start his casting arm twitching in anticipation of a forthcoming contest between fish and fisherman.

After finishing a bowl of Special K with bananas, he locked the front door and walked to his Toyota 4Runner. It had been returned to him only recently after spending too long a time in a body shop in Bozeman repairing the damage inflicted during the apprehension of the murderer of a notable journalist, who had claimed to have an original document which questioned much of what scholars of the Lewis and Clark Expedition had come to agree was accurate. He had become disenchanted with the political in-fighting and union bullying within Massachusetts higher education and, when his wife left him and ran off with a psychology faculty member, he decided to leave higher education behind and begin an entirely new career. After devoting considerable time to a narrowing of potential career possibilities to a handful, he decided to turn his number one hobby into an income-producing adventure. He decided to open a fly-fishing shop. After doing extensive internet research on the best fly-fishing areas in the country and then visiting three of them, he decided to work and live in West Yellowstone, Montana, immediately adjacent to Yellowstone National Park and centered in the region recognized as the premiere fly-fishing area within the lower forty-eight states.

The drive from his cabin to West Yellowstone took about ten minutes. U.S. highway 191 was as straight as an arrow and unless he got trapped behind a slow semi or R.V., he could set his cruise control at sixty-three mph, only three mph over the speed limit, and never touch the brake during the ten mile drive. What a refreshing difference from the Massachusetts Turnpike during rush hour. He usually used this time to think about those things he needed to address when he arrived at his shop or the decisions facing him regarding the business. Occasionally, he would think about non-business related matters, as was the case now. He found himself thinking about his social life or, to be more accurate, the lack of such. Oh, he had friends. Most were related to the business. The fishing guides and employees he hired and worked with were certainly good people, but not the in-depth, meaningful friends one needed for the sharing of intimate and personal matters. All the guides and employees had their own lives away from work where they found the depth of friendship either with a spouse, family members, or an intimate relationship with a woman or man. He had none of those and, if he were honest with himself, he was most bothered by a feeling of longing and loneliness which he attributed to the lack of a meaningful relationship with a woman. His current situation was not healthy. He certainly would rather be in a meaningful relationship with a woman and he felt he had been well on his way having such a relationship with Beth Richardson when their relationship had fizzled. He wasn't sure what had happened or why. He continued to harbor strong feelings for her and he thought she had felt the same about him. They had drifted apart over the past several months and he couldn't put his finger on what had happened to cause it. He realized they were both busy with their work. Maybe it was nothing more than that, at least he hoped there was nothing else. Whatever the reason, he concluded, he wanted to see her again and hopefully rekindle their relationship.

Entering West Yellowstone, he parked by the Book Peddler, as he did almost every morning before going to his shop, to pick up a large coffee to go and one of Susan Nesbitt's homemade and freshly baked scones. Susan owned the Book Peddler for about as long as he had owned his shop. She was a diminutive, outgoing, and personable go-getter whom he enjoyed as a friend. If he didn't know better, he would be convinced he was addicted to Susan's scones. When a morning went by when he didn't have one, he would almost suffer from withdrawal symptoms.

Taking the scone and coffee with him, he drove the three blocks from the Book Peddler to his shop, parked behind it, and entered through the rear door. He had seen two float boats, each hooked to a pickup truck. One belonged to Kevin Mancuso, a guide that worked for the shop during the summer and fall, and the other to Blake Poole, a guide that guided only when all the other guides were booked. Today was one of those days, so Blake would be taking a husband and wife to the Madison River for an all-day fly-fishing float down the river.

Parker asked, "You guys all set or do you need some help before taking off?"

"I'm good to go," replied Kevin, "and Blake's outside loading the last few things he needs. We both expect our clients to show up in a few minutes. What's on your plate today?"

"Not much. I will be the only one in the shop this morning since Jim and Dick are also guiding." Jim Hill and Dick Wells were two of Parker's long-term employees. Dick was a longtime resident of the Yellowstone area that was an acclaimed expert fly-tier and knew more about fishing sites, water conditions, insect hatches, and the when, where, and how of fishing in the Yellowstone area than Parker could hope to learn over a lifetime. Dick had become the second-in-charge around the shop and Parker knew he didn't have to be at his shop every day, all day, because of Dick's ability to manage it. Dick was in his early 50s and as fit and trim as a 35-year old. The only hint at his age were grey areas appearing on his temples and throughout his dark brown hair. He stood about six feet tall and couldn't weigh more than 170 pounds. He had pleasant features and carried himself well. Jim Hill was a Colorado-born-and-bred entrepreneur and a graduate of the University of Colorado Business School, where he had been a top student in his MBA class. He had been on the fast track to a high six-figure salary as an executive with REI when he left it all to become a fly-fishing and ski bum. After a year devoted to fishing and skiing in the Big Sky, Montana, area, his severance pay and savings were gone and he was in need of a job. With his business and organizational skills, he managed the business side of Parker's shop—accounting, payables, catalog sales, web sales, and inventory control, along with serving as a fishing guide. He was in his mid-thirties with dark brown hair which he wore in a bed-head look. For years he had lifted free weights so his neck, shoulders, torso, and arms were muscular. His face was narrow with a somewhat pointed nose and small mouth. When he smiled, glistening white teeth, which he claimed had not been artificially whitened, were displayed. Parker had overheard women in town refer to Jim as a "hunk" and he certainly did not lack for a social life. As far as Parker knew, Laurie and Jim were seeing each other, although around the shop they gave little indication of it.

"Laurie will be here this afternoon and if Sid is available, I'll ask him if he can join Laurie," said Parker. Laurie Black was Karen Black's daughter and she was a spitting image of her mother. Laurie was in her early twenties with coppery skin stretched taut across wide cheekbones beneath large, oval dark brown eyes. Her mouth, normal size at rest, blossomed into something larger and sensuous when she smiled, a set of white teeth framed by pale lipstick and rendered whiter against the duskiness of her skin. Parker wondered if there was some Native American blood in her genes. She had a penchant for wearing jewelry with vivid, colorful clothing, a throwback to early days when she and her mother lived in Southern California. She had an outgoing personality which benefited her work, especially with the men that frequented the shop. She was a godsend in that she had retail experience having worked in a sporting goods store in Carlsbad, California. Parker paid her well for filling in for Dick, Jim, or he at the shop, but every penny he paid her was well worth it. She was a part-time student at the University of Montana in Missoula, Montana, studying fishery sciences. Her master's thesis was focused on whirling disease and its spread through contact with objects placed into water, such as boats, wading shoes, rafts, and float tubes. Sid Caruth was in his late twenties. Parker had hired him about one year earlier. He was tall and lean with long, sandy-colored hair. Every once in a while he sported an earring and a temporary tattoo. His eyes were set deep in his face making him look like he was half asleep. He had recently married and chose to begin graduate studies at Montana State University in Bozeman, Montana. His wife Teri and he were renting a small cabin in Hebgen Lake Estates, ten miles north of West Yellowstone and one mile from Parker's cabin. "If Sid can't come in, I'll stay with her until closing this evening. If he can come in this afternoon, I'll have an afternoon free. Maybe I'll finally be able to fish that stretch of the Firehole River you and I have talked about investigating."

Looking out the front window, he saw a man and woman, all decked-out in fly-fishing gear, get out of a Cadillac Escalade. "I bet that's the Kerrigans," said Parker. "Check out their outfits. Maybe we should call them Mr. and Mrs. Ovis. It looks like they are wearing every piece of fly-fishing clothing, have every piece of fly-fishing equipment, and have clipped to their fishing vest every fly-fishing gadget Orvis ever made. Several thousands of dollars right there. Kevin, you're going to have one interesting day!"

Parker watched Kevin as he greeted the Kerrigans and helped them into his truck. Watching them drive away, with the float boat securely hooked behind, he laughed to himself as he pictured Kevin with the Kerrigans all day. Something told him all the fancy and latest Orvis fishing stuff hid the fact that the Kerrigans were amateurs in their fly-fishing abilities. For sure, Kevin had his work cut out for him if the Kerrigans were going to catch any fish.

"Good morning," said Blake, as he walked into the shop. "I left my clients across the street finishing breakfast. They're going to walk over here as soon as they finish and then we'll be on our way. We're going to float the Henry's Fork River through the Box Canyon section. They requested to float it even after I explained how rough the water is in that section of the river. You know our motto—'Gold Medal gets you to where you wish to fish', so I'm taking them where they requested to go. Here they come now. Let me know when you need me again."

Parker watched as two men got into Blake's pickup and then the pickup, with the float boat attached, drove off. West Yellowstone was just coming to life and he doubted many customers would be coming into the shop during the next hour, so he spent the time checking the inventory of fishing flies and replenishing those which were low in number. He had stockpiled the types of fishing flies he knew would be the most popular based on buying patterns of the past three years. The winter months were when Dick, Jim, and he tied hundreds of fishing flies which constituted the stockpile for the summer and fall fishing seasons.

The late morning hours were devoted to helping customers in selecting fishing flies, giving advice about fishing places throughout Yellowstone, and selling fishing licenses for Yellowstone and a few for Montana. A few minutes before noon, Laurie entered the store. "Hi, Parker. How's the morning gone?"

"Pretty routine. Steady flow of customers, but no big money people. I spent quite a bit of time replenishing fishing flies and catching up on the mail."

Laughing, she replied, "You mean you didn't sell a pair of those new goretex waders . . . the $450 ones? Can you believe the price of those? A wader is a wader, if you ask me. As long as it keeps me dry, I don't care how fancy it is." Walking to the rear of the shop, she hung your coat on a coat-tree. Walking back to the counter, she said: "Did you hear about the body found near the Sylvan Lake picnic area?"

"No," replied Parker, "I haven't listened to any news or checked the internet for news at all this morning. What's going on?"

"The news was rather spotty. Not many details. A man was found dead in a car near the Sylvan Lake picnic area. That's all that was said."

"I suppose we'll hear more details later," replied Parker. "The Yellowstone administration has certain procedures which will be followed. Bruce Dickson will probably take charge until it is determined how the death occurred and where it occurred."

"Do you need any help in the shop later today? I'm not doing anything specific the rest of the day," said Laurie. "I can stay all day if you want me to stay."

"That would be great. I might take a few hours and fish a section of the Firehole where I haven't spent much time. Before taking clients there, I need to check it out for myself. It is about a two-mile walk from the Fountain Flats parking lot, so before I ask clients to walk four miles roundtrip, I better make sure the section is worthwhile to fish."

"Sounds like something worthwhile," replied Laurie. "You don't get much time for yourself, so do it. I'll be fine."

CHAPTER 4

Monday morning
8:30 a.m.
Behind the Sylvan Lake Picnic Area, Yellowstone National Park

Bruce Dickson, Director of Law Enforcement and Security for Yellowstone National Park, parked his van behind the National Park Service Explorer parked in the parking area in front of the Sylvan Lake picnic area. Bruce was a career national park employee that had worked his way up the law enforcement career ladder arriving at his current position a few years earlier. He was in his early fifties and was showing signs of aging as evidenced by a graying of his hair, a flattening of his buttocks, and the beginning of a pot belly. He knew his stuff and was well respected for his knowledge and thoroughness. Exciting the passenger side of the van was Jessica Samuels, the Assistant Director of Law Enforcement and Security. Jessica was tall with an athlete's frame. She had dark hair, more black than brown, which hung straight to just above her shoulders. Her eyes were a bright blue and her skin was unblemished. Even in the drab everyday uniform of the National Park Service, she exhibited a certain feminism which, at times, could become sultry and even sexual in nature. Rumor was that *Playboy* magazine had once approached her about doing a feature about women career employees in the National Park Service. Several of the male employees had discreetly looked through several issues after hearing the rumor, but never found anything. Nevertheless, the rumor continued, probably due to her attractiveness.

Bruce recognized Kurt Bostick and walked toward him with Jessica at his side. "Kurt, good to see you again," said Bruce. "I think you know Jessica Samuels. What do we have here?"

Shaking his hand, Kurt said, "Bruce, it's good to see you too. I think the last time we were together was the retirement party for Jason Goodwin." Reaching across to shake Jessica's hand, he continued, "Jessica,

I remember you being there was well. What we have, Bruce, is the body of a man in a car behind the picnic area. Rick discovered it early this morning. It probably was there overnight. Rick didn't open the car door to look more closely. He said he only looked through the windshield. Neither of us touched anything. We didn't want to contaminate any evidence in case we're dealing with something more than death by natural causes. I was also careful where I walked. Rick may have left some shoeprints when he walked to the car this morning, but his can easily be separated from any others. In fact, I did see some shoeprints, which I think came from the driver's side of the car. Other than Rick, no one has been near the car. Rick and I have kept people away and traffic moving, waiting for you to arrive and take over."

"Sounds like you and Rick handled it well," replied Bruce. "Jessica, please get the casting kit from the van. Also, bring the evidence kits. I think we should follow standard procedure and treat the scene like a crime scene until we can rule out any foul play."

"Sure thing," replied Jessica. She walked to the van, opened the doors in the rear, and walked back carrying what looked like a large suitcase while pulling a wheeled suitcase behind her.

"O.k. Kurt, if you and Rick will keep traffic flowing and any curiosity seekers away, Jess and I will take pictures of the shoeprints and then get some casts of them," said Bruce. "We will then open the driver's door first and look inside before we check the body."

"Anything you need Rick for anymore? I'd like him to continue his visual tour of the region in case there is something else out there that requires our attention," replied Kurt.

Turning to Rick, Bruce said, "Rick, I'll need a statement from you for the record. You can do that in the next day or two. E-mail it to me and copy Kurt. Other than the statement, there's no need for you to hang around. Jess and I are o.k. to go from here by ourselves."

"O.k. Bruce," replied Rick, "I'll be on my way. I hope this doesn't turn out to be anything other than a death by natural causes. Kurt, I'll check-in with you later today."

"Sure thing," responded Kurt. "Good work this morning, Rick. I'll look for your statement soon."

As Rick drove away, Bruce said to Kurt, "While Jess makes casts of those shoeprints you saw, I'm going to see if there is anything of interest in the car, other than the body of course. We won't examine the body until we are confident we haven't overlooked anything that might serve as evidence should this turn out to be more than a routine death. The fact that the car is parked behind the grove of trees and away from the picnic parking lot argues against a heart attack or stroke, since when those things happen, usually the driver loses consciousness and the car goes off in a crazy way and ends up sideways or against some obstacle which stops it. To me, it looks like the driver drove the car behind those trees. I don't like the looks of this from here, but hopefully I'm wrong. What we don't need is something funny. Let's go Jess."

CHAPTER 5

Monday Morning
7:15 a.m.
On the Bank of Soda Butte Creek, Yellowstone National Park, Wyoming
Near the Slough Creek Campground, Yellowstone National Park, Wyoming

The serenade of the Slough Creek wolf pack, coupled with the musical chorus of numerous songbirds, signaled another morning had arrived with all the splendor and wonder which defined the soul of Yellowstone. She had arranged her schedule and gone AWOL, so to speak, in order to watch the Slough Creek wolf pack. She knew if she didn't get going soon, it would be too late to catch them in their morning routine. Rolling up her sleeping bag, she laid it in the back of her Explorer next to her uniform, again noticing the place on the right sleeve of her jacket where a button was missing. She took off her sweatsuit and quickly dressed in her everyday uniform.

The breeding pair of wolves in the wolf pack had denned in the side of a rocky ridge adjacent to Slough Creek. The den had been spotted by a couple of tourists fishing the Creek. The fact that the wolves had chosen to den so close to Slough Creek had led to the closure of a one-mile stretch of the Creek to all public activity, including hiking and fishing. Some complaints had come into the Visitor Services Office from visitors that felt they were being deprived of their right, as taxpayers and purchases of Yellowstone entrance passes and fishing permits, to hike and fish wherever they chose in Yellowstone. However, a large majority of visitors supported the closure as most visitors, many of whom came to Yellowstone to hike its numerous trails or fish its waters, were also supportive of the wellbeing of all wildlife in Yellowstone.

Leaving her overnight sleeping spot, she drove the few miles to the turnoff for the Slough Creek campground. Parking on the northern edge of the campground, she headed upstream, following the trail which paralleled the Creek. She hiked for about one mile before leaving the trail for a spot on top of a small hill. Taking a pair of binoculars from a case, she scanned the ridge directly across from her on the opposite side of Slough Creek. There. What an incredible sight! She watched as two wolves, one larger and darker than the other smaller and lighter one, frolicked with several pups. Both had collars which enabled wildlife experts to track the wolves. A decision had been made when wolves were introduced in Yellowstone to utilize satellites to monitor the movement of wolves and provide pictures of the wolf packs as they moved, reproduced, and formed new packs. The satellite photos were incredible in the detail they included and had proven invaluable during the discussions surrounding whether wolves were making a habit of killing calves and lambs rather than elk and deer. She surmised the larger one was daddy wolf and the smaller mommy wolf with their recently born children. She wondered how those bent on reversing the successful recovery of wolves in Yellowstone could advocate removing all wolves from Yellowstone. She marveled at these majestic animals and how they were enjoying their time of play with their offspring, oblivious to the accusations, hate-mongering, and war of words over whether or not to delist the wolf from the official list of endangered species. She focused her binoculars and continued to watch for several minutes as the wolves seemed to sense they were on-stage and decided to cooperate. She continued to watch them until the adult wolves decided there had been enough playing and sent the pups scurrying back into the den. The male wolf was soon joined by several others and together they began to trot away from the den and over a hill, taking them out of Beth's sight. Realizing the wolves weren't coming back for some time, she put the binoculars back into the case and headed back toward the campground.

Back at her Explorer, she unlocked it and slid into the driver's seat. Checking her satellite phone, she saw the blinking light. She knew something important must be going on, otherwise her satellite phone wouldn't have been called. She listened to the message. "Beth, it's Ryan. Call Kurt as soon as you can. There's been a death in Yellowstone. Brenda called to let you know. Also, call me and let me know when you will be at the office. Thanks." She wondered what this was all about. No way to know until she talked with Kurt. Remembering the policy about only using satellite phones for emergencies, she reached into her purse, withdrew her Blackberry, found Kurt Bostick's number, and pushed the call button.

"Kurt Bostick speaking."

"Hi, Kurt. This is Beth. Ryan left me a message saying Brenda called earlier and asked that I call you. Ryan sounded serious. What's up?"

"I thought you should know," replied Kurt, "early this morning, Rick VanHousen found a body in a car parked off the road by the Sylvan Lake picnic area. He notified me and I called Bruce. He and Jessica are on their way. That's where things stand now."

"You said Bruce and Jessica will be at the scene soon. Bruce will know what to do. Did Rick say anything about his suspicions about cause of death? What we don't need is a homicide. I think we've had our fair share of those over the past couple of years."

"I know what you mean," replied Kurt. "Rick didn't spend any time investigating the body. He played it by the book, as did I when I arrived, and tried not to contaminate any evidence. Hopefully, Bruce and Jessica will be able to determine cause of death."

"I guess you're right," responded Beth, "we'll have to wait and see what Bruce finds out. I just thought of something, has anyone contacted the Superintendent? Also, what about the FBI? I certainly hope and pray it isn't a homicide, but if I'm wrong, it's the FBI's show."

"I don't know about the Superintendent, but I did tell Brenda to alert Janet VanKampen, just in case. You want to notify the Superintendent or you want me to do that?"

"I'll do it," replied Beth. "Good thinking to let Janet know, just in case. Keep me informed, Kurt, should you hear anything else. Good work and please convey to Rick the same."

"Will do, Beth. I hope for all our sakes this doesn't turn out to be anything but a routine death."

She shuddered to think of another homicide in Yellowstone. The last one had occurred too close to home and she didn't wish to duplicate the emotional rollercoaster which she had experienced. No sense worrying about it, she concluded, since whatever would be would be, but she certainly hoped if an autopsy was performed it would rule out any foul play. Taking her Blackberry again, she called her office.

"Hello, Beth Richardson's office. This is Ryan Belgrade speaking. How may I help you?"

"Ryan, its Beth. I'm just heading for the office. I should be there in about 45 minutes. I talked with Kurt and don't have much information. Anything of high importance waiting for me?"

"Nothing urgent. Mostly routine stuff. The Superintendent has asked you to cover an afternoon meeting for him with the bison management task force. That begins at 2 p.m.

"Thanks, Ryan. I'll see you shortly." She started the Explorer and before she began to drive, she breathed deeply and tried to quell her nerves. She needed to put the death out of her mind until there was more information forthcoming from Bruce Dickson.

CHAPTER 6

Monday morning
8:30 a.m.
Terrace Apartments for Yellowstone Employees, Yellowstone National Park, Mammoth Hot Springs, Montana

Last night had been a terrible night of tossing and turning with only brief interludes of sleep. She couldn't shake the anxiety and remorse of knowing she was an accomplice in a murder. What had she been thinking? How had it come to this? She knew the answers but knowing them didn't make dealing with the reality of how she had contributed to the death of another human being any easier.

Becky Greenbrier, Assistant Director of Visitor Services within Yellowstone National Park, stared into the mirror and hardly recognized the person staring back at her. She looked terrible. Dark semi-circles under her eyes and an overall look of exhaustion gave her a zombie-type look. She needed to do a major piece of work on her face before she dared show herself around the office. As she applied her makeup, she thought that certainly the body had been discovered by now and Bruce Dickson was probably already at the scene taking charge of the investigation. She knew Bruce and how meticulous he would be. She knew he would take his time and make sure that all the t's were crossed and the i's dotted. He probably had taken that dingbat Jessica Samuels along with him. Thank goodness being Bruce's lackey was no longer Becky's job. Having been able to transfer to the Visitor Services Office had been a godsend, but not what she deserved. She deserved much more and she was going to get it.

Dressing in the same drab green uniform of the National Park Service day after day was such a downer. Why couldn't the Superintendent allow some individuality in dress? She wanted to show off her body and get the attention of men. Once she had their attention, it was so much easier to manipulate them. She was sick and tired of the uniformity the Yellowstone muckity-mucks imposed upon her. That was one of the reasons she had allowed herself to be talked into assisting with the murder. It meant taking down Beth Richardson and there was nothing that would be more satisfying than watching her nemesis destroyed. After all, Beth didn't deserve the promotions she had been given. She sure didn't earn or deserve being the second in command in the entire Yellowstone administration. Everyone knew she had been given the Associate Superintendent's position not because she earned or deserved it, but because she was providing sexual favors to the powers that be. How else could she have gotten the appointment? Her job should have been mine. I deserved it; not her. I've been with the National Park Service longer than she. The way men drool over her is sickening. The way she struts around the administration building thinking she is God's gift to the National Park Service is maddening. Taking the button from the sleeve of her uniform jacket had been a stroke of genius. Since only six people within the Yellowstone administration had that type of jacket, the button would lead directly to Beth, after the jackets of the other five employees had been checked and no buttons were missing, at least the probability that none of the other jackets were missing a button from their sleeves was low. The hair had been almost too easy to obtain. She knew Beth kept a hairbrush in the women's restroom. It had been a piece of cake to take several strands of Beth's hair from the brush. The shoe had been more difficult. She knew she couldn't just take one of Beth's shoes and leave the other, so she decided to take a pair. She counted on Beth thinking she had misplaced the shoes and not dwell on it or think anything about it. Again, since all the muckity-mucks kept extra pairs of shoes in their offices, so that they could switch from ones they used in the field to ones they wore for social and ceremonial occasions, it had been easy to take the pair of field shoes. The shoes were the same manufacturer and style as the shoes of the other officials of Yellowstone, but the size would narrow the possibilities considerably, maybe even to Beth's shoes. If not directly to her, at least the investigators would be directed to checkout her shoes. The hair, shoeprints, and the button should seal the deal. Yes, Beth was going down. With her out-of-the-way, Becky was in. A much newer and bigger apartment came with being the Associate Superintendent. While Beth lived in that newer and bigger apartment, Becky was stuck in this dingy and cramped apartment. Her miserable situation was all going to change and very soon. How sweet it would be. With Beth out of the way, Becky would certainly be appointed Associate Superintendent, even if she had to use her body to gain the favors required to land the job. Using her body wasn't new to her. She had done it before and would probably do it again. Anything to get ahead. She knew men still found her attractive and she wouldn't hesitate to use sex to first hook them and then blackmail them.

Checking herself in the mirror, she was satisfied the dark circles had been covered. Her auburn hair fell softly to her shoulders. Her complexion was still good and her body hadn't yet begun to spread or sag. It wouldn't be long, she realized, and she would begin to show signs of entering middle age. She needed to use her physical assets now and not wait. Closing the door behind her, she walked the two blocks to her office in the administration annex building of Yellowstone. As she walked up the stairs to the second floor of the building, she could hear the murmuring of voices in the offices she walked past. Stopping in the women's restroom to check her makeup and hair one more time, she saw Nancy Myerson, an administrative assistant in the Law Enforcement and Security Office.

"Hi, Becky," said Nancy, "have you heard about the death near the Sylvan Lake picnic area?"

"No," responded Becky, "I just arrived. What's up?"

"Bruce Dickson called this morning to report that Rick VanHousen discovered a body in a car parked near the Sylvan Lake picnic area. That's all I know. He said he would call back once he had something more definite to share. The Superintendent is attending the meeting of national park superintendents at Jackson Lake Lodge and Bruce called him there. The Superintendent called after talking with Bruce and said that Beth would oversee everything and serve to coordinate the involvement of the medical examiner. Ryan was informed and he was going to let her know what was going on and what the Superintendent said, but Ryan said she wasn't coming into the office until later this morning. He was going to call her on her satellite phone to see if he could reach her."

Trying to act casual, Becky replied, "Did you say the body was in a car near the Sylvan Lake picnic area?" She felt a sense of panic coming on as she realized there was now no way to get away from what happened. What if something had been left in the car or around it someplace that could be linked to the killer or even her?

"Yea, that's what Bruce said. I guess we'll have to wait for more info. Well, I better get back to the office. There may be some other issue or crisis that has to be dealt with. It seems every time I leave the office for a few minutes, the phone rings, a text arrives, or the e-mails pile up. Have a good day, Becky."

Nancy turned and walked out the restroom, leaving Becky to mull over what she should do, if anything. They had agreed last night, during the drive back from the Sylvan Lake picnic area, to lay low and not contact each other unless it was an emergency. They each had disposable cell phones, which they agreed they would use only once, and then discard. The anxiety she was feeling only grew as she contemplated what she had gotten herself into. Probably not a crisis yet, she concluded. Don't overreact, she told herself. She needed more information before she was going to do anything rash.

CHAPTER 7

Monday
10:00 a.m.
Behind the Sylvan Lake Picnic Area, Yellowstone National Park, Wyoming

Kurt watched as Bruce and Jessica processed the scene. Jessica had taken numerous photos of the shoeprints which he had seen by the driver's door. She then made a plaster cast of the most defined shoeprint. She had also taken photos of the ground around both the driver and passenger doors. Bruce had placed some items into a few plastic bags and then labeled them. Kurt knew they were taking care to follow procedure since no one knew whether the victim had died from natural causes or had been killed. He heard Bruce yell across the distance from the car to him: "Kurt, please call Byron Henderson. I need him to come here and conduct an on-the-scene examination of the body. I don't want to disturb the body until Byron gives the o.k. to do so." Byron Henderson was the coroner and medical examiner for Gallatin County. He, or his designee, did all the medical examinations for the National Park Service in Yellowstone. Yellowstone didn't employ its own medical examiner as the number of deaths in Yellowstone was only a handful every year. It was much more economical to contract with the Gallatin County medical examiner's office for services than to have a Yellowstone employee on the payroll.

"Be right on it," responded Kurt. He took his satellite phone and called his office. Karen Voss, his administrative assistant, answered. Karen and her young daughter had moved to Jackson, Wyoming, from Grand Rapids, Michigan, following the tragic death of Karen's husband. He was one of the passengers on United Flight 93 when it crashed into the ground near Shanksville, Pennsylvania, after the passengers overwhelmed the terrorists that had highjacked the plane on September 11, 2001. Karen had recently married. She told Kurt while she still grieved her first husband, the new surroundings of Jackson and the understanding of her husband helped her to spend time grieving only occasionally.

"Hello, Kurt Bostick's office. How may I help you?"

"Karen, it's Kurt. Would you please contact Beth's office and see if anyone has contacted Byron Henderson yet. If no one has, please call Byron's office and ask him to come to the Sylvan Lake picnic area. Bruce wants to have Byron process the body. Call me back and let me know when Byron thinks he will be able to be here. There's not much else we can do around here until Byron gets here and does his thing, so tell him to come as quickly as possible."

"Will do." As Kurt was placing the phone back into his Explorer, Rick walked over to him.

"The DMV called back." Glancing at a small piece of paper he held in his hand, he said, "The Lexus is registered to a Michael Valentine. DMV has his residence as Big Sky. He registered the car only a few months ago. I've got a call into the Montana State Patrol to see if they have anything on him. Same with the Gallatin County Sheriff."

"Now that we have a name, will see if Byron finds identification on the body once he gets here. If there is identification and it says Michael Valentine, then we can be fairly confident we have identification. One other thing. When Karen calls me back, I'll have her contact the FBI. Janet VanKampen will want to be kept informed of what's going on, just in case the FBI needs to be involved." Janet VanKampen was the FBI special agent and agent-in-charge of the FBI's Billings, Montana, office. The FBI was automatically responsible for investigating any homicide occurring in a national park or monument. Although Kurt assumed this death was not a homicide, it was best to at least alert Janet. He heard his phone ring in the Explorer. Probably Karen calling him back.

"Kurt Bostick speaking."

"Kurt, it's Karen. I contacted Byron. He said he would get there as quickly as he can. Depending on the traffic, he thinks he should be there in about 45 minutes of so."

"O.k., Karen. Now, please do me one more favor. Call Janet VanKampen's office in Billings and let her know what is going on here. Tell her until we have a definite finding, we think we have a death by natural causes. If it's not, she definitely will have to be involved."

"Sure thing. I'll call back after I talk with someone there."

"Is there anything else going on this morning in our regions? No one has called me. Has anyone called the office? No fights between visitors going after the same parking place or an injury to someone?"

"Nothing has come in here, so it looks like we're having a calm morning," replied Karen. "I'll let you know if anything pops."

"Thanks, Karen." He saw Bruce and Jessica walking back from the car to their van, so he walked over to them and asked, "What do you think? Please tell me it looks routine to you."

"Can't say anything for sure," responded Bruce. "Until Byron can run tests, we can't rule out a homicide. I sure hope it isn't, but all we can do is wait. Did Byron say when he would be here?"

"He told Karen he hoped he would be here in about 45 minutes, depending on traffic," responded Kurt. "Is there anything else I can do before he arrives?"

"Just keep everyone away from walking between the picnic area and the car," said Jessica. "In fact, it would be best if no one was allowed to use the picnic area. I'll put some of the orange cones I have in my Explorer across the parking area. To play it safe, the picnic area and all the ground between it and the car should be protected. Until we know more, we need to think of this entire area as a crime scene." Looking at Bruce, she continued, "I don't think there is any need for both Bruce and me to hang around anymore. I know Bruce has several matters he needs to attend to back at the office, so Bruce, if you want to leave, I'll stick around. Byron will let me know what his preliminary findings are before he leaves. I'll stay here to hear what he has to say."

CHAPTER 8

Monday
Noon
Fountain Flats Parking Area, Yellowstone National Park, Wyoming
Two Miles South of Ojo Caliente Spring Along the Firehole River, Yellowstone National Park, Wyoming

Parker parked his 4Runner in the small parking lot at Fountain Flats. He opened the rear hatch and withdrew his waders, pulling them up over his lightweight polartech underwear. The Firehole River never ran cold, so he didn't need anything heavy under the waders. He sat on the rear bumper while he put on his wading shoes. Taking his fishing vest and fly rod, he closed and locked the 4Runner and began the two-mile walk to a section of the Firehole which he wanted to fish to determine how good a fishing spot it was before taking any clients to it. This two-mile walk was one of the many secrets which Yellowstone held for those willing to venture away from the roadways and established trails in Yellowstone. Even with all the natural beauty and magnificent thermal features along the walk, a four-mile roundtrip wasn't something most fly-fishing clients would relish if the fishing was only mediocre. As he walked, he passed several fumaroles, small boiling ponds, and numerous small geysers spewing hot water and steam into the air, making the bank of the Firehole River look like a mysterious adventure ride in an amusement park. Bison and elk grazed in the high grasses of the small meadows which were separated from each other by clumps of lodgepole pine. The sky was a deep blue, the color that was only achieved in the skies of the West. He thought back to the dreary, gray, overcast sky of Massachusetts and how the continual grayness only added to feelings of gloom that so many residents of the eastern United States possessed. Sunshine, a few puffy white clouds, intense blue skies, and steam from the fumaroles, boiling ponds and geysers blended together into a fairy land scene which was unduplicated anywhere else in the country.

Walking near the bank of the river, he kept his attention on the surface of the water watching for trout rising to eat some insect floating on the surface. He didn't expect to see any trout rising as the overhead sun usually forced the trout down toward the bottom of the river to escape the bright sun which made it possible for predators to see them in the first two feet of clear water. As he walked, his thoughts once again drifted to his feelings of loneliness. He longed for companionship with a woman of like mind and spirit. He knew what ailed him. It was the feelings of rejection and mistrust which had plagued him since his former wife walked out on him. He realized he was allowing these feelings to define any potential future relationship which might develop with a woman. He had spent time with several women since moving to West Yellowstone, but only one had affected him in a manner which he would call significant. The other women had been pleasant enough, but there had been no chemistry between them and him. There was one exception. Beth Richardson. She, too, was pleasant, but it was the combination of her personality, values, and humor which separated her from the others. Plus, she was the most wholesome woman he had ever known. Nothing pretentious about her. Of course, her beauty was unmatched, testified by the fact that men of all ages couldn't help but give her a second, third, or even fourth look whenever she was in their presence. He knew she was self-conscious about her attractiveness and she tried to downplay it. He enjoyed her not obsessing about how she dressed, her makeup, or hair. What you see is what you get was how she presented herself, and it was very refreshing after being around so many women that spent enormous time and money trying to make themselves into something they weren't.

There definitely was chemistry with Beth or, at least, there had been. He wondered if she had felt toward him in the same way. He felt their relationship had been moving toward one which would be deep and lasting, but then something had caused it to be derailed. He couldn't put his finger on what the issue or problem might have been that caused them to back away from each other. He worried it was something he had done. Not purposefully or knowingly, but something had happened. She certainly hadn't done anything to turn him off. As he neared the section of the Firehole River he wished to fish, he vowed that he was going to call her yet today and try to begin anew to establish their relationship.

Watching the surface of the water, he didn't see any activity which would indicate the trout were feeding on insects floating on the surface of the water. He opened the fly box containing his soft-hackle nymphs and selected a size 14, soft-hackle, peasant tail nymph. He tied it onto a 6 foot, number 4 tippet. He waded into the river until the water level was between his knees and thighs, a depth of water in which trout would feel safe from overhead predators such as ospreys, hawks, or eagles. He also had fished the Firehole River enough to know how deceptive the current could be. In places it became strong enough to sweep a person off her or his feet if the water level approached waist level. Always err on the side of caution he reminded himself. It wasn't wise to take unnecessary risks, especially when he was so far from the main hiking trails from where help, if he needed it, would arrive.

Casting into some water broken in its flow by several boulders, he allowed the nymph to drift with the current through a ninety degree swing until the nymph was directly down from where he was standing. He knew that the majority of strikes by subsurface trout would happen at the bottom of the drift when the nymph was directly down from him and at the full length of his cast. He had learned to count two seconds at the very bottom of the drift before lifting the nymph from the water and casting again a few feet either side of the line of the initial cast, repeating the same 90 degree drift. On the third cast and drift, he felt the characteristic thump signaling a strike by a trout. Firmly pulling his fly rod back to an upright position, he felt the throbbing and thrashing of the fish as it attempted to rid itself of the nymph which the fish had mistaken for a real insect. Several minutes ensued during which the trout, the colorful streak on its sides flashing in the sun, jumped three times trying to dislodge the hook. It was one of the misunderstandings held by people, who didn't fish, that the hook caused the fish pain and that was why fish tried to dislodge the hook. The fact was that fish didn't feel any pain from the hook but reacted to the pressure caused by the tautness of the fishing line as the fish swam in various directions. Imagine if you were tied to a rope which restricted your moving where you wanted to go. You, too, would attempt to rid yourself of the rope.

As the fish tired, Parker reeled it slowly toward himself until he could reach down, hold the fish with his free hand, and release the hook from its lower lip. Releasing a fish without damaging it or even causing it to die from too much ripping of its flesh in order to extract the hook, was much easier when the look was a barbless hook. Barbless hooks were required in Yellowstone and fly-fishers supported this policy overwhelming. For the next two hours, he hooked, landed, and released eleven trout, eight of which were rainbow trout and three German brown trout. Satisfied with the number and quality of the fish he had caught and released, he added this section of the Firehole River to his inventory of sections to which he and the guides would bring clients. He waded out of the water, cut the nymph off the tippet, placed the nymph in his fly box, and began the walk back to the parking area near Ojo Caliente Spring.

Walking along the bank, he found himself realizing how well his life had evolved since coming to West Yellowstone. The Gold Medal Fly-Fishing Shop was a success, his home was very livable and located in a wonderful place along Duck Creek, in only minutes he could lose himself in America's premier national park, and a plethora of diversified fly-fishing opportunities abounded around the Yellowstone area. He had numerous friends and acquaintances. He wasn't going to be rich and that was o.k. with him. If money was important, he would never have resigned his position as president of Sturbridge State University in Massachusetts. He was doing what he wanted to do and that trumped money.

Continuing to walk along the bank of the river, his mind drifted back to his previous thoughts of his life which, he had to admit, wasn't what he wanted it to be. He had no real relationship with a woman beyond a casual and superficial one. Karen Black, Laurie's mother, was an interesting woman. Parker had first met her when she had taken him around the area showing him various cabins and homes. She was partially Native American with a dark complexion, black hair, high cheek bones, brown eyes, and a figure which made her look ten years younger than her actual age, which he guessed to be in the mid-forties. She possessed a pleasant personality and was outgoing. For a few months, she and he had spent time together. Enjoyable times. Nothing intimate. The chemistry simply wasn't there. While they remained friends, that was as far as it went.

His thoughts turned to Jessica Samuels. She was an acquaintance whom, at one time, had tweaked Parker's interest along the lines of a possible relationship. She was fun to be around even given her position as a Yellowstone law enforcement officer. Jessica was more a city person than a rural one. She had confided in Parker that her goal was to obtain a position with a large city's police force as a detective. They had dinner together a few times during which it became evident to him that the chemistry he knew had to exist if a relationship was to blossom didn't exist between them, or at least in his mind it didn't. He had heard via the grapevine that she still wanted a relationship with him which meant he needed to be careful around her so as to not mislead her about the level of his interest in her.

He next thought of Cathy Marsman. She, too, was also an acquaintance. Parker really didn't desire to develop a relationship. She had been overbearing in the past and he had been turned off by how strongly she had come on to him. There wasn't anything to build on with her and furthermore, he wasn't interested in even trying.

He kept coming back to his interest in renewing a relationship with Beth Richardson. He wondered what her reaction would be when he called her. He would soon be in his iPhone's network range and he would call her. He wanted to reestablish their relationship slowly. Nothing too quickly which might scare her away. She was a confident woman and he respected her for her self-esteem. If people didn't know her, they might think she was cocky, even arrogant, mistaking her confidence for arrogance. He would tread slowly and carefully.

Returning to his 4Runner, he placed his vest in the back area and sat on the rear bumper where he took off his wading shoes and peeled off his waders. He stepped into his jeans followed by his Timberland hiking shoes. He broke down his fly rod, placing it into the aluminum tube which served to protect it from damage. Sliding behind the steering wheel, he reached across and opened the glove compartment where he always placed his iPhone when he wasn't carrying it. Turning it on, he placed a call to Beth's office. Ryan Belgrade, Beth's administrative assistant, answered. "Associate Superintendent Richardson's office. How may I help you?"

"Hi, Ryan, it's Parker Williams. It's good to hear your voice. Is Beth there?"

"It's good to hear your voice, too, Parker. Sorry, Beth isn't here. I do expect her any minute. She has several calls to return and numerous e-mails to answer, so I can't promise she'll be able to call you back soon. In fact, she called earlier to tell me about a body being discovered this morning. Until that gets sorted out, I'm afraid she's going to be very busy."

"I understand, Ryan," responded Parker. "It isn't an emergency, so please tell her I'll be patient." Ending the call, his iPhone beeped indicating he had a text message. It was from Laurie. "I hope the fishing proved to be worthwhile. Everything here is fine. Steady flow of customers, but not any rush which I couldn't handle."

He decided to call the shop. Laurie answered. "Hi, Laurie, I got your message. That section of the Firehole is one we want to place on our list. The walk isn't strenuous and passes through some incredibly scenic country, so most of our clients that can walk decently will be able to walk it without any difficulty and get the added benefit of seeing some amazing thermal features. Anything you want me to pick up before I return to the shop?"

"Nothing for me," replied Laurie. "I'm going to walk over to Pete's and get a small order of spaghetti while Sid covers for me. See you in a little while." Pete's Pizza and Pasta restaurant was a favorite with the locals. The various restaurants, which offered pizza on their menus, did a good business, especially Pete's.

He knew discovering a body in Yellowstone was never a routine situation. Beth was going to be up to her ears in handling various details. She certainly wouldn't be calling back for some time. Maybe it was a blessing in disguise as it gave him more time to think about what to say to her and how he should approach the conversation, the first one they had had in quite some time. He wasn't very good beating around the bush and he didn't want to have her wondering what he was trying to tell her, so he decided to be direct and go from broke if and when she called back. As he was beginning, his iPhone rang. Caller id showed it was Beth's office calling. Stopping on the shoulder of the road, he answered, "Hello".

"Hi, Parker. It's Beth. What a surprise to hear that you called. A nice surprise I should add. Long time no talk. I'm sure your life is as crazy as mine, but that shouldn't be an excuse for my not calling you before now. I thought maybe I had done something terribly wrong causing you to write me off, so I hesitated calling you. Whatever I did, I certainly am sorry and ask your forgiveness. I don't like not talking with you and I really don't like not seeing you."

He felt all his planning on what to say and how to say it go out the window. She had totally disarmed him and left him struggling for a response. "Beth, it's so good to talk with you. You didn't do or say anything wrong. It's all my fault. I don't have any excuse for being such a jerk. All I can say is I'm very sorry and I hope you will forgive me."

Laughing, she replied, "Now that we've both been apologetic and have said we're sorry for whatever we thought we did to offend the other, I vote we forget all of it and move forward. You game?"

"You bet I am," he replied, "and the sooner the better. Any chance you will have an evening free in the next couple of days? I could pick you up and, if you agree, we could drive to the Chico Hot Springs Resort for dinner. The dinner menu there is quite outstanding, I'm told." The Chico Hot Springs Resort was located in the Paradise Valley, nestled against the Emigrant Mountain Range, about forty miles north of Mammoth Hot Springs. Hot springs produced water with a steady temperature which was captured in several soaking pools. Accommodations of various types enabled guests to stay overnight or for several days. Physicians often sent patients to the resort and prescribed water therapies. The resort had an on-site restaurant offering appetizing and gourmet meals, especially dinner.

With a teasing tone of voice, she responded, "Dr. Williams, I'm under the impression you are proposing an old fashioned date. Am I correct?"

"If you wish to call it a date, fine with me. I don't care what it's called just so we are able to spend time together. How does your calendar look?"

"I know this is very short notice but this evening will work. Tomorrow evening and Wednesday evening are questionable. Does this evening work for you or is this too short of a notice?"

"You bet it works for me. I'm not even going to check my calendar. I don't care if there is something on my calendar for this evening. It is now cancelled and replaced by dinner at Chico with Beth Richardson."

"Wow! If I didn't know better, I would think I'm being treated rather specially. Am I reading too much into this?"

"No, you aren't reading too much into this. You're special and I want you to know you're special. So, get use to it."

In a teasing manner, she said, "As you say, sir. Oh, by the way, I think you're o.k. too. Now, I didn't say special. I'll save that until after I see if you allow me to order whatever I want from the menu with price being a non-issue. I hear there are some pretty expensive items on the menu."

Warming to her sarcasm, he replied in a joking manner, "If all I have to do to be considered special is allow you to order whatever you want, order away!"

He could hear her laughing as she replied, "O.k., enough of this. I have to get back to work. There's been a death near the Sylvan Lake picnic area. Until we know exactly the what, where, and how of it, I have to make sure we're covering all the bases. What time will you pick me up this evening?"

"I'll be at your apartment around 7:30 p.m. Our dinner reservation will be for 8:00 p.m. I heard something about that death. Nothing alarming, I hope."

"Too early to know," she responded. "Until I hear more, I would only be guessing. Hopefully, it will turn out to be routine. I'll be ready at 7:30. See you then and thanks for calling."

"See you this evening at 7:30."

The feelings he experienced as they had talked were ones he hadn't had for a long time. If he didn't know better, he would say he was giddy. He remembered having similar feelings when his former wife and he were dating and during their first year of marriage. Were these feelings he had while talking with Beth the initial blossoming of a more profound and deeper relationship? What about this death in Yellowstone? Could it involve more than a tourist having an unfortunate heart attack or stroke? For Beth's sake, he hoped not. A death from natural causes, if no complications were involved, was rather routine for Yellowstone's administration. Complications, such as no identification on the body or an accident involving alcohol or drugs, made managing the death more difficult. The worst, of course, was when the death was a homicide. Thankfully for Yellowstone's administration, jurisdiction of homicides occurring in national parks belonged to the FBI, since national parks, national monuments, and national forests were owned and operated by the Federal government meaning a federal authority had ultimate responsibility.

The very thought of a homicide occurring in Yellowstone caused him to reflect on the limited authority he had been given by Janet VanKampen to engage in investigative work on her behalf. The Billings, Montana, FBI Office had a large geographic area to cover and, if truth be told, it had to concentrate the majority of its time and resources dealing with white supremacists groups and various militia organizations scattered across Idaho and Montana. Yellowstone took a back seat and thus, when Agent VanKampen needed to conduct an investigation within Yellowstone, she often used "consultants" as they were called, to conduct preliminary investigations, all the while keeping her informed of their activities and findings. Parker was one of her consultants. She had approached him a while back when a homicide had occurred in Yellowstone and she was unable to assign any of her agents, that were already overwhelmed with existing investigations and cases, to cover it. He had gone to Quantico, the training headquarters for FBI agents, where he went through two-weeks of training focusing on investigative techniques. The training he received was a far cry from the extensive training provided full-time career agents. While his training did include small arms training, he was not to use a handgun unless absolutely necessary for his own protection or the protection of others. He also could not make arrests nor was he allowed to represent the FBI in a public sense. Any requests he might have for laboratory or forensic analysis had to have the prior approval of Janet who would submit the request. He was limited in the expenses he could charge to Janet's office over and beyond the per-diem he was provided. If this death in Yellowstone, which Beth had mentioned, turned out to be a homicide, he might be asked by Janet to assist with the investigation. If that turned out to be the case, he'd have to think about getting involved. Right now, all he could think about was how much he was looking forward to the evening ahead.

CHAPTER 9

Monday
Noon
Behind the Sylvan Lake Picnic Area, Yellowstone National Park, Wyoming

Byron Henderson was wrapping up his inspection of the body. Since Bruce had left shortly after he arrived, he looked for Kurt Bostick. Seeing him standing next to a National Park Service Explorer, he walked toward him. "Well, Byron," said Kurt, "what's your verdict? What was the cause of death?"

"I can't be 100% sure until I get the body back to the lab and do an autopsy, but I don't think he died from natural causes. His pupils indicate something triggered a complete shutdown of his system and it wasn't a heart attack or stroke. I've seen enough to know how the pupils look after a fatal heart attack or stroke. There is also a prick on the back of his right arm. It looks like it came from either a needle or a syringe. A strange place to have such a mark unless it was administered by someone else that was behind him, possibly in the back seat."

Trying to hide his shock, Kurt replied, "You're telling me you suspect someone killed him?"

"If I had to guess based on what I have observed," answered Byron, "I'd have to say yes. But, before we rush to judgment, I need to do the autopsy. Then I can definitely answer your question."

"When will you be able to do an autopsy? If we're dealing with a homicide, we need to alert every Park entrance station to make sure they save the photos from the security cameras for the past 48 hours."

"If I were you," replied Byron, "I wouldn't wait for the results of the autopsy. I'd alert them right now. If this isn't a homicide, you can always discard the photos. You'd probably want to cover all the bases as soon as you can rather than finding out later you would have discovered something important if you hadn't waited."

"You're correct," responded Kurt. "I'll call Karen and have her contact Beth's office and have Beth get the word out. Also, I better call Bruce and let him know what you suspect. He may not want to wait until he hears back from you, with the results of the autopsy, before he contacts Janet VanKampen. Better to alert Janet to the possibility of a homicide so she can decide how she wishes to proceed should it turn out to be a homicide."

"Before you call Karen," Byron said, "would you please help me get the body and place it into the van? There's a gurney in the rear of the van."

"I can't say I'd be happy to help, but I am willing," responded Kurt. "Let's go."

Kurt withdrew a gurney from the rear of the van and held tightly to it as it bounced over the uneven ground to the Lexus. Opening the passenger door, Kurt and Byron removed the body and placed in onto the gurney, covering it with a sheet. They had to walk very slowly back to the van making sure the body didn't slide off the gurney as it again bounced over the uneven ground. Arriving at the back of the van, they lifted the gurney onto the rear of the van and pushed it into the van, closing the doors.

"Kurt, I'll contact you, Beth's office, and Bruce's office when I have the results of the autopsy," said Byron. "Here's hoping I'm wrong and this isn't a homicide."

"I'm with you, Byron," responded Kurt.

As Byron started to walk toward the van, he turned. "I almost forgot, Kurt." He held up a small plastic bag. Inside the bag was a gold button. Kurt recognized it immediately as one of the buttons from the sleeve of the uniform jacket worn by executives of the National Park Service. "I found this under the right leg of the body. Funny place for one of your buttons, don't you think? You need to see that it gets to Bruce."

Kurt looked again at the button and with a look of disbelief he shifted his eyes toward Byron. "I don't like this, Byron, not one little bit."

CHAPTER 10

Monday Afternoon
1:15 p.m.
Food Distribution Center, Old Faithful Complex, Yellowstone National
Park, Wyoming

Lay low and wait it out. Don't act any differently. Follow the same pattern. Go about your business as usual. Don't call attention to yourself. Let it all play out. Above all, don't do anything stupid.

The menial nature of the jobs was almost too much to put up with for too much longer. It had been nearly three months of either loading and unloading boxes of foodstuffs, organizing packaged foods and cans, driving delivery vans, even busing tables at the Snow Lodge restaurant. All necessary in order to blend into Yellowstone's workforce while trying to keep tabs on Richardson. Participating in developing the plan to take Richardson down, while implementing the ultimate revenge on Valentine, was now completed, at least as far as Valentine was concerned. As for Richardson, her success was about to end once and for all.

Valentine was—correction—had been a partner with Victor Barrozo in Media Promotion Group, a multi-media firm specializing in the recruitment of woman for gentlemen's clubs, escort services, and pictorial spreads in such publications as *Playboy, Penthouse,* and *Hustler.* Under pressure, Barrozo had sold his share of the partnership to Valentine. The pressure had come in the form of threats against Barrozo's children, none of which could be traced to Valentine. When Barrozo's daughter disappeared for three days and then, with no explanation given, reappeared, the sale of Media Promotion Group to Michael Valentine occurred only a few days later, prompting rumors about Valentine's involvement in the girl's temporary disappearance. The daughter suffered nervous disorders and hallucinations and had never recovered. She was institutionalized and Barrozo had vowed revenge against Valentine for robbing his daughter of any chance at a normal life. Under Valentine's direction, Media Promotion Group had morphed into a business now specializing in the development of XXX-rated websites and pornographic movies, none of which had been ruled as pornographic by any court thanks to expensive lawyers hired by Valentine.

Nothing about the finding of a body had yet made Yellowstone's internal grapevine or the radio news alerts broadcast internally on Yellowstone's radio information network. It would happen, that was not in doubt. Patience was a necessity. As for Richardson, once the body was discovered, the cause of death pinpointed, and the evidence digested, she would be arrested and charged with the murder of Valentine. Double revenge would be accomplished. But no gloating now. Only a few more days and then goodbye to Yellowstone and hello to a whole new life.

CHAPTER 11

Monday Afternoon
3:15 p.m.
Gallatin County Medical Examiner's Office, Bozeman, Montana

Byron Henderson had double-checked the result. When he had finished the autopsy, he knew Yellowstone's administration would insist he have 100% confidence in his findings, so he had carefully checked all his procedures and tests. No questions remained. No doubt at all. 100% certain. Time to let Bruce Dickson know and let the chips fall where they may. He felt sorry for what Bruce was facing but such was the work they both did. He found Bruce's office number and pushed the call button on his cell phone. A woman answered. "Law Enforcement and Security Office. How may I help you?"

"Maria, this is Byron Henderson. If Bruce is there, I would like to talk with him." Byron had met Maria Wainwright on several occasions and knew her by name.

In her usual jovial voice, Maria replied, "Byron, how are things in Bozeman these days?"

"As well as I can hope for," responded Byron, "but I don't think Bruce is going to be too happy after I talk with him."

"I bet you're referring to that guy that died in Yellowstone. Bruce mentioned he had bad feelings about that one. Maybe it's best that Bruce isn't here. You can convey your not so happy news to Jessica. Is it o.k. if you talk with her?"

"Sure, Maria."

"I'll ring her and tell her it's you calling."

After a few rings, Jessica Samuels answered. "Hi, Byron. What's up?"

"Good morning, Jessica. I have the results of the autopsy of Valentine. I hate to tell you this, but it isn't good. I'll send my findings electronically to

Bruce as soon as we finish our conversation, but I felt it probably is going to create waves for you folks so I wanted to alert Bruce as soon as I could."

"You said it isn't good," replied Jessica. "What do you mean by 'isn't good'?"

"It isn't good because all indications are that Valentine was murdered. The only other possibility is that he injected himself, which I doubt since the muscle structure of his arms shows he was right handed and I doubt he would use his non-dominate hand to push a needle into the back of his right arm."

"So, what you're telling me is that we have a homicide on our hands, correct?"

"That's what I'm telling you," responded Byron, "and what you really aren't going to like is what killed the guy was what you folks use to tranquilize large animals."

Several seconds of silence ensured, followed by a noticeable change in Jessica's voice, indicating her shock at hearing what Byron had told her. "Are you sure, Byron? Absolutely sure?"

"Sorry to say," replied Byron, "I have no doubt. I realized what this might mean, so I checked everything I did. Everything checked out. I'm 100% certain."

"This is not good," responded Jessica. "That this is going to cause waves is an understatement. More like a tsunami. Thanks, Byron, for letting us know. Would you please also copy me on the e-mail you send Bruce?"

"Sure thing. I'm going to send it right now. Good luck. Something tells me you're going to need it."

Jessica sat quietly for several minutes contemplating the consequences of what Byron had told her. Valentine had been killed with a drug used to tranquilize large animals. The type of drug wasn't what was causing her stomach to do flip-flops nor was it the cause of the feeling of dread overwhelming her. Tranquilizers for smaller animals could be obtained rather easily and didn't require a procurement license to purchase. Tranquilizers for large animals were another story. Such tranquilizers were carefully regulated and only organizations or agencies with an appropriate license and personnel certified in the proper handling and use of the tranquilizers could obtain them. Of course, this was before the black market operations one could find on the internet. If obtained legally, almost all such tranquilizers were controlled by zoos, wild animal parks, or the Department of the Interior. Given that Valentine had been found within Yellowstone National Park, the probability that an employee of Yellowstone, with access to large animal tranquilizers, had either used it to kill Valentine or had given it to the killer who, in turn, used it to kill Valentine was probably quite high. Not for sure, but highly probable. Either way, it would mean direct involvement of a Yellowstone employee or employees in a criminal act. She shuddered to think that among Yellowstone employees might be a murderer.

CHAPTER 12

Monday Afternoon
3:30 p.m.
Law Enforcement and Security Office, Administration Building,
Yellowstone National Park, Mammoth Hot Springs, Montana

She didn't need another crisis on her plate. This homicide couldn't have come at a worse time. Thank goodness the investigation fell to the FBI. Maybe she could make lemonade out of this lemon. If she could find a way for her to be Yellowstone's liaison to the FBI's investigation, she might be in on the apprehension of the killer which would elevate her a little higher in the eyes of the upper administration folk that made decisions about promotions and advancements. However, the downside was if she did become the liaison to the FBI's investigation, it was going to intrude on her current investigation of the loss of entrance fee cash. The auditors had discovered several thousands of dollars were unaccounted for from the entrance fee cash paid by visitors entering Yellowstone. The potential for employees to pocket entrance fee cash had been discussed by the Superintendent's Council, the highest policy-making body in Yellowstone's administration, but the technology to implement a fail-safe system was expensive and had consequently been delayed time and time again due to more urgent funding needs.

She knew how the scam was being done and the cash taken. Lifetime passes for every national park or national monument were available to any U.S. citizen age 62 or older. A onetime payment of $10 purchased the pass. When stopping at an entrance booth, the driver need only present the pass and an ID, and the car was allowed to enter. No problem except there was no way to verify if the employee in the booth took $25 in cash from a car, which was the entrance fee for a car driven by a person without a pass, or the driver presented a pass which required no payment of the entrance fee. What an employee, or possibly a group of employees, was doing was taking the cash payment from the driver, keeping it, and reporting on the transaction sheet that a pass had been presented by the driver. Presto. An easy $25. Do it enough times and a sizeable amount of cash resulted.

Recently, a swipe stripe had been added to the back of newly issued passes which included relevant information about the person purchasing the pass. However, there were plenty of "old" passes in use which didn't possess the stripe. Also, the stripe could be compromised by exposure to certain magnetic fields. Extreme heat also sometimes compromised the stripe. The current policy was to allow the car to enter without paying the entrance fee if the stripe was compromised. Anything for the sake of good public relations with visitors was the stated reason. Consequently, there was no record if a compromised pass was used. An employee could report any number of cars entering Yellowstone using a compromised pass when, in actuality, the driver had paid the $25 entrance fee and the employee had kept it.

Jessica had been assigned the task of investigating this scam and identifying the employee or employees "on the take". She had been instructed by Bruce Dickson to be low-key and non-intrusive into the workings of the entrance booths. Easy for him to say. She had to be very circuitous in her work for fear she would alert the thief or thieves that their activities had been discovered. Painstaking and slow work. She had been able to determine the thief or thieves were working the Mammoth Hot Springs entrance. Unfortunately, the Mammoth Hot Springs entrance had the second most separate entrance booths of all the entrances to Yellowstone. Only the west entrance at West Yellowstone had more. Adding to the complexity associated with the Mammoth Hot Springs entrance was the fact that it was open more hours than any of the entrances meaning more individual employees were working the booths. Then there was the public relations problem since many of the employees working the Mammoth Hot Springs entrance booths were career employees, many of whom were long-term, seemingly dedicated, trust-worthy, and honest employees that usually worked the booths to cover for another employee, often a seasonal or part-time employee, that was sick or couldn't make her or his shift that day or evening.

She didn't relish what she needed to do next. She didn't see any other way to proceed. She needed to install a hidden camera in each booth to record every transaction handled by every employee in each booth over a period of time. Her hope was to catch the thief or thieves in action with irrefutable proof. The fly-in-the-ointment was the cost of purchasing and installing the cameras. If and when that hurdle was overcome, there was the problem of when to install the cameras. It had to be done when the booths weren't being used, which meant installation would need to occur in the middle of the early morning around 3 a.m.

The auditors had said about $10,000 was missing in entrance fee cash. The thief or thieves had obviously been at this for some time and might have become overconfident. When she heard the figure of $10,000, she contemplated trying to determine if any of the employees on the list of employees working the Mammoth Hot Springs entrance booths had made an expensive purchase in recent months or taken an expensive trip. Obtaining such information required more wherewithal than she could muster. It might even take a court order, given privacy laws, although it was unclear how much personal information could be obtained from Federal employees working and living within a national park.

Her recent request for the purchase and installation of cameras had been forwarded by Bruce Dickson to the Superintendent's Council. No decision had yet been made. She had her eye on a couple of seasonal employees about whom she felt suspicious. She'd simply have to be patient and catch them in the act, at least that's how she hoped this would turn out.

CHAPTER 13

Monday Afternoon
3:30 p.m.
FBI Office, Billings, Montana

What was she supposed to do? Militia groups stockpiling assault and sniper weapons for who knew what crazy plans; white supremacists threatening to reinstate "white" men to their God-ordained superior place in society; drug merchants establishing distribution centers in numerous cities and towns throughout rural Idaho and Montana; and now this—a homicide in Yellowstone. The call from Byron Henderson couldn't have come at a worse time. Where was she supposed to find an agent with any free time to travel to Yellowstone and spend the time necessary to mount an investigation and carry it forward?

Janet VanKampen, FBI special agent-in-charge of the FBI's office in Billings, Montana, felt the stress she was already under building to an even greater level. Asking for additional agents was a waste of time. She would be laughed at by her superiors. The head-in-the-sky academics in the Denver, Colorado, regional headquarters and the Yale and Harvard egg-heads in D.C., none of whom had spent a day in the field doing the work which brought the results for which the FBI was famous, wouldn't understand the need she had for additional agents. Worse yet, they wouldn't care. However, all hell would break loose and she would be criticized if the Bureau received bad publicity because she was unable to devote the human resources necessary to solve a case, quiet an unruly mob, or control a potential violent situation.

Like it or not, she had the responsibility to investigate the homicide Byron had described. He hadn't provided much information other than the cause of death was an injection of a tranquilizer used on large animals. He said Bruce Dickson had some additional information including the name of the victim. The car, in which the victim was found, had been processed by Bruce, but had not been moved, pending release by her office. Bruce had told her some hair had been found in the car along with a button. Byron was holding the body until she authorized its release to next of kin, assuming there was a next of kin to claim the body. Somehow, she had to have someone with authority to assume responsibility for an investigation, secure the evidence Bruce had described, impound the car and have it transported to the Billings office where the forensic folk could give it a thorough going over, walk the ground around the car to make sure nothing was overlooked, and arrange to have the body released to whomever was identified as next of kin. An idea came to mind. Why not do this time what she had done before? She would conduct an initial investigation and then utilize one of her consultants to continue the investigation. She knew just the consultant she would contact. Parker Williams. He had been very helpful with a recent homicide case in Yellowstone, so he had learned his way around the procedures and policies of the FBI and developed a reasonable approach to conducting an investigation. If he was willing, he would provide a credible presence and also wouldn't step beyond the acceptable boundaries of his limited authority. An extra benefit of having Parker involved was the two of them would work together and be in each other's presence; at least some of the time. When they had worked together before, she thought a relationship was in the making which would lead to bigger and better things. However, it hadn't happened. The relationship had never gotten off the ground. Probably because they lived and had their workplaces nearly 120 miles apart. Hard to have any type of a relationship when it entailed a two-hour drive each way. Maybe by having Parker involved with this homicide, a relationship might blossom this time. She would make it a point to try and make that happen. Finding the phone number for the Gold Medal Fly-Fishing Shop, she placed the call. A female voice answered after four rings. "Gold Medal Fly-Fishing Shop, Laurie speaking."

"Good afternoon. I'm agent Janet VanKampen with the Federal Bureau of Investigation. If Parker Williams is there, I'd like to talk with him."

"I'm sorry, agent VanKampen. He isn't here right now. You could try his cell phone. Do you have his number?"

"I do have his number, but not handy. If you would please give it to me, I'll call it. Go ahead."

"It's 614-326-4962."

"Thanks, Laurie."

"You're welcome, I hope you reach him."

She entered the number into her Blackberry and made the call. After four rings, it was answered. "Hello, this is Parker Williams speaking."

"Parker, it's Janet VanKampen. Long time no speak. I hope you're well and you've been able to do some fishing."

"Janet. What a nice surprise. I'm fine and the fishing is good. How are you doing?"

"The usual, I'm afraid. Up to my eyeballs trying to balance all the different cases we're dealing with right now. This brings me to the second reason I'm calling. There's been a homicide in Yellowstone and I simply don't have any agents available to run the investigation. I was hoping you would be available to take over the investigation from me after I spend some time scoping out the crime scene and collecting the evidence from Bruce and Byron. I really need your help. What do you say?"

"Janet, you've caught me totally off-guard. I really don't know how to answer. I'm not sure about my work schedule or, more importantly, the schedules of my employees. I need to check with Dick, Jim, and the other guides about guided fishing trips and also with Laurie and the other employees to make sure the hours of the shop are covered. I did hear about a death in Yellowstone, but I didn't realize it was a homicide. What can you tell me about it?"

"Nothing more than it's a homicide. I don't have many details. On my drive to the crime scene, I plan to stop by Bruce's office and talk to him as well as pick-up what he removed from the car. I'm also planning to have Byron e-mail me a copy of the autopsy report. Would you please e-mail or text me when you know your schedule and if you can help me out? We can then nail down how we will proceed."

"Not so fast, Janet. I don't know if I will even be available to help. Plus, I haven't decided if I will do it even if I am available. I can't expect my employees to continually cover for me. They have their lives to live too and I don't want them to think I'm taking advantage of them. I'll let you know after I check all the work schedules and look over what guided trips we have booked."

"O.k., I can live with that," she responded. "Please let me know as soon as you can, like yet this afternoon or no later than this evening. As I said, I'm going to the crime scene myself when we finish talking and I'd sure like to have you join me so you can learn everything I learn and, hopefully, take over the investigation." She wasn't about to tell him of her interest in seeing him and spending some time with him, even if it was in the context of inaugurating an investigation. A little time together was better than nothing.

"Please don't assume we have a deal," he replied. "I'll let you know as soon as I can. Talk to you later." As the conversation ended, he thought about Janet, not as a FBI agent, but as a woman. She possessed all the attributes which would attract men-pleasant personality, traditional values, good work ethic, above average beauty, acceptable figure, and the ability to keep confidences. She would be a 6 or 7 on a Bo Derek 1 to 10 scale. Yet, with all she had going for her, he didn't experience any desire to go beyond a working relationship with her. No chemistry existed for him. A nice person for sure. But nothing beyond a friendship. He had to admit, Janet's invitation was intriguing. It wasn't that he was bored. He enjoyed being around the shop and guiding clients now and then, but he recalled the excitement he experienced the last time he had served as an FBI consultant. He would explore the possibility of helping Janet, but only if the shop and scheduled guided fly-fishing trips were covered by his employees. He took the phone again and called his office. "Hi, Laurie, how are things?"

"Quite normal. Nothing out of the ordinary. Sid is here with me. How about you?"

"Something has come up and if you have a few minutes, I'd like you to look over the work schedules for you, Dick, Jim, and Sid for the next few days. Also, check how many guided fishing trips are scheduled for the next several days."

"You want me to check right now?"

"If you can, that would be great. I'll hold." He waited for several minutes while she must have been checking schedules.

"I'm back," she said. "Actually, work schedules are rather light since there are some days when neither Dick nor Jim is guiding. I'm not scheduled at all, although, if you think you need me, I'd be happy to work. I'm trying to earn as much money for tuition as I can."

"As a matter of fact, Laurie, I would like you to work in my place, if that's all right with you. Just being available in the shop during normal hours is what I would need you to do. You wouldn't have to do ordering or inventory or stuff like that. Selling and public relations with customers are what you do so well and, if you would be available for the next few days, you can plan on it. Sound o.k.?"

"Fine with me. I'll plan on it."

"Thanks, Laurie. Go ahead and let Dick and Jim know. I'll talk with you later." That was that, he thought to himself. He didn't have any excuse not to help Janet. It would be a diversion from his normal routine and, if he was honest with himself, he found doing investigative work interesting and challenging. It wasn't something he wanted to do day-in and day-out, but once in awhile it represented a nice break in his routine. He decided to tell Janet he would meet her at the crime scene.

CHAPTER 14

Monday Afternoon
4:00 p.m.
Ford Taurus Traveling South on U.S. Highway 89 from Livingston,
Montana

Maria Wainright answered the phone after three rings. "Office of Law Enforcement and Security, Yellowstone National Park." Maria was the administrative assistant in the Office of Law Enforcement and Security and handled all of Bruce Dickson's non-confidential communications and work. She had worked with Bruce during his previous positions at Yellowstone and was known to sometimes be several steps ahead of him due to her knowledge of how he thought and worked. She not only managed Bruce's office and his work calendar, she kept track of his social life as well, what little there was. Yellowstone employees that knew both Maria and Bruce often speculated that if something happened to Bruce, Maria was fully capable of taking over; she knew the operation of the Office so well.

"Good afternoon, Maria. This is Janet VanKampen. I'd like to talk with Bruce, if I may."

"Good afternoon to you too, Agent VanKampen. Mr. Dickson told me that when you called, I was to interrupt him, so I'll do that now. Please hold while I get him." Janet had to wait only a few seconds before Bruce came on the line.

"Janet, thanks for getting back to me so quickly. How are things with the FBI these days? They still have you protecting us from all those Middle East terrorists or have your bosses in D.C. come to their senses about the real threats to us that live in the Rocky Mountain West?"

"Bruce, you know how it is with vast agencies. The eggheads in D.C. and the academics in Denver think they have all the answers and they really don't know their arms from their asses. If they would ever get off their collective duffs and go out into the field and see what is really going on . . . but, you know all this already and it isn't going to change, so I do the best I can with what I have at my disposal. Speaking of which, I'm on my way to the homicide scene so I can take it off your hands. Parker Williams is willing to take over the routine aspects of the investigation once I'm satisfied with where it is initially, so I've asked him to meet me at the scene. I heard from him a little while ago. Could you meet us too?"

"I'll try, but if I can't, I'll send Jessica. She knows everything I do and she was at the scene with me this morning. I've already told her she is our liaison with you for your investigation, so it makes good sense to have her meet you and Parker. So, you're going to use Parker Williams again. Are you sure he's up to it? I know he seems to have a knack for these types of situations. He certainly proved his ability with the Edgar Hickson and Arthur Nichols homicides, so I guess if you need someone with some knowledge of how to conduct an investigation, he's as good as anyone else. You do need to make sure he doesn't get carried away."

"I know what you mean," she replied, "but I really have no other choice, unless you want to lend me Jessica. I simply don't have an agent to spare. I'm trying to obtain some additional agents, but I have about as much a chance of that happening as I do being the number one pick in the upcoming women's pro basketball draft. Can you lend me Jessica?" Janet hoped her intuition was correct and Bruce would say he couldn't do without Jessica. Having Jessica around Parker wasn't a good idea. Call it what you may, but she sensed Jessica had a "thing" for Parker and having her and Parker working together would provide Jessica with an opportunity to establish a relationship with Parker and Janet didn't want to give her such an opportunity.

"Sorry, Janet," responded Bruce, "I can't do without Jess. We have our hands full with our own stuff. We will work with you and Parker and support him as best we can, but he shouldn't count on us too much. I'm afraid he'll be on his own for the most part."

"I won't give him too much freedom since he is only a consultant and not even close to being a fully trained agent," replied Janet. "Any assistance you can provide him, and me too for that matter, would be appreciated. I certainly understand about Jessica. Give her my best, please. Anything I should know about the murder that you haven't already told me?"

"Nothing I can think of. I suggest you read the autopsy results to get the most comprehensive take. I find them disturbing as they point to the possibility of a Yellowstone employee being involved. After you read it and spend time at the murder scene, if you have questions, let me know. Good luck."

After talking with Bruce, she called Cynthia Jackson, her administrative assistant, and asked her whether an autopsy report had been faxed recently from Byron Henderson's office. Cynthia said one had arrived. Janet asked her to scan it and e-mail it. After several minutes, she checked her e-mail on her Blackberry and saw Cynthia's e-mail with the autopsy report attached. Stopping on the shoulder of the road, she opened the attachment and read the report. It didn't take long for her to understand why Bruce was concerned. When she handed off the investigation to Parker, she would instruct him to concentrate initially on one or more Yellowstone employees being involved in the murder.

CHAPTER 15

Monday Afternoon
3:30 p.m.
Office of the Associate Superintendent, Administration Building,
Yellowstone National Park, Mammoth Hot Springs, Montana

Sometimes she wondered if the reintroduction of wolves into the Yellowstone environment was a wise decision, given the continual uncertainty and finger-pointing of all the special interest groups, both pro-wolf and anti-wolf, which resulted in a massive headache for the Yellowstone administration. In her heart of hearts, she knew the presence of wolves as a primary predator in the Yellowstone ecosystem made absolute good sense as their presence helped control the overpopulation of elk and, to some extent, bison which, in turn, helped rejuvenate the willows and grasses which had a domino effect on maintaining healthy populations of beavers, rodents, birds, and a host of other animals. The presence of wolves also brought thousands of additional visitors to Yellowstone with the expressed purpose of seeing wild wolves living in their natural habitat. The Lamar Valley, referred to as "America's Serengeti," often had hundreds of visitors, sporting thousands of dollars of camera equipment, waiting patiently to photograph a pack of wolves or a single wolf. Just that it was a wolf was all that mattered. The economic impact of the wolf on local economies was in the millions of dollars, as visitors anxious to see a wolf, stayed in hotels and campgrounds, ate in restaurants or purchased food from local grocery stores, purchased gas and souvenirs, and attended local entertainment places. On the flip side, cattle and sheep ranchers were outspokenly hostile to the presence of wolves because wolves didn't respect national park boundaries and learned that killing a slow running calf or lamb was much easier than a faster running elk or a bison calf being protected by an aggressive mother bison. Then there were the animal-rights extremists that somehow believed the killing of any animal, even when the killer was another animal doing what animals had been doing to each other for millions of years without the extinction of species, was wrong, but the killing of unborn babies in a woman's womb was o.k. The bottom line was that the competing forces, using the power of the internet and various social media to whip up hysteria, resulted in Yellowstone officials being caught in the middle and blamed for not solving the problem.

Beth looked at her schedule for the rest of the afternoon. Thankfully, she wasn't scheduled for any public appearances or expected to attend any meetings during the remaining two hours or so. Hopefully, nothing important would intrude to turn the rest of the day into a demanding madhouse of confusing and conflicting requests for assistance or information. The one matter, which could really turn what looked to be a routine afternoon into a chaotic one, was the death near the Sylvan Lake picnic area. Before she did anything, she decided she needed to obtain the latest information from Bruce Dickson about the death. "Ryan, please get Bruce Dickson on the line for me."

"O.k., Beth, I'll give his office a call."

After a minute or two, Ryan responded, "Bruce is out of his office. Jessica is available if you wish to talk with her."

"Sure, Ryan, that would be fine." Feelings of jealousy passed through Beth as she pictured, in her mind, Jessica Samuels. Attractive, not beautiful, but definitely a sexy demeanor coupled with a sultry "come-here" look. Tall, with an athletic frame. Hazel green eyes and a complexion which suggested Hispanic heritage. She didn't hesitate to use her gender to achieve her ends, at least Beth had sized her up that way. Beth had seen Jessica flirt with Parker and, as women are so good at seeing, there was no doubt Jessica had more than a casual interest in Parker. Did Parker have an interest in Jessica? That was the million dollar question. Maybe a subtle question or two during their upcoming dinner at Chico would produce some answers. "Hi, Jessica, I hope you are well. Our paths haven't crossed for some time, so I've lost track of how things are going for you."

"Beth, since you were promoted, I know you must have a million things requiring your attention to say nothing of all the substitutions for the Superintendent you must be doing. I don't know how you do it all."

"Jess, all of us have too much on our plate. The budget situation in D.C. has hurt us badly, as it has all the national parks and monuments. Too many things requiring attention and too few employees or resources to provide the required attention. But, we do the best we can."

"You got that right," replied Jessica. "We better get to the reason for your call."

"I'm calling," responded Beth, "to learn the latest about the death near the Sylvan Lake picnic area. Being Bruce's right hand person, I assume you know the latest."

"I was with Bruce at the Sylvan Lake picnic area so I can tell you about the things we first noticed. I've also read the autopsy report Byron sent Bruce. Beth, I hate to tell you, but we've a homicide on our hands."

"Oh, no, Jess. It can't be! Not another one. Just what we don't need. Has Bruce informed Janet VanKampen?"

"Yes, he did. He also sent her a copy of the autopsy report. In fact, he's meeting her right now at the crime scene to hand her the evidence we obtained and to officially turn the investigation over to her. He's assigned me the responsibility to serve as our office's liaison with Janet's office during the FBI's investigation. But, Beth, I haven't told you the worst."

"You mean a homicide isn't bad enough. What could be worse?"

"If you get a chance to read the autopsy report, you'll see for yourself. I'll fax you a copy. The bad news is the killer injected a massive amount of sucostrin into the victim and you know, as well as anyone, sucostrin is used by us. The killer might be one of our own. Not necessarily, of course, but the probability of a Yellowstone employee being involved, either as the killer or as an accomplice that gave sucostrin to the killer, is increased."

Beth withdrew her breath sharply as Jessica's words sank in. "Jess, I see what you mean. I wonder if the Superintendent has been briefed. Do you know if Bruce contacted the Superintendent's office already?"

"Knowing how methodical and precise Bruce is, I'd be surprised if he hasn't already done so," replied Jessica.

"I'll check anyway," responded Beth. "Thanks Jess, for the info."

"Sure thing, Beth. There's one other thing. Janet told Bruce she would be utilizing one of her consultants to assist her and take over the direction of the investigation once she completes the preliminary work. She said she had asked Parker Williams. Are you still seeing him?"

The directness of the question caught Beth off-guard. If she answered that Parker and she hadn't seen each other for some time, it would encourage Jessica to use her liaison role to be as involved with Parker as possible. If she answered that Parker and she were planning to have dinner at Chico in a few hours, Jessica would certainly spread rumors about Parker and Beth spending the night together at Chico. If those rumors got back to Parker, what she hoped would be a new beginning in a successful relationship could turn out to be a disaster. She knew Parker still carried a cautious skepticism about women and establishing trust between he and she was essential. Rumors about their shacking up could destroy trust in a heartbeat. "We continue to be friends," she answered. She quickly ended any further questioning by saying, "Thanks, again, Jess, for the info. I hope to see you around."

She closed her eyes and leaned back in her chair. She had been hit with a triple whammy. A homicide; a heightened probability of a Yellowstone employee being involved; and Parker working with Janet VanKampen and Jessica Samuels. Beth wasn't sure what bothered her the most. All three were bad news. Two had already happened, so she needed to not let those eat at her too much. The third—the probability of a Yellowstone employee being involved in the homicide—needed to be taken seriously with appropriate attention to media relations as the media often hyped any negative occurrence in a national park and would certainly do so with this situation once they learned a Yellowstone employee might be involved. She could do something about that problem by sending out a directive on the internal communication systems that no one other than Yellowstone's Public and Media Relations Office was to talk with the media about the homicide. It was probably a good thing she concentrated on controlling the story since she didn't want to think about the other two problems.

CHAPTER 16

Monday Afternoon
4:45 p.m.
Sylvan Lake Picnic Area, Yellowstone National Park, Wyoming

He hoped he was doing the right thing. Laurie had said she wanted to work more so he did have the time to devote to an investigation. Since he was in the role of a consultant to Janet, she had ultimate responsibility, meaning if it became too complicated, he could admit he was in over his head and turn the investigation over entirely to her. She would then have to decide how she would proceed.

As he drove around the turn near the Sylvan Lake picnic area, he spied a black, four-door Ford Victoria parked in the picnic area. It screamed FBI. Stopping behind it, he saw the roof antenna and the U.S. Government license plate. Exiting the 4Runner, he saw a silver Lexus parked about thirty yards behind the picnic area. Yellow crime scene tape circled the Lexus as well as about twenty yards out from it. Janet VanKampen and Jessica Samuels were standing together talking near the Lexus. Walking toward them, Janet was the first to note his presence. Stepping to him, she extended her arms around him in a hug, catching him totally off guard and causing him to blush with embarrassment. "Parker," Janet said, "it's so good to see you. Thanks for agreeing to help with the investigation. Do you know Jessica Samuels?"

"Yes, I do," he responded, still feeling the warmth of his blush. Jessica must have also been embarrassed by Janet's show of affection as her look of surprise also showed her embarrassment. Reaching to shake Jessica's hand, he was certain the look she gave him was her way of non-verbally communicating "what's going on between you two?" "Hi, Jess," he said as he shook her hand. "You're looking well. I trust Bruce isn't overworking you."

"Parker, you're looking well yourself," she replied, "the fly-fishing business must be treating you well. I understand you're going to assist

Janet with this investigation. I'm going to be Yellowstone's liaison, so any support you need from us, please let me know." Parker noted a sparkle in her eyes and a slight smile as she was speaking. He interpreted her look as her communicating non-verbally that she intended to provide personal support beyond her official capacity. Not what he wanted. He needed to walk a fine line with her. Support of Yellowstone's Law Enforcement and Security Office was essential because without it, he might as well walk away from this whole matter. At the same time, he needed to keep Jess at arm's length. No encouragement from him to have anything more than a working relationship exist between them.

Janet must have sensed what Jessica was up to since she quickly interrupted any further conversation between Jessica and Parker. "Jessica, why don't you tell Parker what you told me about how you and Bruce found the body, what the scene consisted of, and the evidence you gathered." Turning to Parker, she continued, "I have the evidence now and, in fact, the lab geeks are doing their thing right now with it. I should be hearing from them shortly. When they want to they can turn things around quickly. I also have a copy of the autopsy report which you can read on my Blackberry. I think it would be best for you to take a few minutes now and read the report so we can discuss it together and decide how you plan to proceed before I leave to go back to Billings." Turning back to Jessica, she continued, "You can take off after you brief Parker. While you do that, I have some phone calls to make. I'll use my car phone. Thanks, again, for coming to brief us, Jessica. Give my best to Bruce."

Parker listened as Jessica told him about the photos and casts of shoeprints around the car, the strands of hair recovered from the body and the front seat, and the button found in the car. She also told him the Sunday evening and night recordings from the security camera at the East entrance booth were being reviewed by the technicians in the Billings Office. They agreed the hair would be important to both eliminate possible suspects and to identify the killer, assuming the hair came from the killer.

She described the findings of the autopsy but agreed with Janet that he needed to read it for himself, which he did after thanking Jessica and quickly moving away from her so there wouldn't be an opportunity to engage in personal conversation. He sat in his 4Runner while he read the autopsy report on Janet's Blackberry. He thought he could see how to proceed. Closing the door of the 4Runner, he walked to Janet's car where she was sitting in the driver's seat talking on her car phone. She held up a finger to indicate her conversation would soon end. After a few minutes, she placed the phone in its holder and stepped from the car. "You heard what Jessica had to say and you've read the autopsy report. What are your initial impressions and how do you think you want to proceed?"

Handing her Blackberry to her, he replied, "I think I should begin by getting a list of all Yellowstone employees that would have access to sucostrin. Then check to determine if any of them obtained an amount of it during the past few months. Depending on what I learn, next establish where these employees were last evening after 9 o'clock. Once I have as much information as I'm likely to get, I'll want to interview each of them. I'll need someone to accompany me for those interviews, so you'll need to have someone available to go with me. I want the findings from the lab about the shoeprints and hair as soon as you can get them to me."

"Sounds like a reasonable plan. Like I said earlier, I expect to hear from the lab people soon. There is one problem. I can't provide you with help. You'll have to conduct interviews on your own. Also, when you need some muscle to open up some doors or push some uncooperative people, call the office. I will tell Cynthia to be alert to your requests in case I'm not around. Now, before I leave, let's review a few ground rules. First and foremost, no taking undue risks or playing lone ranger when the situation may be dangerous to you or anyone else's safety. Don't forget, you're dealing with a killer, so err on the side of caution. While you're authorized to carry, your gun should only be used in an emergency or in self-defense. Second, e-mail or text me daily with an update of your activities, findings, and subsequent plans. Even if you haven't made any progress, I want to hear from you anyway. If I contact you, it will be to provide information which I believe will be helpful in the investigation. Finally, carry a copy of your authorization memo with you at all times in case your authority is questioned. Anything you can think of I've overlooked?"

"My mind is going one hundred miles an hour right now, so I can't think of anything. Maybe later." He was uncertain about telling her of his intention to talk with Beth before doing anything in order to get her take on the situation and also to ask her how he could obtain a list of all Yellowstone employees having access to sucostrin. He decided not to tell Janet, at least not now. "I will certainly stay in touch, you can count on that."

"O.k. then," replied Janet, "I'll be going." Before he could react and step away, she pulled him into a hug which brought their bodies together for too long. Releasing him, she walked to her car and drove away, leaving him to renew his doubts about whether Janet didn't have personal reasons for having him working with her in addition to her stated reasons. Pushing aside his thoughts about Janet's real agenda, he took his iPhone and called Beth's office.

"Hello. Office of the Associate Superintendent. Ryan speaking."

"Ryan, this is Parker Williams. Is Beth available?"

"She is, Parker. I'll get her for you."

"Hi, Parker, or should I say consultant-agent Williams," said Beth.

"So you've already heard," he responded. "I wanted to tell you myself before hearing it from someone else. I'm sorry, but I wasn't able to get to you earlier."

"No apologies necessary," she replied, "but I suppose this means our dinner at Chico is out the window." Teasingly, she continued, "I knew you would find a way to get out of paying for dinner."

"You've got it all wrong, Associate Superintendent Richardson," he responded in his own teasing tone. "I've set aside ten dollars to pay for your gourmet hot dog with chips and a coke, so I expect you to live up to your end of the bargain and accompany me to dinner."

She replied laughingly, "Will ketchup and mustard be too much for you to allow me or should I borrow some packets of both from the cafeteria?" Pausing to have her teasing tone subside, she continued in a more serious tone, "I would love to continue this one-ups-man-ship, but I've a meeting I have to get to."

"Before you go," he replied, "I think I need to find out which Yellowstone employees have access to sucostrin. How can I obtain a list?"

"You could say pretty-please," she replied laughingly, "but I must tell you, I think you're barking up the wrong tree. I know sucostrin was used to kill the victim, but that doesn't automatically mean a Yellowstone employee was the killer. I bet sucostrin can be obtained from the internet. Also, don't rule out people that work with large animals in zoos. I know I sound defensive, but I'm having trouble accepting that a Yellowstone employee is a murderer. I know quite a few of our employees and none of them could kill another person. But, I'll be a cooperative, good, little girl and have a list put together of all our employees having access to sucostrin."

"Thanks much. I know, now I owe you big time. Do you think you'll have it by the time we have dinner this evening?"

Once again in her teasing voice she responded, "I knew it was too good to be true. Dumb me. How could I be taken in so easily? I thought I was being asked to have dinner with a man I enjoy being with because he enjoys being with me. Silly me. He's only interested in what help I can give him as he plays Sherlock Holmes. I'll do my best, Sherlock, to have a list to give to you at dinner. One thing you should know, my name will be on the list. The Superintendent will also be there. In fact, all administrators at the upper levels of Yellowstone management have access. Where the difficulty lies is which other employees have access. Although policy says no delegation of authority for handling sucostrin is allowed, who knows how closely it is followed."

"Fair enough," he replied, "and just so you know, if you want to upgrade from chips to French fries with your hot dog, it will cost you an afternoon date for us to hike the Elk Mountain trail."

"You have a deal," she replied. Laughingly, she continued, "with us it's either famine or feast. Don't communicate for awhile and then being together twice in a short period of time. But, if we keep talking and I don't get back to my work, I might not be able to do either. So, before I say adios, what time are you picking me up this evening?"

"By 7:30, but as soon after 7:00 as you can make it.:

"That works for me. I'll try to make it by 7:00. See you then."

Without having the list of Yellowstone employees with access to sucostrin, he wasn't going to be able to do much to narrow the potential employees to a smaller number. As he was thinking through what he could do until he had Beth's list, he received a text message. It was from Janet. "Call me as soon as you can. Some lab results are back." Finding Janet's office number, he made the call.

"Office of the FBI."

"Hello, Cynthia, this is Parker Williams. I have a text message from Janet asking me to call her. Is she available?"

"She's here, but on another line. I don't believe she will be much longer, so I can place you on hold or, if you prefer, I will have her call you as soon as she finishes her call."

"I can wait. Thanks."

The elevator music began to play as he waited for Janet to come on the line. Funny, he thought. Arguably, the world's most powerful and effective crime investigative organization, and it used elevator music just like thousands of hotels and small businesses. Why it struck him as funny he didn't know. But, it did. "Hi, Parker, I wanted you to have the lab results for some of the stuff found at the crime scene. The lab geeks worked even quicker than I expected. It must be my charm and wonderful way of persuading them to place my stuff ahead of everything else. Don't I wish. Truth be told, I bet they didn't have anything to do this afternoon, so my request gave them something to do. I'll make sure to send a complimentary letter to the Director of Forensics. Anyway, here are the results. First, a woman may be involved. The hair samples came from a woman. The lab geeks say her age is mid-30s to mid-40s. Hair color is dark brown or auburn. Of course, the hair may belong to a woman having nothing to do with the murder but we can't discount that it might have come from the killer. Second, the shoeprints are those of a size 7, narrow width, hiking-type shoe, probably Meryl. Could be Timberland as well. Same sole pattern, I guess. The lab geeks think the height of the killer is between 5'6" and 5'8". Both suggest a woman might be involved. Third, the button. It is one found on many types of uniform jackets or blazers. It is used as decoration on the sleeves. Maybe the button came off the killer's jacket. Maybe it didn't. It might have come off when the victim was struggling with the killer before the sucostrin took effect. They were able to lift a fingerprint from the button which has been sent to the fingerprint folks in D.C. They will run it through their data bases. If they get a hit, they will let me know. Anyway, these three, the hair, shoeprints, and button are enough, I think, for you to concentrate, at least initially, on women employees of Yellowstone, age mid-30s to mid-40s, height between 5'6" and 5'8," wearing size 7, narrow width, Meryl hiking shoes, and missing a button from the sleeve of her uniform jacket or blazer."

CHAPTER 17

Monday Evening
5:15 p.m.
Outside the Administration Annex Building, Yellowstone National Park,
Mammoth Hot Springs, Montana

The Yellowstone grapevine was following its usual pattern. Sometimes it seemed to her as good a communication tool as e-mail or texting. It amazed her that with employees scattered across almost one thousand square miles into small groups, rumors, gossip, and sometimes even facts would pass from group to group in what seemed like lightning speed. What made it truly amazing was the fact that only thirty percent of Yellowstone had internet service thereby rendering e-mail, text, and non-satellite cell phones useless. Somehow, news like a murder in Yellowstone spread like wildfire. She first heard the news from Sophia Lopez, a receptionist for Roosevelt Lodge that happened to be passing through Mammoth Hot Springs, having spent her off-day in Livingston, Montana, doing some personal shopping. She told Becky the news when they met in the women's rest room in the administration annex building when Sophia had stopped to take a break during her drive back to Roosevelt Lodge. When Becky asked Sophia how she had heard the news, Sophia responded her cousin, employed in the Snow Lodge at Old Faithful, had sent her a text. Becky remembered the Old Faithful area had full text, e-mail, and cell phone capability.

No turning back now. Her stress level elevated as she realized what she had done couldn't be undone. She was an accomplice in a murder, pure and simple. Her anxiety was high and increasing as she worried whether the false evidence had been discovered and, assuming it had, if anything had been done with it. She had to find out. Not knowing was driving her nuts. She found the number and pushed the call button. "I told you not to call me" was the answer to her call.

"I know, I know, but not knowing anything is driving me crazy. All I've heard is that it has been declared a murder. That's it. What about the evidence? Was it discovered as we wanted?"

"Listen, no more calls. I'm not going to tell you again. I don't know any more than you do. What we can't do is panic. We need to continue to lay low and let things come together. Stick to your normal routine."

"Easy for you to say," replied Becky, "you don't see the bitch like I do. I'm scared she is going to worm her way out of this. Then what? We're left holding the bag. I don't want to go to prison."

"Get a hold of yourself. If people see you acting out-of-sorts or overly nervous, they will wonder why, and we don't need that. Go about your work as normal as possible and whatever you do, don't do anything to draw attention to yourself."

"You don't have to lecture me," Becky responded, "I just want this whole thing to end with Richardson going down. That's why I agreed to be part of your plan. I'm nervous about you forgetting something or maybe you left something behind to make us vulnerable. Don't forget, you're the person that killed him, not me. It's your neck on the line, so you better make sure this works out right. Get me some information before I go crazy."

"Becky, are you threatening me? If so, you better forget that right now. Like I said, when I know more, you will hear it from me. For now, keep a low profile and button your lip. Don't call me again."

This wasn't good. Greenbrier was becoming unhinged. Unhinged people do stupid things. She could ruin the whole thing. She probably had watched too many television mystery shows where one of the perpetrators rats on the other and is excused by the cops for turning into a witness for the cops. Greenbrier had become a liability which required elimination. The sooner the better.

CHAPTER 18

Monday Afternoon
6:10 p.m.
Geyser Apartments for Yellowstone National Park Officials, Yellowstone National Park, Mammoth Hot Springs, Montana

The wolf management task force meeting had been a waste of time. Just what she had expected. With the disagreement between the wildlife agencies of Wyoming, Montana, and Idaho regarding the endangered status, or lack thereof, of the wolf and the Yellowstone administration being the convenient scapegoat for all three to blame for not being able to confine the wolf within Yellowstone's borders, meetings like this were nothing but a bitch session. Add the hostility of the ranching community because calves were easy prey for wolves, and you had a recipe for finger-pointing, blame, and mistrust. All her diplomatic skills had been put to the test. She had about an hour to unwind and get herself ready for her dinner and evening with Parker. She had earlier sent him a text telling him she would be ready by 7:00 p.m. Ryan had left the list of employees having access to sucostrin with her. Smiling to herself, she turned off the lights and locked the office door behind her. The walk from the office to her apartment took no more than five minutes. Entering the apartment, she checked the clock on the kitchen wall. 6:10 p.m. She'd have to hustle, but fifty minutes was enough time for a quick shower and hair styling before Parker arrived.

Drying off and entering the bedroom, she paused to check herself in the full-length mirror on the rear of the closet door. She had to admit, her body had yet to experience any early middle-age spread. The "10" she had been given in the swimsuit portion of the Miss America Pageant would probably be a "9" now if the Pageant were held today. Nothing sagged; nothing required extra pushing or pulling. Dressing in a pale yellow dress, she chose a simple silver necklace, matching tear-drop earrings and bracelet. The dress had been hanging in the closet near her uniform jacket. I have to remember to have that missing button replaced, she thought, and then have the jacket cleaned and pressed. She laid the jacket on the chair next to the closet so she would remember to take it with her in the morning and drop it at the dry cleaners in Gardiner where the owner did some tailoring and repair work on clothes. A touch of lipstick and a quick once-over with hair spray and she was ready for what she hoped would be an evening of good companionship, excellent food, and the basis of a meaningful relationship. Checking one more time in the mirror, she was satisfied with the person staring back at her. Locking the door behind her, she remembered how Parker and she had agreed, when they first began seeing each other, that she would wait for him outside her apartment, weather permitting, rather than having him park, enter her apartment complex, and come to her apartment. There were several benches along the walkway, which passed in front of her apartment complex, and she sat on one to await his arrival. After only a few minutes, she saw his 4Runner driving toward her along the frontage road which paralleled the main highway through Mammoth Hot Springs. As he pulled over to where she was sitting, he parked, walked quickly around the front of the 4Runner to the passenger door, opened it, and in one sweeping motion of his arm, indicated she should enter.

In a humorous tone of voice, she asked, "Is this the new Parker Williams? I kind of liked the old Parker Williams. Does this mean I have to become a different Beth Richardson too?"

"Not on your life," he responded. "You better not change a thing. Now, get in so we can get to Chico on time. Otherwise, all the hot dogs might be gone and you'll have to go without your gourmet dinner."

They exited Yellowstone, passing through the famous Teddy Roosevelt arch, and continued on U.S. Highway 89 toward Livingston, Montana. The Chico Hot Springs Resort was about forty miles north, allowing time for Beth to explain to him the list of fifteen Yellowstone employees having access to sucostrin and each of their roles within the administration and operation of Yellowstone. He told her about his conversation with Janet during which she had told him about the results of the FBI lab tests of the evidence found in the victim's car and the surrounding area.

"I would think size 7, narrow width, Meryl hiking shoe rules out any male employee," said Beth, "assuming, of course, the shoeprints are those of the killer. So, instead of fifteen people to check out, you're down to seven, assuming you agree that a size 7, narrow width shoe is too small a shoe for a man to wear. I should add, I'm one of the seven employees remaining and I wear a size 7, narrow width, Meryl hiking shoe, so you can begin to investigate me right now," she continued laughingly.

"Are you kidding me? You're about as much a murderer as I am. No, I'm down to six women employees. However, I am going to interrogate you, but not about yourself. I'm going to interrogate you about the other six women employees. I especially want your best guess as to which one or ones might be capable of killing another person."

"You don't want much, do you," she replied, "let me think about this for a few minutes."

He knew better than to say anything to her while she was assessing the temperament and likelihood of any of the women on the list to commit murder. After several minutes of silence, she said, "I don't know three of them well enough to even make a guess. I do know that two of the three work at Grant Village and the third at Yellowstone Lake. Besides, I'm quite sure all three are a couple of inches taller than me and I'm 5'8," so they would have to be 5'10" or even taller which would probably mean they wear a shoe size greater than 7. The other three—Gretchen Newberry, Yolanda Gutierrez, and Becky Greenbrier—I do know well enough to make a guess, but it's really only that—a guess. I could be all wrong. Knowing what I do about each, I'd look at Becky first, followed by Gretchen. Yolanda, I really don't think so. She's simply too differential. You know what I mean by differential?"

He replied, "I think so. You mean she is more meek or timid than is normal for most people. She's not aggressive at all."

"Yea, that's it," responded Beth. Too timid. Meek and mild describes her. She is the type that wouldn't step on an ant if she could help it. Not the killer type, if you get my gist."

He replied, "I remember Greenbrier from her being involved with the Edgar Hickson case. Greenbrier is certainly not a Yolanda Gutierrez. Greenbrier's the other side of that coin. She's aggressive, almost bordering on pushy. Why is she at the top of your list?"

"For the reasons you just described, plus, she's a climber," responded Beth. "She doesn't care who she steps on or pushes aside, as long as it benefits her and moves her along toward her goal of being the #1 woman wherever she is at the moment. She would, for example, love nothing more than to have my job and she would do anything she felt she had to in order to get my job."

"Sounds like a nice woman," he replied, "just the type one loves to be around. Is she still working in the Law Enforcement and Security Office?"

"No, she was transferred to Visitor Services. I think Bruce had enough of her flaunting herself and trying to make herself look good at his expense. He orchestrated an internal transfer."

"Now that I think more about Becky, what I remember about her is how she came on to me during the Hickson case," he replied. "I experienced first-hand what you're talking about. Aggressive and pushy. But, enough about Becky. Tell me about Gretchen and then no more about this investigation. I want this evening to be about us."

"About us, I would like that too. About Gretchen. She is a whiner and complainer. I think she must be an only child that was spoiled rotten and got her way all the time by pouting and whining as a child. It has carried over into adulthood. However, this isn't why I think she might be capable of murder. While I haven't experienced it myself, I've heard she has a terrible temper and a mean streak. The combination could be deadly and I'm not saying that as a pun."

"O.k., I'll try to interview both of them as soon as possible. Now, no more about Gretchen, Becky, Valentine, or anyone else or anything related to the investigation. All I want to talk about for the rest of this evening is Beth Richardson, Parker Williams, and the future."

CHAPTER 19

Monday Evening
7:15 p.m.
Room 224, Terrace Apartments for Yellowstone National Park Employees,
Yellowstone National Park, Mammoth Hot Springs, Montana

Why had she been so stupid? Getting high was one thing but to tell her scheme to him was where she really blew it. Since then she had been at his mercy. He had her where he wanted her. If she didn't cooperate, it wouldn't faze him in the least to turn her in and find another Yellowstone employee to run the scam while he continued to take his cut. All this had happened because she had been going stir crazy being isolated away from the action, which she needed to have in order to satisfy an internal craving which she didn't understand. He had offered her the drugs which, he said, would enhance her feelings. That is when she should have said no and walked away. She hadn't walked away and the combination of the drugs with alcohol had been almost too much. When he took her to that place and pressured her to have sex, she hadn't resisted. She had wanted it as much as he. In the euphoria of the moment, she had told him about her scheme. That had been the beginning of the threats and blackmail.

It had started so harmlessly. Only a few hundred dollars every few days. She knew that a few hundred dollars every so often wouldn't be missed. She had told herself not to be greedy. Too much too often and the accounting gurus in the basement of the administration building might discover a shortfall in entrance fee cash. Then her cash-cow scheme would come under investigation.

When he threatened her with exposure, if she didn't cooperate in getting what he said he needed, she didn't think twice since it would result in her getting revenge. What she hadn't counted on was after giving him what he asked for; he demanded a share of the fee money. If he didn't get a share, he said he would tell Yellowstone administration officials about her scheme. She had returned the threat telling him she would expose him as a drug dealer. He had laughed and told her she was a user so if he was exposed, she would be too.

She thought she would feel good about getting revenge. She had never counted on murder and now the revenge wasn't very satisfying as she realized she could be charged with being an accomplice to murder. Her stress level was out-of-sight and she was having trouble even going through the motions at work. When he told her he wanted another session of partying at the place, as he called it, she had lost it. She had screamed at him and told him sex at a time like this was impossible for her. He had responded by telling her there were some drugs at the place which would lower her anxiety and stress. She didn't want to accept his offer but the need to feel better was so powerful she acquiesced. She detested herself for being so weak and detested him for manipulating her.

Somehow, she had to find a way out of this mess. Should she confess everything and hope to gain some leniency and sympathy for coming forth with the truth? It would only be her word against his. What explicit proof did she have to convince the authorities she had been intimidated and manipulated, and had acted the way she had because of pressure from him? Wouldn't it be better if he wasn't able to refute her? If he were to disappear or die, wouldn't her life be so much better?

CHAPTER 20

Tuesday Morning
7:15 a.m.
Home of Parker Williams on Duck Creek, 9 Miles North of West
Yellowstone off U.S. Highway 191, Montana
Gold Medal Fly-Fishing Shop, West Yellowstone, Montana

The song birds sounded extra vociferous filling the morning air with a symphony of sounds like little else in the world. The sunlight streaming through his bedroom windows seemed brighter than usual. Everything around him seemed more alive as he sipped his cup of coffee on the deck of his home and reflected on last evening's dinner with Beth and their conversation.

They had picked up where they had left off several months ago. It was as if there had been no time of absence from each other. Neither of them spent time trying to analyze what had occurred which caused them to drift apart. Rather than looking back and second-guessing what each had or had not been thinking or doing, they shared their ideas and plans for the future, albeit in a cautious manner. The food at the Chico Hot Springs Resort had lived up to its reputation and the atmosphere was superb. It was easy for him to forget about what he would be facing today, an interview with Becky Greenbrier which he would rather not do. He could tell Beth was enjoying the evening as much as he. She, too, seemed to disengage from the pressures and stress of her work and the responsibility of being the second-in-command of the nation's premiere national park.

The drive from Chico to Mammoth Hot Springs had been one of conflicting thoughts and emotions. On the one hand, the intimacy of dinner and their conversation had triggered a desire for the intimacy to continue, even involving physical intimacy. It would have been easy to stop at his home and spend the night together. This wasn't a raw, sexual need on his part but a desire to be with a woman he admired and cared for a great deal. On the other hand, their relationship was back on track and if it continued to develop and blossom, a mutual desire for physical intimacy would naturally result. Call it old fashioned, but one of the many attributes he admired in Beth was her sense of morals and her belief in traditional values. He didn't want to make her chose between compromising her morals and values, or thinking she was pushing him away. In the end, he drove directly to her apartment where they promised to spend Saturday together hiking the Elk Mountain trail and enjoying a picnic.

Closing the slider behind him, he placed his empty coffee cup in the dishwasher and walked to the shower in the master bath. Entering the shower, he allowed the hot water to cascade over him. Finishing this rinse, he stepped onto the bathmat and took a towel, hanging on the towel bar next to the shower, and began to dry himself. As he was drying himself, he looked in the full-length mirror which was on the inside of the bathroom door. Not bad for a 43-year old, he thought to himself. The typical middle-age shape of men-flat rear end, pot belly, receding hair line—were yet to manifest themselves in his body. He did need to exercise more and also watch his calorie intake. Dressing in jeans, a long sleeve, green and white striped cotton shirt, and a pair of Keene walking shoes, he locked the front door of the house, got into his 4Runner, and headed toward West Yellowstone. Arriving in West Yellowstone, he stopped at the Book Peddler to pick up his usual homemade scone and take-out coffee. Saying thanks to Susan Nesbitt, the owner of the Book Peddler, he drove to the shop and parked behind it.

Entering the shop, he was surprised to find Karen Black talking with her daughter, Laurie. For a few seconds, Parker was taken aback by how similar in looks and body shape were Karen and Laurie. It truly was difficult to tell mother and daughter apart. Karen certainly didn't look her age. "Karen, how nice to see you," he said. "It's been awhile. You look terrific. The real estate business must be treating you well."

"Don't I wish," responded Karen, "but I must say I'm doing better than most of my colleagues. The housing collapse and the mortgage mess have affected all of us. You look good yourself, Parker. Must be all those days guiding clients. Now you're the head-honcho on this murder investigation I've heard about. Are you making progress?"

"I've a couple of leads I'm following. Hopefully, they will produce some answers and point me in the right direction. What brings you by our humble shop?"

"Giving my daughter some womanly advice which, of course, she'll ignore. But, it's what mothers do. I'm also picking up some recent pictures of various listings for a client. He leased a home a few months ago north of Mammoth Hot Springs and he is thinking of purchasing a place even before his lease expires. He's got major bucks so if I can make a sale, it will mean a significant commission, some of which can be used for Laurie's tuition."

"If anyone can make a deal work, it's you Karen. Is this guy local or from out-of-state?"

"He lives in Chicago. That's about all I know. He's a secretive guy. Plays things close to the vest. Italian through and through. Barrozo is his last name. Victor Barrozo."

CHAPTER 21

Tuesday Morning
11:30 a.m.
Administration Annex Building, Yellowstone National Park, Mammoth Hot Springs, Montana

She hadn't been able to eat a thing. Her stomach was doing flip-flops. She was a nervous wreck. She had to get a hold of herself before he arrived. He didn't know anything, did he? He had to be fishing. Why her? Why did he want to talk with her? Had the FBI discovered something which pointed to her? Get yourself together. What can they prove? It's my word against theirs. I need to take another Valium. I have to act normal. Don't let him trap me into saying anything I shouldn't. Act dumb. Deny everything. Direct him toward Richardson. I can't take it. I need to know if something has gone wrong.

Taking the second disposable cell phone, she punched in the number. It was answered, "Who is calling?"

"It's me. Parker Williams is coming to see me. He has FBI authorization to ask me questions. What is happening? You told me everything would be smooth with no possibility of anything being traced to me."

"I told you to not call me, unless it was an emergency and this isn't an emergency. Williams knows nothing. No one knows anything. He's on a fishing expedition. Settle down and act normal. Take one of those uppers I gave you. Now, don't call me again."

"What does he know? Why is he coming to talk with me? What do they know about me?"

"I'm not going to say it again. Get a hold of yourself. If he sees you acting nervous or out-of-sorts, he will get suspicious. Let him ask his questions. He's harmless. He's as much an FBI agent as you are a marathon runner. Humor him. Goodbye and don't call me again."

That did it. Greenbrier needed to be eliminated. Tonight. She was unstable and unstable people did stupid things. Tonight.

CHAPTER 22

Tuesday Afternoon
1:30 p.m.
Visitor Services Office, Administration Annex Building, Yellowstone
National Park, Mammoth Hot Springs, Montana

The Visitor Services Office was located in the Administration Annex, a small building a stone's throw from the Administration Building. He entered the office and was greeted by a middle-age woman, whom he assumed to be the receptionist, seated behind a large desk on which a computer and several small piles of paper were located. The woman was plainly dressed in dark brown slacks and a cream-colored blouse. Her hair was cut short and she wore minimal makeup. Looking up from the desk she said, "May I help you, sir?"

Opening his identification wallet which contained his FBI identification card, he responded, "I'm Parker Williams. I called about seeing Miss Greenbrier. Is she available?"

"Becky said to tell you she is outside by the benches next to the Visitor Center. Do you know where the Visitor Center is located?"

"Yes, I do," he responded, "I'm familiar with the Center. Thank you for your assistance."

"Just doing my job," she responded. "I must say it isn't every day we have an FBI agent come by. I hope your visit is about something routine and not serious."

This woman strikes me as a gossip, Parker thought to himself, and would love to spread gossip about why the FBI is talking with Becky Greenbrier. As soon as I leave, I bet she will be e-mailing or texting to as many administrative assistants and secretaries as she can. Can't be helped, he told himself. "Thank you again," he said as he turned and walked out the office.

The Visitor Center was about a five-minute walk from the Administrative Annex. His inquisitiveness was heightened as he contemplated why Becky didn't want to talk with him in her office and chose, instead, to meet him outside. She probably felt there would be no chance for someone, maybe the curious receptionist, to overhear them. Becky obviously wanted privacy. Did it signal she had something important to tell him?

He saw her sitting on the bench farthest from the entrance of the Visitor Center, as far away from people as possible, he thought. Walking to her and extending his hand he said, "Becky, it's nice to see you again." She didn't shake his hand nor did she stand to welcome him. She barely looked at him. She looks awful, he thought. Her eyes were bloodshot, her normally flawless complexion was splotched with red marks, and she seemed to shake now and then. He remembered her as an attractive woman full of confidence. Not so now. Was she fighting a drug problem or was she an alcoholic?

"Parker, I'd be lying if I said I was happy to see you again. We didn't part on the best of terms, if you remember. I really don't know why you want to talk to me and I don't have much time. I heard via the Yellowstone grapevine of your involvement for the FBI with that homicide near Sylvan Lake. If that's what you want to talk about, you're wasting your time. I know nothing."

"Becky, I'm sorry you feel the way you do. I certainly have no ill feelings toward you. You're correct; I do want to talk to you about the homicide. Nothing but routine stuff at this point in time. You remember, I'm sure, from your time with Law Enforcement and Security, how every possible connection with the homicide must be checked out."

"So, what you're telling me is you're checking me out to determine if I had anything to do with the homicide. Sorry to disappoint you, but I had nothing to do with it and I don't know anything about it, so you can move on to your next poor sucker. Can I go now?"

He could see she was shaking more visibly than before and beads of sweat were on her forehead and upper lip. She was definitely very nervous. "You know how things go," he replied, "so please bear with me. Just a few routine questions and I'll be on my way."

"I've told you I know nothing about that homicide. But I suppose, if you must, you must. Make it quick. I can't be gone from the office too much longer."

"Thanks for understanding," he responded. "I'll be brief. Where were you this past Sunday evening?"

"The same place I'm almost every evening. In my apartment watching television, even with the pathetic choice of programs."

"Were you there all evening?"

"Sorry to say, I was. If there was something else to do around this place, believe me, I'd do it. Nope. Little old Becky was bored watching some stupid reality shows."

"Were you alone?"

Laughing, she replied, "Don't I wish I wasn't. A half-way decent guy would certainly be a plus. You interested, Parker? I'm sure I could forget about the past and we could start anew and have some fun."

Embarrassed by her forwardness, he avoided responding to her suggestion. Instead, he said, "I take it you were alone."

"Unfortunately, I was. Alone all night. You'd think a woman like me wouldn't have to spend her nights alone, wouldn't you?"

He wasn't going to rise to her bait, so he responded by saying, "Is there anyone that will verify you were alone?"

"Unless there was someone in my apartment I didn't know was there, maybe some guy hiding in my closet getting a cheap thrill when I undressed for bed . . . I sleep naked you might like to know . . . I'm afraid there is no one to verify my story. You'll either have to believe me or try to prove I'm lying, which I'm not."

"Do you have access to the tranquilizer socostrin?"

"Yes, I do. Why do you ask?"

Did he see an intensifying of her nervousness? She seemed on the edge, ready to come apart. If he told her some facts, maybe she'd break down and tell more than he anticipated she would. "It was used to kill the victim. Since it is used here in Yellowstone, the FBI wants to determine which employees might have been able to obtain it."

"Even if I do have access, so what? I told you I had nothing to do with this murder and I know nothing about it."

"What size shoe do you wear?"

"Size 7."

"Do you have a pair of Meryl hiking shoes?"

"I have the same hiking shoes as all the other Yellowstone employees. Part of the drab, everyone wear the same thing and all look alike mentality of this place. I don't know the manufacturer. I suppose you want to see them."

"Maybe, but not now. Please don't throw them away. There were shoeprints around the victim's car and I may need to compare your shoeprint with those at the crime scene. Routine procedure, nothing more."

"If you want to come by my apartment tonight, you can check my shoes for yourself. Take them with you if you want. Maybe you could stay awhile and we could put all this questioning behind us and enjoy each other's company."

"It won't be necessary for me to get your shoes just yet. It may never come to that. I appreciate your willingness to have by-gones be by-gones, but I need to keep going on this investigation plus make sure the shop is doing o.k. during my absence. I do appreciate your willingness to meet me and answer these questions. If something comes to mind, which you forgot to tell me, please contact me. You can call the shop and they'll let me know you called."

"Still Mr. Cold Shoulder, aren't you? Have you lost all your testosterone? Maybe you're gay. Maybe it's me. You don't think I'm attractive. Oh well, you win some and lose some. You're not the only fish in the pond. See you around, Parker. I hope you find the killer." She abruptly stood up and walked hurriedly past him without saying goodbye or acknowledging him.

As he watched her walk away, he didn't know what to think. Either she was on something which made her nervous and jumpy, or she was hiding something. Maybe both. He had purposely avoided mentioning that Beth had identified Becky as a potential suspect. It had surprised him that Beth hadn't been mentioned by Becky since, as Beth had told him, Becky viewed Beth with disdain and would say or do almost anything to discredit Beth and tear her down. Maybe Becky was indirectly trying to tear down Beth by her suggestive comments to Parker. It hadn't been too long ago that Parker had discouraged establishing a relationship with Becky. Instead, he had pursued one with Beth. In Becky's mind, perhaps her suggestive comments to Parker was her way of getting back at Beth.

Too complicated to think any more about the machinations of women. Nevertheless, Becky would bear watching. Careful watching. She might be a killer.

CHAPTER 23

Wednesday Morning
1:15 a.m.
Outside the Terrace Apartments for Yellowstone National Park Employees,
Yellowstone National Park, Mammoth Hot Springs, Montana

No more delay. Greenbrier was too great a risk to wait any longer. She was losing it and on the verge of blowing the whole thing. She had to be eliminated.

There wasn't the luxury of planning and assessing the pros and dons of different scenarios, nor was there time to do any rehearsing in order to eliminate mistakes. Thankfully, there was some sucostrin remaining, enough to do the job. Using all of it hadn't been necessary with Valentine. Doing it when Greenbrier wasn't expecting it was the key. It wouldn't be as clean as Valentine. There simply wasn't enough time to set it up properly so that Richardson would be blamed for this one as well. That was the way it was. No sense dwelling on what wasn't.

Like most people that work normal hours and leave their place of work at nearly the same time every day, Greenbrier followed a certain routine after leaving her office unless there was something unusual which caused her to deviate from her normal routine. After leaving the Visitor Services Office, she would go to her apartment to change clothes before either walking to the Mammoth Hot Springs cafeteria to have dinner or driving to Gardiner, Montana to dine at the Gardiner Steak House, sometimes with Victor Barrozo, sometimes with other acquaintances from the Paradise Valley area. Tonight, she had gone to Gardiner. Barrozo hadn't come to his Paradise Valley home for this coming weekend, so Becky probably had dined with someone she knew from the Gardiner area. Hopefully, she wasn't staying with some cowboy or ranch hand until later this morning. Killing her now, at this early hour when she was walking along a dark area between her apartment complex's parking lot and her apartment, would present the least risk for discovery.

It was about fifteen minutes after 1 a.m. when Greenbrier's car pulled into the parking lot. She exited her car and began her walk to her apartment, following her usual path. Just a few more minutes. Breathe deep. It had to be done, didn't it? She might become unhinged and decide to spill the beans to protect her own hide. Stop thinking about it and just do it. Get yourself under control. Now. She's not expecting it. "Becky, how was your dinner? You're back quite late."

Reacting surprised, she replied, "What are you doing here? You scared the ba-gee-bees out of me. I thought you said we shouldn't get together or talk until Richardson was arrested."

"I was worried about you after we talked. I wanted to make sure you were o.k. You're o.k., aren't you?"

"I'm fine and I don't appreciate being surprised like this."

As Becky was talking, they were no longer separated, providing the opportune time to use the syringe. There. Into the fleshy portion of her upper arm. Lashing out, Becky twisted her arm causing the syringe to fall into the dirt. Raking her nails across skin, she grabbed a handful of hair as she screamed and tried to run away, stumbling for a few steps and then collapsing as the sucostrin took effect. Grab her under the arms and drag her into the trees next to the apartments. Throw some branches over her, enough to keep her hidden until morning. Look around. No time to clean up. Someone may have heard her screams and come looking to see what the screams were all about. Have to get away and fast. No looking back. No time to find the syringe. Just get away.

CHAPTER 24

Wednesday Morning
7:30 a.m.
Parker Williams' Home on Duck Creek, 9 Miles North of West
Yellowstone off U.S. Highway 191, Montana
Old Faithful Visitor Center, Yellowstone National Park, Wyoming

The serenade of numerous song birds awakened him. He stretched and as the sleepiness departed, his feelings of last Monday came rushing back. He hadn't enjoyed himself as much or experienced such a wonderful several hours in a long time. The evening with Beth had flown by and there was so much more he wanted to say to her. He wanted to be with her again, and soon. Perhaps a hike together or maybe they could attend an evening performance at the Playmill Theatre. He really didn't care what the activity was. He would be content to just sit and talk. All he wanted was to be with her.

Walking into the kitchen, he pushed the brew button on the Keurig coffee maker. In less than a minute, he had a steaming cup of freshly made coffee. Opening the double slider, he stepped onto the deck overlooking Duck Creek. He never tired hearing the sound of it gurgling through its curves. He also never tired of the view over the meadows of Yellowstone framed by the snow-capped peaks of the Spanish Mountain Range. Numerous professional photographers had tried to capture the splendor and awesome grandeur of the Yellowstone area and this particular view ranked as one of the most photographed. Returning to the kitchen, he decided to drive into West Yellowstone, pick up a second cup of coffee and two of Suzy's wonderful scones at the Book Peddler, and stop in the shop to check whether something required his attention. He quickly shaved, showered, and dressed, and was on his way in less than twenty minutes. During the drive, he called Yellowstone's Personnel Office and obtained the office telephone number for Gretchen Newberry. Calling the number, he was able to schedule a time to talk with Gretchen later in the afternoon.

As he parked in front of the Book Peddler, his iPhone rang. The caller ID showed the call was from the FBI Office in Billings. "Hello, Parker Williams speaking."

"Mr. Williams, it's Cynthia Jackson. Janet asks you to call her on her cell phone. She's traveling to Missoula, Montana. She told me to tell you there is some additional information pertaining to the Valentine case which she wants to discuss with you. Do you have her number?"

"Yes I do, Cynthia. I'll call her in a few minutes."

He entered the Book Peddler and walked to the rear of the store where the coffee bar was located. "Good morning, Suzy," he said to Susan Nesbitt, who was placing raspberry scones into the display case. "Good morning to you too," she replied, "I'm surprised to see you around here. I assumed you would be off somewhere doing your FBI investigative work."

He was surprised Susan knew about his being involved with the FBI since she wasn't one to spend time prying into other people's business. "How did you find out about my being involved with the FBI?"

"Parker, are you kidding? It should come as no surprise to you that in a small town like ours, news about any of us travels fast, especially when that news involves something out of the ordinary, like a murder in Yellowstone. I heard about it from Cathy Marsman who stopped in yesterday afternoon for a cappuccino. I don't know from whom or where she heard it, but she couldn't wait to tell me. Are you making progress? Given your track record in helping to solve murders, you should have this wrapped up soon."

"I don't know if I should take what you're saying as a compliment or not, but let's say I'm only helping out with the FBI's investigation. They're short on agents at the present time, so I'm merely helping with the preliminary routine stuff."

Smiling, Suzy responded, "O.k., I get it. You're playing the 'I'm just a peon game' and you're not going to tell me anything meaningful. That's o.k. I understand and respect you for it. But, there's one thing I feel you should know. This is from a friend to a friend. I would want you to tell me if I were in your shoes. So, don't shoot the messenger. The gossip is that Janet VanKampen continues to have a thing for you and she finds excuses to get the two of you together, like claiming she is short on agents. Now, like I said, don't shoot the messenger."

100

Holding back the anger he was feeling, he replied in as normal a tone of voice as he could muster, "No, I'm not going to shoot the messenger, especially a messenger I count as a friend, and I'm not upset with you. Thanks for telling me. You've just proved again why you are a true friend. Please, if you do have a chance to talk with Cathy, convey to her that I think she's living in fantasy land. Now, please, I'd like two of those fabulous scones, the raspberry ones, and a large coffee."

"Sure thing. Here's a large take-out cup." Pointing to where three coffee urns were placed together, she continued, "Help yourself to whichever one you want. Here's the scones. I'll put it all on your account."

He maintained personal accounts at several businesses in town just as numerous West Yellowstone business owners did at his shop. Paying a monthly bill was easier for all involved since the paperwork and recordkeeping was much less. "Thanks, Suzy, for the information and for being such a good friend," he said as he walked out the shop. Sitting in his 4Runner, he began to eat the scones and sip the coffee, deciding to forget what Suzy had told him. Time to get on with the investigation. Calling Janet's cell phone, she answered after two rings.

"Hello, Janet VanKampen."

"Janet, it's Parker. Cynthia said you wanted me to call. You have some additional information about the case."

"Yes, I do. First, let me tell you I read your e-mail report. Good work. Have you talked with Gretchen Newberry yet?"

I will be talking with Gretchen later today. I talked with Becky yesterday. She acted very nervous. She claimed she knows nothing but I'm not sure she's being truthful. I wish we could have someone watch her, but I know that isn't possible. I'm going to tell Jessica about her and maybe Jessica can have someone watch her."

"I'm not so sure involving Jessica is a good idea. She's only supposed to be a liaison, not an investigative person. If Greenbrier makes a run for it, we'll know she has something to hide. Other than that, I think we need something more definite than you thinking she isn't being truthful to place her under surveillance. Now, let me tell you about the information I have received. Hopefully, it will help move things along. The lab geeks dissected the frames of the security camera film and blew them up. It shows Valentine's head was held in place by tying his neck to the headrest. His wrist was also tied to the steering wheel. We believe this was done to make it look like he was driving the Lexus. Given the autopsy results about probable time of death, we believe he was already dead when the Lexus entered Yellowstone which means the investigation shouldn't fall under our jurisdiction, but would be Yellowstone County Sheriff's responsibility. I've already talked with Sheriff Evenhouse. She says the murder could have occurred in Yellowstone in the half-mile between the actual boundary of Yellowstone and the entrance where the camera is located. I doubt that's how it happened, but it can't be ruled out. Bottom line is she wants her cake and ice cream both. She wants us to continue our investigation, while she conducts her own, until it is confirmed one way or the other where exactly the murder took place. Until then, we are to keep each other informed. Unnecessary duplication if you ask me. Also, too many cooks spoil the broth. Unfortunately, for public relations purposes, I couldn't object. I agreed to go along with her. I hope you're o.k. with it too."

"My feelings won't be hurt if you tell me to stop and let her do her thing. I'm fine with turning everything over to her. I can get back to something I know about. Just give me the word."

"Not so fast. I think we should keep pursuing our investigation for a little while longer. If we let go of it now and later it is confirmed the actual murder took place within Yellowstone's boundaries, we would lose a lot of valuable time and possibly allow the killer additional time to work on an alibi."

"I understand what you're saying," he replied, "I'll stick with it for the time being. Is my approach to talk next with Gretchen o.k. with you?"

"Yep. Talk with her and let me know what you learn. I've got to run. Talk to you later."

Laurie, Dick, and Jim were all in the shop when he arrived. They assured him all was well and he wasn't needed for anything in particular. He spent the rest of the morning reading the mail, the majority landing in the round file after a brief scanning of the material. Requesting he be contacted should his attention be required, he walked from the shop to Pete's Pizza and Pasta restaurant where he had a small vegetarian pizza with a Coke. Saying goodbye to Jo, the owner of Pete's, he got into his 4Runner and began the drive to the Old Faithful Visitor Center where Gretchen Newberry worked. As he drove alongside the Madison River, he saw several fly-fishers engaged in fishing along the banks of the river. He entertained thoughts of forgetting his meeting with Gretchen and joining these fly-fishers. But he knew he better not if any progress was going to be made in the investigation. This afternoon he might be talking with a killer and he couldn't afford to provide her with any more time to think about her alibi.

Arriving at the Old Faithful Visitor Center, he parked in a parking place reserved for Yellowstone security personnel. Gretchen's office was located in the lower level of the Center. Her title was Assistant Ranger, but something had occurred to place her into a desk job and not in the field. Depending on what he learned, he might have to do some research into Gretchen's history with Yellowstone. Another area to look into was why she continued to have access to suscostrin. The main level was devoted to numerous education exhibits designed to introduce visitors to the world of geysers, boiling lakes, bubbling hot pots, and the various animal species inhabiting the Yellowstone area. Two or three career rangers and several career naturalists and wildlife experts were available to answer the thousands of questions visitors asked. Gretchen's office wasn't enclosed, as he hoped it would be, but a cubicle with portable walls about six feet in height. "Ms. Newberry, I'm Parker Williams." Reaching to shake her hand, he found her not offering her hand but rather conveying a sense of combativeness and hostility. He continued, "Thank you for allowing me time to meet with you. I'll keep it short."

He put Gretchen's age in the early 40s. She wore her brown hair in a pony tail which made her round face look narrower. She had dark brown eyes which seemed to be trying to size him up. She was neither skinny nor overweight and possessed an ample figure. He estimated her weight to be 140-150 lbs. Without knowing her shoe size, he concluded from her physical appearance that she matched close enough the physical characteristics associated with the assumed killer. "Mr. Williams, I've heard what you're doing and I must tell you, you're wasting your time. I know nothing about the murder by Sylvan Lake and I have no idea who was killed or whom the killer might be. Now, I'd like to get back to my work if you don't mind." She had yet to ask him to sit down and she probably had no intention to do so.

"May I sit? Bare with me, Ms. Newberry, I have only a few questions to ask you and then I'll go."

Motioning to a chair opposite her desk, she replied with disgust in her voice, "That chair will work. If you must ask questions, I guess I can't stop you, although you're barking up the wrong tree. The way I'm overworked around her and unappreciated, I can assure you I wouldn't have time to kill anyone even if I wanted to. But, I'll be a cooperative soul, so fire away and let's get this over with."

"I'll try to be brief," he replied. Taking a small recorder from his shirt pocket, he continued, "Do you mind if I record our conversation? It saves on time and I don't trust my note taking to always be accurate."

"If you must, you must," she responded, "it's fine with me. I've nothing to hide. If it gets this over with more quickly, all the better."

"Good, let's do it." Switching on the recorder, he continued, "First, did you know the victim, Michael Valentine?"

"Are you kidding? This is the first time I've even heard the name. I don't know anyone named Valentine. Did he invent Valentine's Day or valentine cards or something?" The sarcasm in her voice was apparent.

Deciding not to acknowledge her sarcasm, he continued, "Do you know anyone that knew Michael Valentine?"

"Nope, I don't know anyone that knows Michael Valentine. Michael Valentine. Sounds like an all-American guy. Like I said, you're wasting your time asking me these questions."

"Where were you this past Sunday evening?"

"Ha, that's easy. I was where I always am on Sunday evenings. Right here working my rear end off without any recognition or even a 'thank you' from the muckity-mucks. You've seen that mob scene outside. Many of those people have come hundreds, even thousands of miles, to see Old Faithful erupt and someone needs to be here throughout the evening until it gets dark to make sure none of them do something stupid like trying to walk through the steam and hot water to get a close-up picture."

"From what time to what time were you here?"

"Too long, that's for sure and no overtime pay either. To be precise, from ten in the morning to ten at night. You can check with the other people that also have the Sunday day and evening shift with me."

"You never left during that time?"

"Where would I go? There's nothing around here to go to, unless it's West Yellowstone, which isn't what I would call Las Vegas. Sorry, I don't mean to make fun of your beloved little town, but it really leaves a lot to desire for a gal like me that needs some action now and then. I spent the entire twelve hours right here."

"If you would please, give me the names of the other workers that were here with you this past Sunday evening. After that, I'll be going."

She hurriedly wrote the names of four people on a sheet of paper and handed it to him. "Here you are. I've also included their office phone numbers as I know you're going to call them. By the way, why did you decide to talk with me? Who suggested I might know something about this Valentine guy?"

"Gretchen, I trust you understand I can't tell you much, but I can tell you that our preliminary analysis of some probable evidence points to the killer being a woman employee of Yellowstone, between 5'6" and 5'9," with dark brown or auburn hair, and having a 7 shoe size. You match all those characteristics, so I thought I needed to talk with you. Nothing personal, just following where the leads take me. Thanks for your time. If you do come across any information you believe may be relevant to this investigation, please don't hesitate to contact me. By the way, what is your shoe size?"

"Sorry to say, I wear a size 8 & 1/2. I know you're disappointed you haven't found the killer. You'll have to keep looking, I'm afraid."

This time, she offered her hand and they shook hands. As he turned to leave, she said, "I don't know all the women employees here at Yellowstone, but I can think of two that match those characteristics. You probably have both on your list and maybe you've already talked with them."

He wondered if she would identify someone other than the names Beth had given him. "Would you please tell me their names so I can see if I already know about them?"

"Sure. Becky Greenbrier and Beth Richardson. Both match all the characteristics you mentioned. Have you talked to them too?"

"I can't say, Gretchen. Thanks again for your time."

Walking back to his 4Runner, he thought about what Gretchen had told him. He could easily check her alibi. His gut told him she was telling the truth. She had also identified Becky Greenbrier, but only based on the characteristics he had mentioned. For the first time, he realized that Beth matched the characteristics as well, possibly even better than Gretchen or Becky. He had been so quick to dismiss her that he hadn't given a thought to how she would be a suspect if any other person was doing an investigation other than himself. Beth Richardson a murder suspect. Preposterous.

CHAPTER 25

Wednesday Morning
8:15 a.m.
FBI Office in Billings, Montana

"Janet, it's Bruce Dickson. I have bad news. I'm trying to comprehend it myself. Becky Greenbrier has been murdered; at least it looks that way to me. Right under our noses, too. I'm really worried that we may have a serial killer on our hands. There's a needle mark in the back of Becky's arm. Could be the same stuff as used on Valentine. We won't know until Byron does an autopsy. You know, Becky worked for me for awhile. She became too headstrong and wanted to do only the glamour stuff which, you know, doesn't cut it. She must have gotten herself mixed-up in something. We've notified a brother that lives in New Mexico."

"Bruce, this is unreal. Now a Yellowstone employee murdered. Two homicides in three days. This certainly is bad news. What else can you tell me?"

"Becky's body was found this morning around 7:45 a.m. by a cafeteria worker walking along a path from where she lives to the Mammoth Hot Springs cafeteria where she works. She spotted the body and called her boss who told her to stay where she was and not let anyone near the body. Her boss then called my office. When I got there, I taped the scene off and did a preliminary look around. The body was partially covered by pine branches and brush. It looks to me like the killer was in a hurry and tried to cover the body but did a half-assed job. I found a syringe near the body. I bagged it and gave it to Byron. I'm sorry to have to tell you, but there's no ambiguity where Becky was killed. This one for sure is your baby. You need to decide how you want to proceed. I'll keep the area where the body is secured until you or one of your agents gets here. I've also secured her car and her apartment. One last thing. She must have struggled with the killer as I found hair still clutched in her hand. Also, there's some dried blood on a couple of her fingernails and fingers. She may have scratched her killer as well as pulled out some of the killer's hair. I bagged all of it and sent it along with the body to Byron."

"When it rains, it pours," Janet replied, "just what I don't need—another homicide to deal with. Unfortunately, I'm on my way to Livingston because a white supremacist group has taken some hostages and is now barricaded inside Big Sky University's Student Center. Bruce, I don't have any agents to send there right now. Could you spare Jessica for the rest of today? I'm going to have to send Parker and having her assist him would reduce my anxiety level tremendously."

"I know you're in a real bind and I feel for you. I'll tell Jessica to go to the scene and stay there until Parker arrives." Then, in a teasing voice, he continued, "Knowing how Jessica enjoys being around Parker, I'm sure I won't have to twist her arm to do this. You're going to owe me big time for this one, you know."

"Thanks, Bruce, and I do owe you. Pray it doesn't rain in the next couple of hours and wash away any evidence Jessica and Parker may find on the ground. For what it's worth, I'm aware of Jessica's interest in Parker. I'm not sure it's a two-way street, but I'll let them deal with that themselves. Tell you what Bruce. If anyone else dies in Yellowstone, please don't call me. It might just push me over the edge. Talk to you soon."

She had to reach Parker right away, to tell him about Becky Greenbrier and about Jessica's involvement. He wasn't going to like either one. She didn't like having to ask for Jessica's help, not because of Jessica per se, but because Janet didn't want Jessica to be able to be with Parker for an extended time. Call it jealousy if you wished, but the possibility of Parker developing an interest in Jessica as a companion wasn't something Janet wanted to make possible. Unfortunately, she had no other choice. All her agents were already doing double duty. Having Parker going solo with two homicides was too great a risk to take with an inexperienced person like Parker. Damm those jerks in Denver and D.C. She needed more agents, no questions asked. Another problem was the direction of Parker's investigation. Becky Greenbrier's murder suggested the decision to focus on her and the other woman was probably wrong. Given that Valentine and Becky had both been killed in the same manner, it was logical to conclude the same person had killed both. As she thought about it more, she knew she was missing something. What was it? Her instinct told her there had to be a connection between Valentine, Greenbrier, and the killer.

It was a key to solving one or both murders. Finding the connection was now a priority. She found Parker's cell phone number and pressed the call button on her Blackberry. He answered on the third ring. "Parker Williams, speaking."

"Parker, it's Janet. I have bad news, but first tell me if you have new information."

"I don't think I want to hear what you're going to tell me. I don't like getting bad news, at least not in the middle of this investigation. As for what information I've been able to gather, it isn't much. I met with Gretchen Newberry. She's a pretty defiant woman, but my impression after talking with her is she isn't the killer nor does she know anything that would help us. She said she was working until 10 p.m. on Sunday and provided names of four people that would verify her alibi. I haven't contacted any of them yet, but I will."

"Don't bother. My bad news is Becky Greenbrier is dead. Her body was discovered this morning near her apartment at Mammoth Hot Springs. From all indications, she was murdered, much in the same fashion as Valentine according to Bruce Dickson."

"What? You can't be serious! Becky dead. It can't be. What is going on?"

"I know it's hard to believe. Bruce has secured the scene and Jessica is waiting for you to join her to more thoroughly and carefully process the scene. You will also need to process Becky's apartment and her car."

Interrupting her, he said, "Wait a minute, Janet. I didn't sign on to be involved with a second murder. This is totally getting away from me. I'm not sure I should be involved with any of this anymore. This is much bigger than I ever imagined. Two murders in three days. You need to have one of your experienced agents involved in all this, not me."

"Parker, I appreciate your concern, but please don't bail on me now. I need you more than ever. I simply don't have anyone else to turn to whom I trust. You won't be alone with this second one. Jessica will be helping. At least hang in there until I can figure out how to relieve you of at least Becky's murder."

"I don't know, Janet. I'm feeling really inadequate. Jessica being there will certainly be a big help, but I'm not experienced in dealing with multiple murders. Are you sure you have no one else to take over?"

"I'm sure. I wish I could relieve you but I can't. I need you to continue, at least until we get a break on the Valentine case. I'll try and have Bruce and Jessica take over the Greenbrier case, o.k.?"

"O.k., but please don't wait around to have Bruce and Jessica take over."

"I won't," she replied. "Now, when you are processing Greenbrier's apartment, pay special attention to her computer, address books, iPad, if she has one, cell phone, and any printed sheets which might contain names of people that e-mailed her. Look for any messages she may have printed. Also, check around the ground where the body was found for shoeprints or other evidence. Bruce says he found a syringe near the body, but he may have overlooked other possible evidence."

Interrupting her, he said, "Wait a minute. You said a syringe. That tells me Becky was killed in the same way Valentine was killed, so we may be dealing with one killer of both Valentine and Becky. If I'm correct that Gretchen didn't kill Valentine, then I'm out of suspects, at least for now. Let's hope some evidence is found which will point us in the right direction, since we seem to have barked up the wrong tree with Gretchen and Becky."

"Before throwing the baby out with the bath water, check Gretchen's alibi. If it checks out, then we need to go back to square one and review what we learned from Valentine's murder. In particular, assuming Greenbrier didn't kill Valentine, we need to look for a possible connection between Valentine and Greenbrier. If we find that out, it might lead us to some suspects. One last thing, we have jurisdiction over Greenbrier's investigation, not Bruce or Jessica. Keep that in mind. I asked for Jessica's involvement because I didn't want you to feel overwhelmed by taking on too much. But, as soon as you and she have finished processing the scene along with Greenbrier's apartment and car, Jessica can go back to her responsibilities with Bruce. Understand?"

Something was going on here with Janet and Jessica which he didn't understand and didn't want to begin to try and understand. Relationships between and among women had always baffled him and he wasn't about to expend the energy and time required to scratch the surface of the complex fabric of female perspectives and emotions. Whatever it was involving Janet and Jessica, it was their issue, not his, and he would leave it there. Too much was on his plate to give any further thought to Janet and Jessica's issues.

"I understand. Thanks for working this out with Jessica to help. Two heads are better than one, especially when the one head is mine. Once we finish processing the scene, apartment, and car, I'll tell Jessica she can return to her usual role with Bruce. I know that you know I knew Becky. I'm having a hard time accepting she's dead. What had she gotten into or what did she know which caused her to be murdered? Find the answer to that question and we've found her killer and, most likely, Valentine's killer as well. One final question, Becky's computer, cell phone, and whatever else we find, what should I do with them?"

"We need to get all the electronic stuff to the computer geeks in the Denver Office. Overnight the stuff to them. We have special arrangements with UPS and FedEx, so use them. Both have offices in West Yellowstone, Bozeman, Livingston, and Billings. They will crate or package whatever you have. Bring whatever you have to them, tell them to package it for special handling, put the cost on the office account, and have it on the first Delta Express flight to Denver International Airport from West Yellowstone or Livingston, if it is faster, a United Express flight from Bozeman or Billings to Denver. I'll let the Denver Office know to expect something and request that it be analyzed as quickly as possible. Now, I have to run to deal with this hostage situation. Good luck and keep in touch."

Becky Greenbrier dead. While the chemistry between them had never materialized, she wasn't a bad person. Certainly, she didn't deserve to die as she had. Her death was too close to home and he felt a sense of guilt that he hadn't talked to her earlier. Maybe her death could have been avoided if he had acted sooner. Stop beating yourself up, he thought to himself. Jessica would be waiting for him, so he needed to concentrate on obtaining as much evidence as possible rather than speculating about the timing of his interview with Becky. The best he could do now for her would be to bring her killer to justice.

Driving to Mammoth Hot Springs to meet Jessica, his conversation with Gretchen haunted him, specifically her identification of Beth as a potential suspect. He should put it out of his mind. However, it was true. Beth matched the characteristics of the suspected killer—Yellowstone woman employee; 5'8"; auburn hair; wears size 7, narrow-width Meryl hiking shoe; and access to sucostrin. She had even said she was a match. Where had she been Sunday evening? Had she really been camping by Soda Butte Creek? There was no way to verify her story; at least none had come to light yet. Where had she been early this morning when Becky was killed? Stop it, he said to himself. It was ridiculous to give it any more thought. Put it out of your mind once and for all. Beth Richardson was the woman with whom he was beginning to think about spending the rest of his life, not a woman that had killed two people. What was he thinking? Maybe he was overwhelmed and crazy thoughts like this were taking over his mind.

CHAPTER 26

Wednesday Morning
11:15 a.m.
Office of the Associate Superintendent, Administration Building,
Yellowstone National Park, Mammoth Hot Springs, Montana

How could this be happening in America's premier national park? Beth sat at her desk, holding her head in her hands, trying to understand what had happened in only three days in the place she loved and called home. How could she reconcile two murders in three days? One was bad enough, but two was unthinkable. What was so devastating was a fellow employee was the latest victim. She had learned of Becky's death only a few minutes ago. The Superintendent was attending a meeting of the national park superintendents in Salt Lake City, so the news of Becky's death had come to her when Bruce Dickson's call to the Superintendent had been forwarded to her. She had to get control of her emotions as she was the final authority as long as the Superintendent was absent and she was expected to make sure the proper procedures were being followed, which meant, in this case, the involvement of the FBI.

She didn't have much time to think about Becky's murder or if Gretchen Newberry might be the killer of either Valentine or Becky. She had to represent the Superintendent at a ceremony honoring volunteers that provided countless hours of free service in hundreds of different ways throughout Yellowstone. She opened the door of the closet in her office to find her jacket not there. Ugh, she had forgotten to pick it up from the dry cleaners in Gardiner. She had paid the extra cost for express service, so she knew it was ready for pickup. With all the upheaval during the past three days, she had simply forgotten all about it. Fortunately, this wasn't a formal occasion, so she could get by without the jacket. She would wear her everyday uniform instead, although she would have preferred to wear her more formal jacket since she was representing the Superintendent.

She quickly wrote herself a note to pick up her jacket when the first opportunity presented itself, maybe even yet today.

Thank goodness the honoring of volunteers was more about refreshments than the ceremony. She didn't have any responsibilities to perform other than to smile, act interested, and acknowledge her introduction. She made sure she circulated among the volunteers, shaking hands and thanking them for their service. As these things went, small groups of volunteers, that knew each other from working together, formed and it was easy for her to slip away unnoticed. As she walked back to her office, she thought again about the murder of Becky. What had Becky been into that led to her death? Beth needed more information. She realized Parker was probably experiencing overload and would welcome an intrusion about as much as she would if she were in his shoes, but she had to have more information about Becky's death. Taking her cell phone, she called his cell phone number. "Hello, this is Parker Williams speaking."

"Hi, Parker, it's Beth. I've been thinking about you and wanted to know how you're doing. I heard about Becky's murder. I can't believe it. What a shock. I'm really distraught and also very much concerned about how you're doing. Plus, I'm scared. Two murders in so short a time. I'm scared there may be another murder if the killer or killers aren't found soon."

"Beth, it's so good to hear your voice. Thanks for calling. Something's terribly wrong and you're not the only one that's scared. I'm scared too. Right now, Jessica and I are going over Becky's apartment looking for anything that might help identify her killer. Bruce thinks she was killed in the same way as Valentine. If that's true, we may have a serial killer on our hands. That really scares me. I'm feeling totally inadequate to continue with this investigation, no, correction, two investigations. I'm sorry I can't talk any longer, Beth, but I need to take Becky's computer, cell phone, and iPad to Livingston so FedEx can crate it and get it off to the FBI Office in Denver on the next flight. Before I hang up, I do want you to know something. When this nightmare is over, you and I are going to do something special and spend some more quality time together with no interruptions. That's a promise."

"That sure sounds wonderful to me. Heaven knows I need it. Can I ask you one more thing before you go?"

"Sure."

"Did you have a chance to talk with Gretchen Newberry and do you think she might be the killer?"

"That's two questions, but I'll forgive you. I did meet with her. She isn't our killer, at least she didn't kill Valentine and I doubt she killed Becky. Gretchen was working until 10 p.m. on Sunday. She says she never heard of Michael Valentine and doesn't know anyone that might know him. You were correct in your assessment of her being cocky and arrogant, but she isn't our killer. Now, I have to get back to work. Thanks, again, for your concern."

She felt much better after talking with Parker. Just his voice had a calming influence. She realized he was rapidly becoming more than a friend. She wanted to be with him more than occasionally and she wanted to continue to talk with him about his ideas, plans, and dreams. If she were still a teenager, she could say she had a crush on him. As a mature woman, having a crush didn't cut it. She was very fond of him and felt an emotional link with him like she had never felt before with a man. Could she be falling in love? Was this the man she had dreamt about meeting and with whom she wanted to spend her life?"

Enough of such thinking. She had a mountain of work to get to, both hers and some of the Superintendent's which had been forwarded to her. Looking over an analysis of the distribution of improvements to campgrounds throughout Yellowstone, her intercom buzzed. "Yes, Ryan."

"Beth, there's a couple of officers from the Park County Sheriff's office asking to speak with you."

"Park County Sherriff's office. Why do they want to see me?"

"They didn't tell me. They're very insistent they speak with you. Should I send them in?"

With so much work to do, she didn't need this. But, it was important to maintain positive relationships with all the law enforcement agencies surrounding Yellowstone. "Sure. Send them in." Walking from behind her desk, she extended her hand to greet the two people as they entered her office. The man was dressed in a dark blue suit, white shirt, and red tie, the typical dress of a person attempting to convey power and authority. He was short and stocky and of Latin or Hispanic heritage. The woman wore a dark brown pant suit with a white blouse and a small strand of pearls, most likely ornamental. She was the opposite of him, being tall and slim. She was small boned and had the look of a well-trained athlete. She had light brown hair and brown eyes which darted around Beth's office as if she was expecting something to jump out. "Welcome," said Beth.

"Associate Superintendent Richardson, I'm Deputy Carlos Medina and my colleague is Assistant Deputy Ann Vogelzang." He withdrew his Park County Sheriff's identification from the inside of his suit jacket and passed it to Beth who glanced at it to give him the satisfaction of having her follow his lead. She noticed him giving her an up-and-down-her-body-look, staring at her breasts longer than necessary. A sexual creep she thought that uses his position of power to intimidate and take advantage of women. The woman stood to his side in a posture which conveyed a subordinate role to him. Beth wondered if they were a good cop, bad cop tandem which worked together or if they had just come together because someone in the Sheriff's Office thought a woman should be along when Medina met with a woman. Medina continued, "We'd like to ask you a few questions about the murder of Michael Valentine. As you may know, there is some uncertainty regarding the jurisdiction over the case. At the present time, the FBI is continuing to carry out its investigation. Our office is also doing our own investigation since it may turn out the murder was not committed in Yellowstone, but in Park County. Am I making myself clear?"

"I'm aware of the ambiguity regarding the jurisdiction," replied Beth. "I wasn't aware you were carrying out your own investigation. Isn't that a duplication of effort?"

"Some might call it that," he replied, "but we would rather think of it as supportive work. Sometimes the FBI and other law enforcement agencies have differing interests and it pays for each to pursue their own investigation. Now, as for why we are here, allow me to first tell you that you have the right to have a lawyer present if you wish. Deputy Vogelzang and I will wait until your lawyer arrives if you chose to exercise this option."

"Deputy Medina, why don't you tell me what this is all about. I know about Michael Valentine's murder because my friend, Parker Williams, was requested by FBI Agent VanKampen to assist with the investigation. Why would I need a lawyer?"

"Ms. Richardson, I'll ask the questions if you don't mind. Do you wish to have a lawyer present?"

"Why would I need a lawyer? Oh, that's right. I'm not supposed to ask any questions. No, I don't need a lawyer."

"Ms. Richardson, did you know Michael Valentine?"

"I know he was the murdered man found near the Sylvan Lake picnic area this past Sunday evening."

"Did you know him personally?"

"No, I did not know him personally." She noticed the two of them making eye contact after she answered. What did that mean?

"Where were you Sunday evening?"

"I attended the speech and dinner at the Buffalo Bill Historical Center in Cody after which I spent the night camped in a spot near Soda Butte Creek."

"Were you camping along?"

"Yes, I was alone."

"Is there anyone that can vouch for your camping?"

"I purposely wanted to camp alone, which I did. I wanted to be close to where I thought the Slough Creek wolf pack would be in the morning so I would be able to watch them, which I'm pleased to say I did. I didn't tell anyone about camping that night. I wanted to have a night alone to relish in this wonderful national park."

"You said you camped by Soda Butte Creek. That would mean you entered Yellowstone through the Cooke City/Silver gate entrance, correct?"

"You've got that correct."

"I understand there are security cameras at each entrance of Yellowstone which record each vehicle entering, isn't that so?"

"You're correct again. You've obviously done your homework." Don't smart off, she said to herself. No sense to come across as defensive. Go with the flow and soon it will be all over.

"If we were to look at the recording from Sunday evening of vehicles entering Yellowstone through the Cooke City/Silvergate entrance, we would find your vehicle recorded, which I believe is a National Park Service Ford Explorer with government license plate USG 7631."

"Unfortunately, when I was driving through the entrance, I noticed the security camera was missing. I assumed it must have malfunctioned sometime earlier and was taken away to be repaired. So, you won't find a record of me or any other vehicle entering that night." She noticed the meeting of eyes again as well as Deputy Vogelzang writing in a small black notebook.

"What did you do the next morning?"

"As I told you, I wanted to watch the Slough Creek wolf pack, so I drove from where I camped by Soda Butte Creek to the Slough Creek Campground and hiked to a good spot from which to watch the wolves. There's a small hill which provided a good location from which to view the area where the wolves den. Luck was with me since two adult wolves, I assume the alpha male and female, were visible for quite awhile. Even the pups spent several minutes in view. Quite a show. When they decided it was time to move on, the pups went back into the den with the female wolf and the male took off, probably to join the other wolves of the pack for their hunt. Is that enough detail for you, Deputy Medina?"

"Thank you," Miss Richardson. "Did you hike back to your Explorer then and leave the area?"

"You've got that right. I drove right back here."

"Did anyone see you during the time you were hiking back to your Explorer?"

"Not that I know of. There was one car parked in the campground parking area, but I didn't see anyone around the car or anywhere else, for that matter."

"What size shoe do you wear, Ms. Richardson."

"Something tells me you already know, Deputy Medina, but for the record, I wear a size 7."

"Do you own a pair of narrow-width, Meryl hiking shoes, size 7?"

"I do. One pair is in my apartment. The other pair I'm wearing right now."

"Do you have a uniform jacket which you wear to more formal events?"

"Come on, Deputy Medina, we're all adults and professionals to boot. You obviously know a great deal about me already, so why play this game of gotcha questions? You already know the answers to the questions before you ask. You know I have such a jacket. All senior officials of the National Park Service do. I'd show you mine but it's currently at the dry cleaners."

Ignoring her attempt to get him to cut to the core of why they were questioning her, he continued, "What is the name and location of the dry cleaners and why is your jacket there?"

Patience, Beth, patience, she said to herself. Don't lose it now. Stay civil and see where all this is going. "It is the only dry cleaners in Gardiner. I brought it there to have a button sewed on a sleeve after which I wanted it dry cleaned and pressed." She saw them glance at each other again and

Assistant Deputy Vogelzang gave a slight nod to Medina while she closed the notebook and stepped to the side of Beth's desk.

"Ms. Richardson, Deputy Medina said, "I'm having a hard time believing you. Let me tell you why." Again, she noticed him giving her the once over. Sex creep, she wanted to say. "You said you never knew Michael Valentine. You lied. You've known Michael Valentine for some time. He was one of the judges in the Miss Illinois pageant in which you participated and, as I'm sure you fondly remember, won. Didn't Mr. Valentine, as one would say, come on to you during the pageant? Didn't he threaten to tell the world about your father's indiscretions if you didn't give in to him? Didn't you send him running when you countered by threatening to go public with his offer to you to vote for you if you, shall we say, entertained him? Didn't you threaten to go public with his interest in you if he didn't give you his first place vote? You see, Ms. Richardson, we checked the voting record of the judges in that year's Miss Illinois pageant. Guess what? Michael Valentine cast his first place vote for you. And surprise, surprise, without his vote you wouldn't have won. You would have finished as runner-up, meaning no Miss America pageant for you and, consequently, no full-ride college scholarship. And, didn't Michael Valentine come back Sunday evening to proposition you again and threaten to expose your father if you didn't cooperate? Didn't you arrange to meet him after the meeting at the Historical Center so you could kill him? How am I doing so far?"

She couldn't believe what she was hearing. She wasn't able to formulate the words for a response. She was numb. Who did this guy think he was? Where was he coming from? Who was setting her up? Get a hold of yourself. This was no time to panic. Think clearly. The truth would come out and she'd be out of this mess.

"Deputy Medina, nice try, but you've got it all wrong. Nothing but conjecture and speculation on your part. Now that you mention the Miss Illinois pageant, I do remember one of the judges suggesting he and I spend time together in his hotel room. I don't remember his name. As a contestant, we were kept somewhat secluded and separated from the judges, but one of the judges managed to corner me in a hallway in-between sessions. He did threaten to make public some things about my father and I did tell him that if he did, I would tell the sponsors of the pageant what he was doing. That's as much as what happened. Somebody has fed you a crock. I'm surprised a professional like you would be sucked into such a fantasy without checking all the facts, not just the ones you find interesting. I suggest you quit wasting your time and mine and instead, join forces with the FBI and find the real killer of Michael Valentine. Forget about this separate investigation nonsense. Why don't you share your information with the FBI and work with them to find the killer of Becky Greenbrier? You do know about her murder, don't you? Now, I'm not going to answer any more of your questions without my lawyer present. So, you can leave now. Don't worry, I'm not going to go anywhere. If you believe you have enough evidence to arrest me, go ahead. But before you do, please know that I'll sue you, the Sheriff, and the Park County Commissioners for harassment, wrongful arrest, and loss of career and compensation when I lose my job because of your overzealous pursuit of the wrong person based on someone's feeding you false information. Oh yes, I'll make sure that the Cody, Bozeman, Livingston, and Billings newspapers are told how you harassed me and weren't willing to check out all the facts before accusing me. I also will tell them how you seem to be fascinated with my breasts, given the way you stare at my chest."

His face crimson and with fire in his eyes, he responded in a biting tone of voice, "Nice speech, Miss Richardson, but you haven't heard the last from us. We are waiting for the results of a comparative analysis of the hair taken from Valentine's car and body. You see, we are cooperating with the FBI. Agent VanKampen told my boss that all the findings from the lab work would be made available to us. Since you're so confident of your innocence, you won't mind us taking a sample of your hair with which to do our own comparison, now would you?"

"I probably shouldn't," she replied, "and, if my lawyer was here, I'm sure I'd be told not to cooperate without a proper warrant, but I'm going to go against my best judgment." Taking a scissors from her desk drawer, she cut a few strands of her hair and handed them to Assistant Deputy Vogelzang who placed them into a small plastic bag. "There you are."

"Ms. Richardson," Deputy Medina replied, "please don't leave the area. If there is anything you want to tell me, here's my number." He handed her a business card. "Thank you for your time and cooperation, Miss Richardson." He opened her office door allowing Assistant Deputy Vogelzang to walk ahead of him and then closed the door behind him.

This was unreal. It was unbelievable. She couldn't believe what had just taken place. She was being accused of murder. She was being setup to take the fall for killing Michael Valentine. Sure, he had threatened to expose her father if she didn't respond to his sexual overtures. Yes, she had threatened him back. But, those things were buried in her past, or she thought they had been. Who knew about them? How had Deputy Medina learned of them? Come to think about it, the man staring at her during the meeting at the Historical Center must have been Valentine, although he looked much different that she remembered him looking as a judge for the pageant. Why did Medina ask her about her uniform jacket? Why did he want a hair sample for a comparison? Could it be that somehow, some of her hair had been placed in Valentine's car? Why else would Deputy Medina want a sample of her hair for comparison purposes? Someone had gone to great lengths and taken huge risks to pull this setup off. Who wanted her so badly out of the way? Who hated her so much to kill Michael Valentine and try to pin it on her? What about Becky Greenbrier? Was she mixed up in this in some way or did she have nothing to do with any of this? If she did, what was the connection? If she didn't, why was she killed in the same way Valentine was killed? Many questions, no answers. It did no good to formulate question after question and have no answers. She wouldn't get anywhere doing that. She needed to think clearly and devise a plan to prove she hadn't had anything to do with Michael Valentine's murder or, for that matter, Becky Greenbrier's murder. She knew what her first step should be. Talk to Parker and get his advice. Her instinct told her there wasn't much time before Deputy Medina had the results of the comparison and, if she guessed correctly that her hair had been planted in Valentine's car, he would be back with a warrant for her arrest for murder.

CHAPTER 27

Wednesday Afternoon
12:15 p.m.
Gardiner River, Two Miles North-East of Mammoth Hot Springs,
Yellowstone National Park, Montana

Beth's text message had rattled him. As soon as he recovered from the shock of her message, he had called her to fill in the gaps of her text. It had been an emotional conversation for both of them. When her tears began to flow and her voice trembled, his heart ached for her. He wanted to be able to reach across the miles separating them and take her in his arms and comfort her. More than ever, he resolved to turn over every stone until the true killer was apprehended, freeing Beth from the grip of uncertainty and dismay.

Someone was out to destroy her. Someone knew things about her past which she believed had vanished from anyone's knowledge except for Michael Valentine and the person that had told Valentine about Beth's father's indiscretions. Her logic seemed solid. Valentine had told someone about his overtures to her and her rejection, and about her father. That someone was either Valentine's killer or had passed the story on to someone else. He realized a chain of story passers might exist between Valentine and the eventual killer, but he had to start somewhere and it might as well be at the beginning of the chain. He had debated whether to tell Janet about the two sheriff deputies. He didn't want to get her into any trouble with another law enforcement agency should she admonish the Sheriff. After all, the deputies were from Park County meaning the Park County Sheriff had approved sending the deputies to confront Beth. On the other hand, Janet had placed her confidence in him and trusted him to keep her informed. In the end, he had called her. Her reaction was predictable. After calling the Sheriff names he hadn't heard expressed in a long time, she had settled down and thanked him for letting her know. She told him to keep investigating and not to be concerned about her. She told him she was e-mailing a report she had received from the FBI's Chicago Office about Valentine's background.

After only a few minutes, an e-mail from Janet arrived with an attachment which was the report on Michael Valentine's life as unearthed by the FBI's Chicago Office. Reading through the report, he had to force himself to concentrate or what he was reading as his mind kept wandering back to thinking about Beth and the craziness of her being accused of murdering Valentine. Beth had to have been setup. By whom was the question. Was he being so supportive and loyal to Beth because of his feelings for her or was he the world's biggest fool? Was Beth not the wonderful woman her thought he to be but rather a calculating con-artist that could turn on the charm, warmness, and caring demeanor when she needed to and yet be a ruthless killer underneath the compassionate and caring exterior? No, it was impossible. He was ashamed for even thinking Beth wasn't the woman he knew she was. Monday evening's time together had sealed the deal for him. She simply couldn't be someone totally different than the person he had been with for several hours.

The report didn't provide much information or present any possible leads. Valentine's business ventures were described. He and his partner, a Victor Barrozo, had parted on less than amiable terms. Barrozo had accused Valentine of orchestrating the kidnapping of Barrozo's daughter which had resulted in the daughter being severely traumatized and finally institutionalized. The report included no additional information about Barrozo but did state that additional information would be forthcoming following a more in-depth investigation by the Chicago FBI office of Victor Barrozo.

Valentine had certainly been a womanizer, maybe even a sex addict, if there was such an addiction, as had been debated in the media and among so-called addiction experts during the Tiger Woods scandal. Several of his women "conquests", so to speak, had been willing to talk with the FBI agents. They recalled Valentine making comments, during his times with them, about a woman he "had a thing for" for several years and wouldn't give up trying to "have her." Another finding of the FBI agents was Valentine's purchase of a condo in Big Sky Village. Big Sky Village was a combination of homes and condos, surrounded by an 18-hour golf course, with retail stores, restaurants, and golf, ski, and fishing shops located in a retail center, all at the base of the Big Sky ski area and resort. Big Sky was about forty-five miles north of Yellowstone on U.S. highway 191 midway between West Yellowstone and Bozeman, Montana. Why had Valentine purchased a condo in a ski and golf resort in southwestern Montana far away from any night life or attractions? Many people viewed the area as being-in-the-boondocks. There were no indications that Valentine was a golfer or skier. If he wanted to hang out with the rich and famous and be seen around golf and ski celebrities, he would have purchased a condo in Aspen or Vail, Colorado, or Sun Valley, Idaho. If his sexual appetite was for more and more conquests of women that hung around where the rich and famous went, it wouldn't be Big Sky, Montana. Could it be Valentine learned of Beth working in Yellowstone and living in Mammoth Hot Springs, which wasn't far from Big Sky? A final clue, which the report mentioned, was that Valentine had purchased tickets, several weeks in advance, for all the events held in the Buffalo Bill Historical Center which involved Yellowstone information or activities. He had done so from his office in Chicago showing he'd been planning for some time to be in Cody. Why purchase tickets for every event unless he wanted to make sure he was attending when he thought Beth might be attending?

All this added up as Valentine having a long-term infatuation with Beth, which began with the Miss Illinois Pageant and culminated with his purchase of a condo at Big Sky, so he could be near her and watch for an opportunity to be near her and, in his mind, fulfill his fantasies. Parker shuddered at the thought of Valentine confronting Beth and attempting to force her to compromise her morals. As that other contestant had shouted, Valentine was indeed a "slimebag". Even so, he had been murdered and that was an act which shouldn't go unpunished.

What connected Beth and Valentine was the Miss Illinois pageant where Beth was a contestant and Valentine was a judge. According to Beth, she had not heard from him or seen him since the night of the pageant. He next showed up dead near the Sylvan Lake picnic area in Yellowstone National Park. Where was he just before he was murdered? Since he had a ticket for the speech and dinner at the Historical Center on Sunday evening, he probably was in attendance, most likely to confront Beth which, according to Beth, he had not done. He must have left the Center hoping to confront Beth at a later time. Did he leave with someone? Had he come with someone? He had only purchased a single ticket so he probably came alone, most likely hoping to leave with Beth. About three hundred people had attended the event, so maybe someone would remember seeing Valentine. How do you talk with three hundred people and who were these people? Most likely, they were people from throughout the greater Yellowstone area. A futile effort for sure, but it might have to be attempted. He thought about placing an advertisement in the *Cody Enterprise*, Cody's newspaper, asking anyone that attended the event to send him an e-mail. Maybe he would get lucky and someone would respond that recalled seeing Valentine and someone with him.

Given the time of Valentine's death, it had to have occurred somewhere near the east entrance of Yellowstone. The security camera at the East entrance had recorded his Lexus entering with what the FBI lab technicians had been able to show to be his neck tied to the headrest and his wrist to the steering wheel. The conclusion Janet reached was this was done to give the impression of Valentine driving the car. Most likely, the killer was driving the car, probably by sitting on the floor on the passenger side of the car and reaching across under the dash to control the car for the few feet through the entrance. An agile person would have been able to do it. Why go through the trouble of tying Valentine's head to the headrest and wrist to the steering wheel? Why was it important to have Valentine's car enter Yellowstone with his body made to look like he was alive and driving the car?

A nagging thought had been with him for some time and he couldn't shake it. Was he concentrating so much on Valentine's murder and not enough on Becky Greenbrier's murder? It simply couldn't be a coincidence that she and Valentine were both murdered in the same fashion and in close proximity time-wise. How was Becky connected to all this? The most logical explanation was she knew too much and her killer was afraid she would tell someone what she knew. Either that or she was blackmailing her killer and the killer had become fed up with the blackmailing. Beth had told him how Becky had reacted when Beth was chosen as Associate Superintendent. Becky had reacted very jealously. He, himself, had experienced Becky's jealous nature during a prior encounter when he was involved with an investigation of the murder of Edgar Hickson. Perhaps her jealousy of Beth had gotten the best of her and she had been drawn in by the killer.

There was also the money found in Becky's apartment. Jessica had found it under a loose floorboard in the back of Becky's bedroom closet. Ten thousand dollars in 5s, 10s, and 20s. Was stashing money in such a way typical of Becky? If so, why did she also have a savings account at the Yellowstone Credit Union which showed, according to the account records Jessica found in a file in Becky's desk, monthly electronic deposits of $200 from Becky's pay? The savings account never totaled more than

$2,500 since Becky withdrew small amounts periodically. Unless she had winnings from gambling or a lottery, how did she accumulate $10,000? Was the $10,000 the result of payments from someone she was blackmailing? Was it hush money? Did she offer herself as a sexual partner for money—a prostitute? If she did, she must have been very discreet since none of the other people living in the Terrace Apartments remember seeing men with her or men going to her apartment. Before leaving a few minutes earlier to return to her work at the Law Enforcement and Security Office, Jessica had talked with Becky's neighbors in the Terrace Apartments. They knew Becky and thought of her as a good neighbor that minded her own business and didn't come across as trying to be secretive.

His mind was so jumbled with bits and pieces, which didn't seem to fit together into any meaningful composite, he knew what he had to do to settle his mind before he tried to fit the bits and pieces together. He had to do what he had done before when he needed to reduce ambiguity and uncertainty. He had to fish. The Yellowstone area offered more and different fly-fishing opportunities than anywhere else in the lower 48, so he didn't have to go far to be fly-fishing on a river or stream which supported a healthy population of trout. Only a few miles from Mammoth Hot Springs was the Gardiner River, which cut across the north-central region of Yellowstone and was a tributary of the magnificent Yellowstone River. The drive to the Gardiner River went past the administration building and he toyed with the idea of stopping and surprising Beth with an impromptu visit. He thought his support, shown by physically being in her presence, would give her a boost. No doubt she needed a boost. Pulling off the road and parking on the shoulder, he sent her a text. He waited several minutes wondering if she would respond. As he was about to continue driving, he received a text reply. "So wonder to hear u. love to see u. can't. tied up. bummer. later." He was disappointed, but not surprised. Beth had a demanding position which left her with little discretionary time. It reminded him of what his life was like when he was president of Sturbridge State. He sure didn't miss that life. Parking in a small parking area near the Gardiner River, he put on his hip boots, withdrew his fly rod and reel from the rear of his 4Runner, placed the reel on the rod and threaded the line through the rod's guides. Before entering the water, he surveyed the surface of the river to determine if any trout were eating insects from the surface of the water. He saw no activity. He surmised the trout were content to eat nymphs which were drifting subsurface in the current. He tied a size 14, golden stonefly nymph on the end of his 4x tippet. Entering the water, he waded carefully to a place where the water was a few inches above his knees and he could cast to the water breaking around and over several mid-size rocks creating safety for trout from overhead predators like eagles, hawks, or ospreys. Casting above the broken water, he allowed the stonefly to drift, under the surface, into the broken water area. Counting two seconds at the end of the drift before he withdrew the stonefly to cast again, he didn't feel any strike. He cast two more times in the same area, allowing the stonefly to drift into the broken water. Same result. No strikes. All his experience told him there were trout in this particular spot in the river. He also knew trout could be very finicky, wanting to eat only a certain kind, size, and color of insect. Sort of like people that want to eat berries, but will pass on blueberries or blackberries, which they will eat almost all the time when available, to eat only strawberries. Different berry, different size, different color. Fish and people were sometimes very much alike. O.k., he'd play the trout's game. Clipping the golden stonefly from the end of the tippet, he tied a size 18, sparkling green colored, bead-head, caddis pupa. A much different looking fly than the golden stonefly; much smaller, different color, different insect. Casting into the same water and allowing the caddis pupa to drift subsurface into the broken water, he was rewarded with a strong strike as the pupa drifted to a position almost directly down from him. Pulling back firmly to set the hook, he fought the trout for several minutes before bringing it to him. Reaching into the water, he grasped the trout and gently released it. It was a beautifully colored brook trout, about 11 inches in length. He continued to fish a 100-yard section of the river before he felt satisfied that he had had a successful "fix" of fly-fishing which cleared his mind.

Walking back to his 4Runner, he began to organize his thoughts into three areas: what he knew about the two murders; what the probable reasons were; and what he didn't know. Reaching his 4Runner, he opened the back, broke down his fly rod, placing it and the reel into the back of the 4Runner. Taking off his hip boots, he placed them next to the rod and closed the back of the 4Runner. Sliding behind the steering wheel, he opened the storage compartment under the dash and withdrew a writing tablet. He wrote three columns across the top, labeling them "Know," "Probable Reason," "Don't Know," and began to write. When he finished he studied the columns. There were probably some matters he had overlooked. Nevertheless, he saw the steps he needed to take next.

CHAPTER 28

Wednesday Afternoon
2:00 p.m.
Outside the Student Center, Big Sky University, Livingston, Montana

Talk about a disaster waiting to happen. Two diametrically opposed philosophies in a clash of power with neither side showing any sign of backing off. The white supremacist group demanded a location in the Student Center, similar in size and visibility to the Gay, Lesbian, Bisexual, and Transgender advocacy organization's university-subsidized location in the Center. The university administration refused to recognize what it called a hate-based group. To escalate their claim of discriminatory treatment by the university administration, the supremacists had taken hostage two gay male students and two lesbian female students, and were presently locked in the office of the Gay, Lesbian, Bisexual, and Transgender organization. Heightening the tension was the fact that the supremacists had weapons and gas masks, showing they had planned ahead in case tear gas would be used to drive them from the office. They were media smart as evidenced by their text messages to media outlets to explain that the university had ignored their earlier requests for fair and equitable treatment and they had no other option to bring attention to their situation than the taking of hostages. They stated they didn't wish to harm anyone or bring negative publicity to bear on the university. All the university had to do, they stated, was to guarantee the supremacists the same status and treatment as the Gay, Lesbian, Bisexual, and Transgender organization, and the hostage situation would end peacefully with no one being harmed. The university administration, most notably the university president, had dug in its heels and refused to negotiate with the supremacists, the president stating that no hate-based group was going to push the university or him around. The situation became further complicated when the media reported that one of the two female student hostages was the daughter of the speaker of the Montana House of Representatives. It was well known that the Speaker was an antagonist of the university president and had disagreed with the president on numerous occasions regarding university policies. Given that the budget of the university depending on state funding support and all state funding for state-supported colleges and universities had to be approved by the House of Representatives, where the Speaker had enormous power and influence over how the representatives voted, an entirely new dimension was heaped onto this tension-filled drama when the Speaker went on television to say he thought the university needed to negotiate and reach a compromise, thereby allowing the hostages to be released.

In the midst of this mess was Janet VanKampen. She was expected to not only bring this potentially explosive situation to an end, but to do so without any violence occurring and providing no opportunity for those, that were out to discredit anything the FBI did, to be able to do so by second guessing any action she did or didn't take. She thought of all the second guessing, accusations, and finger-pointing of blame which occurred subsequent to the killing of Osama Bin Laden by Navy Seal Team 6 in Pakistan. No matter how this mess turned out, she was bound to be criticized by someone, somewhere. Her phone rang. Caller ID showed it was the Park County Sheriff's Office. She thought to herself, now what? I don't need this. She thought about not answering, but then realized she better take the call. "Hello, Agent VanKampen speaking."

"Agent VanKampen, please hold for Sheriff Evenhouse."

Janet had met Sarah Evenhouse several months earlier during a meeting of law enforcement officials from around the greater Yellowstone region. Janet remembered Evenhouse as a no-nonsense, level-headed, we-do-it-by-the-book person. "Janet, it's Sarah. I understand you're handling that hostage situation at the university. If it were me, I'd storm those idiots and show them who's boss. We can't have renegade groups like the supremacist's taking over our educational institutions."

"Sarah, I wish it were that easy. The supremacists have weapons. Imagine the outrage and backlash if one of the hostages was wounded or, God forbid, killed during our storming, as you call it, of their location."

"Sometimes you have to take the bad with the good. No one is above the law. Those supremacists have to be shown they aren't above the law. But, enough about your situation. You aren't going to do what I suggest, so no reason to waste my breath. I'm calling you as a courtesy. Two of my deputies are on their way to arrest the Associate Superintendent of Yellowstone National Park, a woman by the name of Beth Richardson, for the murder of Michael Valentine. The comparison of the hair from Richardson and the hair found on Valentine's body and in his car show one and the same. The button found in Valentine's car is the same as on the uniform jacket worn by her and other Yellowstone officials. An extra bonus, if you want to call it a bonus, is the lab was able to lift a fingerprint from the button and it is Richardson's fingerprint, meaning the button came from her jacket. Her shoes match the shoeprints from the murder scene. She had the motive. She was in the same location as Valentine when he was killed. She has no verifiable alibi for how she spent Sunday evening after the shindig at the Buffalo Bill Historical Center. It's a slam dunk. We have our killer. Richardson killed Valentine."

CHAPTER 29

Wednesday Afternoon
2:15 p.m.
Office of the Associate Superintendent, Administration Building,
Yellowstone National Park, Mammoth Hot Springs, Montana

She had been up most of the night unable to sleep. Her concentration through the day had been lousy. Her mind kept going over and over what had happened over the past few days and how she had been falsely accused. Following her instinct, she had decided to place a call to her parents. No one had answered, so she left a message for either of her parents to call her at her office. As she was beginning to look over her schedule for the next day, her intercom buzzed. "Beth, your mother is holding on line 1".

"Thanks, Ryan. Hi, Mom. I wanted to call and see how you and Dad are doing."

"Oh, honey, it's so good to hear from you. Other than the usual aches and pains that go along with aging, your father and I are doing o.k. I wish your father wouldn't watch as much of those cable political opinion shows as he does. He gets too excited about some of the things he hears. But, I suppose if that is the worst thing he does, I can live with it. I'm sure there are some things I do which bother him as well. So, how are you doing?"

"I'm fine, Mom. As you can guess, there is no chance to sit around and contemplate my navel. There's always plenty to occupy my time."

"I'm sure your work has plenty of interesting twists and turns, but what about your outlook for finding a soul mate? You're not getting any younger, you know?"

"Interesting you should ask, mom. There is a man with whom I'm enjoying myself. Anything serious is a long way off, but for now, I'm liking it."

"That sounds wonderful, Beth. Your heart will tell you if he's the one for you. I know you'll tell us more when you're ready. Your father isn't here right now, otherwise I'd have you talk with him."

"You can give him my love," replied Beth. "There's a favor I'd like for you to do for me, mom. The album you made about the Miss Illinois Pageant, would you find it and then take the program for the final night and fax a copy to my office?" Beth remembered the program listed the names of the final contestants as well as the sequencing of program activities. Beth couldn't remember the names of the other finalists. She felt if she could see the names and activities of the final night of the pageant, something might be triggered in her memory which might open up a new line of inquiry about a connection between Valentine, his killer, and possibly Becky Greenbrier. Maybe it was grasping at straws, but nothing else seemed to be working. Parker was doing the best he could, she knew, but she needed to help him more if she could.

"I'll be happy to do that, honey," responded her mother. "You want to relive that evening, I suppose. It sure was an exciting and fun evening. Seeing the glow on your face and the sparkle in your eyes was worth all the effort you put into getting there. Too bad that shouting match had to mar what was a wonderful evening for so many people. Are you planning to come visit us soon?"

"I'm not sure about my calendar, mom. Maybe I'll be able to get away for a few days. You said something about a shouting match. What shouting match? I don't remember any shouting," Beth responded.

"Of course you don't," replied Beth's mother, "you were so surprised and overwhelmed when you won that I don't think you would have heard a bomb going off. Besides, you were so surrounded by the media you couldn't have noticed anything happening even if you had wanted to."

She wanted to know more. She never knew shouting had occurred. Who shouted at whom and about what? Not that knowing now would have any importance. She was curious by nature and her curiosity was piqued. "I'm curious, mom, do you remember what the shouting was about?"

"I sure do. I was so upset with those two people shouting at each other when the evening was a festive one. I was on my way to the restroom to freshen up when the woman contestant you beat out starting yelling at one of the judges. He shouted something back to her, trying to get her to stop, I think, but it didn't work. He started to walk away and she shouted at him again. Then several people came up to me to congratulate me on your winning and I started to talk with them, so I don't know what happened after that."

"That's all interesting, mom. I didn't know anything about the shouting before now. I guess I was so caught up with the media and all the people offering congratulations that I missed anything going on around me. Well, mom, I have to run. You have the fax number for my office, don't you?"

"I certainly do. I'll find the program right away and fax a copy to your office. I do hope you'll be able to come and spend some time with your father and me. Bye, honey."

"Thanks, mom, and give my love to Dad." She glanced at the clock on her office wall. Time to forget about her situation and concentrate on some work which she had put off for too long. Try as she may, she couldn't shake feelings of anxiety and frustration. There wasn't anything on her schedule for the remainder of the day which promised to be extra difficult or personally annoying. Yet, she didn't feel good about the rest of the day. Shake it off, she thought. No sense creating unnecessary anxiety. She walked into the outer office where Ryan was sitting. "You can expect to receive a fax at any minute. When it arrives, please bring it to me right away. In the meantime, is anything happening later this afternoon that I don't know about?"

"The only thing I know about is you have a late afternoon meeting with the Gardiner Chamber of Commerce, although I could call the Chamber office and tell them you aren't going to be able to make it. The meeting agenda they sent a few days ago looked quite boring, if I may say so. Nothing is listed that concerns Yellowstone."

"Great idea. Go ahead and call The Chamber. I'm going to hunker down in my office and work through some stuff I've put off." As she closed the door to her office, she heard the fax machine beep. Most likely the fax from her mother, she thought. I'll wait to see if Ryan brings it in. After only a few minutes, her intercom buzzed.

"Beth, the fax you were expecting arrived," said Ryan. "Shall I bring it in?"

"Please." Her office door open and Ryan handed her a couple of sheets. "Thanks, Ryan." She took the fax and began to scan the program looking for the names of the contestants that, along with her, comprised the finalists. They were listed on the inside cover. As she read the names to herself, she tried to recall the person and anything she remembered about them. She was concentrating so intently, she almost didn't hear the intercom buzz again. "Yes, Ryan."

"Those same two deputies from the Park County Sheriff's office are here and want to see you. Shall I send them in?"

What could they want? She had answered their questions and told them everything she knew. She really didn't have time for more of their foolishness. However, she knew she should cooperate lest she be accused of being uncooperative which could find its way to the Superintendent which she wanted to avoid occurring. "Have them come in, Ryan."

Deputies Vogelzang and Medina walked into her office, both looking grim and determined. Not a good sign, Beth thought. "Miss Richardson," said Deputy Medina, "you're under arrest for the murder of Michael Valentine. You have the right to remain silent. Anything you say may be used against you in a court of law. You are entitled to legal representation. You are to come with us." Assistant Deputy Vogelzang took a pair of handcuffs, which were hanging from her belt, walked behind Beth, and handcuffed Beth's wrists together. Taking her by the arm, Vogelzang gently pushed Beth toward her office door. Deputy Medina opened the door allowing Beth and Vogelzang to walk from the office.

With a shocked look on his face, Ryan said, "What's going on, Beth? Why are you handcuffed?"

"Ryan," replied Beth, "there's been a terrible mix-up. I'm sure everything will be sorted out very soon. Please do two things for me as soon as you can. Let the Superintendent know I've been arrested by the Park County Sheriff for the murder of Michael Valentine, which, of course, is absolutely not true. Also, call Parker Williams and tell him the same thing. Ask him, also, to contact the best criminal lawyer he can find and have that lawyer come to the Park County Law Enforcement Center in Cody."

"I don't understand," responded Ryan with a look of utter disbelief on his face. "How can you be accused of murdering anyone?" Looking defiantly at the two deputies, he continued, "You must be wrong. Associate Superintendent Richardson isn't anymore a murderer than I am. You're making a huge mistake."

"It's o.k., Ryan. Please do those two things for me right away."

Assistant Deputy Vogelzang gently pushed Beth into the hallway, down the stairs, and out the entrance door to where a dark brown Ford, with the seal of Park County, Wyoming, was parked. Beth was thankful no employees had been in the hallway or on the stairs to witness her humiliation of being led handcuffed, like a criminal, by two Park County Sheriff deputies. Beth was pushed gently into the back seat of the car. As the car drove away from the administration building, she wondered if she would ever see the building or her office again.

CHAPTER 30

Wednesday Afternoon
2:30 p.m.
On U.S. Highway 20 Traveling Toward the East Entrance of Yellowstone
National Park, Wyoming

The call from Ryan Belgrade had turned his world upside down. The shock of it hadn't yet subsided. He was so upset he couldn't remember what Ryan had said after saying Beth had been arrested and charged with murder. He had been totally out-of-sorts for several minutes before he slowly gained back some semblance of functioning normally. He had gained enough where-with-all to call Ryan back and ask him to repeat what he had told Parker earlier. He realized Beth was counting on him to do what she had told Ryan to tell him. He couldn't let her down. What he wanted to do was get his hands on those deputies and pound some sense into them, futile as that might be. Instead, he did what Beth had asked him to do. He had called Janet VanKampen and requested her recommendation for the best criminal defense attorney she knew. Janet had replied that there was no need for an attorney as Janet would contact Sheriff Evenhouse and tell her to release Beth since, obviously, a mistake had been made. Janet had called him back after several minutes with the disheartening message that Sheriff Evenhouse had refused to release Beth saying only that irrefutable evidence proved Beth had killed Michael Valentine and a bail hearing was scheduled for the following day. Janet had apologized profusely and said she was going to contact the Park County Commissioners she knew and have them direct the Sheriff to release Beth. Upon Parker's insistence, she told him the best criminal defense lawyer she knew was Marcia Farrington, who had an office in Billings and was licensed to practice in Wyoming as well as Montana.

Janet had called Farrington. She had next called Parker, asking for as many details about Beth's situation as he could provide. Farrington's conversation with Parker ended by her agreeing to take Beth as her client and saying she would notify the Sheriff as to that fact and tell them Beth was not to be interrogated without Farrington, or someone she designated, being present. In addition, she was going to tell the Sheriff she expected full disclosure of the reasons for Beth's arrest.

Farrington wasn't going to be able to meet with Beth until Thursday morning, meaning Beth would be in the Law Enforcement Center overnight without any support or seeing any familiar faces. He couldn't allow that to happen. He needed to be there. He wanted to be with her. He realized he probably wouldn't be allowed to see or talk with her unless he could convince those holding her he was entitled to see her. He thought for several minutes and then realized he had a way to be able to see her. He realized he was investigating the murder of Becky Greenbrier with the blessing of the FBI. He could use his FBI authorization to see and talk with Beth. It's worth a try, he said to himself, as he made a quick call to his fly-fishing shop and told Dick to oversee everything and not to expect him to be in the shop for a few more days.

The drive to Cody seemed much longer than usual due to his impatience and the uncertainty regarding how successful he would be when he did arrive at the Law Enforcement Center. The drive provided time for him to devise an approach to see Beth which he felt might work better than his initial idea. He had called Marcia Farrington and explained what he had in mind. She had responded that his idea was highly unusual and if it wasn't Sheriff Evenhouse with whom they were dealing, the answer would be no. However, Marcia felt it would serve Evenhouse well to be confronted with Parker's approach, so she had agreed he could it.

Entering the Law Enforcement Center, he was greeted by a woman sitting behind a counter. He assumed she was the receptionist. The woman looked to be in her early fifties. Her hair was more gray than brown and tied in a bun which seemed to be perched on the top of her head like a speckled cinnamon bun. She had glasses perched on the end of her nose and, glancing over the glasses, she said, "Good morning."

"Good morning," replied Parker, "I'm here to meet with our client, Miss Richardson."

Looking down at a sheet of paper on her desk, the woman replied, "Deputy Medina is the officer-in-charge of Miss Richardson's case. You'll need to talk with him. I'll see if he can meet with you." She lifted a phone and pushed two buttons. After a few seconds, she said, "Deputy

Medina, there's a gentleman here that says his client is Miss Richardson and he wants to meet with her." She paused for several seconds listening to whatever Medina was saying in response. Returning the phone to its holder, she said, "I'm sorry, sir. Deputy Medina says that a woman lawyer is representing Miss Richardson. Only her lawyer can see her."

"Please contact Deputy Medina again," replied Parker, "and inform him that I am Marcia Farrington's assistant and I have been authorized by her to meet with her client. Deputy Medina can contact Ms. Farrington if he doubts me." The poor woman, thought Parker. She looks to be all be-fuddled. She's caught in the middle and is looking for someone to get her out of this situation. In as kind a voice as he could project, Parker said, "How about I help? Let me get you out of being caught in the middle. If you call Deputy Medina again for me, I'll talk to him so you won't have to."

She didn't hesitate; relief showing across her face that she had been rescued from what appeared might be a confrontation. Handing Parker the phone, she said, "Deputy Medina should answer." After three rings, a man answered.

"Yes, Margaret."

"It's not Margaret, Deputy Medina. My name is Parker Williams, an assistant with Marcia Farrington. Marcia has authorized me to meet with her client, Miss Richardson. If you doubt what I'm telling you, you may contact Marcia. She will verify everything I've told you. In the meantime, I'd appreciate seeing Miss Richardson."

"Now, wait just one minute. Farrington didn't say anything to me about an assistant. Furthermore, she told me she herself would be coming tomorrow morning. What did you say your name was?"

"Parker Williams. You are correct that Marcia is coming tomorrow. She decided she didn't want to wait that long before hearing from Miss Richardson so we could better prepare for the bail hearing. Now, I'd like to see Miss Richardson."

"Parker Williams . . . Parker Williams. I've heard about you. You own that fly-fishing shop in West Yellowstone. You've also been involved in a couple of homicide cases in Yellowstone. Now you're telling me you're an assistant with Marcia Farrington. What are you trying to pull, anyway?"

"I'm not trying to pull anything and I resent your accusation. Why don't you call Marcia? I'm sure she would love to tell the judge at the bail hearing how you refused to allow our client her right to meet with her lawyer when her lawyer was requesting to have her assistant meet with the client."

"Whom do you think you are, Mr. Williams, threatening me? I don't respond well to threats."

"I'm not threatening you, Deputy Medina. I'm giving you an opportunity to not make a huge mistake. And, while you're at it, you may want to contact FBI agent VanKampen of the Billings office of the FBI. She has authorized me to interrogate Miss Richardson about the murder of Becky Greenbrier. I plan to do that when I'm meeting with Miss Richardson. If you doubt me on this too, I have an authorization memo from the Director of the FBI which you're welcome to read."

"You have to be kidding. You, an FBI agent? No way, baby. You stay right where you are. I can't wait to see this so-called authorization."

Withdrawing his FBI authorization memo from his shirt pocket, he handed it to Medina. Medina turned a shade of crimson as he read the memo which was on FBI letterhead and signed by the Director of the FBI in Washington, D.C. The memo stated that Parker was authorized to assist Special Agent Janet VanKampen in whatever activities and actions she deemed to have him undertake. Janet had been able to obtain several such authorizing memos from the Director as a quid-pro-quo for having so few agents assigned to the Billings office and her accepting the position as agent-in-charge. Parker assumed the other consultants utilized by Janet possessed the same authorizing memo, the only difference from the one Parker possessed being the name of the consultant being authorized.

With a look that could kill, Medina said, "I don't know how you obtained this memo and I can't believe Agent VanKampen would allow inexperienced people like you to function like an FBI agent. The FBI must really be hard up and in a sad state of affairs to have people like you playing FBI agent."

Parker could tell this was going to be a battle of wills which might turn ugly, but he decided he wasn't about to back down. "Deputy Medina, I really could care less what you think of me or Agent VanKampen or, for that matter, the FBI. I'm sure Agent VanKampen would be happy to discuss the track record of the FBI with you, but she has more important matters to deal with than petty jealousy of a small law enforcement agency and its mediocre staff. Now, before I have to ask Agent VanKampen to contact your superior, I believe that would be Sheriff Marilyn Evenhouse or, better yet, the County Commissioners, please take me to see Miss Richardson and, by the way, I expect to be able to talk with her confidentially with neither you nor any other individual listening in from a hidden microphone."

Deputy Medina looked at Parker with steely eyes and for a few seconds, Parker thought his approach and strong words were going to backfire. Then he saw Medina's shoulders sag as he lowered his eyes, a sign of resigned defeat. "O.k., Williams, you win this time. But, I'm warning you, don't cross my path again with your high and mighty attitude, or you'll be sorry."

"I wouldn't think of it, Deputy Medina. Please take me to see Miss Richardson." Without saying a word, Medina turned in an exaggerated manner and walked briskly toward the same door through which he had entered. Parker followed him through the door into a hallway where a uniformed guard sat immediately adjacent to a gray door farther down the hallway.

"Harry," Medina said, "please take Mr. Williams to the conference room. Also, please have Judy escort Miss Richardson to meet Mr. Williams in the conference room."

"Sure thing, Deputy Medina. Shall I tell Judy to remain with Miss Richardson and Mr. Williams?"

"No, not in the conference room, but immediately outside the room. Mr. Williams and Miss Richardson will be alone in the conference room. Also, please make sure the microphone is turned off." Turning to Parker, he continued, "There you are Mr. FBI wan-na-be. Harry will escort you to the conference room where Miss Richardson will meet you. When you finish, Harry will escort you back here. One last thing. Beth Richardson is a murderer. You and Marcia Farrington are going to look like fools. Don't say I didn't warn you." Turning quickly, he walked from the room leaving Parker with the guard Medina called Harry.

"Please come with me," Harry said as he gestured for Parker to follow him. Harry entered a series of numbers of a pad next to the gray door which caused an audible click which Parker interpreted as the electronic locking mechanism being disengaged. Opening the door, Harry indicated Parker should walk through the doorway. Entering another small room, Parker saw a uniformed woman guard seated next to another gray door. On another wall, at a 90-degree angle from the gray door, was another door. This one was wooden with a small window on the upper portion. "Judy, this is Mr. Williams," said Harry, "he's here to meet with Miss

Richardson. Please escort Miss Richardson here to the conference room. I'll bring Mr. Williams to the conference room."

The woman guard, whom Parker assumed was Judy, entered some numbers in a pad adjacent to the gray door. Parker heard the same click as before. Judy opened the door and walked through the doorway, closing it behind her. Hearing another click, Parker assumed the gray door was locked. Only then did Harry take a key from his pants' pocket and open the wooden door. "This is the conference room you will use," Harry said. Entering the room, Parker saw a plain wooden table and four metal chairs, two on each side of the table. All the chairs were bolted to the floor as was the table. On the table was a small black box with a red button. "If at any time you wish to contact Judy, just push the red button," said Harry. "It activates a signal outside the room and Judy will look through the window to determine if the signal is because you are finished or you need assistance. You are not able to open the door. It is electronically locked and can only be opened by entering the proper sequence of numbers on the pad on the other side of the door. Do you have any questions before I leave?"

"Two," replied Parker. "When will Miss Richardson be here and how long may I talk with her?"

"She will be here momentarily and you'll have fifteen minutes. After fifteen minutes, Judy will escort Miss Richardson back to her cell and I will escort you back to the reception area." Harry then walked from the room, leaving Parker to wait for Beth to arrive. As he waited, his mind was racing. His emotions were at the surface, ready to boil over. He was concerned for Beth's wellbeing and worried the situation she was in would permanently scar her. Her whole life—career, reputation, friendships, earning power—hung in the balance. He trusted Janet's opinion regarding the abilities of Marcia Farrington, but even the best lawyer couldn't make incriminating evidence go away. Additional evidence proving Beth's innocence had to be found. Better yet, the person or persons responsible for planting the false evidence must be exposed. He heard the click of the door just before it opened.

CHAPTER 31

Wednesday Afternoon
3:15 p.m.
Dormitory for Yellowstone National Park Employees, Old Faithful
Complex, Yellowstone National Park, Wyoming

It had worked! The plan and its execution had been flawless. Beth Richardson had been arrested and charged with murder. She was going down. The Yellowstone grapevine was working like a charm. The news had spread like wildfire. By this time, every employee throughout Yellowstone was talking about Beth Richardson being a murderer. Simply wonderful.

Was it time to vamoose, leave this place behind, and get on with a new outlook on life knowing double revenge had been achieved? However, leaving quickly might raise questions. But, so what? Questions among Yellowstone employees meant nothing. Let them ask all the questions they wanted. Who cares? Oh, how sweet it would be to be there when the word spread that Richardson had been found guilty. It would be icing on the cake. In the big scheme of things, what were a few more days? Getting to this point had been such a long time in coming. A little longer to achieve the final payoff—Richardson convicted of murdering Valentine—was worth it. No, stay put. Don't leave, at least not now. Double revenge. So, so sweet.

CHAPTER 32

Wednesday Afternoon
4:15 p.m.
Conference Room, Park County Law Enforcement Center, Cody, Wyoming

Beth wore an orange jump suit with the words "Park County Sheriff's Department" across the left chest area. Her hair was disheveled and her eyes were puffy, indicating she'd been crying. As the door closed, his emotions overcame him and he rushed to wrap his arms around her and hold her close. "Beth, Beth, I'm so sorry, "he said in a broken voice as she began to sob in his arms. He wanted to say more but words stuck in his throat as he too felt tears flowing down his cheeks. Her body trembled in his arms and her sobs continued as they remained standing locked in a mutual hug.

Slowly her sobbing stopped, as did his, and they released each other. "Look what I've done," she said, pointing to his shirt front where her tears had turned the light blue color to a dark blotch. "I've made a mess of your shirt." Turning slowly, as if she were a model displaying a fashion designer's latest creation, she continued, "Don't I look terrific? Now you know how I truly look most of the time." She was obviously trying to bring some humor into a horrible situation.

"Beth, I came as soon as I heard from Ryan what they had done to you. This is simply outrageous. What can they be thinking? Don't they realize you've been framed?"

"Where are my manners? I haven't even thanked you for coming," she replied. "I didn't expect to see you, or anyone else, until a lawyer showed up. How did you manage to get past the watchdogs out there? They're probably watching us through that window over there," pointing to the window which Parker assumed had one-way vision glass enabling someone to look into the room without being seen from the inside.

His emotions now under control, he responded, "It's a long story and it isn't important. Let's just say that I'm here in a two-fold capacity. I'm assisting your lawyer whose name, by the way, is Marcia Farrington. She'll be here tomorrow morning to meet with you. My second role is as an FBI consultant authorized to interrogate you regarding the murder of Becky Greenbrier. In reality, of course, I'm doing neither. Rather, I want to know anything you learned from the deputies about what they believe they know which convinced the Sheriff you're guilty of killing Valentine. We know it's a lie, but if I knew what they believed, I could get to work undoing it and, at the same time, expose whomever set you up." Looking at the clock on the wall, he continued, "We have only about ten more minutes before they make me leave, so tell me everything you learned."

"Medina and Vogel . . . ah . . . , whatever her last name is, the woman deputy, I can't remember her last name, they were closed lipped for most of the drive here from Mammoth Hot Springs, so I didn't learn much. The woman deputy did most of the talking and it seemed to me that she and Medina weren't on the same page. I sensed some hostility between them. She did say the hair comparison was a lock, those were her words, so I assume she meant the hair found on Valentine and in his car match mine. How they got there is anyone's guess. Then there's the button and my jacket missing a button. Apparently, the button found in Valentine's car is the same type of button on the uniform jacket worn by senior people in the National Park Service. There are only six of us in Yellowstone with that uniform jacket so I assume my jacket was the only one missing a button. Then, the shoeprint by Valentine's car is from the same type and size shoe I wear everyday around work. All I can think of is when I discarded a pair of shoes, someone took them and used them to make shoeprints around Valentine's car. Lastly, my camping overnight on Sunday can't be substantiated, so they probably think I'm lying about where I was Sunday evening after the event in Cody."

"There's nothing to be done about the hair comparison," replied Parker. "Somehow, someone took some of your hair and planted it on Valentine and in his car. What we need to do is find that person or persons. The button could have been taken from your jacket, assuming it is even from your jacket. I bet that button is used on numerous uniform jackets besides the ones you and the other senior officials wear. So, that isn't going to carry much weight as evidence against you. Your explanation about the shoeprints makes sense. As for the overnight camping, are you sure no one saw you or your Explorer around Soda Butte Creek on Sunday evening or early Monday morning before you left for the Slough Creek Campground? All we need is one person to have seen you or your Explorer, and the case against you unravels."

"It was dark, the camera at the Cooke City/Silvergate entrance was missing, there was no one working the entrance station, and no vehicle passed me after I entered Yellowstone. I didn't see anyone or any vehicles the rest of the night or the next morning around Soda Butte Creek. There was one car at the Slough Creek Campground, but I can't recall the type of car or what state license plate was on it. Besides, they can say I could have driven to Slough Creek very early Monday morning after killing Valentine the night before." Smiling as best she could, she continued, "I should have invited you to join me for my overnight camping. You could have been my alibi plus we probably would have enjoyed being out there under all those stars all by ourselves. Unfortunately, you weren't with me and I'm afraid there's no one to verify my being there."

"Finding the person or persons that set you up, that's the key," replied Parker. "Is there anything, even the remotest possibility, you can think of why someone would want to set you up? Anyone, past or present, that might hold a huge grudge or be so jealous of you to go to any extreme to get back at you?"

"I've been racking my brain all the time I've been here trying to answer those questions. Unless there's someone that picked me totally at random and is getting his or her kicks from seeing if she or he can get away with framing someone they picked at random while also committing murder, I can only come up with two people and neither of them makes any sense. In fact, one is dead, so even if she did set me up, it's too late to confront her. The other is ancient history and I can't even remember her name." The gray door clicked and the woman guard entered the room. "Time's up. I'll take you back now, Miss Richardson."

"Please, Judy," said Parker, "just another minute. I have one more matter to discuss with Miss Richardson and it won't take long."

"O.k. Mr. Williams, you have one more minute and then no more. I'll be right outside the door."

"Thank you," replied Parker. The door clicked behind Judy as she exited the room. "Quick, Beth, tell me anything you can think of about the two people you think may have set you up. I don't care if one is dead and you can't remember the name of the other. It gives me a place to start and right now, I have no other place any better."

"The one that's dead was Becky Greenbrier. She was furious when I was promoted to Associate Superintendent. For some reason which escapes me, she thought she should have been given the job. She might have been so resentful and jealous, I suppose, that she could have tried to frame me for Valentine's murder. But that would mean Becky killed Valentine and I really can't see her as a murderer. The one whose name I don't remember was a contestant with me in the Miss Illinois pageant. The day after the pageant, I heard from one of the media people interviewing me at the time that she accused me of providing sexual favors to one of the male judges in exchange for his vote. Totally absurd and preposterous. Add that my mother remembers a shouting match between a contestant and one of the male judges. It's a possibility, I suppose, that the contestant that shouted was the same contestant that accused me. I had my mother fax a copy of the final evening's program of the pageant to Ryan. In fact, I was beginning to look through it to see if I remembered any of the names of the contestants or judges when Medina interrupted me and subsequently arrested me. I just remembered now that when Medina first came to question me, he mentioned Valentine as one of the judges. I hadn't remembered his name until Medina mentioned it and I was going to look for it in the program when Medina arrested me."

The gray door clicked, opened, and Judy walked in. "Miss Richardson, please come with me. Mr. Williams, Harry is waiting outside the room for you. Please remain in the room until Miss Richardson and I leave. Harry will come and get you." Taking Beth by the arm, Judy led her from the room. After they had exited, Harry entered.

"Mr. Williams, please come with me." Holding the door open, Parker walked from the room wondering if the information Beth had provided would be a dead-end, like everything else had been so far, or might prove to be just what the doctor ordered.

CHAPTER 33

Wednesday Afternoon
4:15 p.m.
Outside the Student Center, Big Sky University, Livingston, Montana

The training at Quantico for FBI agents hadn't included "here's how you deal with pompous politicians and arrogant university presidents" seminars. Throw in some idealistic students and know-it-all university faculty and you have a recipe for a Ruby Ridge-type standoff on steroids. The Speaker of the Montana House of Representatives had been on local television and quoted in the Livingston newspaper demanding the university president give the student group, which called itself 'Equal Treatment for All Students', what it wanted so the Speaker's daughter, along with the other students being held, would be released unharmed by the group. The university president, not to be upstaged by a politician, let alone the most powerful politician in the Montana Legislature, had also appeared on television and been quoted in the newspaper saying that the university would not negotiate with terrorists and politicians should keep their noses out of university business and do their job of solving the fiscal nightmare which was the state budget. Upon hearing they were being called terrorists, the leader of the Equal Treatment for All Students group threatened to act like terrorists beginning with the torture of the Speaker's daughter. Not to be undone by anyone and in its typical not-knowing-what-they-were–talking-about manner, the university's faculty senate voted to hold a sick-out to show the faculty's support for the student group

Special Agent Janet VanKampen felt like telling everyone where they could go and what they could do, and then walking away from this mess. This was a no-win situation and yet, she was expected to pull off a miracle where everyone would be pleased with the result, no one would be injured or hurt, both physically and in their egos, and the FBI would be seen as the great mediator and solver of all difficult situations. What a joke. She had no more of an idea how to solve this mess than she had of bringing Nancy Pelosi and Russ Limbaugh to respect each other. To make matters worse, there was the deteriorating situation in Yellowstone. Parker Williams had sounded like a grasshopper in a frying pan when he called to tell her about the arrest of Beth Richardson and to ask for the name of the best defense lawyer Janet knew. She needed Parker to remain focused and non-emotional. He seemed far from either and that created a dilemma for her. If she pulled him from the investigation, it would mean she agreed with Sheriff Marilyn Evenhouse that Beth Richardson had killed Michael Valentine. If she didn't pull him, it meant an upcoming confrontation with Marilyn was inevitable. Plus, because of Parker's apparent emotional and mental state of mind, he might do something which would be very damaging to Janet and the reputation of the FBI. Sure, right now she felt like she could care less about the reputation of the FBI, but she knew her feelings were only temporary. The FBI was her life and deep down, she respected and admired the Bureau and wanted to enhance its credibility and reputation, not hurt them. Besides, a confrontation with Marilyn Evenhouse might be fun, especially if the irrefutable evidence she claimed to have as the basis for charging Beth Richardson with murder wasn't so irrefutable after all. Knowing how good a lawyer Marcia Farrington was, it only made sense to give her time to delve into the details of Evenhouse's findings. As for Parker, Janet would make it clear to him that he wasn't to say or do anything related to Beth Richardson's arrest without first passing it by Janet. Have him on a short lease, she decided, was necessary if the Valentine and Greenbrier murder cases were to be kept under control.

CHAPTER 34

Wednesday Evening
7:00 p.m.
Gold Medal Fly-Fishing Shop, West Yellowstone, Montana

Throughout his drive back to West Yellowstone, the look on Beth's face, as she had left the conference room, haunted him. Even the wondrous sights all around him, which made Yellowstone such a special place, couldn't shake the feelings of anger he felt about how Beth had been treated and the lack of clues as to how to prove she had been framed. It was time to pursue an entirely new angle beginning with what Beth had told him at the end of their conversation. Beth had pointed to Becky Greenbrier as being jealous enough to frame Beth. The trouble was Becky had been murdered, suggesting that someone killed her to either keep her from talking or because she had been blackmailing someone that had enough of her blackmailing. The $10,000 Jessica had recovered from Becky's apartment suggested she had been paid to do something, either blackmailing or something else. Her bank accounts and deposit records for the past two years had shown the $10,000 had come from some other source than her work. The personal information obtained by the FBI staff in the Billings office had found no lottery or gambling winnings, no inheritance, or any source of money totaling $10,000. The fact Becky had been killed using the same tranquilizer as had been used to kill Valentine and the murders were only three days apart were strong indicators she was mixed up in the Valentine murder and had paid the ultimate price for her involvement. Parker concluded from everything learned about Becky Greenbrier that she had participated in the murder of Michael Valentine and been involved in setting up Beth to be charged with his murder.

Stick with it, he said to himself. Somehow, Becky Greenbrier was a key to finding whomever had been behind Becky's participation in framing Beth and, most likely, the killer of Becky and Valentine. What had been

Becky's role in all this? What had she done in helping to frame Beth? There had to be something. Had anything been learned from the evidence gathered from the murder scene? These questions were rolling around in his mind as he parked behind the shop. He had decided, during his drive from Cody, he needed to check-in with his employees and find out what, if anything, required his attention. Entering the shop through the rear entrance, he saw Laurie at the counter talking with a man and Dick seated at the fly-tying bench. He didn't want to interrupt Laurie in the middle of her conversation, so he walked over to Dick. "Dick, it's been a few days since we talked. Thanks for staying late this evening. How are you?"

"Parker, it's good to see you. I'm fine. The more important question is, how are you? To be honest, you look somewhat frazzled."

"Frazzled is a good word for how I feel. I can't seem to make any headway with this Valentine murder situation. It's really frustrating. Maybe I'm not cut out for this amateur FBI agent stuff. Leave it to the pros, which I'm not."

"I feel for you," replied Dick. "I know I wouldn't be worth anything as an investigator. I'll stick with my fly-tying, catching fish, and guiding clients. Speaking of which, we've had a steady stream of clients wanting us to be their guides. We've been able to handle all the requests. I've had to tap into our backup supply of peasant tail nymphs and elk hair caddis dry flies to keep up with demand. A couple clients caught several nice size rainbows and browns using those flies and you know how quickly word travels among fly-fishers. Everyone coming into the shop to purchase flies wanted several of each."

Laughing, Parker responded, "Tomorrow it will be some other fly. We've seen it happen time and time again. Someone will catch fish using "x" fly and the rush to purchase "x" fly will be on. I certainly appreciate your watching over things, Dick. I couldn't be doing this amateur FBI stuff if I didn't have you. Is there anything you need me to do before I try again to get somewhere with this investigation?"

"There is one thing. The Sage fly-rod representative stopped in. He wanted to talk to you about a special promotion involving the shop and Sage. He didn't volunteer what the promotion involved and I didn't ask. He said he would call you in a few days"

"Sage always has top quality products so I'll be curious to listen to his spiel. Anything else?"

Nodding toward Laurie, Dick replied, "Only to say that she is a godsend, but you already know that. She is simply wonderful with customers. Of course, it doesn't hurt that she is one good looking young woman. The younger male fly-fishers seem to purchase more than they attended to purchase after talking with her. Anyway, let's make sure we don't lose her or our revenue will probably be cut in half."

"Right on, Dick. Laurie sure is a keeper. If you do need me for anything, call or text me." He saw that Laurie was still engaged in conversation with the same customer as before. The customer, a young man, was holding a pair of wanders in front of him, looking in a mirror to determine if the size was correct. The waders were the high-end Simms goretex ones which, if sold, meant a nice profit for the shop. She smiled at Parker and gave him a wink indicating the sale was a sure thing. He smiled back and gave a slight wave as he exited the shop out the rear entrance. He'd have to think about a bonus for Laurie, he decided.

Back in his 4Runner, he found Janet's cell phone number and called it. On the third ring she answered. "Janet VanKampen speaking."

"Hi, Janet, it's Parker. I was able to see Beth and talk with her. Thanks for supporting my idea to be able to get to see her. Based on a couple of things Beth told me, I have a hunch that Becky Greenbrier may be a key to finding the real killer of Valentine. What were the results of the lab's analysis of the evidence found at Becky's murder scene?"

"Parker, are you sure your feelings for Beth aren't clouding your thinking? It's no secret you and Beth were seeing each other awhile back. Maybe it's time for you to bow out of the investigation. You've done everything I've asked you to do, but it seems to me that, as much as you don't like to admit it and, I confess, I find it hard to believe myself, the evidence against Beth is strong. Her hair on Valentine's body and in his car, shoeprints matching her shoes around Valentine's car, a button missing from her uniform jacket, with her fingerprint on it, found in Valentine's car, a history of a questionable relationship with Valentine, and no credible way to verify where she was when Valentine was murdered are enough to conclude she killed Valentine or, at least, is involved in his murder. I'm sorry to say, less convincing evidence has resulted in a conviction in cases of which I've been aware."

"What's this about a fingerprint? I hadn't heard about that until now," replied Parker.

"Beth's fingerprint is on the button. It verifies the button is hers."

"I know it looks bad," he responded, "but I know Beth and she isn't a murderer. My emotions aren't clouding my judgment. She has been framed. The question is by whom? Answer that question and you have your killer. Janet, if you want me off the investigation, I'm o.k. with that. You're the boss. But before I'm back to Parker Williams, fly-fishing shop owner and everyday citizen, tell me about the evidence found at Becky's murder scene. Also, has the report on that Barrozo guy come from the Chicago FBI people yet?"

"I don't want this to cause hard feelings between us," she replied. "I still hope we can see each other socially, maybe do some fishing together, and some other fun stuff,"

"No hard feelings, Janet. I was actually thinking about suggesting to you that I bow out of the investigation. Now about the evidence and the report."

"Oh yes, the evidence and the report. First, the evidence. The lab geeks say the hair found clutched in Greenbrier's fist was from a man. Also, the hair was colored. The ingredients of the coloring solution are different. Not from your ordinary, over-the-counter hair coloring solution. It's a solution found in Latin America. Comes from some plant which is somewhat rare. I don't remember the name of the plant. Expensive stuff, I'm sure. The scrapings from Greenbrier's fingernails were from someone other than Beth. This, combined with the colored hair being from a man, rules out Beth as Greenbrier's killer. However, I doubt if that will have any bearing on her arrest for killing Valentine. That's it for the evidence. As for the report, it has a lot of interesting stuff, but I don't think it provides any solid evidence to support Barrozo being involved in Valentine's murder. I'll fax the report to your shop."

"Thanks, Janet, and thanks for giving me the opportunity to help with the investigation. I'm sorry I wasn't more helpful. What I'm really sorry about is that I wasn't able to help clear Beth of this ridiculous charge against her. As for helping you again in the future, I think I'll pass for awhile. I'm pulling for you to find Becky's killer. Whatever she was mixed up with, she still didn't deserve to be murdered. Maybe we can do some fishing together sometime down the road, but for the foreseeable future, I'm going to concentrate on my business."

He said a quick goodbye before Janet could say anything more. So, he was officially off the investigation. The key word was "officially". He might not be officially involved with the investigation any longer, but that didn't mean he couldn't unofficially pursue his own investigation. He'd have to be more careful, that's all. He had the authorization memo to use if he had to, making sure Janet didn't find out he was using it. There was simply no way he was going to stay on the sideline while the woman he was so fond of and cared a whole lot about was in a life and death struggle about which no one else seemed concerned.

He had a couple ideas what to do next. He hadn't told Janet about either and he certainly wouldn't now. She seemed to be in the camp with those that believed Beth had killed Valentine. He couldn't let Janet know what he was doing. She had told him the evidence found at Becky's murder scene ruled out Beth as Becky's killer. Of course Beth hadn't killed Becky. What Janet apparently didn't realize was she also had provided information which could prove important down the road.

CHAPTER 35

Thursday Morning
9:30 a.m.
Park County Law Enforcement Center, Cody, Wyoming

Beth paced around her cell. Last night had been miserable. She hadn't slept more than a few minutes at a time. The reality of her situation had become a weight bearing down on her. She had racked her brain trying to understand how the false evidence against her had been obtained and, more importantly, who might have done the planting of it. She knew she focused better when she was moving instead of being in one spot. Thankfully, she was the only woman being detained in this area of the Law Enforcement Center so she didn't have to contend with other women prisoners. Her meeting with Marcia Farrington had gone as well as it could, she concluded. Marcia had said the evidence was what she referred to as "maybe" evidence. Maybe this; maybe that; or maybe something else. Maybe her hair was on Valentine's body and in his car because she had been with him. Maybe her hair was on Valentine's body and in his car because someone had placed them there. Maybe the button found in Valentine's car came from her uniform jacket because she had been in Valentine's car and struggled with him as she killed him; maybe the button had been taken from her jacket by someone that then planted it in Valentine's car or gave it to the killer and the killer planted it when killing Valentine. Maybe the shoeprints around Valentine's car came from Beth's shoes, maybe from someone else's shoes identical to Beth's shoes. Maybe, maybe, maybe had been the theme Marcia was going to pursue. She stressed, of course, the best approach to dismissing the case was to have verification Beth had been on her way to the camping place by Soda Butte Creek when Valentine was murdered, had been camped by Soda Butte Creek all night, or, best of all, find the person or persons that had framed her. The best news Marcia had given Beth was although bail was normally not granted in a murder case, since the Superintendent had personally vouched for guaranteeing Beth wouldn't take-off and would be accessible at all times, the bail judge might be sympathetic and grant bail. The bail hearing was scheduled in a few minutes. Until then, all she had was to think about her situation and how to extricate herself from it. The support of the Superintendent was a huge plus. When the charges against her were dismissed, she now felt confident her career wouldn't be harmed, thanks to the Superintendent's belief in her.

The troubling aspect of her situation was all her eggs were in two baskets; Marcia Farrington, to get the bail judge to release her on bail and to obtain a no guilty decision should she go to trial, and Parker, to find the person or persons that set her up. To be so dependent on two people wasn't her nature. She had always been resourceful and able to solve her own problems without depending on someone else. She assumed she would be on administrative leave when she was released on bail, so she would have time on her hands. Depending on the stipulations the bail judge placed on her release, she might be able to help Marcia prepare her defense and Parker with his investigation. She liked that thought, as it meant Parker and she could further their relationship while she contributed to finding the person or persons that framed her.

She heard the click of the gray door opening followed by Marcia Farrington and Judy. "Let's go meet the judge," said Marcia, gesturing Beth to follow her out the door.

"I'm ready when you are," replied Beth. "The sooner I'm out of here the better. No offense, Judy."

"I don't take it personally, Miss Richardson," responded Judy. "I'd want out of here too if I was in your shoes. For what it's worth, Miss Richardson, I hope the judge let's you out on bail. I've seen a bunch of criminals in my time around here and you don't seem to be a criminal to me."

"Thanks, Judy, I appreciate that. It means a lot. Your instincts are good too. I'm not a criminal and I trust everyone will know that soon."

"Come on, let's move it," said Marcia, "we don't want to keep Judge Roscoe waiting."

CHAPTER 36

Thursday Morning
9:45 a.m.
Administration Building, Yellowstone National Park, Mammoth Hot
Springs, Montana

In a strange way, he felt relieved. He had thought about it last night and again this morning. No more Janet VanKampen looking over his shoulder or having to be kept informed. No more daily status reports to be prepared and sent. No more trying to live up to the standards of FBI agents. He was free to come and go as he wished and to do what he wanted, when he wanted. The only drawback was he had to exercise caution if and when he had to use his FBI authorization memo. Hopefully, he wouldn't have to use the memo at all, or at most, no more than once or twice.

He parked in a visitor parking space outside Yellowstone's administration building at Mammoth Hot Springs. If he remembered correctly, Beth's office was on the third floor, down the hall from the Superintendent's office. He entered Beth's outer office where he was met by Ryan Belgrade. Ryan and he knew each other from previous times when Parker had stopped to visit Beth. "Hi, Ryan. How are you holding up?"

"Lousy, Parker, plain lousy. This situation with Beth has us all upset, including the Superintendent. Beth isn't any more a murderer than I am. When those two deputies came and arrested her, I couldn't believe it. How can this be happening? What can we do?"

"Ryan, I'm as dumbfounded as you. Beth's been framed and we have to find out who set her up. The FBI hasn't ended its investigation although to be brutally honest, I don't see the FBI trying too hard given Beth's arrest. I can't see the FBI going head-to-head with the Park County Sheriff. One law enforcement agency would be saying the other one is incompetent and incapable of conducting a sound and forthright investigation. Isn't going to happen, I'm afraid."

"We can't just sit back and do nothing," replied Ryan. "There has to be something we can do."

"There is, Ryan, and together, you and I are going to do it. I'm going to need your help, trust, and your pledge to keep everything confidential if we're going to help Beth."

"You know you can count on me, 110 percent, and I know there are others around here that will gladly help as well," responded Ryan.

"I'm sure that's true," said Parker, "but we're going to have to keep it as quiet as we can. Otherwise, what we're doing might backfire and end up hurting Beth rather than helping her. Here's where trust and keeping everything confidential come into play. You'll have to trust I know what I'm doing and keep everything you hear from whomever and everything I tell you to yourself. You tell no one. Not even the Superintendent, FBI, or, above anything, anyone with the Park County Sheriff. Keep everything to yourself. Do we have an agreement?

"I'm not sure why you're so secretive, but I trust you and will keep anything you tell me or what I might see or hear from others totally confidential. If it means freeing Beth, you have my pledge."

"Excellent, Ryan," responded Parker. "To begin with, give me a copy of what Beth's mother faxed Beth and what Beth was looking at just before she was arrested. You keep a copy for yourself. Don't show it to anyone else. Do you have access to a computer and the internet other than here at the office?"

"Sure. I've a computer with internet access in my apartment."

"Great. Use it and not your office computer for what I'm asking you to do. Please do profile searches and social network searches on every one of the final contestants in the Miss Illinois Pageant. Do the same for each of the judges. If there is anything which strikes you in the slightest way as being unusual, flag it and send it to me in an e-mail. I mean the slightest thing. Also, you believe many of your fellow employees throughout this building would help to get to the truth about Beth's whereabouts the evening Valentine was murdered. I'd like to you to go around to every department and office in this building and ask each person—from the janitor to the Superintendent, don't skip anyone—if they can think of any way to verify that Beth was not with Valentine after the meeting in Cody ended. Maybe someone was driving the Chief Joseph Highway the same time she was and remembers seeing a National Park Explorer. Maybe someone wanted to view the Sough Creek wolf pack too and spent the night near Soda Butte Creek in a tent or an R.V. and saw Beth's Explorer. I know it's a long shot, but we have to try everything we can think of doing."

"I'll get on seeing people right away and I'll do those searches this evening using my personal computer. At least it will give me something positive to do other than get more anxious and angry about how Beth is being royally screwed."

"Thanks, Ryan. Now, please make me a copy of that program." Ryan pulled open his desk drawer, withdrew what Parker assumed was the program, and walked to a copy machine where he proceeded to make a copy. Handing Parker the copy, he said, "Beth's a wonderful person to work for. She treats everyone with respect and values every one of us. She doesn't deserve what has happened to her. Please, Parker, find the person that framed her."

"I intend to do just that, Ryan, with your help. I'll be awaiting your contacting me with the information you discover."

Exiting the administration building, Parker got into his 4Runner. Before starting it, he reached over to the passenger seat where he had placed the FBI report on Victor Barrozo after reading it earlier. The report painted a picture of a wealthy man whose habits and lifestyle were routine, but then again, not routine. He had apparently used the money he obtained from Valentine, when Valentine bought out his share of their partnership, to purchase the franchises of several Chipotle Mexican Grills in Illinois, Indiana, and Wisconsin. He lived alone in Oak Brook Estates, a posh western suburb of Chicago, in a multi-million dollar home with a live-in chef, housekeeper, and landscaper/gardener. His one son was a vice president in Barrozo, Inc., the parent company of the various Chipotle restaurants. His only daughter had been declared insane and institutionalized following a three-day unaccounted absence which affected her mental health from which she never recovered. Barrozo spent untold hours with his daughter and had spent hundreds of thousands of dollars pursuing numerous treatments and engaging mental and medical specialists. Friends and business associates said he never recovered from seeing his daughter become irrational and withdrawn, and his change in demeanor contributed, they stated, to his divorce which occurred shortly following his daughter's institutionalization. He kept to himself, friends stated, and showed no signs of overindulging in alcohol or being involved in lavish living, which he could certainly afford. Caregivers with the care facility where his daughter was institutionalized stated they heard Barrozo, on occasion while sitting with his daughter, that was essentially non-communicative and could burst out screaming obscenities for no reason other than something happening in her mind, to say to his daughter, "don't worry, honey, he is going to pay for what he did to you". The "he" was assumed to be Michael Valentine, although Barrozo never used Valentine's name nor was there any proof Valentine had been involved in the three-day absence of Barrozo's daughter.

Bank account records showed Barrozo had leased a home for a year in Paradise Valley through Paradise Valley Enterprises, a real estate company specializing in the leasing of upscale homes in the Paradise Valley of Montana. Barrozo's leased home was about twelve miles north of Gardiner, which was only a few miles north of Mammoth Hot Springs and the northwest entrance to Yellowstone. The agent of Paradise Valley Enterprises with whom Barrozo had worked said Barrozo was close-lipped, almost secretive, and never disclosed the reason for leasing the home. After signing the lease agreement and paying the entire year's lease in advance, no communication had occurred between Barrozo and Paradise Valley Enterprises. More recently, he had engaged Karen Black to find him a home to purchase in the Yellowstone area. Parker made a mental note to talk with Karen about Barrozo.

Barrozo had one credit card, a Visa Platinum card, which records showed he used extensively for what appeared to be nearly all his expenses, suggesting he used cash very sparingly. A strange twist was the billing address for payment of his charges was a post office box in a post office substation located near his office, suggesting he meant to keep the charges away from prying eyes. Reviewing his credit card charges over the past six months showed a pattern of charges for round-trip airfare from Chicago to Billings every eight to ten days with rental car charges for two days at the Avis car rental agency in the Billings airport. Occasional charges at a few restaurants, especially the Gardiner Steakhouse, during the same two days, were mostly in excess of $80 indicating Barrozo didn't dine alone. Several wait staff of the Gardiner Steakhouse recalled Barrozo having dinner with a woman that sometimes was in a National Park Service uniform. A general description of the woman was provided by the wait staff. It was very close to one for Becky Greenbrier.

The most interesting set of credit card charges were recent, having occurred this past Saturday, Sunday, and Monday. Barrozo had flown into

Billings from Chicago late Saturday afternoon, renting a car from the Avis car rental agency at the airport. The next credit card charge occurred on Sunday for lunch at Bubba's Barbeque restaurant in Cody followed by dinner at the Prime Cut restaurant in Cody. Both were for less than $30, indicating Barrozo ate alone. The next charge was at the Holiday Inn in Cody for Sunday night. On Monday morning, a charge for a rental car at Avis in the Billings airport was recorded. The car was returned at 10:15 a.m. The final credit card charge was at a Starbucks in O'Hare International Airport in Chicago early Monday afternoon, forty-five minutes after United Express Flight 4217 from Billings landed.

On the personal side, all but one of his business acquaintances and friends didn't show any unusual relationship with Barrozo. The one, however, sent a flag up the flagpole. Barrozo and the current Secretary of the Interior were college fraternity brothers. After college, they had drifted apart but had renewed their friendship following the appointment of the Secretary. Airline flight records showed Barrozo had taken several trips between Chicago and Washington, D.C. since the Secretary had been appointed. In addition, Barrozo's bank records showed two large contributions to the election campaign of the President a few weeks before the November election. Speculation was that Barrozo had been encouraged by his soon-to-be-appointed Secretary of the Interior friend to financially support the President's campaign to assure the Secretary's appointment, should the President win the election.

Was this the break Parker had been hoping to find? Bless the FBI and its incredible means to obtain information in short order. It seemed to Parker that he had found Valentine's murderer. Rather than being delighted, he was cautious. What was nagging at him was what was Barrozo's reason for setting up Beth to take the fall? Beth didn't know Barrozo. Nothing suggested Barrozo knew Beth. Could the answer lie with the woman seen dining with him at the Gardiner Steakhouse? If the woman was Becky Greenbrier, she was dead. Dead people don't talk. Had Barrozo killed Becky in order to silence her?

The combination of Barrozo's motive—revenge for his daughter's condition which he blamed on Valentine—and the Saturday afternoon-Monday morning trip into Billings, with dinner at the Gardiner Steakhouse and overnight in Cody on Sunday night, were too much of a coincidence to be passed over without more in-depth investigation. Barrozo could have killed Valentine, had an accomplice pick him up from the Sylvan Lake picnic area using a different rental car, stayed overnight at the Holiday Inn in Cody, returned to Billings on Monday morning in time to return the rental car and fly to Chicago. Even without an airline record showing Barrozo had returned Tuesday night, he could have hired a contract killer to kill Becky. Parker could feel his heart beating more rapidly. He felt he was getting closer to freeing Beth and apprehending the real killer of Valentine.

CHAPTER 37

Thursday Morning
10:00 a.m.
Outside Yellowstone County Law Enforcement Center, Cody, Wyoming

Beth couldn't help herself. She hadn't been able to hold back the tears of gratitude when the Superintendent had appeared before the bail judge to personally plead for her release. The Superintendent had taken personal responsibility for her full compliance with whatever stipulations were laid down by the judge. Having just finished thanking the Superintendent, she turned to Marcia Farrington. "Now what? I'm rather restricted in what I can do and where I can go. What do I do all day? Watch soap operas and eat bon-bons?"

"Beth, you're a lucky woman, at least for now. This is the first time Judge Roscoe has granted bail for a murder suspect. Without the personal appearance of the Superintendent, I'm not sure the judge would have granted bail. What you can't do now is something to cause your bail to be rescinded. You heard the judge's warning. Don't speak to anyone about your situation. Stay away from the media. Don't answer your phone without first knowing who's calling. Don't respond to e-mails or texts about your situation. Media people are clever. They will use e-mail addresses and text addresses which seem harmless to you. Don't fall for their tricks. Be overly cautious. I know it's the pits, but it's much better than going back to that cell. Take my advice and stay in a motel somewhere, tell the Superintendent and me where you're staying and no one else. Buy one of those disposable cell phones. Call me whenever you are feeling really down. Be careful where you go to eat. You'll probably become sick and tired of fast food, but it might be your best bet to stay inconspicuous for the next few days. Remember, I haven't stopped working for dismissal of all the charges against you with appropriate damages. We're going to win this thing."

"Thanks, Marcia, for everything you're doing. I'll take your advice. I'll try not to bug you too often. I do need to pick up a few things from my apartment before I find a place to hide out. I need a ride back to Mammoth Hot Springs to get some things from my apartment. Can you arrange transportation for me?"

"Surprise, surprise. Once I knew the Superintendent was going to personally vouch for you, I was counting on Judge Roscoe granting you bail so I rented a car in Billings and had it driven here by a friend that visits her daughter who lives in Cody, every Thursday. It's for you to use. It's parked around the corner. A blue Ford Fusion. Here are the keys. Before you go to the car, check to make sure no media goons, with or without cameras, are lurking around. One more thing. Forget about your apartment. Stay away from it for a few days. The media will be watching it. Who knows, maybe the killer is watching it as well. Stop at a WalMart or Target and purchase some inexpensive clothes, if that is what you want to get from your apartment. Here's five hundred in cash. Try not to use your credit cards or personal checks for awhile. Stay in touch."

Marcia walked away leaving Beth to realize she was free for the first time in two days. She also felt she was alone without anywhere, in particular, to go. Contrary to her life before this nightmare began, she had nothing to do. No office to go to. No telephone calls, e-mails, or texts to return. No meetings to attend. No presentations to prepare and deliver. No reports to prepare and distribute. No work plans or strategies to prepare. She felt like a fish out of water. Walking from the Center, she turned the corner and saw a blue Ford Fusion parked down the block. Doing as Marcia had suggested, she looked both ways, several times, looking for someone intent on the car that might be a media person ready to pounce. Seeing no one, she walked quickly to the car, unlocked the door, and slid behind the steering wheel. The car started immediately. Driving away, she looked in the rearview mirror after each turn. She didn't see any car following her. After several turns, some back upon the way she had just come, she was satisfied no one was following her.

Pulling between two parked cars in the Stagecoach Mall in Cody, she turned off the car and thought about her next actions. She needed to take a long shower to wash away the smells of the cell she had been in and change into fresh underwear and clothes. Could she risk going to her apartment to do all that? She would probably be seen by someone, even if she waited until dark. Then there was the ever lurking media with which to be concerned. Marcia had suggested she stay away from her apartment, find a motel, and hunker down. That didn't sound very satisfying. She needed an alternative. Someplace away from the possibility of the media hanging around while providing her the opportunity to do some walking outside and also communicating, albeit, cautious communicating. Having a computer with internet capability would be a big plus.

She looked at the stores fronting the mall and saw a sign for Casual Western Wear. Perfect, she thought. She would purchase a new set of western-styled clothes. Her purse and its contents, which had been taken from her when she was booked at the Law Enforcement Center, had been returned to her intact when she was released. Fortunately, along with the $500 Marcia had given her, she had enough cash to last several days if need be. She agreed with Marcia that she didn't want to use a credit card or personal check with her name on it. Maybe Marcia and she were being paranoid or overly cautious, but no sense risking having a store clerk recognize her name and alert the media.

About one-half hour later, she emerged from the store dressed in women's Levis, a button-down light yellow blouse, an imitation leather belt with a large silver buckle, and a light blue bandana tied around her neck. All that was missing were cowgirl boots. She couldn't accept paying the retail price for comfortable cowgirl boots. Maybe later, if she could find a pair at a discount store or on e-Bay. For now, her low-styled hiking shoes would have to do. The clothes she had worn into the store were in a bag which she placed in the trunk of the car.

During her time in the store, she had hatched an idea which was risky and might ruin the progress she felt had been made with Parker. Nevertheless, if their relationship was going to go anywhere, this would be a good test. She decided to have a go at it. Driving slowly around the mall, she had almost completed a full circle when she saw a store which she'd been hoping would be located at the mall. Parking again between two parked cars, she walked to the store conscious of looking in all directions to spot anyone that might have recognized her, especially any media people. Satisfied she wasn't being watched or about to be approached, she entered the store, found what she'd hoped to find, purchase it with cash, and returned to her rental car. Opening the package, she withdrew the prepaid cell phone and read the instructions for its use. Easy enough. Now for the tricky part. Her cell phone was being retained by the Sheriff as evidence—why she couldn't fathom—so she didn't have telephone numbers readily available. She would have to obtain the cell phone number she wanted in a circuitous manner. Turning on the phone, she called 684-411, the phone information number for the West Yellowstone area. An automated response requested the name of the person or business for which the telephone number was sought. "Gold Medal Fly-Fishing Shop in West Yellowstone," she said.

"One moment, please," the automated voice replied. Following a few seconds of silence, the automated voice said, "The number is 684-916-3749."

Disconnecting, she called the number. "Good afternoon, Gold Medal Fly-Fishing Shop. This is Laurie speaking. How may I help you?"

Hoping to disguise her voice should Laurie recognize it, she raised the tone of her voice and replied, "I'm a clerk in FBI Agent Janet VanKampen's office. I'm supposed to relay a confidential message from Agent VanKampen to Mr. Parker Williams. I can't seem to locate Mr. Williams' cell phone number. I'm hoping someone with his business could provide it to me."

"Sure thing. I have it right here. It's 684-379-1204."

"Thank you. You've been most helpful. Goodbye." Ending the call, Beth was surprised how nervous she had felt. She didn't like having to mislead anyone, but the circumstances provided no other option. Now for the make or break part of her plan. Calling Parker, he answered after two rings. "Parker here."

Breathing deeply, she replied, "Hi, Parker, it's Beth. I've been released on bail. Marcia did a superb job, as did the Superintendent who personally came to the bail hearing and vouched for me. I'm under some restrictions and that's why I asking you to consider something unusual." Before she could continue, Parker interrupted.

"That's wonderful, Beth. I'm so happy for you. Good for the Superintendent. That should tell you how highly you're thought of in Yellowstone's administration. Nothing you ask me is going to be unusual. I'm so happy right now."

"Don't commit to early, Mr. Happiness. Here's the deal. Marcia suggested I not return to my apartment because the media might be camped out waiting for me to appear. She suggested I locate where the media wouldn't look. She suggested a motel, but that seems so uninviting, especially after spending time in that dinky cell. I'd like to use your place for a few days or as long as I have these stipulations on me which the judge imposed as a condition of my bail. I'm not suggesting anything other than my using the guest bedroom and bath. I'll try not to intrude on your normal routine or personal space."

Laughing, Parker responded, "Are you kidding? I don't care how much you intrude or mess up my routine. Of course, you can stay at my place. The whole place is yours, not just the guest bedroom and bath. There's plenty of room. The media know nothing about my place. It would be ideal. Where are you now? When might you get to my place?"

"Thanks for your understanding. I'm still in Cody. I'm in need of a decent meal which I'm going to have here before I head out. I should be to your place sometime this evening."

"There's a key to the house under a moss-covered rock next to the planter on the rear deck. Use whatever you need or want. The code to the security alarm is 4321. Please make yourself at home. I won't be there for awhile. At least not until tomorrow morning. I'm following up on a lead, which I can't tell you about, not because I don't want to, but I have nothing really to share yet. Now, I need to tell you that I'm no longer an FBI consultant on the case. Janet thought it best I not continue for reasons I'll tell you when we can talk together. I may no longer be official, but, as I said, I'm not stopping my investigation. I'm going to find out who framed you if it's the last thing I do. You should also know, Ryan's helping me. He's been great. Now, drive carefully, make yourself at home, and I'll see you tomorrow sometime."

It was so good to hear his voice and to know he cared enough for her to not question her but accept her request without hesitation. She realized he was willing to risk his reputation for her sake. If it was discovered she was residing at his home, the rumors and gossip about them shacking up would spread like wildfire. She couldn't worry about that, she decided. They would have to be discreet, that's all. Both of them had much more to be concerned about beginning with helping Marcia build a defense should Beth have to go to trial.

Before leaving Cody, she purchased some groceries at the Albertsons grocery store on the northern edge of town. She didn't want Parker to think she was a classic free-loader. If she was going to stay in his place for most, if not all of the near future, she could at least provide good home prepared food for Parker and herself. Maybe, just maybe, she might show her domestic side and prepare him some special meals. Home cooked food for a change. She smiled inwardly. What's that saying? Oh yes. The way to a man's heart is thru his stomach. She was about to see how true that was.

CHAPTER 38

Thursday Evening
7:30 p.m. Central Standard Time
Home of Peter and Mary Ann Richardson, Peoria, Illinois

Here he was. Beth's girlhood home. He had called as soon as his flight landed at the Springfield, Illinois, airport. Fortunately, Beth's mother was home and yes, she would be delighted to meet a friend of their daughter. How delighted she would be when she learned the reason for his visit was debatable. No parent wanted to hear about the troubles of a child and when the troubles included an arrest for murder, he could only guess at the anguish she would feel. He would be as diplomatic as he could be, but he always believed full truth was better than half truth. He would assure her of Beth's innocence and promise she would eventually be fully exonerated.

The home was a typical Midwestern ranch home. All brick with a one-car attached garage. Homes like this were built in the boom construction years following World War II when very few homes sported two or more cars. The home was on a large lot, probably 1/3 acre. The landscaping was immaculate reflecting the pride the Richardsons obviously had in their property.

He rang the doorbell. The door was opened and he couldn't hide his surprise. The woman greeting him could be Beth in thirty years. She had the classic beauty of a mature woman who took pride in her natural appearance without artificially attempting to look modern or chic. Her silver hair was styled in a page boy cut. Small silver earrings and a silver necklace were the only jewelry pieces he saw other than a silver wedding band on her left forefinger. She wore black, tailored slacks, black and white blouse, and black flat shoes. Her eyes gave off the same sparkle he had seen so often in Beth's eyes. "Mr. Williams, welcome to Peoria and our home. Please come in."

Reaching to shake her extended hand, he replied, "Mrs. Richardson, it is so nice to meet you. Thank you for allowing me time to visit with you. I must say that Beth didn't warn me to expect such a look-a-like. I'm not sure who's more beautiful, mother or daughter."

Smiling, she responded, "Come now, Mr. Williams, flattery will get you nowhere, at least with me. I always told our daughter beauty comes from the inside. The external can be altered but the internal remains constant. May I get you some coffee or ice tea? I also have coke, 7-up, or fruit juices."

"Ice tea sounds wonderful."

"Please take a seat wherever you like. I'll be back in a jiffy. I'm sorry my husband isn't here, but he's with his golfing buddies playing an evening round in a tournament for seniors." She left the room, apparently to get the ice tea. Looking around, he saw several framed pictures of a younger Beth with her parents. He was tempted to look more closely at a few of the pictures but decided against it since he didn't want Beth's mother to think he was forward. He sat on the couch as she came back into the room carrying a tray with two classes of ice tea and a plate of some type of small bar. She placed the tray on the coffee table in front of the couch. Taking a glass, she sat down on the opposite end of the couch and turn to face him more directly. "Please help yourself to some homemade lemon bars. They're especially tasty with ice tea. Now, Mr. Williams, I suppose you've come all this way to question me about this ridiculous accusation about my daughter murdering a man."

Attempting to hide his relief at not having to be the person to first tell her about Beth's situation, he replied, "You've just taken a huge burden from my shoulders. I didn't know how I was going to tell you. I'm curious. How did you find out?"

"A reporter from the Cody newspaper called and wanted us to react to the news of Beth's arrest. We didn't give him the time of day. Of course, we were in shock for awhile. Then we called the Sheriff's office in Cody to find out what was going on. The deputy we talked with, I don't remember his name, wouldn't let us talk to Beth, but he did tell us she had a lawyer and he would have the lawyer call us, which, of course, never happened. He probably never contacted Beth's lawyer. However, Beth's lawyer, Miss Farrington, did call us to tell us that Beth had been released on bail. That's a good sign, isn't it?"

"Marcia Farrington is an excellent lawyer and we are certainly encouraged by Beth's release on bail. However, she's far from being out-of-the-woods. We need to clear her permanently and that's why I wanted to talk with you and your husband. I've been working with the FBI on the investigation and there are some loose ends I want to tie down. I hope you can help me do that."

"I'll certainly try. Anything my husband and I can do to help, we'll do it. It must be terrible for Beth. It sure was thoughtful of the Superintendent to personally vouch for her. Miss Farrington told us about that. How can anyone with half a brain believe Beth is a murderer?"

"Mrs. Richardson, I believe someone set up Beth by planting false evidence in the victim's car. That's what I need to prove. There's someone out there that dislikes your daughter immensely or is extremely jealous of her. I need to find that person. Beth, herself, may have provided a clue as to whom this person might be. As I understand, she asked you to send her a copy of the program of the final night of the Miss Illinois Pageant in which Beth was a final contestant. I have a copy of that program with me." Reaching into his shirt pocket, he unfolded the copy which Ryan Belgrade had given him. "Mrs. Richardson, I'd like you to tell me everything you can remember about the Pageant, especially any interactions Beth had with anyone—other contestants, judges, pageant workers—anyone. Please try to not leave out anything which you might think is inconsequential or unimportant. Would you mind if I record our conversation? I don't want you to not remember something you might mention which doesn't seem important now but may become extremely important later."

"I don't mind at all. While you do that, I'll refill your glass and add some ice. One of my pet peeves is servers in restaurants that refill your glass of ice tea or lemonade and don't also add additional ice. It isn't called ice tea for nothing."

Retrieving the recorder from his rental car, he knew what would take place over the next hour or so might provide the missing piece of the puzzle regarding whomever set up Beth and probably murdered Michael Valentine. Then, again, it might result in another dead end. Beth's mother was sharp as a tack, but would she be able to remember enough of the happenings of an event, which took place several years ago, to provide valuable information?

Reentering the room carrying his glass of ice tea, she said, "Beth was a gangly, uncoordinated girl and a so-so student throughout elementary and middle school," said Mary Ann Richardson. Parker had turned on the recorder and was listening carefully. "She was shy and Peter and I worried she would be an unhappy high school student. Were we ever wrong! Somewhere around thirteen or fourteen, she changed physically and that seemed to usher in a totally different person. She because self-assured, her self-esteem soared, she blossomed socially, her grades improved, and her outlook on life became joyous and happy. Please don't think I'm bragging, but she excelled in anything and everything."

"The Miss Illinois Pageant," replied Parker, "how did that come about for her?"

"The mayor of Peoria, at that time, received a nomination form from his brother that was a member of the Board of Directors of the Pageant. Peter and the mayor were both members of the downtown Rotary Club. You can probably guess the rest of the story."

"Let me think," responded Parker. "The mayor told your husband he wanted to nominate Beth and your husband thought it was a good idea. The mayor nominated Beth and, as they say, the rest is history. Do I have it right?"

Laughing, she replied, "You missed an important first step, but don't feel badly. I wasn't aware of it either. Beth had to enter, and win I should add, a local pageant in order to be invited to the Miss Illinois Pageant. She chose to enter the Miss Peoria pageant. She won it."

"Can we stay with the Peoria pageant for a minute? Did anything happen during the pageant which could have caused someone to want to get back at Beth several years later?"

"The Peoria pageant was small, low-key, and lots of fun for the girls. For their parents and families as well. The girls all knew each other and got along fine. No jealousy among them since the pecking order, so to speak, had been worked out prior to the pageant. The girls all went to the same high school, with the exception of a few girls that attended the Catholic high school. I hope you understand when I say this, but there was little doubt Beth would win. In fact, the girls joked among themselves that the pageant should be called 'Beth Richardson's inauguration'. No, I can't think of a single person that would have been so upset or angry with Beth to carry a grudge for these many years."

"That's o.k.," Parker replied. "I didn't want to possibly overlook something that happened which might provide a clue to the identity of the person or persons responsible for framing Beth. Please go on."

"The Miss Illinois Pageant was entirely different. It was large and was held in the Fine and Performing Arts Center in Springfield, which is our state capitol. As I recall, there were seventy-five contestants in the beginning, all of whom had won a local pageant, just like Beth had. The competition level was high and the intensity of many of the contestants was off the charts. I suppose, because the winner automatically qualified for the Miss American Pageant and the scholarship money was significant, the intensity was ratcheted up. Also, the contestants didn't know each other which didn't add to a congenial atmosphere. The rules were too many and too picky as I recall. I know Beth didn't enjoy it nearly as much as she did the Peoria pageant."

"In a minute, I want you to concentrate on the final evening of the Miss Illinois Pageant. Beth asked you to send her a copy of the program for that final evening, so I'm assuming Beth thought something happened that evening which could provide a clue to whom might have carried a grudge. But first, like the Peoria pageant, is there anything you remember about the Miss Illinois Pageant prior to that final evening?"

"I remember the tension we all felt throughout the entire pageant. I remember the disappointment of the contestants that were eliminated. I remember how cool and collected Beth seemed to be, although she says she wasn't. Those first two evenings were pretty cut and dried, as I recall. Nothing happened involving Beth or, for that matter, any of the other contestants."

"O.k., now for the final evening," he said, as he opened the copy of the program which Ryan had given him. "Just like before. Do you remember anything happening?"

"You can imagine how we felt when Beth was declared the winner. You know how they dramatize the whole thing; second runner-up, first runner-up, and build to the climax. My emotions were going big time, that I know. How Beth maintained her poise is still something I marvel about. What I remember, besides the elation of Beth winning, was the nasty shouting match I witnessed between one of the contestants and one of the judges. I told Beth about it when she called the other evening. I think it's what prompted her to ask me to send her a copy of the program."

Beth hadn't mentioned a shouting match to him when he had last talked with her. She had told him about the program, but not the reasoning behind her requesting her mother to send a copy. Was there something Beth remembered or thought she remembered which prompted her to ask her mother to send a copy of the program? He needed to talk with Beth. He'd do so right after he finished with her mother. "This shouting match you remember," he said, "tell me about it."

"Beth had won and the media people were all bunched around her, taking pictures, asking her questions, you've seen how pushy media people can be, I'm sure, so I left the area where she and the media people were and was on my way to the women's rest-room to freshen up, check my hair, you know, what women do. In the hallway on the way to the restroom, I saw one of the contestants and a judge shouting at each other. Both of them were quite animated, especially the woman contestant. She was yelling at him and he was trying to get away from her, but not very successfully. I would say she was out of control. It was a very uncomfortable moment for me."

"I bet it was uncomfortable for you," he responded. "You said when you told Beth about it, she asked for the copy of the program. Do I have that right?"

"Yes, she wanted a copy of the program after I told her about the shouting match."

Beth must have wanted to check something about that evening, he thought. Probably something to do with the shouting match. "Tell me about the shouting match," he asked.

"It happened quite some time ago, so I don't remember too many details," she replied. "I hope you understand. Beth was surrounded by the media wanting to have an interview with her, take her picture, those kinds of things. I was on my way to the women's restroom when I became aware of one of the judges and a contestant shouting at each other. I was in a hallway and they were only a few yards away from me, so I could hear them very clearly. There was nowhere for me to go, so I stopped momentarily, hoping they would either turn around and go down another hall or pass by me. The contestant, I believe it was the woman that was the first runner-up, was hysterical. Out of control. She was screaming. The judge shouting for her to shut-up and then he stormed past me. Almost knocked me over. The woman screamed at him again and then she turned around and went down another hall."

""The woman contestant," responded Parker, "she was the first runner-up you said. Do you remember her name?"

"I believe her first name was Vanessa. I don't remember her last name. She is listed in the program, so you can find her last name there."

"You said the judge shouted back to the women, 'shut up'," said Parker. "Do you remember what the woman shouted?"

"Not the exact words, if that's important. I do remember her screaming at him something about his trading his vote for sex and he was going to pay for doing it, something along those lines."

Opening his copy of the program, he said, "There were ten final contestants. Their names are listed in alphabetical order. Vanessa Cortez. Is she the woman you saw and heard screaming?"

"I can't be certain, but I believe it was her. If I could see her picture, I'd be able to be sure."

"Do you remember which judge it was?"

"Since there were only three male judges, it had to be one of the three," she responded. Again, I can't be certain, given how long ago this occurred, but I think it was him." She pointed to a name. Michael Valentine.

"That's all I can remember about the pageant," she said. "I'm so worried about Beth She must be terribly worried and very distraught. She's innocent and we must find a way to prove it."

"Mrs. Richardson, we are going to prove she's innocent. Believe me, we are. Thank you, again, for allowing me to be here with you. "I'm sorry I wasn't able to meet your husband. Please give him my best and tell him we are going to prove Beth is innocent."

"I will do that, Mr. Williams," she replied. "Beth is fortunate to have you as a friend and to have you working on her behalf. Please keep us informed and if we can help, please let us know. We'll do whatever we can."

After exchanging a few pleasantries, he said goodbye. He drove the rental car only a few blocks and stopped in front of a Wendy's. It wasn't too late to call. Taking his iPhone, he called his home, hoping Beth was there and would answer. After five rings, the voice message came on. It was strange listening to himself say he couldn't answer right now but would return the call soon. Beth, if you're there, please answer, he thought. He waited, but she didn't answer. He hadn't told her to feel free to check his messages, so leaving one for her wouldn't do any good. He'd have to wait until he saw her to have her tell him about Vanessa Cortez.

What he could do now was find out more about Victor Barrozo. He turned on his iPhone, pushed the Safari icon, and waited while it logged into the internet. He went to Google.com and entered the name Victor

Barrozo. His screen showed numerous listings. However, the most recent listing caused Parker to feel like he'd been punched in the stomach. The listing was from the *Chicago Tribune* newspaper. It was an article describing the outcome of a meeting Barrozo and the Assistant Secretary of Interior had in Cody this past Sunday evening immediately after the conclusion of the event held at the Buffalo Bill Historical Center. Parker could care less about the outcome of the meeting. It was the meeting itself which affected him. Barrozo couldn't have killed Valentine. Barrozo had a perfect alibi in the person of the United States Assistant Secretary of the Interior.

CHAPTER 39

Thursday Evening
8:00 p.m.
Gardiner Apartments for Yellowstone Employees, Yellowstone National Park, Mammoth Hot Springs, Montana

Ryan Belgrade felt good about himself. He had done something important which, he hoped, would help his boss. Maybe, he thought, when she finds out what he did to help her, she would think more about him as a man in whom she could be interested rather than her administrative assistant. He admitted to himself, he was infatuated with her. So what? He kept his feelings under wraps around the office and the other employees in the building. Yes, he thought about her when he was alone. He wondered how she would feel in his arms; how kissing her would feel. Was it wrong to think about her like that? He didn't think so. Who knows? Maybe she had similar thoughts about him.

Parker Williams had asked him to dig for information about the contestants and judges listed on the Miss Illinois Pageant program. Parker had also asked him to talk with as many of the employees in the building as he could to determine if any of them had heard something from someone about Beth's camping overnight on Sunday evening by Soda Butte Creek. He had managed to talk with only a few and hadn't learned anything significant. He'd talk with the rest on Friday. As he was leaving the office earlier this afternoon, he saw he had a voice message. Maybe it was from one of the employees he had already talked with that had remembered something he or she forgot to tell Ryan. He would log into the office phone system and listen to the message after he talked with Parker.

He had learned some interesting stuff. He bet Parker would find it interesting as well. He wanted to call Parker as soon as he could, but not where he might be overheard. Parker had warned about confidentiality and being discreet. What he could do, however, was send a text message.

He took his Blackberry and sent a cryptic message, "Fd inter info, call me." Within a few minutes, he heard his Blackberry chirp, indicating a text message had been received. "Go to secure phone, text me #". Parker wanted him to go to a secure phone and text him the number of the phone. Wouldn't his Blackberry do? He would go outside to a place where few people went and wait for Parker to call. Fortunately, it was dark, so chances were no one would see him. Folding the sheet of paper on which he had written the information he wanted to tell Parker, he locked his apartment door behind himself and went out the building walking toward Crystal Falls Terrace. About fifty yards before the walkway to the top of where the Crystal Falls Terrace began, he took a sharp right turn. There wasn't a path or trail to follow, but he had gone this way several times when he wanted to have total peace and quiet. It never ceased to amaze him how alone one could be with the quiet of nature and be just a stone's throw from the hordes of visitors and cars that never ventured from the roadways of Yellowstone. Yellowstone employees and true lovers and supporters of Yellowstone shared a common humorous fact. Ninety-eight percent of the two million annual visitors to Yellowstone saw only ten percent of Yellowstone.

Walking through a stand of lodgepole pine trees, he came to the place where he knew he would be alone. He sat on a fallen log. The only sound breaking the absolute stillness was the gurgling of a small creek on its way to merge with the Gardiner River. Taking his Blackberry, he sent another text message to Parker, "call this #, secure". He would enjoy the stillness while he waited for Parker's call.

CHAPTER 40

Thursday Evening
8:30 p.m.
Home of Parker Williams on Duck Creek, 9 Miles North of West
Yellowstone off U.S. Highway 191, Montana

The key to his home was where Parker said it would be. She felt funny as she opened the front door and walked into his home. She had been in his home before and had even stayed overnight in the guest room. She remembered that evening well. They had talked intimately, sharing with each other their hopes and plans. That was when she felt closeness to him and was confident their relationship would move from friendship to a deeper one. They had not been sexually involved that evening. She knew they shared common values and morals, and she was thankful they did. It was a rare commodity these days to find two adults who continued to hold to their morals in the face of an increasing "it's o.k. to do anything as long as it doesn't hurt anyone" attitude across society.

He had told her he was embarrassed by the size of the house. One person didn't require nearly the amount of space nor the number of rooms comprising the house. She smiled as she contemplated two people living in the home, each with their own living area, so to speak. It would be interesting to see how Parker and she would find living under the same roof, separate but yet together at times. Hopefully, it wouldn't be for too long. Not because they would find the arrangement to be unsatisfactory, but because the charges against her would be dismissed and she would be able to return to her normal routine.

Having stayed in the guest room before, she knew where it was located and what to expect. The guest bath was located adjacent to the guest room. She didn't have anything with her—no cosmetics, no tooth brush, no personal items other than the clothes she was wearing when she was arrested, which were now stuffed in the bag she had used when she purchased the western clothes she was now wearing.

Might as well make myself at home, she thought. A hot, lingering bath sounded wonderful. She wanted to wash the remnants of the Law Enforcement Center from her body and hair. She wanted to go back to wearing her normal clothes rather than the western duds. She just didn't cut it as a cowgirl. She took her clothes from the bag and placed them into the washing machine, adding some Tide laundry soap which she found in the cabinet above the washer and dryer in the laundry room. Parker had told her he had replaced the hot water tank with a Reni tankless hot water system, so she knew there would be plenty of hot water for her bath, as well as the washing machine. Was he domestic enough to have an iron and ironing board, or did he take the clothes needing ironing somewhere to be ironed? If he did iron his own clothes, where would he place the iron and ironing board? The laundry room was the logical place, but neither was there. Maybe he didn't iron, but she didn't want to give up until she checked more places. Other than the laundry room, the closets seemed the most logical. She looked in the closets throughout the home, with the exception of the master suite. Would she be violating his privacy if she looked in the closet in his bedroom? She hesitated before the door. Entering his bedroom, she felt, would be taking a step toward more intimacy. That was o.k. with her. She hoped it would be the same for him.

The master suite was larger than she had envisioned. Probably due to the king-size bed. She had envisioned a queen-sized bed. She smiled. A king-sized bed for one person. Certainly more than enough room to toss and turn. Then a thought crossed her mind which she knew she couldn't allow herself to dwell upon. Maybe someday she would find herself in this bed.

In the corner of the room, near the walk-in closet, was an ironing board with an iron standing on end. So, he did his own ironing, or at least some of it. Apparently, he kept the ironing board in the closet but hadn't bothered to fold it and put it away after using it. Now, she had to decide. Should she iron her clothes here in his bedroom or take the ironing board and iron out of his bedroom to somewhere else in the house? Ironing here was maybe taking her invitation to live here at little too far, she thought. She folded the ironing board and carried it and the iron from the room.

Closing the door behind her, she had a similar thought as before. I wonder if and when I might be back in this room?

Back in the guest bedroom, she stripped off her clothes, hanging the blouse and jeans in the closet. Laying her underwear on the bed, she entered the tub, filling it with hot water. She hadn't found any bath oil or bubble bath to add to the water. She smiled as she thought that he probably hadn't contemplated a woman taking a bath. She also felt good knowing that if women were regular occupants of the guest room, there probably would be bath oil, bubble bath, or scented soap in the bathroom. Men, she knew, were almost entirely shower-takers, as she also was most of the time.

Letting the hot water soothe her muscles, she thought about how she had gotten to be here and what, more importantly, needed to happen to get her back to her normal life. She needed a break. Someone had to come forth with a piece of information and the ball would start rolling until the person or persons that had framed her were identified. She felt frustrated with the restrictions placed on her by the bail judge because it meant she had to depend on others to find that someone or that new bit of information. To someone used to doing things herself, it was difficult to wait on the sideline while the game was taking place without her participation.

Toweling off, she went to the laundry room where she transferred the clothes from the washer to the dryer. She felt self-conscious and, strangely enough, somewhat naughty to be walking naked around Parker's home. To be honest, she liked the feeling. Parker's home was private enough, she knew, so no one was going to see her or surprise her by entering the house, yet to be naked in the home of the man for whom she had feelings and desires for more intimacy, was exhilarating. Retreating to the guest bathroom, she busied herself drying and brushing her hair until she heard the dryer beep, indicating the clothes were dry. She took the clothes from the dryer and dressed in the laundry room. The mutual feeling of a clean body, washed and brushed hair, and clean clothes was wonderful. The smell of the Law Enforcement Center had been washed away.

While she was in the tub, she heard the telephone ring several times. She assumed the caller had left a message. She wasn't going to be so presumptuous of Parker's invitation to make herself at home that she would answer when the telephone rang or listen to messages left by callers.

That would be going a little too far. Yet, if Parker was trying to contact her, a telephone call to his home was the only way to do so since she had no cell phone or computer. Unfortunately, Parker used a laptop and iPhone, which he carried with him, so there was no computer in the home. If there was, it might not be password protected, which would enable her to gain access to her e-mail and also the internet. No such luck. She'd have to wait until he showed up. In the meantime, she checked the refrigerator and pantry to see what she might be able to add to the groceries she had purchased.

CHAPTER 41

Thursday Night
8:15 p.m.
Fifty Yards from the Administration Building Alongside Crystal Springs
Terrace, Yellowstone National Park, Mammoth Hot Springs, Montana

The stillness was shattered by the ringing of his cell phone. Looking at the screen, the caller ID said "Parker Williams". He answered after the second ring. "Hi, Parker. I'm in a secure place. No worry about being overheard."

"It's good you've taken the precautions you have, Ryan. It sounds like you've some good information. Let's have the important stuff now and then when we both have more time, you can give me all the details. I've paper and pen, so fire away."

"O.k., let me give you this in no particular order. I'm not sure what's most important or what takes priority over something else. You'll have to be the judge of that."

"Sure enough," replied Parker, "I'm ready."

"First, Becky Greenbrier was seen a couple of times outside the food distribution center at Old Faithful. Bud Forester, who saw Becky outside the food distribution center, said she was pacing back and forth and appeared to be agitated. When Bud said hello to Becky, he said she almost jumped out of her skin and didn't want to talk with him, so he went on his way. He then saw her again the next night but didn't bother to try and talk with her since she had blown him off the night before. The question is, why would Becky be outside the food distribution center two consecutive nights?"

"Sorry to interrupt, Ryan, but did Bud see anyone near Becky or someone walking away from her?"

"He didn't say nor did I ask him. Maybe you'll want to follow up on that with him although I think we may have a clue about whom Becky might have been there to see. I'll get to that in a minute."

"Sorry to interrupt," replied Parker. "I'll keep my mouth shut until you finish."

"Second, I spent quite a bit of time doing various internet and Facebook searches on the contestants. Leaving out Beth, eight of nine final contestants have, what I would call, normal, routine, cut-and-dried lives. Six are married with kids; two are divorced, also with kids. All eight live in the Midwest—Illinois, Indiana, and Michigan. I checked the public records in the city or town clerk's office where each lives. All are listed as owners or co-owners of homes. Mortgages and property taxes are paid up. Credit ratings are good. All-in-all, there is nothing in any of their lives suggesting they aren't fine, upstanding citizens going about the business of raising a family and living normal lives."

"Throw Beth in with the lot," responded Parker, "and you have nine of ten. I have a feeling you're going to tell me something different about number ten."

"Vanessa Cortez is her name. She seems to have chosen a much different path for her life than the others. She dropped out of college, was arrested for possession of a controlled substance, was twice charged with soliciting, although there is no record of convictions, and had a DUI. This is what is strange. She apparently has disappeared. There's no information on her since about three months ago. Nothing. Nowhere. Nada."

"Did you say Vanessa Cortez?"

"That's her name. Why do you ask?"

"She is one of the contestants in the Miss Illinois Pageant in which Beth was also a contestant. I can't believe this is just a coincidence. You said she has disappeared. That is strange too," replied Parker. "She has to have left a trail somewhere at some time. Driver's license, car insurance, credit cards, bank accounts, rental or mortgage payments, or cell phone agreement. Something."

"That's how I see it," responded Ryan, "but I couldn't find a thing. Maybe someone doing a more detailed search will find something. I struck out. Last, but not least, remember Becky Greenbrier being outside the food distribution center? Well, something about that seemed strange to me, so I contacted Human Resources to get a list of all the employees in the food distribution center. I figured Becky may have been waiting for one of them. Just a hunch on my part. I know Tom Berkshire in Human Resources, so I asked him for a list of employees and also asked him if any of them had ever come to H.R.'s attention, you know acting differently or doing something which prompted H.R. to be notified. He pointed out one employee, Yolanda Mendez. She had been hired only two months ago. Came out of the blue one day, according to Tom, and filled out an application for seasonal work. Tom said if I wanted to see her application, he would fax a copy, as long as I treated it confidentially. I didn't ask for it, pending our conversation. Why I'm telling you this is Tom said she's been sent two payroll checks and none have been cashed. Tom said that suggests she might be an illegal or working under a false name. He said they were going to wait to confront her until after the next payroll period, which is ten days from today. Finally, and I don't know if this might mean anything, Tom said she was a real looker that knew she was and tried to use it to influence the male H.R. employee who took her application. Very beautiful and sexy were Tom's words. He said she carried herself like a model or the way women in beauty contests do."

CHAPTER 42

Friday Morning
7:00 a.m. Central Standard Time
Abraham Lincoln Capital Airport, Springfield, Illinois

His head was still spinning. He had driven to the airport to catch the first airplane flight to Bozeman. He had stayed overnight in a Hampton Inn on the outskirts of Springfield. He turned in the rental car, all in a mental state of confusion, as what he had learned from Beth's mother and Ryan Belgrade kept tumbling through his mind. What did it all mean? Did any of it mean anything? How did any of it fit together? Was it all circumstantial or were there connections between the murders of Michael Valentine and Becky Greenbrier? Was the case against Beth about to unravel or was there nothing in any of this to help Beth? He felt out-of-sorts and frustrated. He needed to be home, digging into all he had learned. Instead, he was about to have a three-hour flight and then another two-hour drive from Bozeman.

He couldn't waste five hours. He needed to take the bull by the horns. Call in all his chits. Do whatever it took to get the ball rolling to find the killer of Michael Valentine and free Beth. He would do it and he would start right now. He had fifteen minutes before he would have to board his flight. Enough time to make some calls and, if need be, send some text messages. The first call was to his shop. He knew the shop wasn't open yet as it was only 5:00 a.m. in West Yellowstone. He knew Laurie would be opening the shop in two hours and would check voice messages. "Hi, Laurie, it's me. I don't have much time to explain. If, after what I tell you, you think you won't be able to open the shop, don't open. Laurie, you must go immediately to my home. Even if it is early, don't wait. Beth Richardson is there. Tell her to drive to Bozeman and meet me at the airport. My flight is scheduled to arrive at 9:15. This is extremely important, Laurie. Thanks so much. I'll owe you big time."

His next call was to Janet VanKampen. He expected his call to go to her voice mail so he wasn't surprised when it did. "Janet, it's Parker. I'm reinstating myself as your consultant on the investigation of the Valentine murder. You can fire me for good later if you want to, but right now I need the authority. I may be close to finding Valentine's killer. Probably Becky's killer too. I wouldn't be doing this if I didn't believe this was extremely important. Don't bother to try and talk me out of it. If I mess up, you can charge me with impersonating an FBI agent. Trust me, Janet. That's all I'm asking. Trust me on this."

Too long a message, but hopefully she won't check her voice messages until later. He needed as much time as possible before she sent someone, or maybe she would come herself, to corral him. Looking at his watch, he had five more minutes before he needed to board the flight. Time for one more call. Again, he knew he would need to leave a voice message. "Office of Law Enforcement and Security. We are unable to answer your call. Please leave a message and we will return your call as soon as possible."

"This is Parker Williams and this message is for either Bruce Dickson or Jessica Samuels." The airport information system announced the final boarding call for his flight. Would he have time to leave his message? "Bruce or Jessica, I've just been told to board my flight, so I have to be brief. Please listen carefully. It's extremely important. Please send someone to keep tabs on an employee that works in the food distribution center at Old Faithful. Name is Yolanda Mendez, although I don't believe that's her real name. Her real name, I believe, is Vanessa Cortez. She is working as Yolanda Mendez at the food distribution center. I believe she is mixed up in the Valentine and Greenbrier murders. You may also want to obtain a search warrant for her room and car. That's all I can tell you right now. Sorry, but I have to get on this plane. Please trust me. I can't overemphasize the importance of this. Thanks much. I'll owe both of you. See you soon."

He made it on the airplane jut as the lead flight attendant began to close the entrance door. "Nothing like cutting it close sir," she said with the cookie-cutter smile which all female flight attendants seemed to possess. He settled in his seat and exhaled a huge breath. Three hours of thinking, sorting, and strategizing lay ahead.

CHAPTER 43

Friday Morning
7:00 a.m.
Gold Medal Fly-Fishing Shop, West Yellowstone, Montana

Parker had sounded high strung and almost desperate. Not like him at all, at least the Parker Williams she had come to know and respect for the past several years. Her respect had actually become more of an interest to develop a personal relationship with him, even though he was more than ten years her senior. She realized she was engaging in wishful thinking because Beth Richardson was someone special in Parker's eyes and her arrest for murder had to be affecting him in a profound way. Laurie had never met Beth, but the word about her was she was friendly, personable, and honest. Everyone that did know her remarked how attractive Beth was and unpretentious at the same time. At one time, Laurie had envisioned her mother, Karen Black and Parker becoming an item, but it had never gotten off the ground. Now, she was glad it hadn't. Otherwise, there would be absolutely no hope for Parker and she to develop a relationship, assuming Beth was out-of-the-picture.

She told Dick about Parker's call and request. Dick said he didn't have any clients to guide or other responsibilities outside the shop, so he would be able to keep the shop open while Laurie was gone. She grabbed her purse and car keys, and drove north on U.S. highway 191, covering the nine miles to the turnoff just before the highway passed over Duck Creek. Parker's home was a short distance in from the highway on a rise which sloped down to Duck Creek. A blue Ford Fusion was parked alongside the garage. She parked in the driveway and knocked on the front door. If Beth was in the house, would she answer? If Beth wasn't in the house, who was? Whose car was parked alongside the garage? It had Montana license plates, so it either was a local person's car, perhaps a house cleaning person, or a rental car, most likely from a Bozeman rental car agency. If

Beth wasn't in the house, perhaps she was somewhere near outside. Laurie would have to find her. Did Parker have house guests? What she did know is Parker wouldn't be a happy camper if she didn't find Beth and deliver his message. She noticed a peep-hole in the door. If Beth was on the other side, hopefully she would see a woman and be less nervous about opening the door.

Laurie was about to knock again when the door opened a crack and a folded sheet of paper fell onto the landing as the door closed and the lock clicked. She reached down and unfolded the sheet of paper. Printed as "Mr. Williams isn't here. Please use this sheet to leave a message. When you finish, knock again." Laurie walked back to her car and located a pen in her purse. On the other side of the sheet, she wrote, "Beth, Parker called me and asked me to personally deliver an important message to you. I'm Laurie Black. I work for Parker in his shop. No one else is with me." She walked back to the front door and knocked. She heard the lock click and the door opened a crack allowing her to slip the sheet of paper through the crack. The door closed again and the lock clicked. After a few seconds, the lock clicked and the door opened. "Hi, Laurie, I'm Beth Richardson." Extending her hand, Beth continued, "I'm sorry to have treated you like an intruder, but I'm forced to act strangely these days. Please come in. Would you care for a cup of fresh brewed coffee? I finally figured out Parker's fancy coffee-maker."

So, this is Beth Richardson, thought Laurie. No wonder women and men agreed she was beautiful. Even through her eyes, jealous eyes as they were, Laurie had to agree. A feeling of jealousy swept over Laurie as it dawned on her that here was the woman that had aced out her mother and would ace out Laurie too. "Let's sit on the couch over there," said Beth, as she walked toward a three-seat couch, facing the moss rock fireplace, which dominated the east wall of the great room. Laurie had never been in Parker's home nor had her mother, so she was taken back at the size of the interior. All this for one person, she thought. Rather ridiculous. Her mother's home could fit into this space at least twice. "I'm o.k. with nothing to drink," responded Laurie. "I should get back to the shop as soon as I can. Dick's the only person there. Let me tell you what Parker wanted you to know. If you're going to meet him, you'll have to get going as soon as you can."

"Meet him? What do you mean? He knows I'm here," replied Beth, "so should I wait here or does he expect me to go somewhere else?"

"Somewhere else," responded Laurie. "He wants you to meet him at the Bozeman airport. He said his flight would take about three hours, so he should be to Bozeman in a little more than two hours, just enough time for you to get to the airport from here."

"Bozeman airport, what for? What's he doing there? Where's he coming from?"

"He didn't say. He was obviously in a hurry. He was adamant about telling you to meet him at the Bozeman airport. Now, I really have to be getting back to the shop."

Walking to the entrance door, Beth said, "Laurie, thanks for coming. Parker has told me so many good things about you. If you had called his home telephone, I wouldn't have answered. Parker probably realized I wouldn't answer his home phone so he sent a trusted friend."

"You're too kind," replied Laurie. "You know, for what it's worth and it isn't much right now, you certainly don't seem to me to be a murderer. I'm sorry this has happened to you. I'm pulling for you to get out of this mess. Be assured, I won't tell a soul, not even my mother, about your being here. Take care."

Beth watched Laurie drive away. Why did Parker want her to meet him at the Bozeman airport? Where had he been and for what reason? She could use the telephone in the house to call him, but his iPhone wouldn't be turned on in the airplane. She could stay here and call him, but he wouldn't have sent her that message through Laurie if that is what he had wanted. She decided she should do what he asked. Hopefully, her questions would be answered in person in a short time.

CHAPTER 44

Friday Morning
8:30 a.m.
Outside the Student Center, Big Sky University, Livingston, Montana

With the press conference concluded, Janet was anxious to depart this funny farm and get back to the work awaiting her in her office, which she hadn't been able to address thanks to the pig-headedness of the university administration. This entire fiasco would have been over a long time ago if the university president wasn't such an ego-maniac and pompous ass. In the end, he was made to look foolish, as the chairman of the University's Board of Trustees had intervened and directed the president to compromise with Students for Equal Treatment, the student group demanding equal treatment with the Gay, Lesbian, and Transgender student organization. Looking like a whipped dog, the university president had hastily called a press conference in which he blabbed about the good of the university and its commitment to diversity and equality for all. The bottom line was Students for Equal Treatment was given space in the Student Center, the daughter of the Speaker of the Montana House of Representatives and the other hostages had been released unharmed, and no violence had occurred. Janet was credited with a masterful piece of negotiation, although she knew it would have been much different had the student leaders of Students for Equal Treatment wanted to make a spectacle and not been intent on achieving a non-violent outcome.

Driving back to Billings, she had listened to her voice messages and checked the text messages she had received during the past few hours. She couldn't believe the message from Parker. Give a man an inch and he would take a mile. In a way, she couldn't be angry with him. Annoyed, but not angry. One of the reasons she had wanted him to be one of her consultants was his stick-to-a-tive-ness and work ethic. On the other hand, he was ignoring her direct order and playing lone ranger, something that if her superiors ever found out, she would be history in terms of advancement in the Bureau. She'd probably be banished to a posting in northern North Dakota, never to be seen or heard again. Parker's message was very specific. He must believe he was on to something important and needed the cover of his authorization to accomplish what he wanted to do. It had to be something related to the case against Beth Richardson. Janet did think the case against Beth was weak. Too much "maybe" evidence, which Marcia Farrington would make sure a jury understood. Janet had to tread carefully because she didn't want to be out-front, leading a charge to discredit Marilyn Evenhouse's case. Embarrassing and humiliating another law enforcement official wasn't done. If Parker did manage to show Beth hadn't murdered Valentine, Janet would declare ignorance of Parker's activities and let the chips fall where they would with Marilyn Evenhouse.

She tried Parker's phone again. Still no answer. She could text him, but he could always claim he hadn't received her text. He probably wouldn't answer or reply as he most likely thought she would chew him out. Maybe it was better that he didn't answer. They would avoid having a confrontation over the phone which might leave her no choice but to send one of her agents to corral Parker and sit on him, so to speak. This time she'd leave a voice message. "Parker, it's Janet. I don't know what you're up to, but you better be careful. You don't have my approval and if push comes to shove, I'll say I wasn't aware of your intentions and I'd have to charge you with impersonating an FBI agent and recommend prison time. Sorry to be so harsh, but I really don't have any other choice. Whatever you do, don't call my office. Only call my cell or text me. I hope this doesn't blow up in your face."

CHAPTER 45

Friday Morning
8:30 a.m.
Office of Law Enforcement and Security, Administration Building,
Yellowstone National Park, Mammoth Hot Springs, Montana

Parker's call had caught her off guard. She wasn't sure to take him seriously or caulk it up to a man desperate to save the woman he wanted to please. Jessica had held out hope she would be that woman but she knew she was only kidding herself. Parker had a thing for Beth Richardson. Obviously, he would do anything to try and prove she was innocent of the charge against her. Jessica herself had a difficult time envisioning Beth as a murderer. She wasn't the type. Becky Greenbrier was another story and Jessica would have easily believed Becky could be a murderer. Not Beth Richardson.

Parker had sounded so insistent. Doing what he asked, without any more justification than what he had said, was dubious at best. Watching this woman employee, let alone obtaining a search warrant for her living quarters and car, was over-the-top. No judge would grant a search warrant without more justification than Parker had conveyed. In fact, he hadn't conveyed any real justification at all.

Using one of their in-house employees to keep tabs on another employee would spread like wildfire on the Yellowstone gossip express if word got out. Nothing stayed secret for very long when a Yellowstone employee was involved in something mysterious, let alone two employees. As much as Parker was counting on her, she couldn't do what he wanted. He would be disappointed, she knew, but he would get over it. The most negative result, she surmised, was a barrier would be created between Parker and herself. Forget about any romantic relationship. That thought depressed her. Maybe there was a way, somewhere in the middle, to be responsive to Parker's request while avoiding the embarrassment for the Department and herself, should watching this woman employee be a mistake. The only way to accomplish this, she concluded, was for her to do the watching under the guise of checking the various security cameras around Old Faithful. There were some twenty-five security cameras around the Old Faithful area since, of the two million visitors to Yellowstone every year, nearly one and one-half million spent some time in the Old Faithful area. With so many people congregated in one area every day of the season, trouble and problems were inevitable. The security cameras were meant to supply visual clarification to what often were conflicting descriptions.

"Joan, I'm going to Old Faithful to check our security cameras in that area. I'll probably be staying overnight in one of the vacant rooms in the employee dormitory. Bruce should be back later today. Please let him know where I will be."

"Will do, Jess. Should I direct callers to your voice mail while you're gone?"

"Yes, I'll check my messages occasionally. One last thing. If a man named Parker Williams calls, please tell him I'm at Old Faithful checking out the security cameras."

CHAPTER 46

Friday Morning
10:00 a.m.
Employee Dormitory, Room 317, Old Faithful Complex, Yellowstone National Park, Wyoming.

Maybe it was time to blow this pop stand. There was nothing more to do here. Double revenge had been achieved. Valentine had paid the ultimate price and Richardson was close to paying the same price. Too bad about Greenbrier but she had been too great a risk to leave hanging. It was still unbelievable that Richardson had been granted bail. She must have promised someone sexual favors down the road to be granted bail. How else could it have happened? Where had she gone? Where was she living? Was she alone or with someone? As long as nothing surfaced to question the findings of the Sheriff, Richardson was going down. No sense to hang around any longer. This cold climate was the pits as well. How awful to live where the temperature didn't go above seventy-five degrees, even in July and August. Blow this pop stand and head for warmth. Maybe Florida or Arizona. Possibly Mexico, if it could be done without having to show a passport. If illegals could get into the U.S., how difficult must it be to get into Mexico illegally? Above all, leave no trail. No ability to locate. Disappear. Time to go pack what little there was to take. Travel lightly was the motto. Leave no trace. Leave Yellowstone to the bison, elk, and wolves. Rot in prison, Beth Richardson. Good riddance.

CHAPTER 47

Friday Morning
10:15 a.m.
Gallatin County International Airport, Bozeman, Montana

The three-hour plane trip had seemed much longer. He was anxious to see Beth and share with her everything he had learned. He hoped Beth had been at his home when Laurie arrived to convey his message. If she wasn't at the airport, he'd wait fifteen minutes in case something had slowed her down. If she still hadn't showed, he hopefully catch up with her later at his home.

The airplane taxied to the gate and passengers began to deplane. He could now turn on his iPhone. It beeped, indicating he had at least one message. If it was from Beth using a pay phone, he would be disappointed she wasn't coming to the airport. The first message was from the Montana representative for Simms waders and wading boots. He wanted to stop by the shop, when Parker was there, to show him the new line of merchandise. Parker saved the message. He'd let Dick handle it. The next message was from Janet. Listening to it, he breathed an internal sigh of relief. At least she wasn't forbidding him to go ahead. She didn't say absolutely not. She wanted him to be careful and to realize he was on his own if everything came crashing down on his head. Fine with him. He could live with that. No other messages. None from Beth.

Walking from the plane, he looked for Beth. He didn't see her. Was she coming? Wait a minute, he thought to himself. She didn't know which flight he had taken, so he shouldn't expect her to be at the gate. Her waiting in the main concourse area seemed more logical. He hurried to the main concourse. Sure enough. She was standing close to where she thought he would arrive. She spotted him about the same time he saw her. A large smile broke across her face as they closed the distance between them. Oblivious to whom might see them, they came into each other's arms in a mutually embracing hug. Neither spoke for several seconds, seemingly lost in the warmth of the moment. She broke the trance-like silence first. "This better be good, making a fugitive girl spend two hours driving to such a romantic place as the Bozeman airport."

"And here I thought it was my irresistible charm that drew you," he responded. "Nevertheless, I'm glad you came. I have lots to tell you and we need to get back to West Yellowstone and possibly to the Old Faithful area. Let's get going."

"Aye-aye, sir," she replied, as she gave a mocking salute. "If you haven't thought of it, we have two cars here. How are you going to tell me everything you want if we are in separate cars?"

"We'll leave your rental car here. I'll call Marcia Farrington and tell her to have it picked up and turned in. She rented it in Billings, so picking it up here won't be a big deal. I'll tell here it's here at the airport. On the way out, we will stop at the car so you can put the keys under the floor mat along with the parking stub. You'll have to drive my car so I can make some calls and maybe send some text messages."

"So now I have to be your chauffeur," she said with a smile. "What's next, be your chief cook and bottle washer?"

Laughing in return, he replied, "You didn't think you could stay in my house for free, did you? Now, let's get to the car so we can get out of here and on our way."

After placing the keys to her rental car under the driver's side floor mat along with the parking ticket, Parker called Marcia Farrington and left her a voice mail message explaining the location of the car and where the keys and parking ticket were placed. As they drove U.S. highway 191 south toward his home, he told Beth everything he had done and learned, including the visit with her mother. When he first mentioned going to see her parents, she showed quite a bit of emotion. Continuing to describe his time with her mother, she became more like her normal self, even making a joke about her mother probably sizing up Parker as a potential marriage candidate.

He could tell she was her normal self when she quipped, "You now have your two girl friends doing your bidding. Nice work on your part. When this is all over, I suppose I'll have to thank them for their help. Maybe I can throw a celebration party and you'll be surrounded by the women in your life! I'll invite Laurie too and why not her mother, Karen? Wouldn't you love all the attention you would receive?"

"Come on, Beth, get serious," he replied, "in case you've forgotten, you're still accused of murdering Valentine. This is not time to be talking about celebrations or parties."

"You're right," she responded, "I'm sorry. I do want to thank them when this nightmare is over, but I shouldn't be putting the cart before the horse. Now, there's something I want to do and, I'm sorry, but I must keep it a secret, even from you. Please don't lecture me about playing cat and mouse. This will only involve two private phone calls to two people I trust as much as I trust you. I'm going to need to use your iPhone since I don't have my own. Mine's at the Law Enforcement Center being held as evidence. Don't ask me what they think they're going to find incriminating on my phone, but so be it. When we get to your home, please allow me to make these calls without questioning me. O.k.?"

Trying to remain calm and not raise his voice, he responded. "I don't like it, but I can tell I'm not going to be able to talk you out of it, so I'm going to trust you know what you're doing. While you are making your calls, I'm going to contact Jess. I want to know if she was able to obtain a search warrant. By the way, I believe Yolanda's name is really Vanessa Cortez, your fellow contestant in the Miss Illinois Pageant. I'm concerned she might slip away and sterilize everything before she departed."

"Vanessa Cortez, really? I think she was the first runner-up. What is she doing in Yellowstone?"

"I'm hoping Jessica is finding the answer to that question right now," he replied. My guess is Vanessa is in the middle of Valentine's murder. Maybe Becky's too. Vanessa may be the killer we've been looking for."

"Wouldn't that be nice? I'll make my calls while you talk to your girlfriend Jessica," responded Beth.

CHAPTER 48

Friday Morning
11:00 a.m.
Outside the Employee Dormitory, Old Faithful Complex, Yellowstone
National Park, Wyoming

This isn't what she thought she'd be doing as Assistant Director of Law Enforcement and Security for Yellowstone National Park; watching the entrance to the employee dormitory at the Old Faithful Complex. If the office or she were swamped with work, she wouldn't be able to be doing this stakeout. Parker had been so insistent and she had to confess she would like to help stick it to the Park County Sheriff's Department, especially Carlos Medina, who had been a suggestive pig more than once with her. His suggestive overtures had been such a turn-off, yet he wouldn't back off. She would love to be able to make him eat humble pie.

The entrance door opened and a woman came out carrying a box. Was she Yolanda Mendez or Vanessa Cortez? Pick your name. At this point, it made no difference. Jessica would go with Vanessa Cortez. The woman opened the truck of a black, small car. Grabbing her binoculars, Jessica focused on the woman. Dark hair, olive complexion, and, even from far off and through another woman's critical eye, a marvelous figure. If it was Vanessa, it looked like she was getting ready to take off. As Jessica watched the woman walk back toward the dormitory entrance, she asked herself, what should I do? I can't stop her since I have no grounds to hold her. Besides, I don't want to alert her that I'm watching her. But, I can't just let her drive away. What should I do?

As she was thinking of a way to detain Vanessa, the entrance door opened and Vanessa, or whom Jessica thought was Vanessa, came out carrying some clothes over her arm. Sure enough, she was leaving. To where? Anyone's guess, but she must be stopped.

Vanessa went back into the dormitory. During her walk, Jessica thought she saw her look toward where Jessica was parked. Jessica wondered if she'd been spotted. Nothing to do about it now. If she had been seen, she had no choice but to drive away. Jessica didn't feel she could do that given Vanessa's apparent intention to leave. It hit Jessica what she had to do to detain Vanessa. She had to do it now. Don't think about it. If she was caught, it would take a whole lot of explaining. She slipped from the car and staying in the shadows as much as possible, she crouched next to Vanessa's car. Withdrawing the knife she carried in her fanny pack, she jabbed it as forcefully as she could into the driver's side front tire. The hissing sound of air escaping caused her to look around to see if anyone had heard it and might come to investigate. Time to get away from here before Vanessa returned. She moved quickly and silently back to her Explorer, breathing a sigh of relief that no one had apparently heard or seen her. It was a good thing she hadn't stayed longer by Vanessa's car or taken the time to puncture another tire because no sooner had she slid behind the steering wheel than Vanessa came out the dormitory entrance carrying what looked to be a small travel pack and a purse. Jessica held her breath as Vanessa started her car and began to drive away, stopping after only a few feet. Vanessa got out of her car and looked at the front driver's side tire which was as flat as a pancake. Jessica could see the frustration on Vanessa's face as she kicked the tire, the side of the car, and then walked briskly back into the dormitory.

Thinking Vanessa might call Yellowstone's mobile automobile repair service to come and repair the tire, Jessica called Joan. "Hi, Joan, I don't have much time to explain and please make the call as soon as we finish this conversation."

"Sure thing, Jess."

"Please call the automobile mobile service and tell them they are not to go to the employee dormitory at Old Faithful should a call come from a woman to have her tire repaired. I don't care what excuse they want to use, but they are not to go. If a woman does call, I want to know about it. Thanks, Joan, talk to you later."

"You got it. I'm calling them now. Take care."

Jessica hoped she hadn't done the wrong thing. If this woman wasn't Vanessa, Jessica had made a huge mistake. Even if she was Vanessa, was there any evidence she was involved in Valentine or Becky's murder? Jessica hoped her interest in Parker as a man hadn't clouded her thinking. If she had made a mistake, she was responsible for a totally innocent and uninvolved fellow woman employee having her plans sabotaged.

CHAPTER 49

Friday Morning
11:45 a.m.
Home of Parker Williams on Duck Creek, Nine Miles North of West Yellowstone off U.S. Highway 191, Montana

Beth had finished her two phone calls and was presently sitting on the deck with a glass of ice tea. She looked calm, too calm, thought Parker. She knew something he didn't and it bothered him she was withholding something from him. She said she was expecting a return call from whomever she had talked with on her second call. Parker was preparing lunch as he, too, was waiting for a return call from Jessica.

"I wish you'd let me do something to help you," said Beth, as she slid the slider open and stepped into the great room. "I'm not a total klutz in the kitchen, I'll have you know. I do have some domestic talents, in spite of what my mother might have told you."

"Your mother said nothing about your domestic skills," replied Parker. "In fact, we didn't do much talking about you at all. We spent almost all our time having your mother describe events, as she remembered them, from the final evening of the Miss Illinois Pageant."

"The way you said she described the shouting match between Vanessa Cortez and Valentine I can see how Vanessa might still carry a grudge after these years. If she does, it would explain her wanting to get revenge against the two people that she believed kept her from winning, Valentine and me. But murder? That seems to be much too much a response to not winning a state pageant. After all, being first runner-up wasn't too shabby."

"I'm still hoping you'll let me in on why you had to make those secret calls, but I'll pass for now. You're lucky I can't bug you right now since I need to watch the salmon filets so I don't overcook them."

She replied laughingly, "Where did you learn all this gourmet cooking stuff, master chef?"

"It's none of your business. You don't tell me some things, so I can play the same game. Now, go back outside while I zap the potatoes."

His iPhone rang as Beth was stepping onto the deck. She picked up the phone and said, "Sorry, it's not your girlfriend. It's my call back." She closed the slider behind her leaving Parker to wonder what she was being so secretive about and with whom.

CHAPTER 50

Friday Morning
11:50 a.m.
Outside the Employee Dormitory, Old Faithful Complex, Yellowstone National Park, Wyoming

Jessica's cell phone vibrated. She had placed it on vibrate so no ringing would sound and possibly occur when Vanessa was outside and might hear it. Caller ID showed the call was from Joan. "Hi, Joan."

"Jess, it's a good thing I called Carl when I did. He just called me and said it wasn't but five minutes after I called that a call came in from a woman employee at the employee dorm at Old Faithful requesting to have a tire repaired." Carl McCall was Yellowstone's employee that worked the day shift for the automobile mobile service.

"Good work, Joan," Jessica replied. "Did Carl say anything else about what the woman said?"

"Nope. He was anxious to get off the phone as he said the phone line needed to be available for incoming calls.

"O.k., thanks again," Joan. "I'll be back to the office soon."

She felt she had done all she could. If Vanessa found some employee to change the tire on her car, there was nothing Jessica could do about it. There simply wasn't anything concrete she could use to hold Vanessa. Some fake charge could be dreamed up, she supposed, but doing something like that, with the potential backlash if it was discovered the charge had been made up, was above her pay grade. Her boss, Bruce Dickson, would have to make a decision about something like that and bringing Bruce into this situation at this time, with all the explaining that would have to be done, didn't seem like a good idea at all. She decided to call Parker and let him know the situation and tell him she was leaving the scene.

CHAPTER 51

Friday Morning
11:55 a.m.
Home of Parker Williams on Duck Creek, Nine Miles North of West
Yellowstone off U.S. Highway 191, Montana

Beth stepped into the great room with a wide smile spread across her face. Handing Parker's iPhone to him, she said, "Good news. Very good news. I won't know for sure until tomorrow morning, but if it's true, it's the break I need."

Turning to face her, Parker replied, "Care to share your good news?"

"Not yet. If it turns out to be a big nothing, I don't want you or anyone else to feel you have to console me. You're not alone in being in the dark until tomorrow morning. I'm not going to tell Marcia Farrington either. Boy, that salmon looks wonderful. My congratulations to the chef."

He was going to try again to persuade her to tell him what it was that had raised her spirits earlier, even before this recent call, and especially now after this call. She was riding high, no doubt about it. As he started to try and persuade her, his iPhone rang. Caller ID showed the call was from Jessica Samuels. "Jess. Where are you?"

"Right where you asked me to be," responded Jessica. "I've been watching the employee dormitory here at Old Faithful and your hunch was correct. Vanessa, if it is her, is planning to take off. She won't be going anywhere for a little while since her left front tire is as flat as a pancake and the automobile mobile service isn't able to help her. However, there are plenty of male employees around that might want to play knight in shining armor and help out the lady in distress by changing the tire. If that happens, I'll bet she takes off as quickly as she can."

"Jess, you said you don't know for sure if the woman is Vanessa. Are you thinking 50-50 chance or 70-30 or what?"

"I'm guessing in the 90-10 range, but there's always the possibility I could be wrong. Look, Parker, there's nothing more I can or should do here. I've overstepped my authority already. Don't ask me how because I don't want to lie to you. I've done what I could. To tell you the truth, I'm not proud of it. But, it's done and I'll have to live with it."

"I'm very grateful, Jess. However, we need for Vanessa not to leave. Isn't there something you can do to hold her a little while longer until I can get there and use my FBI authority to question her? How about telling her you want to question her about that entrance fee cash scheme you told me about? That, or maybe a search warrant?"

"You've got to be kidding, Parker. No judge on this side of sanity would grant a search warrant. What would be the grounds? Maybe this or maybe that? There is nothing definite to bring to a judge. Plus, there's no time to do the warrant and get it to a judge. Something tells me she's going to use her beauty and that marvelous body of hers to get some hormone-hyped guy to either fix the tire or lend her his car."

"I know, I know," responded Parker with so much exasperation in his voice that Beth reached across the table, at which they were sitting, took his hand, squeezed it, and held up a finger to indicate she had an idea. He continued, "I think we're close to finding the real killer of Valentine and to lose a suspect, right at the time were making some sense out of this mess, can't happen. Thanks again, Jess. Talk to you soon."

Beth said, "Let's go." Getting up from the table, she continued, "I hate to leave this good lunch but we need to get to that dormitory before Vanessa leaves. Take your last bite of salmon and then let's move it."

"I've got a better idea," he responded. "I'll go and you stay here. Remember, you're under strict stipulations and besides, this could be dangerous and no sense you taking unnecessary risks."

Laughing, she came right up to look him directly in the eyes. As she did, her composure changed. She became very serious and he could see determination in her eyes. Her words were forceful and she almost spit them out. "If you think I'm not going to confront Vanessa, you're sadly mistaken. In case you've forgotten, I'm the one accused of murder. I'm the one that spent time in that cell. I'm the one whose reputation is on the line, along with my career and ability to earn a decent income. So, forget it, buddy. I'm going and that's that. Now, you have any other stupid comment to make?"

He knew enough to not even try to respond, let alone attempt to dissuade her. This was a side of Beth Richardson he knew existed, but had rarely been exhibited, at least in his presence. Determined and not to be denied was how he would describe her demeanor. "I think you've said it all, at least for now. It's going to take us a while to get there, so I suggest we make tracks."

CHAPTER 52

Friday Afternoon
Noon
Behind the Parking Lot Adjacent to the Employee Dormitory, Old Faithful
Complex, Yellowstone National Park, Wyoming

That had to be the person, sitting there so high and mighty as if no one could see her. It was a woman and the uniform she was wearing meant she was a Yellowstone employee. Well, she was in for a big surprise. Whom did she think she was dealing with? A dummy? Did she think a tire going flat for no reason wouldn't raise a question or two? Didn't she realize that sitting in a National Park Service Explorer and looking at the employee dormitory for fifteen minutes straight was a giveaway? Time to find out what she was doing here besides making car tires go flat.

Walking quietly and keeping to the shadows, Vanessa approached the rear of the Explorer in which Jessica Samuels sat wrestling with whether she should stay until Parker arrived or take off. Jessica knew every minute longer she stayed, she risked being discovered and with it a host of questions she'd be asked by her boss about her reasons and purposes. On the other hand, Parker needed help and if this Vanessa was whom Parker believed her to be, she just might have someone change the tire for her and be able to slip away during the time after Jessica left and before Parker arrived. A knocking on the driver's side window startled her and broke into her thoughts. She turned to see a woman holding what looked like a 38-caliber handgun at her and motioning to lower the window. Jessica immediately thought of her own handgun. Where was it? Did I even bring it? Looking again at the woman, Jessica recognized her as the woman she had been watching get ready to take off. Vanessa Cortez. Vanessa tapped on the window with the handgun, indicating this time with a more vigorous hand motion, that she wanted Jessica to lower the window. Who knows what Vanessa might do if I don't do what she wants?, thought Jessica. Turning the ignition key to the "on" position, Jessica pressed the button to lower the window. In a defiant voice, Vanessa said, "Didn't think I'd see you out here, did you? Did you have fun making my tire go flat? I wonder what your precious Superintendent will say about one Yellowstone employee pulling such a nasty stunt on another Yellowstone employee, or did you do it for some other reason than just a prank?"

Jessica was so stunned she wasn't sure if she should answer and, if so, how she should answer. How could Vanessa know about her puncturing the tire? No one had seen her, she was sure. She'd deny it and see where things went. "I don't know what you're talking about, but what I do know is your threatening an office of the law and if I were you, I'd put the gun away and leave before I arrest you." Looking for an opening, Jessica continued, "By the way, do you have a permit for that gun? If not, I'll add that to the charges against you if you don't lower the gun right now and walk away."

"Tough talk from somebody that is looking at a gun, not holding one. A Law Enforcement and Security Officer to boot. In case you haven't noticed, I have the gun and you have nothing, so just shut up and give me the keys to this Explorer. I always wanted to have one of these to use like all you big-shots. I need wheels. My car is indisposed, if you haven't noticed."

"Taking the Explorer will add another charge against you," replied Jessica. "If you walk away right now, I probably could forget any of this happened. I could also call the car repair service and use my influence to have them come and repair the tire."

"You really are something. What a comedian. Nice try, but no go. I already called those car service bozos. I was told they were booked solid for the next few hours. As for taking your Explorer, do you think I care about another charge against me? One more isn't going to make any difference. Now, quit stalling." Looking at Jessica's waist where a pair of handcuffs hung from her belt, Vanessa continued, "Those handcuffs you have on your belt, let's have them, and the key. We wouldn't want you going anywhere, now would we?"

"You're making a huge mistake," Jessica responded.

"That's for me to worry about. I'm not going to ask again. Keys, please. Both sets. The handcuffs too. I'd hate to start on your kneecaps with this gun. They tell me shattered kneecaps mean you won't ever walk again. Think of spending the rest of your life in a wheelchair."

Reluctantly, Jessica handed the keys and the handcuffs to Vanessa. Taking them, Vanessa pulled Jessica's left wrist against the steering wheel and used the handcuffs to cuff Jessica's left wrist to the steering wheel. "That should hold you while I'm gone. I won't be long. I'm going to get my stuff from my car and then we'll be on our way."

Jessica watched as Vanessa walked toward her car. If they were going to leave in Jessica's Explorer, she needed to leave something behind that would alert the people, which would eventually search for her, to what had happened. But what? Looking around the Explorer, she realized she could reach into the small compartment between the driver and front passenger seats. The compartment was part of the center console. Opening it, she felt around, trying to identify the contents. Hold it. She hadn't thought that it still was in the Explorer. Perfect. It should do the trick. Taking it from the compartment, she palmed it in her right hand. Would she have an opportunity to drop it outside the Explorer without Vanessa seeing her? Distracting her for only a few seconds, when the door was open, would work. If Vanessa caught her, would she lose it and use her gun? If she had already killed, why would she not do it again? Jessica's anxiety level skyrocketed and a gripping fear overcame her as she watched Vanessa return carrying a small suitcase and some clothes over her arm. Opening the rear hatch of the Explorer, Vanessa said, "Can you believe this is all I have to take with me? Pretty Spartan, huh? Travel lightly, I'd say. There are a few more things back in my room, but nothing that can't be replaced. Besides, when someone decides to check the room after they don't hear or see me for a few days, I'd like them to think I'm still around. I'm leaving stuff around to make it look like I'm still around and living there. Some of the stuff has my name on it. I'm Yolanda Mendez, if you care to know. At least that's what everyone thinks around here. Can you believe that bird-brain guy in H.R. never asked me for my identification when I applied for the crummy job? He was too interested in stealing looks down my blouse. I purposely didn't wear a bra that day, so I made sure he could get an eyeful. I haven't even cashed my payroll checks. I would probably have been asked to show identification, and I don't want that. I left those checks in my room. Whomever eventually checks the room will think I haven't left yet. Who would leave payroll checks behind?" Walking to the driver's door and opening it, she continued, "Here's the way we're going to do this. I'm going to uncuff you and then you and I are going to walk around the Explorer to the passenger door. Then, you're going to sit in the passenger seat and be a good girl while I cuff you to the headrest. Then, I'm going to come back to the driver's seat and we'll be off together. Do we understand each other? Remember, I have the gun, so I wouldn't try any funny stuff if I were you."

Uncuffing Jessica, Vanessa indicated she should get out of the Explorer. Walking slowly around the Explorer with Vanessa behind her, just as Jessica was behind the Explorer, a car drove into the parking lot. Both Vanessa and she were startled by the quick appearance of the car. Vanessa stepped in front of Jessica to stop her from making any signal to the driver of the car. Now, thought Jessica, and she quickly dropped what had been clinched in her right hand and used her foot to push it under the rear of the Explorer. As quickly as the car had appeared, it turned and headed across the parking lot driving away on one of the roads leading from parking lot. "For a minute there, I thought you had been able to summon one of your fellow law officers. Good thing for you it wasn't or you'd know what it feels like to be shot. Now, move, before someone else shows up." Walking to the passenger door, Vanessa opened it, pushed Jessica into the seat, grabbed her left hand, cuffed it to the steering wheel, and locked the door. Never taking her eyes from Jessica, Vanessa walked around the front of the Explorer, sat in the driver's seat and inserted the key into the ignition. She next uncuffed Jessica's left hand, placed it against the column of the headrest, and cuffed it again. Jessica had thought about making a move to disarm Vanessa during the few seconds her left hand was free, but Vanessa had never lowered the gun or taken her eyes off Jessica. "If you wonder where we're going, we're leaving this miserable place. We're leaving Yellowstone through the east exit. There's someone I want you to meet. Settle back and enjoy the ride. If you behave yourself, I just may spare your life. On the other hand, maybe not."

CHAPTER 53

Friday Afternoon
12:45 p.m.
On the Loop Road between Madison Junction and the Old Faithful
Complex, Yellowstone National Park, Wyoming

They had made good time. Thankfully, there had been no traffic jams
caused by elk or bison on or near the road causing visitors to stop on the
road to watch or photograph the animals. Also, they had not encountered
any R.Vs. traveling ten or fifteen miles an hour causing massive traffic
backups. There were few places on the curvy, two-lane roads to pass another
vehicle, especially R.Vs. The speed limit on all roads in Yellowstone was
forty-five miles per hour and they had been able to maintain a steady fifty
to fifty-five miles per hour hoping no traffic enforcement patrol vehicle
would stop them. Beth reached across and placed her hand on his arm and
said, "Have I told you how much I appreciate all you've done for me? You
could have walked away when Janet pulled the plug on you. You're quite
the guy, you know." Leaning across the front seat, she kissed him on the
cheek.

He couldn't resist making a wise-crack, like she often did with him. In
as serious a tone of voice as he could muster, he responded, "So, the only
time I get kisses anymore and told I'm a good guy is when I help you when
I'm not supposed to. I guess I'll take what I can get."

"So, now you're feeling sorry for yourself," she replied. "Well, let me
tell you something, Mr. I'm-feeling-sorry-for-myself. When this mess is
over, I'll show you what real kisses are all about. And you won't have to do
anything to earn them. They are going to be free and yours for the taking,
assuming you want them, that is."

"Promises, promises," he responded. "I'll believe it when it happens.
At least I can think about it and hope for the best Now, before I start

fanaticizing too much, let's decide what we hope to do when we get there and how we want to do it."

"If Vanessa hates me as much as it seems," replied Beth, "if I confront her face-to-face, she might become so agitated she'll confess right then and there. Maybe you first confront her as an FBI agent, tell her you're taking her into custody for further questioning, and then when you and she get into the car, I'll be there. Maybe the sight of me will push her over the edge and she'll realize her game is up."

"It's as good a plan as any other, I suppose," he responded. "I still don't like your being involved, but I lost that battle already."

"You sure did," she interrupted very abruptly, "and don't forget it."

"What we have to be prepared for is her having a weapon," continued Parker. "If she does, all bets are off." Pointing to the glove compartment, he continued, "My gun is in there. I'm going to have it with me when I confront her."

They drove on in relative silence for several miles each absorbed in one's own thoughts. Pulling into the parking lot for the employee dormitory at the Old Faithful Complex, he saw only a few cars in the lot. No sign of a National Park Service Ford Explorer, which would indicate Jessica was here. She had left. He had hoped she would stay. He was disappointed she hadn't, although he could understand her reasoning. Was one of the cars Vanessa's or had she left too? Her room was on the third floor of the dormitory, but on which side? If it was the side facing the parking lot, had she seen them drive into the parking lot, assuming she was still here and in her room? Turning to face him, Beth asked, "What do you think? Time to fish or cut bait?"

"If she's still here and in her room, she may have seen us and will make a break for it out another exit when she sees me head for the entrance. Assuming one of these parked cars is hers, my bet is she goes for it and tries to drive away. So, I say you stay right here and if you see a woman hurrying toward one of these parked cars, you lay on the horn. I'll come as fast as I can. I'll leave the keys in the 4Runner so if push comes to shove and she makes it to a car, don't be timid. Get close enough to shoot out her tires. I'll leave the gun here with you."

She looked at him like he was talking nonsense. "What if she has a gun and you don't? We believe she's killed before. Why don't you take the gun? If she does make it to her car, I'll ram it from the front. I'd much prefer to deal with damage to your 4Runner than damage to you."

"No deal. The gun stays here with you. I'll take my chances. Now, here goes." He stepped from the car and walked toward the dormitory entrance. He knew he'd been short with Beth but he didn't want her to argue with him about having the gun. He wanted her to have maximum protection. If anything happened to her, he wouldn't be able to live with himself. Concentrating on what he was about to do, he entered the dormitory. A directory was listed on the wall by the set of elevators. Next to the elevators was a stairway. Best to take the stairs, he thought. The directory listed room 317 for Vanessa Cortez. Here goes, he said to himself, as he started up the stairs.

CHAPTER 54

Friday Afternoon
12:45 p.m.
FBI Office, Billings, Montana

"Janet, there's a Ryan Belgrade on the line. He says he's calling on behalf of Beth Richardson and it's very important he talk with you. He said it could be a life or death matter. You want to talk with him or should I put him off?"

She hadn't felt good about the way she had treated Parker when he told her he was using his FBI authorization. Sure, she hadn't forbid him to use the authorization. She had chosen him and pulled some strings to obtain the authorization in the first place, so she should have enough confidence in his decision-making process to allow him to utilize the authorization if and when he felt he needed it. During the drive back from Livingston, she remembered a similar time in her own career when she had told her superior she was going to follow her instinct. Her superior had been lukewarm in his support and she remembered how she had been turned off by his approach and response. She didn't want to add to the disillusionment Parker might be experiencing because of her response to his serious undertaking so she decided she would talk with Ryan Belgrade, even if what he was wanting to tell here wasn't from Parker per se. "I'll talk with him, Cynthia," she replied. "Hello, Mr. Belgrade. I understand you have something from Beth Richardson which she wishes for me to know. Please fire away."

"Hello, Agent VanKampen. Beth Richardson speaks very highly of you. Thank you for taking my call. Beth specifically asked me to contact you directly. I'll repeat verbatim what she told me to tell you. She said there was proof about where she was and what she was doing the night Michael Valentine was murdered. She said several photos existed providing the proof. She said she wanted you to know this as you would know what to do."

"Hold it, Mr. Belgrade. Tell you what. If you allow me to call you Ryan, I'll allow you to call me Janet. We don't need this formal stuff."

"Fine by me, Janet," he replied.

"Let me tell you, Ryan, what I think I heard you just tell me. As I understand what Beth told you, there are photos proving she was camped overnight where she said she was. Do I have that correct?"

"You got it," responded Ryan. "This means she couldn't have killed Valentine, doesn't it Janet? She can go free now, can't she?"

"If those photos indeed exist—and I'm not saying they don't—it would sure confirm her alibi. Where are the photos, Ryan? Did Beth tell you?"

"I asked her the same question," he replied. "She answered by saying the photos would be forthcoming in due time and she wanted to deliver them personally to Deputy Medina and Sheriff Evenhouse."

"Oh, I bet she would," responded Janet. "Do you know where she is right now? I'd like to talk with her."

"No, I don't. She didn't say and I didn't ask. Sorry I can't be more helpful."

"You've been more helpful than you know, especially for Beth," replied Janet. "If you hear from her again, please tell her how pleased I am and that I'd like to talk with her as soon as possible. Thank you, again, Ryan."

This wasn't the first time, in her career, when a case which appeared locked-up took a dramatic turn. Everything she had heard about Beth Richardson was that she was a straight-shooter. If she claimed photos substantiating her alibi existed, then Janet was going to accept her claim as fact and act accordingly. However, before doing anything, there was something which had been nagging at her for sometime which she wanted to do first. The full scope and power of the FBI was about to be unleashed to find an answer.

CHAPTER 55

Friday Afternoon
12:45 p.m.
In a National Park Service Ford Explorer Driving Toward the East Entrance
of Yellowstone National Park, Wyoming

Jessica wasn't sure of anything. She wasn't sure where they would be headed after they left Yellowstone. She wasn't sure what Vanessa intended to do with her when they arrived at wherever they were going. Most of all, she wasn't sure of Vanessa. Jessica had been around killers when she worked for the Kansas City Homicide Division prior to joining the National Park Service. Vanessa didn't have the demeanor, act like, or talk like a killer. Not that she didn't have a mean streak about her, but the cold ruthlessness, which was part-and-parcel of the nature of murderers, wasn't in her. If Vanessa was a killer, she wouldn't be risking her future by taking Jessica with her. She would have killed Jessica a long time ago. Jessica began to think another person was involved with Vanessa, someone else who killed Valentine and probably Becky too, and had used Vanessa to get to Valentine and Becky. Was Vanessa an accomplice while the real killer was someone else? Jessica's gut told her "yes". She decided to try and draw Vanessa out and test her theory. "Why did you murder Michael Valentine and frame Beth Richardson?"

"Oh, please, why don't you just go for the gold, sweetheart," responded Vanessa. "You don't tiptoe around, do you? I'm sure you'd like to know, but that's for me to know and you to find out. I'll tell you what. You aren't going anyplace nor are you going to be talking to anyone, at least if I have my way, so let me tell you a few things about the high and mighty Beth Richardson."

There was someone else involved, thought Jessica. Interrupting, she said, "So, if you're not calling the shots, who is?"

"Not so fast, law enforcement big shot. I call my own shots. Do you want to know some things about her majesty or would you rather keep her on that fake pedestal you've all put her on? She has all of you bluffed, you know."

"To tell you the truth," responded Jessica, "I'd much rather you tell me why you killed Michael Valentine and framed Beth Richardson for it. That's much more interesting to me that hearing more about Richardson's achievements and successes. I'm sick and tired myself of hearing all about that stuff. As far as I'm concerned, I wouldn't be sad for one minute if I never heard anything more about Beth Richardson." Jessica said this to try and gain some of Vanessa's confidence and have her open up about Valentine's murder and also Becky Greenbrier's murder. Deep down, she knew she was jealous of Beth, but not nearly to the extent she was putting on. She wanted to have Vanessa begin to think of Jessica as an ally against Beth.

"So, Miss Perfect has gotten to you too. I bet you haven't had to live, for as long as I have, with her screwing you out of what was rightfully yours, along with thousands of dollars and a probable career in the movies and television. She never earned anything on her own. Everything has been given to her and if you haven't noticed, it's always men giving to her. She uses her looks and body, even better than I do I think, to get what she wants. Well, not this time. This time she's been outsmarted and revenge has finally happened."

"Isn't murder going too far to exact revenge for something that occurred several years ago?"

"Easy for you to say. Look at you. You have a very good job with promotions and higher salaries ahead as your career unfolds. Me. I have nothing except my looks and body. Soon, those are going to not be as attractive to men as they are now. I have to make my mark now and that includes destroying Beth Richardson."

Now to go for the jugular, thought Jessica. Either Vanessa was going to confess to killing Valentine or she was going to tell Jessica that she helped kill Valentine. "Don't make a terrible mistake and take the fall for whomever used you to get to Valentine. You aren't going to get away with this. Why do you think I was watching the dormitory? Our department is on to you as is the FBI. If you give this up now and tell me who the real killer is, I'll do everything I can to tell everyone how cooperative you were in helping us get the killer."

Laughing, Vanessa responded, "You've got to be kidding. Nice try, but I'm in this so far that nothing I do or say will get me out of it. No, I'm heading to a place where no one will find me. I made it this far, didn't I? With a little well-timed blackmail, I can do rather well. Add a false identity with documents to back it up, have a steady flow of bucks from blackmail, and I'll be just fine."

CHAPTER 56

Friday Afternoon
1:00 p.m.
Room 317, Employee Dormitory, Old Faithful Complex, Yellowstone National Park, Wyoming

Either Vanessa had left her room for a little while and would return or she had skipped out in a hurry, leaving quite a few personal belongings behind. Perhaps she was deliberately trying to mislead anyone wanting to talk with her by making it look like she was returning. There was really no reason for him to hang here even if she was returning. If she did return, it might not be for a considerable time. Besides, his gut instinct said she had bolted.

Beth had stayed in the car ready to sound the horn if Vanessa showed up outside. No horn. If Vanessa was on the run and leaving Yellowstone, she could use any one of the five exits, although the South and West exits were closer than the other three. The first question to answer was not which exit she would use, but how was she traveling? Utilizing his FBI authorization identification number, he had called the license plate numbers of the five cars in the parking lot to the Montana DVM, including the car with the flat tire. All except that car were registered to Yellowstone employees, none a woman. The car with the flat tire was a stolen car which was registered to a Frederick Lawson of Cody. Unfortunately, law enforcement officers in Yellowstone were not informed, in a timely manner, of vehicles stolen outside Yellowstone, or for that matter, most other crimes as well. Lawson's car had been stolen with almost no worry of being apprehended in Yellowstone unless the thief was stopped in Yellowstone for a traffic violation or other suspicious activity. Had Vanessa stolen Lawson's car and now stolen another to make her run for it? If she had, the only way to identify the car was to pull the registrations of all the cars owned by Yellowstone employees living in the dormitory, although that didn't guarantee that someone else hadn't parked in the dormitory parking lot and Vanessa had helped herself to that person's car. A futile effort, he decided, and a huge waste of time.

Walking back to his 4Runner, he wondered what spot Jessica had used to watch the dormitory. She would have wanted a good line of sight and yet stayed as out-of-sight from the dormitory as possible. He looked around the parking lot, trying to think like Jessica had thought. Probably over there, he thought, looking toward a place across from where Beth waited for him in his 4Runner. Looking toward the place, he spotted something on the ground. Funny, he thought, that wasn't a place where many people would chose to park, so why would trash be on the ground there? There were numerous vacant places to park much nearer the entrance. Someone had parked there, he surmised, and dropped something. Most likely a piece of trash thrown indiscriminately from a parked car. Since he wanted to see if his reasoning for where Jessica had parked to watch the dormitory was correct, he walked toward the piece of trash to determine if Jessica may have parked near that place. Might as well pick it up and toss it into a trash receptacle. Keeping Yellowstone free of trash was in his blood, so he always picked up trash whenever he could without thinking about doing it. Picking it up from the ground, he saw immediately it wasn't trash. Far from it. It was an instruction brochure for the tracking device carried in every Yellowstone vehicle. He had seen the same instruction brochure in Beth's Explorer. She had once told him that every National Park Service vehicle used at Yellowstone had a tracking device because of the large distances separating vehicles from each other and the requirement to know where each vehicle was located in such a vast geographic area. A National Park Service vehicle had been parked here and the brochure from that vehicle had been discarded. Why? He thought about it as he walked to his 4Runner. It had to be, he said to himself. He didn't believe in coincidences. It would be too great a coincidence for this brochure to be in this place at this time and not be from Jessica's Explorer. His reasoning had to be correct. Jessica had indeed parked here. She had watched the dormitory from here. She had left but not without leaving evidence that she'd been here and more importantly, she'd left not of her own choice. She wanted whomever found the brochure to know she'd been forced to leave. "Bless you, Jessica," he said quietly. "I know what vehicle Vanessa is using to make her escape. You've also told me how to find her."

CHAPTER 57

Friday Afternoon
2:00 p.m.
Somewhere Over the Beartooth Mountain Range between Billings, Montana, and Cody, Wyoming

One bad apple spoils the barrel or was there more than one bad apple? The information she had requested had made it clear there was at least one bad apple. She needed to determine how wide the rot had spread. Cody was in the jurisdiction of the FBI office in Cheyenne, Wyoming, so it was proper protocol for her to alert Agent Leo Dirkse of her presence in Cody and the reason for her coming to Cody. She had faxed him the report she had received. She had the report saved on her iPhone and had a hard copy in her attaché.

Was there a connection between the Valentine and Greenbrier cases? She'd been around enough of these types of situations that she didn't place much stock in coincidences. Nevertheless, there were too many coincidences to not conclude there was a connection. She still couldn't figure out what the connection was and that bothered her.

The airplane made a routine landing and taxied to the private plane area of Cody's Yellowstone Regional airport. Deplaning, she spotted a tall, gray-haired man in a dark suit standing next to a black, four-door Ford Taurus. Extending his hand, he said, "Janet, welcome to the home of Buffalo Bill Cody, although he didn't live her all that much. Thank goodness he spent quite a bit of time here, enough so the town could be named after him and the Historical Center located here. Was your flight o.k.?" Leo Dirkse was the agent-in-charge of the FBI's Cheyenne office. He had flown from Cheyenne to meet Janet.

"Leo, there's no better way to view the Rockies than to fly over them in a small plane, as long as the weather cooperates, that is. Thanks for meeting me. I don't relish this anymore than you probably do, but it has to be done, and the sooner the better. This has to be handled forcefully, yet delicately. I'll bring you up to speed while you drive. We can also talk about strategy on the way. A life may be on the line and we can't make any mistakes."

CHAPTER 58

Friday Afternoon
2:00 p.m.
Alongside Buffalo Bill Reservoir, Five Miles West of Cody, Wyoming

"Jessica is both a smart woman and a courageous one," said Beth. "When this is all over and I have a chance to talk with her, I'm going to ask her how she managed to drop that instruction brochure. I know I have one in my Explorer, but I have no idea where it might be. Thinking to leave such a good clue, under what I'm sure was extreme duress, was quite the feat. All I want now is for her to be safe and sound."

"You and me both," replied Parker, "especially since I'm the one that asked her to stake out the dormitory and watch for Vanessa. Somehow, something went wrong. You're right. Jess is smart and she would have been careful. Something happened. Thank goodness there wasn't any blood around where we found the brochure. That's a good sign." Hearing his iPhone beep, he quickly looked at the screen. "I've a text from whomever is in that plane following Jessica's Explorer. Her tracking device is working superbly." Handing his iPhone to Beth he continued, "Here, you read the text while I continue to drive."

When they began their drive from the Old Faithful area, Beth had called the Superintendent's office and secured one of Yellowstone's small airplanes to fly toward Cody with its tracking device turned on. She knew that the plane would be able to track the movement of Jessica's Explorer assuming the tracking device in Jessica's Explorer was turned on. Parker and she had been anxious to learn if the airplane had been able to lock-on to Jessica's tracking device. The airplane had texted her a few minutes ago that it had a lock on Jessica's tracking device and would be sending texts periodically to Beth's satellite phone regarding the movement of Vanessa and Jessica.

Taking his iPhone, she read the text. "The Explorer has exited the tunnels and is still headed toward Cody, so they're not very far ahead of us. You keep driving and I'll keep reading the texts as they come. I hope whomever is in that plane sending us this text realizes we need several texts a minute if we're going to find Jessica and Vanessa in Cody. Too bad we can't alert the local authorities, but we can't run the risk. How ironic. We're lay people trying to catch a criminal and hopefully, apprehend a killer, and local law enforcement isn't involved because we can't trust them. Something really wrong with this picture, don't you think? If we could trust them, we could have them lay down those strips with the spikes in them. If Vanessa drove over one, she would have to stop. However, we can't trust the local cops. Plus, there are all those other cars with innocent people on the highway. Hey, get this. Another text from our friends overhead. Jessica's Explorer is headed in the direction of the Law Enforcement Center." Laughing, she continued with sarcasm dripping from her voice, "My favorite place to hang out."

"The Law Enforcement Center," he responded in a surprised voice, "why would Vanessa go to where she could be arrested for kidnapping, assuming someone in the Center has enough smarts to see that Jessica isn't going along on her own volition with Vanessa? I know a quicker back way to the Center. We might even get there before Vanessa does."

Taking several turns onto various streets and passing on both the left and right sides of slower cars, he crested the hill where the Law Enforcement Center was located. "Looks like we're a few minutes too late," said Beth. Pointing to a National Park Service Explorer parked near the entrance to the Center, she continued, "I bet that's Jessica's Explorer. I can't see anyone inside it. It looks like Vanessa and Jessica are in the Center. This is really bizarre. A murderer walking into the Sheriff's office with a hostage. Go figure."

"I can't figure," answered Parker, just as his iPhone beeped indicating another text message had been received.

"It's from the plane telling us they're heading back to Mammoth Hot Springs and wishing us good luck," said Beth. "Remind me to have the Superintendent personally thank whomever is in that plane."

His iPhone beeped again. Beth began to read the text message. With a smirk on her face, she handed him the phone. "This is from your second girlfriend and boss. You need to read it. Things could get real interesting in a few minutes."

Taking his iPhone from her, he read the text. It was from Janet. "P. don't know where u r. Have breaking info. I'm head to Cody. Go to Sheriff office."

"Looks like we're going to have company in a few minutes," he said. "I wonder what the breaking information is which has her coming all the way from Billings. I better reply so she knows we're here too." He quickly typed a reply and sent it. Turning to Beth, he said in a direct manner, "I've three things to say to you. First, I'm going into the Center to find Jessica and confront Vanessa. Second, you're staying here. Third, cut the crap about girlfriends. Janet's my boss, temporary boss I should add, and that's it. Jessica is a nice person and that's as far as that goes too. Now, after I leave, lock the doors. If I'm still in there when Janet arrives, tell her what's going on and make it clear she is not to come barging in waving her FBI badge. Are we together on this?"

Reaching across to place her hand behind the far side of his face, she pulled his head close to her. Looking directly into his eyes and with a determined look on her face, she replied, "I hear you and I'll drop the girlfriend stuff. But, if you think I'm going to sit here and twiddle my thumbs while the man I care about than any other male on the face of the earth goes into that place by himself, you're loony tunes. Get this straight. I'm going in with you. Now, let's not debate this. Jessica needs our help, so let's get to it."

Before he could begin to reply, she opened the passenger door and exited the 4Runner. Realizing he had again been outmaneuvered, he exited on his side of the 4Runner, checking to make sure his 22-caliber gun was in the holster in the small of his back. Standing next to her, he said, "At least listen to me this one time. I've have the gun so please stay behind me. If Vanessa's going to start shooting, let's not give her two targets."

His ego is damaged and he needs some stroking, she thought to herself, so let him play protector and lead warrior. Under her breath, she bad-mouthed the bail judge that had stipulated she couldn't have her gun back. "O.k. Sir Galahad, I'm behind you. Lead on."

No one shouted for them to stop nor did they see anyone as they walked slowly toward the entrance and cautiously opened the door. The lobby was empty. The reception desk and counter were empty. Papers were scattered across both suggesting the receptionist had left quickly in the middle of working. Parker looked behind the counter. The computer screen had writing on it with the cursor blinking in the middle of a word in an unfinished sentence. An open purse was on the floor next to the empty chair. A Starbucks coffee was on the desk next to the computer. "Either the receptionist is in the potty," said Beth, "or she hightailed it out of here as fast as she could. Probably not her choice to leave. No woman I know leaves an open purse unless she hasn't had time to take it with her. I'll go check the restroom."

"Hold it," spat out Parker in a whisper, "you'll do nothing of the sort. She would have finished typing the sentence before leaving for the restroom. Vanessa's got her along with Jessica." As he was talking, he heard voices from the end of the hallway. "It sounds like they're in a room down the hallway. Let's see if we can't take them by surprise."

He reached behind his back and withdrew his handgun. Would he use it if Beth or he were threatened? Would Vanessa have a gun? She must, he concluded. How else could she hold Jessica hostage? Did Vanessa have her own gun or was she using Jessica's gun? He could hear his heart pounding in his ears as he slowly inched forward down the hallway toward where he heard the voices. As he moved toward a room at the end of the hall, the voices became increasingly loud. Everything then happened so fast that he was momentarily paralyzed. The voices became shouts. A woman and man both shouting. He heard the woman shout "you slimy, greasy pig," followed by two gunshots and a woman's scream. Oh no, please don't let it be Jess, he silently pleaded as he ran to the door of the room. Flinging open the door, he found himself staring at the barrel of a handgun pointed at his chest.

CHAPTER 59

Friday Afternoon
2:15 p.m.
Room 102, Park County Law Enforcement Center, Cody, Wyoming

Held around her chest by a woman he didn't recognize, but guessed to be Vanessa Cortez, was Jessica Samuels. Vanessa had a gun pointed at Jessica's head. Next to Jessica was another woman, dressed in a dark business suit, being held in a similar fashion by a man dressed in a blue oxford shirt and light yellow tie, also with a gun pointed at the woman's head. He didn't recognize the woman but he recognized Deputy Medina immediately. Summoning courage he didn't realize he had and speaking in the most authoritative voice as he could muster, Parker said, "I'm FBI agent Parker Williams and I'm ordering both of you to release those women and drop your guns. Additional FBI personnel are on the way so you won't be able to get away. Make it easy on yourselves and give it up. Deputy Medina, I don't know what you're doing, but the murderer of Michael Valentine is Vanessa Cortez, the woman holding Jessica Samuels. Take her into custody!

Medina responded in a sarcastic tone of voice, "My, my, look what we have here, Vanessa. Our make believe FBI agent ordering me around. Listen to me, Williams; I don't care if President Obama authorized you to be a boy scout or if Navy Seal Team 6 is on the way. If the Sheriff and the Yellowstone cop aren't going to die right here, along with you and some others before I'm done, I'd suggest you drop your gun and move aside before one of these lovely ladies gets hurt real badly. Besides, you've got it all wrong. The murderer of Valentine was already found and arrested. She's standing right behind you. Now, drop the gun."

Whispering in his ear, Beth said, "The woman he's holding is Sheriff Evenhouse."

As Parker was considering his next move, Sheriff Evenhouse said, "Wise up, Carlos. Your game's up. Give it up now and it will go much easier on you."

"Shut up, Marilyn. Why should I listen to anything you say? You've been a nagging pain in the ass and you've treated me like crap. Think you're so smart, don't you? You couldn't even see an elephant under your nose, that's how naïve you are. Sorry, but we're doing this my way. Now, we're all going to go outside and then Vanessa and I are going to take the Explorer and get out of here. If anyone tries to stop us, precious Marilyn will get it first and then our Yellowstone cop. Understand make believe FBI agent? Now everyone, move nice and slowly. If anyone tries to pull a fast one, they will have the Sheriff's blood on their conscience."

They moved slowly down the hall and out the entrance. "Stop," said Medina. Before anyone could respond, Beth stepped from behind Parker had walked slowly toward Jessica and Vanessa. "Hi, Jessica, and you too Vanessa. It's been a long time, Vanessa. I guess you're doing this because of me. Why don't you do what you want with me? Isn't it me you want to hurt? Jessica hasn't done anything so how about I exchange places with her? Take me. Let her go."

Beth was now standing only a few feet from Jessica. Parker wanted to yell "no, no". What was Beth trying to prove? Before he could say or do anything, Medina barked, "Go ahead, Vanessa, it makes no difference to me. Make up your mind and be quick about it. We need to high tail it out of here."

Pushing Jessica aside, Vanessa said to Beth, "You're right. It has been a long time. Too long. You've tormented me even since you stole the title away from me. I've waited a long time to get revenge. Now, I'm going to get it. I was hoping you'd spend your life in prison or even be executed, but since that isn't going to happen, I'm going to extract my own revenge." Keeping the gun pointed at Beth while she turned to Medina, she continued, "This is where we depart Carlos. You can play Mr. Tough-Guy with the FBI if you want, but former Miss Illinois and I are taking off. There's something I've wanted to tell you for some time and I guess this is as good a time as any. If you really want to know, I detest you. You're a small man with a small mind. After I blow this amateur hour, I'm going to find me a real man. Oh yes, you're also lousy in bed. I only pretended when you thought you were Mr. Macho Lover. As your unfortunate sidekick back in there told you, you are a greasy, slimy pig. You're a sad specimen of a neutered man that doesn't have the gonads to . . ."

Shouting over her, Medina replied in an almost hysterical voice, "I'll show you who has gonads, you two-bit, over-the-hill, washed-up beauty queen whore." Aiming the gun toward Jessica and Vanessa, it exploded in a single shot. Jessica and Vanessa both screamed. Vanessa slumped to the ground clutching her shoulder which quickly was covered in blood. She lay on the ground moaning. Jessica recovered quickly and picked up Vanessa's gun, pointing it toward Medina who still held Sheriff Evenhouse. "She needs to get to a hospital or she may bleed out," screamed Jessica. Beth quickly ran to the entrance where a pack of hand towels lay next to the door. A laundry service had recently dropped them by the door. Grabbing the pack of towels, she ripped open the pack. Bending down over Vanessa, she said to Jessica, "Push these as tightly as you can across her chest and around her arm. They should help to slow down the bleeding if you keep pressure on them. Let's help her sit up. That will help too." With Jessica's help, Beth and she were able to get Vanessa into a sitting position. As Vanessa moaned, Jessica kept pressing against the towels, which had become blood-stained.

"How touching," said Medina, in a sarcastic voice. "Now our beauty queen and Yellowstone cop are playing nurse." In an angry tone of voice, he continued, "Let her be. I was going to have to eliminate her anyway. I couldn't have her talking, now could I? I was getting tired of her too, just like I'm tired of talking with all you losers. You want to keep me here, don't you, until your FBI buddies show up. Sorry to disappoint you." Pointing at Beth with the gun, he continued, "Miss beauty queen, come here and make it snappy. As for you, Miss Yellowstone cop, you'd best drop the gun or our beloved Sheriff isn't going to be with us much longer."

"Beth, no," shouted Parker, "we can't trust him."

Looking at Parker for a fleeting second, Beth gave him a wink and a slight nodding of her head as she rose from kneeling by Vanessa and walked to Medina.

"Today's your lucky day, Marilyn," said Medina, as he pushed Marilyn Evenhouse away and grabbed Beth. "Sorry to say, but she's a whole lot better looking than you, Marilyn, and her body is certainly much better proportioned. For a red-blooded guy like me, what more could I ask for? Nothing personal, you understand, but I don't think Mr. half-baked FBI agent is as likely to try anything funny if she's with me rather than you. Bye-bye everyone. Oh yes, one last thing. Marilyn, you may want to check Ann. She tried to play tackle football and ended up taking a bullet to her leg. Don't worry, I checked her myself. Only a flesh wound. I told her to hold my handkerchief tightly against the wound. See what a nice guy I am? I'm sure she's in some pain, so I suggest someone check on her after the beauty queen and I are gone." Pulling Beth with him, he pushed her toward and into the Explorer. Following her into the driver's seat, he started the engine and drove from parking lot just as a black, four-door Ford Taurus drove past it toward the entrance.

CHAPTER 60

Friday Afternoon
2:10 p.m.
Parking Lot, Park County Law Enforcement Center, Cody, Wyoming

Janet had spent most of their drive from the airport going over the Valentine case with Leo Dirkse and listening to his take on what Ryan Belgrade had told Janet which, together with the report she had showed Leo, had launched her on this trip to Cody and her contacting Leo in the first place. He had reacted like she suspected a veteran agent would, especially one seeing retirement on the near horizon and not wanting to mess it up. He felt she didn't have proof other than the words of a person charged with murder. Truthfully, he had confided, if he were twenty years younger and not nearing retirement, he too would be doing what Janet was doing. As it was, he said he wouldn't be the one to do the confronting. In fact, he would stay behind in the car while Janet did the heavy lifting. If something popped, he would be ready to assist, but he wasn't volunteering to do anything.

"I understand fully, Leo," said Janet. "No sense risking being dinged by the mukkity-mucks just before retirement."

"Thanks for understanding my situation," Leo replied. "If this works out well, I hope you'll put a plug in for me when you do your report. It wouldn't hurt to have a positive statement from a fellow agent to keep the eggheads in D.C. off my back for my final few months."

"You've got a deal, Leo. How much longer before we get there?"

"Only a few minutes," he replied. Just then Janet's iPhone beeped indicating she had received a text message. Accessing it, she read it and then said, "Parker's at the Law Enforcement Center and is going in. He says Vanessa Cortez is there and has Jessica Samuels as a hostage."

"A hostage situation," exclaimed Leo in a voice a few levels higher than normal. "This changes everything. I need to call in our Hostage Recovery and SWAT teams."

Responding as calmly as she could, Janet said," Leo, a minute ago you said you didn't want any part of this scene except to get credit when it worked out for the good. Now you want to escalate a possible . . . we don't know for sure . . . hostage situation into a full blown circus. You'll have every media person within fifty miles of here falling all over each other and asking stupid questions. What if it goes bad? What if Jessica Samuels really is a hostage? She's a Yellowstone law enforcement officer and, heaven forbid, what if she gets killed? If that were to happen, the media will crucify you and you can kiss most of that retirement pension goodbye. Instead of cashing your retirement checks and playing golf, you'll be cashing food stamps and playing solitaire in Nome, Alaska."

She could see the wheels spinning in Leo's head. Leo turned to her and said, "Have it your way. But, if this goes bad, it's your ass that's going to be fried, not mine."

"That's a nice way to put it, Leo," she responded. "You're right. If this goes badly, my career is shot. But, I'm willing to take the risk. As for you, you've made a smart decision. You can always call in the troops if necessary, but I wouldn't rush into doing it. When we get there, I'm going to go inside and hopefully work things out without anyone getting hurt. Keep your phone on and I'll text you to let you know the score."

As they drove into the parking lot of the Law Enforcement Center, a National Park Service Explorer sped past. She didn't have time to tell Leo to follow it before she blinked her eyes to make sure she was really seeing what she thought she was seeing. In front of the entrance was a scene she hadn't expected. Was this for real?

CHAPTER 61

Friday Afternoon
2:15 p.m.
Outside the Entrance of the Park County Law Enforcement Center, Cody,
Wyoming

Janet blinked her eyes and looked again at the scene in front of her as she jumped from the car. Jessica Samuels was kneeling on the ground helping a woman that had obviously been shot. Marilyn Evenhouse was running into the Center shouting that she was going to call for two ambulances. Parker Williams was running toward his 4Runner with a gun in his hand. "Parker, Parker," she shouted, "what happened?"

Shouting in return, Parker said," Too much to tell you now. Medina has Beth. I'm going after them. Jessica can fill you in. Someone inside is hurt. I'll text you when I can." Before Janet could tell him to stop, the 4Runner sped from the parking lot.

"Leo," she shouted, motioning him to join her. "You wanted to get credit for one more take down. Here's your chance. This is your territory, so you'll get all the credit for neutralizing a hostage situation and helping to solve two murders. I'm going to take your car and you're going to stay here and take charge. I suggest you get paramedics and ambulances here a.s.a.p., then alert local and state police to be on the lookout for a National Park Explorer with a man and woman inside. Make sure you tell them this is a hostage situation and the man has a gun. Have them set roadblocks on all major roads out of Cody. Get statements from Jessica Samuels, the Yellowstone Park law enforcement officer assisting the woman that has been shot, and Sheriff Evenhouse. She's inside where there's also someone that's hurt. Get some of your agents to tape off the entire area and keep the media at bay. You'll want to be the person talking to the media. Give yourself and your office all the credit. Call or text me when you can. I'm off."

Returning to Leo's car, she drove from parking lot. Where had Parker gone? That fool. What did he think he was doing running off by himself with no backup? Stopping at the side of the road, she sent two texts, one to her office requesting a helicopter be dispatched to Cody and the other to Parker. "I'm behind you. Where are you? Are you following Explorer?" Would he, could he answer her text? If he didn't, she wouldn't know where to go. Cody wasn't a large town, but big enough when you didn't know your way around. Her experience told her Medina would make a run for it away from Cody. If he did, the roadblocks should get him. There were four major highways in and out of Cody, one from each direction. He probably wouldn't head west since that would bring him into Yellowstone with its limited roads and easy places to establish roadblocks. Also, Beth Richardson would be known to most Yellowstone employees that would be on the lookout for her once the word spread she was a hostage. No, not into Yellowstone. Either east or north, she concluded. Her iPhone rang. The caller ID showed Cheyenne FBI office. "Hello, this is Janet."

"Janet, it's Leo. Things are under control here. Both shooting victims are on the way to the hospital. The paramedics said they both will make it. The victim in the Center was an assistant deputy named Ann Vogelzang. Deputy Medina, the guy we came to confront, shot her as well as Vanessa Cortez. He's the guy that has the hostage, a Park official named Beth Richardson. He took a National Park Service Ford Explorer. The Explorer is used by Jessica Samuels, a Yellowstone law enforcement officer, whom the paramedics say helped save Vanessa's life. I got all this from her and Marilyn Evenhouse. I'm going to talk with them some more after our conversation. The Cody police, Park County Sheriff Patrol, and both the Wyoming and Montana State Police have been alerted and are establishing roadblocks as we speak. It's only a matter of time until we find this Medina character. I hope we're not too late for Beth Richardson's sake."

"Good work, Leo. I'm hoping to hear from Parker Williams momentarily. If and when I hear more, I'll let you know. How's the media treating you?"

"I thought over what you said and I've decided to have Marilyn join me when I talk with the media in a few minutes. Jessica Samuels too. There's more than enough credit for everyone and they certainly deserve it."

"I like that, Leo. You're doing the right thing. Tell Marilyn and Jessica to please not mention my name. Not Parker Williams either. Only you should be seen as the presence of the FBI. Hope to see you soon with Medina in tow."

CHAPTER 62

Friday Afternoon
2:45 p.m.
Behind the Number 4 Green, Olive Glenn Golf and Country Club,
Cody, Wyoming

"How long do you believe you can stay here before the FBI or your friends in the Sheriff's Department figure out you didn't leave Cody? You've been around the Sheriff's office long enough to know there are probably roadblocks already in place on every road out of Cody," said Beth. "Sooner or later they're going to conclude you stayed in Cody. Then it will only be a matter of time until they come to this place."

"Shut up. I don't want to tell you again. I don't need you telling me what I already know. You've overlooked the most important reason I'm going to get out of this," replied Medina. "You. You're my insurance policy. As long as I have you, no one is going to stop me. I'm going to ditch this Explorer and get another car, and then we're going to make tracks. So, just shut up and let me think."

Beth knew he was correct. As long as she remained with him, no one would force him to give up for fear he would harm her, possibly even kill her. She hoped Vanessa was o.k. and also Ann Vogelzang. Medina had told her how he shot Vogelzang when she tried to tackle him after Vanessa had come into the Law Enforcement Center with Jessica and told Medina they had to leave immediately. For sure, both Vanessa and Vogelzang were to a hospital by now. She wondered what Parker was doing. It would be just like him to throw all caution and concern for his own safety aside in an all-out personal effort to free her. When this was all over, she vowed to tell him she wanted to know if he had the same strong feelings about her as she did about him and, if he did, there was no more keeping their feelings and emotions at arm's length. First, she had to free herself from Medina before Parker, or anyone else for that matter, tried to free her. Medina wasn't going to give up without a fight and that meant people would be hurt, possibly killed.

Medina had driven directly to a large equipment shed on the golf course. He obviously knew about it. It had vacant space to accommodate a vehicle as large as the Explorer. She hated to admit it, but he was correct in thinking it would be awhile before anyone thought to check an equipment shed on a golf course for a fugitive with a hostage What worried her the most was the more time Medina had to think, the greater the possibility he would decide to make a run for it without her. He would soon realize, if he hadn't already, that Parker and the others would be looking for a man and woman and might overlook only a man, especially if he was in a car other than the Explorer. Plus, Medina might decide he could make a faster get-away without someone else slowing him down. Once he realized and thought about both of these possibilities, he wouldn't hesitate to kill her or hurt her enough where she'd be unconscious and unable to get away herself. She had to free herself. She needed to distract him and get the gun away from him. She looked around the shed for the umpteenth time, trying to identify something she could use to disarm him and immobilize him. Something to hit him solidly over the head would do nicely. Funny, she thought, as she again saw the mattress in the corner of the shed. Why a mattress among the lawn mowers, weed-wackers, law tools, and numerous hoses?

"I see you're looking at the mattress. Wonder why it's there? You don't think this is the first time I've used this shed, do you? Come on, how would I know about it if I hadn't been here before? This place is an equipment shed during the day and my love-nest during the evening and night. I provide some happy pills to the grounds workers and they allow me to use this place during the evening and overnight if I want to. Vanessa and I used it often. Several other women have been here as well. If Marilyn was better looking and Ann had a pair of headlights like you, I would have treated them to the thrill of their lives. Maybe I'll let you experience a thrill before we leave."

That's it. Medina used this shed for his trysts with women. She felt her heart pound and sweat begin to form as she thought about Medina forcing her to have sex.

"The more I think about it, the more I like what I'm thinking," he said. "Why not enjoy our time together, limited as it's going to be? You'd be pleasantly surprised by my ability to bring ultimate pleasure to a woman. Contrary to what Vanessa said, she enjoyed every minute with me."

Incredible, she thought. At a time like this, how could this slob be thinking about sex? As she shuddered inwardly at the thought of him forcing himself on her, an idea began to form in her mind. Yes, if that was the only way to be able to disarm him, she would have to think about making him believe she was interested.

"You know," said Medina, "Valentine was a scumbag. He destroyed a whole lot of folk. In particular, he hurt my friend's daughter badly and caused a whole lot of anguish for her and my friend. Somehow, Valentine found out about my little drug distribution setup and started to blackmail me. He thought he could continue to blackmail me. I had to make him stop. I asked him nicely to stop and he just laughed. I even introduced him to Vanessa and she tried to get him to stop. He used her for sex but then told me he would be doubling the amount of money I had to pay him. That was the last straw. When Vanessa told me about her desire to take you down and that Valentine had been a judge in your pageant, two and two came together. Pretty ingenious of me, don't you think, to kill Valentine and make it look like you did it? Nothing personal, you understand."

This isn't good, thought Beth. He's confessing to me which means he wants to unload on me since he has decided to kill me and I won't be able to repeat his confession to anyone should he be caught. I've got to act quickly, she decided. To act, I need to divert his attention long enough to reach under the seat. Keep him talking. He won't kill me as long as he's talking. "What about Becky Greenbrier. Why was she killed?"

"Vanessa learned from some Yellowstone employees that Becky was very jealous of you and resented your being given your position instead of her. She believed she deserved the position and you used sex to get it for yourself." With a lustful look and lurid tone of voice he continued, "Looking you over, I can sure see how you could use sex to get what you wanted. I'll admit I'm thinking I might like to sample the goods. Reaching across and placing his hand on her breast, he continued, "I'm wondering if these are really all yours or if you've been helped out with some enhancements?"

What a creep, she thought. Resisting the impulse to push his hand away, she realized this was her opportunity. I can divert him. All I need is a few seconds. How I hate this, she thought to herself. I'm lowering myself to his level, but I've got to do it. With as sexy a voice as she could muster, she responded, "Vanessa is a beautiful woman but she lacked two things which I have and she wished she had. I beat her fair and square because I'm all real and she isn't. I'll prove it to you. You can see for yourself I've had no help. It's all me."

Before he could object or think of something to say, she opened the passenger door. "Hey," shouted Medina, "what do you think you're doing?"

"I thought you said you wanted to sample the goods. I'm willing, but not in this cramped front seat. I guess if that mattress is good enough for Vanessa, it's good enough for me, but only if you sweep it to make sure there aren't bugs on it. Go sweep it and I'll join you as soon as you finish." She unbuttoned her blouse and shrugged it off, leaving her dressed in only her bra. "Now hurry," she continued, "before I change my mind."

She thought Medina's eyes might pop out his head. Staring at her bra, he mumbled, "I guess I'm about to find out if you were kidding about being all you." He opened the driver's door and almost ran to where a broom was leaning against the wall near the mattress. "Please, Jessica, Beth whispered to herself, "please don't have removed it."

CHAPTER 63

Friday Afternoon
4:00 p.m.
Lobby of the West Park Hospital, Cody, Wyoming

He was distraught with worry and frustrated with the lack of information. Where was Beth? Had Medina hurt her or possibly killed her? Why hadn't the Explorer been spotted? He had come to the hospital to check on the status of Vanessa Cortez and Ann Vogelzang. Not surprising, Marilyn Evenhouse was in Ann Vogelzang's room keeping vigil. She had greeted Parker warmly and apologized for accepting Medina's advice and rushing to judgment about Beth's guilt. Ann Vogelzang would shortly be receiving a sleeping drug which would place her into unconsciousness for several hours. Jessica was keeping a similar vigil in Vanessa's room. When Vanessa's condition was more stable, she would be placed under arrest and charged with being an accomplice in the murder of Michael Valentine and possibly also Becky Greenbrier.

"She's asleep," said Marilyn, as she sat in the chair next to Parker. "The doc told me she's out of the woods but it will be several days before the damage to the nerves and muscles in her shoulder and upper arm can be determined. She may never be able to resume her duties if she can't fully function with a damaged shoulder or arm. I feel so responsible," she sobbed as tears streamed down her cheeks. "I continued to believe Medina even after Ann told me she felt there were too many unanswered questions. What a fool I was. I need to resign. The people of Park County need a Sheriff that isn't misled so easily and so headstrong to boot."

"Marilyn, please don't do that. You have a distinguished track record and no one will blame you for the actions of a deranged man. You acted properly on the evidence before you. Beth could produce no verification of her alibi and you had the hair sample along with the shoeprints and button with Beth's fingerprint on it. The election for Sheriff is more than one year away. Let the voters decide if you should continue."

His iPhone rang. The caller ID showed the call was from Janet. "Janet, do you have him? Is Beth safe?"

"I'm sorry, Parker, we haven't found him yet, but we will. I'm beginning to think he hasn't left Cody. The roadblocks have turned up nothing and the Explorer hasn't been found either. I'm thinking the Explorer is in a metal building or somewhere the tracking device can't detect the signal. He may have abandoned the Explorer in a metal building and now has another vehicle. Leo's going to keep the roadblocks for awhile, but I bet they don't result in anything other than some kids with booze or pot in their cars."

"I know you and Leo are doing all you can," replied Parker, "but we have to find him soon," the concern evident in his voice. "Beth could be hurt. She may need medical attention. We've got to find her."

"I know, I know," responded Janet, in as compassionate a voice as she could muster. "We're not going to let up until we get him and her too. Do you know how Ann and Vanessa are doing?"

"I'm here at the hospital with Jessica and Marilyn. Ann and Vanessa are no longer critical. Both will make it. Leo has been here monitoring their progress and keeping tabs on the search."

"Thank God," replied Janet, "they're going to be o.k. Tell you what. Talk to Marilyn. Maybe she has some ideas where Medina might hole up in Cody or where he might hide the Explorer. Let me know if she suggests some places to look."

"Good idea. Marilyn is here with me. Please, Janet, let me know as soon as you learn or hear anything."

"Will do. We're going to find Medina and Beth. You can go to the bank on it. I'll be in touch."

Turning to face Marilyn Evenhouse, he said, "Do you know of places where Medina might go in Cody to hole up or hide the Explorer? The roadblocks have turned up nothing, so Janet thinks he may have never left Cody and is waiting for things to quiet down before he makes a run for it."

"I know this is going to sound funny," she answered, "but I really don't know much about Carlos. He did his job, fairly well I might add. He kept to himself most of the time and didn't socialize with the other employees with the exception of trying to socialize with Ann. It was more like trying to get her into the sack if you ask me. I could tell he wanted her to be more than just his partner on the job, if you get my drift. I think he had a kind of macho attitude toward women, especially women he found attractive or sexy. Ann is certainly attractive and can, at times, come across as sexy. Other than these observations, I can't think of anything else which might help us discover where he's hiding."

"Besides his interest in Ann, did he date anyone or spend time with a woman?"

"There were rumors about his womanizing, but nothing concrete, at least not that I know of. He never mentioned dating or spending time with a particular woman."

"How about male friends?"

"Like I said, he didn't socialize or mingle with other employees, men included. The only time I heard him mention a man was when he said he played golf with some guy."

"Did he do anything else besides playing golf when he wasn't working?"

"He never mentioned or talked about anything around the office, so I really don't know. He showed up for his shifts on time, performed his job, and left after his shift was over. If I needed him for extra hours or for a special assignment, he almost always did them without complaining. Seems like a model deputy, doesn't he? Did he ever pull one over on me."

"You're far from alone, I'm afraid. He misled a whole bunch of people. He's a killer dressed in a Deputy Sheriff's clothes. One last thing and then you'll probably want to check on Ann. Do you know if Medina had a favorite restaurant or bar in town? If he had, maybe someone there may know something to help us find him."

"I think he watched his alcohol intake, so a favorite bar might not exist. I do know he often ate at the Rib and Steak Grill. He especially liked its baseball cut of sirloin steak."

Marilyn and he shook hands and then she left to return to Ann Vogelzang's hospital room. He walked to his 4Runner, drove toward downtown, and parked in front of the Rib and Steak Grill. He needed to do something. The lack of progress in finding Beth was really getting to him and his frustration level with himself for not being smart enough to figure out Medina's actions was intensifying. He needed a break and he was going to discover that break, come hell or high water. Entering the Rib and Steak Grill, he flashed his FBI identification and asked for the

253

manager. In a few minutes, a smallish woman wearing a light blue western blouse, tight-fitting jeans, boots, and a pink scarf walked up to him and extended her hand. Shaking her hand, he noticed a large gold ring on her finger and two smaller gold rings on other fingers. "I'm Sherrie Carlson, the manager. It isn't every night we are visited by the FBI. I hope we're not in trouble."

"You're not in any trouble that I know about," replied Parker. "I'm hoping you can help me locate one of your regular customers. Perhaps there's someplace we can go for a few minutes away from the noise and activity."

"My office will work," she responded. "We'll have privacy." He followed her through the restaurant noting that the overwhelming choice of the customers was steak with a baked potato. The smell was wonderful and made him realize he hadn't eaten for some time. His thoughts immediately went to Beth. Had she eaten anything since leaving his home? If not, she had to be hungry too. He promised himself he would take her to any restaurant she wanted and she could order whatever she wanted, price being no object.

"Please, ah, I'm sorry, I haven't even asked you your name," Sherrie Carlson said as she indicated he should sit in a chair in front of her desk.

"Parker Williams and please call me Parker. I trust it's o.k. to call you Sherrie."

"Certainly o.k. with me," she replied. "How can I help you?"

"I understand Deputy Sheriff Carlos Medina frequents the restaurant quite often. I'm trying to locate him. I'm wondering if he mentioned to you, or any of your wait staff, places where he liked to hangout or spend time."

"I know Deputy Medina. He was, and I emphasize was, a regular customer for quite some time but he isn't welcome here anymore. He made one too many suggestive comments to a couple of my women wait staff and touched them in inappropriate places, if you get my point. I haven't told anyone about any of this before now because I didn't want to be blackballed by the Sheriff's department."

Parker responded, "So, Medina acted inappropriately toward some of your wait staff. That would be enough, I grant you, to keep him away. Besides his inappropriate behavior, is there anything else you can think of which might provide some indication where he might hole up to get away by himself?"

"One of my women wait staff told me he told her he knew a place, where he played golf, where she and he could go and be alone with nobody bothering them. He told her he would pay her well to party with him, his choice of words, not mine I should add. As far as I was concerned, that was the straw which broke the camel's back. This woman is a single mom working two jobs to make ends meet and take care of her child and herself and that slob Medina treated her as if she was a whore."

"Sherri, I need you to be as accurate as you can be in remembering, as best you can, where Medina said this place was located. It may be the clue I need to find him."

"Let's not trust my memory," replied Sherri. "Amy is working tonight. She's the woman he propositioned. Let's have her tell you what she remembers." She left him sitting in her office for only a few minutes before she returned with a tall brunette woman, probably in her early 30s, with green eyes and a soft, almost glowing complexion. Not a striking beauty, but certainly more attractive than not. She was wearing a white blouse and black skirt partially covered by a white apron with Rib and Steak Grill stitched across the top. She said, "Parker, please meet Amy Wiseman. Amy, this is Parker Williams with the FBI."

Shaking hands, Parker took the lead. "Amy, Sherri has told me about your unfortunate episode with Deputy Sheriff Carlos Medina and his inappropriate suggestions and behavior. Please know everything you tell me will remain absolutely confidential. I don't mean to embarrass you, but I need you to tell me, as fully and accurately as you can remember, precisely what he said to you the times he propositioned you."

"I'll try my best to remember," she responded. "Over the past six months or so, he had been flirtatious with me and made comments about how nice I looked, what a great figure I had, how I could make a whole lot of money practicing the oldest profession in the world, stuff like that. I didn't think too much about it, to tell you the truth. I'm kind of used to men trying to flirt with me, looking me over, winking, and those sorts of things. I didn't bother to tell Sherri about those kinds of things because I didn't want to cause trouble. Besides, I usually get very good tips from men that do those sorts of things, so I overlook their harmless looks and words. Of all the men, I have to say that Deputy Medina was the most persistent and aggressive. I didn't like the way he would stare at my chest and then smile and wink at me. So when he offered to pay me to have sex, I thought I better tell Sherri. He hasn't been back since and I don't miss him."

"Amy, again, I'm sorry you have to relive this situation, but I need to know exactly his words, as you recall them, when he propositioned you," replied Parker in as non-accusatory voice as he could muster.

"He told me he knew a place, where he played golf, where we could be alone without anyone knowing we were there. He said he would pay me well to party there with him. He said I would enjoy every minute of it. I wasn't very nice to him, but I was angry at him for thinking I would throw away my values and morals for money." She blushed as she continued, "I told him, if he was in such a great need, to go play with himself."

"Amy, you've been most helpful," replied Parker. "I assure you all you've told me will be held in strictest confidence." Turning to Sherri, he continued, "Thank you for letting me barge in on you and take you and Amy away from your busy work. Hopefully, I'll be able to return in the near future and enjoy one of those baseball cut sirloin steaks." Shaking their hands and thanking them again, he walked from the restaurant to his 4Runner. Taking his iPhone, he found Janet's number and pushed the call icon. After three rings, Janet answered.

"We're still looking, Parker," said Janet, "all our leads have fizzled. He can't hold out forever. Do you have anything for the good-of-the-cause?"

"I might, but it's too early to tell for sure. I need to checkout a couple of things and then I'll let you know."

"Hold on, buster," she replied in a stern voice. "If you have something, I want to know about it. This guy is armed and dangerous and you're not to do anything that might put you or Beth Richardson at risk. Now, what is it?"

"Sorry, Janet, fire me if you wish. I promise I'll tell you after I checkout some things. I'll keep in touch." Before she could respond, he ended the call.

CHAPTER 64

Friday Afternoon
4:15 p.m.
Olive Glenn Golf and Country Club, Cody, Wyoming

The only golf course in Cody was the Olive Glenn Golf and Country Club. It was located only a few blocks from the Law Enforcement Center. Could it be that Medina hadn't gone but a few blocks and was laughing about the roadblocks and the various law enforcement agencies running helter-skelter like chickens with their heads cut off trying to locate him?

Parker drove down the driveway which led to the main building of the club. The parking lot was about one-third full indicating some golfers were probably having dinner, after finishing their rounds of golf, along with some non-golfers that had chosen to have dinner that evening at the club. He drove slowly up and down each lane between the rows of parked cars looking for Jessica's Explorer. It wasn't here. Had Medina managed to abandon the Explorer along one of the residential streets bordering the club and stolen another vehicle from one of the homes? If he had, was that car now parked among these cars? Maybe Medina hadn't come to the club at all? Parker could be on a wild goose chase.

Since Parker didn't have any other ideas to pursue, he decided to stick with checking the buildings of the club. Where to begin? Medina had propositioned Amy about being with him where they could be alone. That meant a place with privacy. Away from where golfers and other users of the Club's facilities would be. That would rule out the pool area, locker rooms, and eating areas. All those places lacked privacy. If Medina and Beth were here, they would probably be in a meeting room of some type which wasn't in use. What other places existed for them to hide out? Would they be parked somewhere on the golf course? Perhaps in or hidden by a grove of trees?

Even if he felt privacy was important for Medina and Beth to be hiding, he thought he best look around those areas which were more public. He wouldn't put it past Medina to be in plain view, with his gun hidden but pointed toward Beth, looking like a couple passing time together at the club. Best to check out all the places, in and around the buildings, before venturing from them and onto the grounds.

He made sure his gun was securely in its holster in the small of his back. Entering the primary sitting area of the main building, he slowly scanned the area. No Medina; no Beth. He asked two couples, sitting on opposite ends of the room, if they had seen a woman dressed in a National Park Service uniform accompanied by a short, heavy-set Hispanic man. Neither couple had seen anyone resembling either Beth or Medina. He next entered the restaurant. Same result. As he was about to begin to check the various meeting rooms, his iPhone rang. The caller I'd. showed the call was from Janet VanKampen. "Hello, Janet, what's up?"

"You tell me," she replied in a sharp tone of voice. "Where are you? I don't want you going after Medina on your own. I'm pulling your authorization. Now, tell me where you are so we can have some Cody police officers take over."

"Janet, since you've just fired me, I don't have to listen to you. I appreciate your concern and your offer of help, but no thanks. A show of force by gun-toting cops could easily set off Medina. I can't risk that happening, not as long as he has Beth. Besides, I'm not even sure Medina and Beth are where I think they are."

"Parker, you can be so exasperating! Medina isn't going to give up easily. We've learned enough in the past hour to convict him of killing Becky Greenbrier, running a drug distribution operation, and being an accomplice to stealing cash from the National Park Service. We found sucostrin in a locker he used at the Cody Recreational Center along with several pounds of cocaine. We found a listing of payments Becky Greenbrier had made to Medina in exchange for Medina not blowing the whistle on Becky's entrance fee skimming scheme. Medina knows he is going away for a long time, maybe even to death row if he gives up, so he's not going to do that. He's extremely dangerous and you shouldn't give it any thought to trying to apprehend him yourself."

"Janet, I'm not going to do anything stupid. I'm also not going to allow this madman to hurt Beth or anyone else for that matter. I promise

I'll contact you if I feel I need help." He ended the call before Janet could respond.

The meeting and conference rooms were across the hall from the restaurant. He realized he'd be a sitting duck when he first entered each room should Medina be waiting for anyone to enter the room. He'd have to take that chance. There was no other option. Reaching behind his back, he withdrew the gun from its holster. He placed himself tightly against the wall as he opened the first meeting room door. Stealing a look around the corner of the door into the room, he saw it was empty. He felt the adrenalin subside resulting in a tired and somewhat depressed feeling. No letup. See this through to the end. No turning back, not while Beth's life might be hanging in the balance. Repeating his entry into the first meeting room, he entered the other meeting rooms and the conference room. Same result. No Medina; no Beth.

He exited the building and headed for the building housing the golf pro shop and the locker rooms. His iPhone rang as he neared the building. The caller I'd. showed no name but the telephone number had a local area code. He didn't need to be talking with a solicitor or hear some recorded political statement about a forthcoming school board election. He wouldn't bother answering. Let it go to voice mail. If the caller left a message, he'd listen to it later. No sooner had he decided to not answer the call than his phone rang again. This time, the caller ID showed Janet VanKampen. Maybe Medina and Beth had been found. He answered. "Janet, I hope you're calling to tell me you've got Medina. Is Beth safe?"

"I wish I could tell you both of those things. What I am going to tell you is that we just tracked down Medina's drug supplier. A two-time loser that works out of Casper. The drugs come in on a private airplane from Logan, Utah. Yea, I know, Mormon country, so go figure. Anyway, this loser told us Medina mentioned once that he first stored the stuff in a shed before moving it to the locker in the Rec. Center. Unfortunately, he didn't know what type of shed or its location. If we find where Medina stashed the drugs, we also may find Beth. Is this what you're doing too, checking storage sheds?"

"No, I'm not, Janet, but you should keep at it. I told you already, I'm not sure what I'm doing is going anywhere, so you should continue to follow any and all leads. The main thing is finding Medina and Beth as soon as possible."

"Are you going to tell me where you are and what you're doing?"

"Janet, please. I'm not sure about anything right now and I'm worried sick about Beth. I hope you understand why I'm not sharing with you what you are asking me to tell you."

"Let me try one more time," she responded, "this time with good news. Beth is entirely off the hook. The wolf research team at Yellowstone had leased time on a satellite which took pictures, even at night using heat-seeking thermal technology, of the Slough Creek wolf pack. I guess one part of the research program is to keep tabs on the wolves at night. See if they spend the entire night in the den or leave it now and then. Anyway, last Sunday evening, the satellite took pictures which showed a human body in a sleeping bag near Soda Butte Creek. Enhancement of the photos clearly shows a National Park Service sleeping bag with a person inside. Also, expanding the photos to wider shots shows a National Park Service Explorer parked nearby. Reversing the focus to a small one and zooming in on the license plate shows the license plate number of Beth's Explorer. She was camped where she said she was Sunday evening. According to the guy that called me to tell me all this, Beth had called him and instructed him to only tell her if there were or were not satellite pictures of the Slough Creek Campground and Soda Butte Creek area. He said he called back, not to her office and not to her cell phone either . . . he didn't remember the number he called . . . and told some guy, that refused to identify himself, that several photos existed. This guy asked him to describe the photos, which he did. This guy then told him to e-mail the photos to Beth's office and not to anyone else. Apparently, the research fellow said he knew about Beth's arrest and the more he thought about the photos, he realized the photos would help support her innocence, so he decided to send them. Thank goodness he did."

"That is good news, even if it comes somewhat late in the game. There's going to be egg in some faces over this one. Marilyn told me she thinks she should resign. I tried to talk her out of it. If this information about the satellite photos became public, she'd be crucified. I hope you can keep them confidential. They aren't necessary now that we know Medina is the killer."

"I'll certainly try, but there are no guarantees in this business. E-mails have a habit of being forwarded or distributed all over the place."

"Thanks, Janet, for telling me. Please let me know the minute you find Medina. I'll do likewise." He ended the call before she could begin to argue with him again about where he was or what he was doing. No sense getting them both upset. He wasn't going to change his mind nor was she.

One thing Janet had said had him thinking. Janet had said Medina used a shed to temporarily store drugs, but the type and location of the shed wasn't known. Janet was checking storage sheds. What if it wasn't a storage shed Medina used, rather another type of shed?

CHAPTER 65

Friday Afternoon
5:00 p.m.
Room 327, West Park Hospital, Cody, Wyoming

Vanessa Cortez was resting comfortably and was in a talking mood. Marilyn Evenhouse had brought in a recorder. She wanted to capture Vanessa's words in case she tried to alter her story down the road. Lieutenant Angie Hernandez sat in a corner of the room. She was there as a witness in case Vanessa later claimed to be abused or coerced into talking. Vanessa had already been read her Miranda rights and she had waived her right for an attorney to be present. The doctors had said no more than fifteen minutes and then the session had to end. If Vanessa had a good night's rest and there were no complications, she could be interviewed for thirty minutes in the morning. Marilyn Evenhouse didn't want to waste any of the next fifteen minutes so she skipped the preliminaries and got right to the meat of the matter.

"Vanessa, what is your relationship with Carlos Medina?"

"Carlos and I first met in the bar area of the Erma Hotel. I was looking for work in Yellowstone so I could learn as much as I could about the habits of Beth Richardson. I spent hours outside her apartment and the administration building at Mammoth Hot Springs watching her. I wanted to determine her habits. The only reason I came to this out of the way place was to get revenge for what she did to me. I must admit I never thought it would work out this way. Carlos is going to kill her before any of you find him, so he's going to extract my revenge for me."

"So, you met Medina in Cody one night," replied Marilyn Evenhouse. "How did you and he end up planning to kill Michael Valentine and Becky Greenbrier?"

"Do I have to spell it out for you, Sheriff? He had access to drugs; I was lonely and wanting someone to help me get to Richardson; he seemed to be highly sexed; you can complete the picture I'm sure. During one night's party, as he called our sex and drug-filled times together, I told him about my desire to get revenge on Richardson. He told me how he wanted to kill Valentine. I couldn't believe it was the same Michael Valentine as the Michael Valentine that was a judge for the Miss Illinois Pageant in which Richardson and I were contestants. That bitch Richardson used sex to get Valentine to vote for her, you know. Otherwise, he would have voted for me and I would have been Miss Illinois and on to stardom."

"Carlos and you put together the plan to kill Valentine," responded Marilyn. "What about Becky Greenbrier?"

"Killing Becky was never part of the plan. She hated Richardson almost as much as me, so it was easy to get her to obtain some of Richardson's hair, a button from her jacket, and a pair of her discarded shoes. They lived quite close to each other, you know, and they worked fairly closely to each other as well, so it wasn't too hard for Becky to pull it off. She took some of Beth's hair from a hairbrush which Beth used when she touched up her hair in the women's restroom. Women working in the administration building kept hair brushes in the restroom. The button was clipped from Beth's uniform jacket after she hung it on a coat rack in the Mammoth Hot Springs cafeteria. The fingerprint was a gift. I'm not sure how Becky got one of Beth's hiking shoes. Anyway, Carlos found out about Becky's scheme of taking cash from Yellowstone entrance fees and used it against her. He probably forced her to have sex along with blackmailing her for money. Becky became too squirrely when Richardson was released on bail. She was on the verge of breaking down and spilling everything. Carlos decided to eliminate her, as he called it. Murder I call it."

A nurse had entered the room as Vanessa was finishing her answer. "Sheriff Evenhouse, you'll have to end now. Doctor Parson's orders."

"One more question and I'll go," replied Marilyn. Before the nurse could object, Marilyn asked Vanessa, "Where might Deputy Medina have taken Beth Richardson?"

"Most likely the same place he took me and the other women he seduced," responded Vanessa, in a sarcastic tone of voice, "to his hide-a-way on the golf course. Real romantic, huh? He loved to brag about all his conquests, as he called his trysts with women. But, I'm sure you're too late. He has killed Richardson by now and is long gone."

CHAPTER 66

Friday Afternoon
4: 45 p.m.
Olive Green Golf and Country Club, Cody, Wyoming

Medina and Beth were not in the main building, golf pro shop, or locker rooms. If they were here at all, it had to be somewhere else. But where? Sitting in his 4Runner, he felt terrible. He not only had let Beth down, he was allowing a killer to make a fool of him. What ate at him the most was not knowing if Beth was alive or not, or if she was injured and suffering. He was contemplating what to do next when his iPhone rang. The caller ID showed no name, just a number, and a local number. Was it the same number which had called before and he hadn't answered? He had to hand it to whomever it was, she or he was being persistent. Nothing else to do, so I might as well answer, he thought.

"Hello, Parker Williams speaking."

"Why didn't you answer the first time I called?"

He couldn't believe it. Was it really Beth? "Beth, is it you? Are you o.k.? Where are you?"

"That's three questions and, if I remember correctly, you allowed me only two so which one don't you want me to answer? Yes, it's really me and I'm o.k., but I would dearly love to have someone take this slimy monster off my hands so I can get a shower somewhere and something to eat. I'm grubby and hungry."

"Beth, I'm so relieved. I was so worried. Are you sure you're o.k.?"

"When you didn't answer my earlier call, I called information for the Sheriff's Office and also for Janet VanKampen's office. I'm using Medina's phone, but neither number was in his phone. Can you believe that? Wouldn't you think a Sheriff's deputy would have the phone numbers for his own office plus the other law enforcement agencies in the area? I haven't heard back yet from Marilyn or Janet, so if you want to beat them to the punch and arrest Medina, you better come quickly. Hold it, the phone is ringing. I better answer it. Who knows who might be calling Medina. Maybe some of his drug buddies. He told me about his drug operation along with a whole lot of other things. Quite a guy. I'll tell you all about it later. I need to answer this call. By the way, I'm with Medina in an equipment shed at the golf course."

Before he could tell her how close he must be to her, the call ended. Equipment shed. So that was the type of shed. And here at the country club. Near, but oh so far. He drove around the back of the main building to a gravel two-wheel track which headed out onto the golf course. After a few minutes, he saw a metal shed with several large riding lawn mowers outside. This had to be the shed, he concluded. Parking his 4Runner, he ran to the shed, as fast as he could, aiming for a small door on its side. Opening the door, he entered the shed and almost began laughing at the spectacle before him.

CHAPTER 67

Friday Afternoon
4:45 p.m.
Main Lounge, West Park Hospital, Cody, Wyoming

Janet had been shocked to learn from Cynthia that Beth Richardson had called the office in Billings. Janet assumed Beth had called to tell Janet she had escaped from Medina. The call back telephone number Beth had left wasn't familiar to Janet and it couldn't be Beth's cell phone since Beth's cell phone was being held at Marilyn Evenhouse's office as evidence in the Valentine murder. The number had a local area code suggesting that Beth had somehow obtained a cell phone from a local resident or was calling from somewhere local using a landline phone. Calling the number, Janet wasn't surprised to hear Beth's voice but she was surprised by what she said.

"You are calling Deputy Sheriff Carlos Medina but this is Beth Richardson, not Carlos Medina, answering."

"Beth, it's Janet Vankampen. What a pleasant surprise. Are you o.k.?"

"Janet, thanks for calling back. I'm fine. A little grubby and hungry, but other than that I'm not the worse for wear. I have something here you want and I'm anxious for you to have him. He told me he killed Valentine just past Pahaska Tepee, so he belongs to you since he killed Valentine within Yellowstone."

"I'd be delighted to take Medina off your hands," replied Janet. "Tell me where you are and Leo and I will both come."

"Janet, please don't take this personally, but I'm going to wait for Parker to arrive before I tell you where Medina and I are hanging out. Don't worry, he isn't going anywhere. He's somewhat incapacitated at the present moment. An ambulance isn't necessary but you may want to have him checked over by a doc, especially his face and eyes."

"Beth, this isn't the time for us to argue. Just allow me to say that Parker is operating on his own. I withdrew his authorization some time ago. He's only an ordinary citizen without any authorization. He can't arrest anyone. He has no idea how to handle a killer like Medina. It would be better if Leo and I handled Medina."

"I'll remind Parker about his having no FBI authorization, but I doubt he'll care. I certainly don't. He isn't interested in arresting Medina. That's for you to do. All I know is he was the only person that stuck with me through thick and thin, so now I want him to be the first to experience the fruit of his labors and have the first crack at Medina. You'll get your chance with Medina, I promise. I'll call you soon."

Medina began to moan again as the shot she had given him after subduing him with the bear spray, which she had taken from under the front seat of Jessica's Explorer when Medina had left her alone for several seconds while he cleaned the area around the mattress in the shed. Medina had been so intent on what he thought was Beth's willingness to engage in sexual activity with him that he had turned his attention away from her for several seconds. A few seconds was enough time for her to get the bear spray from the holder under the front seat, get close to Medina, pull the pin, and spray him in the face. Bear spray was meant to turn away a charging bear. It acted like mace on steroids. Medina never had a chance. He went berserk, screaming and clutching at his eyes. It was easy for Beth to get the key to the handcuffs from his front pants pocket and cuff him to a large lawnmower in the shed. A shot of pain killer and another of Benadryl, which were standard fare in the medical kits carried in every National Park Service vehicle, and Medina was off in la-la land. The Benadryl must be wearing off since Medina was starting to move. If he became too active, another dose of bear spray would keep him in check, although she wouldn't blast him full force. She didn't want to possibly damage his eyes permanently. She'd only give him a short blast making sure to stay away from directly spraying into his eyes. At least enough to subdue him so she could administer another dose of Benadryl if she needed to do so. If that didn't do the trick, she could always use Medina's gun to keep him at bay. The sound of a vehicle stopping outside the shed signaled the arrival of Parker, she assumed. Might as well give him something to remember. She walked over to Medina and pushed him to the ground.

CHAPTER 68

Friday Afternoon
4:50 p.m.
Equipment Shed behind the 4th Green, Olive Green Golf and Country Club, Cody, Wyoming

He didn't know whether to keep staring at the scene before him or rush over and take her in his arms. She may have said she was grubby, but to him she looked magnificent. Hair disheveled; her uniform wrinkled and dirtied almost beyond recognition; streaks of dirt on her face; Beth had never appeared more beautiful to him than at this moment. There she stood with on foot on the chest of Carlos Medina, her arm raised high in a gesture of triumph, and standing straight with the look of a conquering gladiator. Best of all was the huge smile gracing her dirt-streaked face. "How long are you going to stand there before you come over here and give me the embrace I deserve? I sure could use it," she said, in a strong tone of voice.

Ever the humorist, he thought, as he rushed to embrace her. Hugging tightly, he felt her body tremble and the sobs began to wrack her. Feeling totally inadequate, he could only manage to say repeatedly," It's all o.k. now. It's all over." Her sobs slowly became less until they were holding each other in silence. Her face rose to meet his in a kiss which was intense, yet gentle. Their intimacy was broken by a moan from Medina who was struggling to sit. For the first time since entering the shed, Parker looked at Medina. Medina's face was swollen in places and covered with red splotches. His eyes appeared to be swollen shut. He obviously couldn't see much, if anything, since he seemed to not notice Parker's presence. "I'd love to continue our embrace," said Beth, "but I vote for another time and place. I think we need to get some medical attention for our friend and we should call in the troops and let them take over. You with me or would you prefer to start again where we left off?"

269

Laughing, he replied, "You can't guess? I would much prefer to start again but I agree a different time and place would add something. Let's get the troops here so we can finally put this nightmare behind. I say we let Janet know where she can find Medina and then we take off before she gets here. I'm sure you'd love to take a shower and get something to eat. Should I call Janet?"

"Sure, you call her. She's expecting a call. I called her when I was waiting for you to arrive. I thought she should know Medina was no longer a threat and was under control. I didn't tell here where we were, however. I wanted you to be the first one here. Frankly, I wanted some time alone with you to emotionally discharge, so to speak, before the circus begins. Call it being selfish, but I wanted to be with you, not a bunch of hyped-up cops or FBI agents." They again came into each other's arms kissing again as deeply as before. His feelings were strong and he wanted their intimacy to not end. But he knew it must, at least for now. Ending the embrace, he said, "Thanks for thinking about me. I, too, don't want to share you with anybody right now." Taking his iPhone, he called Janet's cell phone. After three rings, she answered.

"Parker. Beth called. She's o.k. and she has Medina. Marilyn told me Vanessa told everything about how she and Medina planned the killing of Valentine and the framing of Beth. Vanessa also said there is a shed Medina used at the golf course. Leo and I are on our way there now. I'm hoping to hear from Beth so we know precisely where she and Medina are located so we can have medical personnel check her out. Make sure she's really o.k."

"Janet, I assure you, Beth is fine. She doesn't need medical attention but Medina does. To be specific, I'm with Beth and Medina right now. We're at the Country Club in an equipment shed behind the 4th green on the golf course. Medina was sprayed with bear spray. His face is a mess. In particular, tell the medical people to pay attention to his eyes."

"You say you're with Medina? How did you find him? Did you have to use your weapon?"

"Janet, relax. I didn't have to do a thing to subdue Medina. Beth did that before I arrived."

"You're kidding me, right? How did she do that?"

"Janet, I'll tell you everything later. Beth will as well. Just so you know, I really don't care about the authorization. You can have it back as far as

I'm concerned. I've had enough investigating to last a lifetime." Winking and smiling at Beth, he continued, "I've much more important things on my mind right now and I plan to do some personal stuff in the near future. Now, I suggest you, or whomever is authorized, get here to arrest Medina. You will find him handcuffed with the key to the cuffs and his gun nearby him but far enough away where he can't get to them unless he's Houdini. I know you want and need to interview the star witness, but you'll have to wait to do that. Your star witness and I won't be here when you arrive and please don't try to find us. Beth will contact you when she's ready. I'm sure you'll have enough on your plate to occupy you for the next day or two. One last thing. It would be nice if Marilyn Evenhouse received some credit and positive publicity out of this. Have fun, Janet. Talk with you later."

"Very good, Dr. Williams," Beth said in a somewhat laughing voice, "aren't we protective and assertive I might add. I feel like you might just want me all to yourself for awhile and I don't mind at all. If we're going to get away by ourselves, we need to blow this place in the next minute or so. Otherwise, your girlfriend . . . oops, sorry, I forgot my promise . . . will be here and neither of us will be able to get away. We'll leave the Explorer here and take your 4Runner. By the way, you're very observant. I very much need a shower and then a dinner, a huge dinner with all the extras. Let's make sure Medina is securely cuffed and then let's go."

They both checked to make sure the handcuffs were secure. Placing the key to the handcuffs and Medina's gun near to where he sat propped against the lawnmower, they walked hand-in-hand to the 4Runner. He opened the passenger door for her and then went around the back and slid behind the steering wheel.

"Before we take off, please come here for one more minute," she said. He leaned over across the middle console. Placing her hands gently on his cheeks, she continued, "Thank you for believing in me. During the terrible parts of the past several hours, I vowed that if I got out alive, I wasn't going to procrastinate any longer regarding my true feelings about you and about us. If it's o.k. with you, I'd like to take my shower at a wonderful place I know about on Duck Creek. I bet there's even some food in the refrigerator. We'll lock all the doors, disconnect the phones, pull down the shades, keep on only a minimum number of lights, and leave cell phones in the 4Runner, which we'll park away from the place so anyone coming by will think no one is there. I know I don't have a nightgown and I for sure don't have any clothes to wear while I'm washing and ironing this dirty uniform, but as long as it doesn't bother you, I'm not going to let either of those bother me either." Kissing him, she continued, "Now, let's get out of here before it's too late."

POSTLUDE

Monday Morning
10:00 a.m.
Conference Room in the Yellowstone Administration Building, Yellowstone
National Park, Mammoth Hot Springs, Montana

Janet VanKampen placed the recorder on the conference room table. Marilyn Evenhouse had done likewise only a minute or two earlier. Beth and Parker were already sitting on one side of the table waiting for Janet and Marilyn to adjust their respective recorders. They were using the conference room in Yellowstone's administration building. The room was adjacent to the Superintendent's office suite and only a few doors away from Beth's office. Reporters from the Cody, Billings, Bozeman, Livingston, and Jackson newspapers, television news anchors from NBC, CBS, and ABC affiliate television stations in Billings, Bozeman, and Idaho Falls, Idaho, representatives of several radio stations, and Kelly Moore, Director of Public Relations for Yellowstone and Editor of Yellowstone's monthly newsletter, *Yellowstone in Perspective,* were outside the building awaiting a media conference where Beth, Janet, and Marilyn would be present. They had agreed to provide information and answer questions about the apprehension of Carlos Medina and his arrest on the charge of murdering Michael Valentine and Becky Greenbrier, and kidnapping and threatening Beth Richardson. Janet had asked Parker not to appear at the media conference and he had readily agreed. Janet and he agreed it was best if his involvement in the Valentine murder investigation and his pursuit of Medina be kept under wraps as much as possible.

Three nights and two days had passed since Janet and Leo Dirkse had found Carlos Medina handcuffed to a large lawnmower in the equipment shed behind the 4th green of the Olive Glenn Golf and Country Club in Cody. Beth and Parker were not there when Janet and Lou arrived and try as she might, Janet had been unable to reach either Beth or Parker

Friday night and all day Saturday and Sunday until Beth called her around 8:30 p.m. last night. Janet had sent text messages and e-mails, and left several voice messages on Beth and Parker's cell phones. Janet had driven to Parker's home to determine if he might be there in seclusion. The thought did enter her mind that Beth might be there with him and the feelings of jealousy swept over her even during this stressful situation when her superiors in the FBI's Regional Office in Denver, Colorado, were increasing the pressure on her to have her provide the media with another "isn't the FBI wonderful?—look what we've done for you" story. Parker's home had been locked and all the window shades down. Only a light on the main floor shone through the shades. There were no lights showing from the second floor. Parker's 4Runner was no place to be seen. Janet had looked in the garage. No other vehicles were there either. She looked in his mailbox, which was located where his driveway met the gravel road from U.S. highway 191 and saw mail from the past several days was undisturbed. She had contacted the Montana office of AT&T and requested a run-down of Parker's phone calls since Friday evening. No calls had been made from his home or his iPhone. She concluded he wasn't in his home which meant Beth wasn't there either. She had asked Bruce Dickson to have someone from his office check Beth's apartment. Bruce reported her neighbors, living on either side of Beth and across the hall, hadn't seen her for several days nor had they heard any activity or sound coming from her apartment. Janet learned that Beth had sent a text message to Ryan Belgrade telling him not to expect her in the office on Monday morning and asking him to inform the Superintendent. Frustrated, Janet had returned to Billings. She realized she'd been outsmarted and didn't like it. Even more troubling was the recurring thought of Beth and Parker possibly being together and having the opportunity to develop their relationship further while Janet could only wonder where they were and what they were doing.

All that was in the past. What counted now was that Beth was here and ready to recount her time with Carlos Medina. "I think we're all set and ready to begin," said Janet. "Marilyn, are you ready?"

"I'm as ready as you are," replied Marilyn. "You ask your questions first, Janet, and I'll follow with any questions I might have which you haven't covered."

"Works for me," responded Janet. "Beth, are you all set?"

"Before you begin with your questions, I'd like to know all you've learned over the past forty-eight hours or so about Medina, Vanessa, Victor Barrozo, and Becky Greenbrier," replied Beth.

"I'd like that too," chimed in Parker.

"I guess we can do that, can't we Marilyn? So you know, we're still awaiting some information from the Border Patrol in Tucson, Arizona, so we don't know yet all we need to know about Medina's drug supply and distribution networks," responded Janet.

"That's o.k. I think Beth and I are more interested in the connections among Medina, Vanessa, Barrozo, and Becky, and how Beth fit into all of it," said Parker.

"Do you want the short or long version? Some things I can't tell you because the investigation is continuing," replied Janet. "As I said, we're awaiting information from the Border Patrol. There's also investigative work underway in Mexico, in cooperation with the Mexican authorities. Other than that, I can give you the short or long of what we've learned."

Turning to look at Beth, Parker said, "It's up to you, Beth. You want all the details or those that involve you?"

"I don't need to know all the details," replied Beth, "but I do want to know how Becky fit into all this. She was a Yellowstone colleague of mine and even though we weren't friends, I won't feel right without knowing what forces were at work to cause her to be killed."

"Sure enough," responded Janet, "the short version. Carlos Medina was employed by Victor Barrozo as the security heavy-hitter in a media promotion company when Valentine and Barrozo were partners and co-owners. When Barrozo's daughter went missing, or should I say kidnapped, which most people knowledgeable about the situation believe, Medina was in charge of an internal investigation to find her. The Chicago police and the FBI office in Chicago were the official designated investigators, but according to the records provided by them, neither put much stock in the kidnapping scenario. They believed it was a routine teenager-fed-up-with-being-controlled-and takes-off-scenario, so not much was done by either the police or the FBI to find Barrozo's daughter. Barrozo, on the other hand, pushed the kidnapping theme. Medina, for whatever reason, probably wanting to please his boss, pursued Valentine with vigor and attempted to pin a kidnapping charge on him, even lacking evidence to do so. Medina did all he could, legally and illegally, to place the blame on Valentine.

"So, the connection between Medina and Valentine goes back several years," said Parker, "but why did Medina want to kill Valentine?"

"When Valentine became sole owner of the media corporation, he abruptly fired Medina, according to other employees of the corporation that were working there at the same time Medina was. Apparently, Valentine did so without providing Medina with any warning or severance pay. Medina found himself out on the street. At the time, Medina was divorced and had custody of two small children. He filed for unemployment but was turned down because Valentine's lawyers said that Medina had voluntarily resigned his job. Money and skilled lawyers won out, I'm sad to say. Because he didn't have an income, Medina was forced to depend on welfare. His ex-wife saw an opportunity to tell the custody judge that Medina was incapable of supporting the children. Medina lost custody of the children. According to sources interviewed by Chicago FBI agents, Medina made it known he was going to get Valentine if it was the last thing he did."

Shaking her head in understanding, Beth said, "So what else is new? Lawyers and money win out again. Valentine carried a grudge, I take it, and when the opportunity to get to Valentine presented itself in the person of Vanessa Cortez, he took advantage of it."

"You got that right," responded Janet.

"I now understand the connection between Valentine, Barrozo, and Medina," said Parker. "Vanessa. I think I know the connection, but let's hear what you've learned."

"Vanessa and Medina met each other initially at the bar area of the Erma Hotel in Cody. As you probably can surmise, they became sexually involved, utilizing the equipment shed Medina took you to Beth. Vanessa told us she told Medina about her past, in particular the Miss Illinois Pageant and her obsession with getting her revenge for you screwing her out of winning the pageant, as she put it. She told Medina you had slept with one of the judges in exchange for his vote. Vanessa told us she happened to mention Valentine's name to Medina and he, as Vanessa described it, went ballistic about how Valentine had treated him, was responsible for Medina losing custody of his children, hurt Barrozo's daughter for life, and the rest of the stuff I've already told you."

"Imagine that," said Parker, "a random comment by Vanessa about Michael Valentine set this whole plan of theirs into action and resulted in the death of two people. Had she not mentioned him, Medina wouldn't have had any thoughts about using Vanessa to get to Valentine."

"All we have so far is Vanessa's story," responded Janet. "Medina isn't talking, at least not yet. When he does, which he eventually will, he may tell a much different story. It really doesn't matter who first told whom about Valentine."

"Janet, what's still missing for me," said Beth, "is how Vanessa knew I was living and working in Yellowstone and how Medina and Vanessa lured Valentine to Cody the evening of the Assistant Secretary's speech and dinner at the Buffalo Bill Historical Center."

"Remember Beth, all we have to go on so far is what Vanessa has told us. She may be telling us only bits and pieces. There may be things she isn't telling us. There could be distortions or untruths in her story, but it is all we have to go on for now other than the report from the Chicago FBI office and what Leo Dirkse and his agents have uncovered."

"I understand the limitations," responded Beth, "but tell me what Vanessa said and whatever the FBI has uncovered."

"Vanessa told us she knew you wanted to have a career in the National Park Service. Apparently, you mentioned your career ambitions during one of the interviews you gave during the Miss Illinois Pageant. Vanessa googled you and learned you had recently been promoted to Associate Superintendent of Yellowstone. She came to Yellowstone and obtained the part-time job in the Food Distribution Center, supposedly to be able to monitor you and determine when best to take you down, as she put it. By the way, when we asked her what she meant by 'take you down', she smiled and said, 'that's for me to know and you to figure out'. After she met Medina, he contacted Barrozo. He told Barrozo that Medina had arranged for a beautiful woman to be available waiting for Barrozo in his house, outside of Gardiner, if Barrozo was interested. A sidebar, should you wonder, is that according to Vanessa, Medina and she didn't spend any time together in Barrozo's house. Medina felt he would be violating the trust Barrozo placed in him if he did. Go figure that one. Anyway, Medina got Barrozo to find out where Valentine was living in Evanston, Illinois, a suburb of Chicago and passed on the information to Medina. Another sidebar. Vanessa said Barrozo knew nothing about Medina's and her plan to kill Valentine. So far, we haven't been able to pin any charges of complicity to commit murder on Barrozo. He has cooperated fully with us. We will continue to investigate him, but it looks like he really didn't know what was going on."

"I'm still waiting to learn how Valentine got sucked into coming to Cody," said Beth.

"Once Medina knew where Valentine lived, he contacted the Evanston police department. Using his position as Deputy Sheriff, he was able to obtain Valentine's telephone number and e-mail address. According to Vanessa, Medina them used Vanessa to make an anonymous call, probably using a pre-paid, throw-away cell phone, to call Valentine and leave a message telling him you were in Yellowstone. She also sent him an e-mail, using a computer in the Cody public library, telling him you often attended events at the Buffalo Bill Historical Center which involved Yellowstone stuff. Valentine must have wanted desperately to see you. According to Vanessa, he responded immediately to an e-mail address Vanessa gave him which Medina had established for doing his drug distribution business. Valentine wanted to know the dates and times you would be attending events at the Center. Once Valentine responded, Medina and Vanessa knew they had Valentine hooked. Since the Center publishes its events well in advance, they knew the dates and times. What they didn't know was whether or not you would be attending the events involving Yellowstone stuff."

"I'm following it all so far," said Beth, "but how did Valentine know I would be at the Center last Sunday evening and how did Medina know Valentine would be there?"

"Enter the marvelous information tool called the internet and your own, I don't mean you personally Beth, but Yellowstone's own internal newsletter. The visit of the Assistant Secretary and your being Yellowstone's representative was all over Yellowstone's website and listed as an upcoming event in the newsletter. Remember, your interview with Kelly Moore? Front page in the newsletter. Vanessa saw it and told Medina. He had an anonymous e-mail sent from a computer at the Cody library to Valentine telling him to look on Yellowstone's website for interesting information. That's how Valentine happened to be at the Center last Sunday evening, the same evening you were there."

"After the event ended, Medina must have been waiting for Valentine," said Parker. "Somehow, Medina got the best of Valentine and was able to inject the suscostrin into Valentine's body. If I remember correctly, the autopsy report said Valentine had a needle mark on the back of his upper right arm. It could be that Medina was hidden behind the driver's seat in Valentine's car and was able to give the shot into Valentine's arm from behind him."

"That seems plausible," replied Janet, "although we won't know for sure until Medina starts talking."

Beth asked, "Did Medina kill Valentine inside or outside Yellowstone's boundary?"

For the first time, Marilyn Evenhouse spoke, "We don't know. The only person that knows for sure is Carlos. Frankly, I'm not going to make an issue out of it. Janet and Leo have been gracious to give me credit for apprehending Carlos, which I don't deserve." Looking directly at Beth, she continued, "and you have been very understanding and gracious for not bad-mouthing me or the Sheriff's Department for our horrible blunder in arresting you and mistreating you as if you were a criminal capable of murder. I still can't believe I was suckered into believing Carlos. If I had to guess, Carlos killed Valentine at a convenient place somewhere along the highway before entering Yellowstone. However, Carlos wanted to make it look like the murder occurred in Yellowstone since he knew the FBI would then have jurisdiction and it would pursue the murderer with the full resources of the FBI. Besides, Vanessa and he wanted to frame you so he wanted to make it look like the killing occurred inside Yellowstone. By doing so, they thought it would point the finger at a Yellowstone employee at least that was their thinking according to Vanessa."

"Marilyn, please don't beat up yourself over what happened to me," responded Beth. "The evidence was there. Any law enforcement official worth their salt would have done what you did when confronted with the evidence before you. The fact I couldn't prove where I spent Sunday night following the event at the Center only contributed to making me look guilty. I should have remembered the satellite images and pictures associated with the monitoring and tracking of the Slough Creek wolf pack much earlier than I did. If I had, you would have known the evidence was manufactured and Medina would have been placed on the defensive. Ann Vogelzang wouldn't have been shot and her career wouldn't be jeopardized. I'm hoping for her full recovery."

"The docs are quite optimistic she will regain full use of her arm and shoulder," replied Marilyn. "Ann told me she didn't feel right about how Medina was handling the investigation, but stupid me, I ignored her. Doesn't say much for my competence level, does it?"

"Marilyn, don't even go there," responded Parker. "You're a very competent Sheriff that made a legitimate, understandable mistake. Now, no more about it." Looking toward Janet, he said, "How did Becky Greenbrier fit into all of this? Why was she killed?"

"The Yellowstone grapevine brought Vanessa and Becky together. Vanessa learned about Becky's unhappiness with not getting the position of Associate Superintendent, your current position, Beth. Vanessa sought out Becky and together they shared their anti-Beth Richardson feelings. Vanessa told Becky about Medina and the plan to frame you for Valentine's murder if some evidence incriminating you could be obtained and placed at the murder scene. Becky, Medina, and Vanessa met on a few occasions to decide what could be obtained in the way of evidence. Becky volunteered, according to Vanessa, to obtain the evidence, namely your hair, your shoes, and the button from your uniform jacket. Of course, either Medina or Becky or both saw an opportunity to engage in some 'partying', as Medina called his sexual activities. He provided some drugs to enhance their 'partying' and Becky found herself in deeper than she probably ever wanted to be. Becky's first mistake was getting involved with Medina in the first place. Her second mistake was telling Medina about her scheme of taking Yellowstone entrance fee cash. Medina blackmailed her for a portion of the cash she skimmed by threatening to send an anonymous letter to Yellowstone's Law Enforcement and Security Office with a copy to the Superintendent, exposing Becky as the perpetrator of the fee cash scheme."

"All, or a portion, of the $10,000 Jessica found in Becky's apartment," said Parker, "I assume was money Becky had accumulated from her fee cash scheme or did Medina pay her for obtaining the stuff to use to frame Beth?"

"We don't know the answer to that yet," responded Janet. "Maybe some of both." When Medina gets around to talking, we'll learn the answer. Maybe there was some pay-for-sex money thrown into the pot as well. Only Medina knows the answers."

You said you think Barrozo is clean," said Beth. "Why the big home in Paradise Valley? Why did he come out here so often? Who was the woman he was seen eating dinner with at the Gardiner Steakhouse?"

"Baroozo told us he rented the house so he could test whether he wanted to have a retreat place in a totally different location in the country. He felt he needed to be around it often to make a fair judgment about whether such a place made sense for him. He said the woman was Becky. Medina had arranged for Barrozo to meet Becky, probably trying to suck Barrozo into the plan and then turn around and blackmail him. We had to push Barrozo for him to admit that Becky tried to seduce him the two times they had dinner together at the Gardiner Steakhouse. If Becky told Barrozo about the plan to kill Valentine and frame you, Beth, we only have Barrozo's word that he knew nothing about it. Unless we learn something different, we are going to accept what he told us as the truth."

"I'm satisfied for now," said Parker. In a sarcastic tone of voice, he continued, "I think the three of you should meet with your adoring media."

Giving him a light punch on the shoulder, Beth said, "Maybe you should join us after all. All those media clowns will wonder how three women, with no man present, could have pulled this off. Capturing Medina and freeing me, without a male presence certainly couldn't be accomplished. You want to join us and play Mr. Macho Man?"

"No thanks," replied Parker, "those media goons will fawn all over you three. Sort of a modern day Charlie's Angels. I'm perfectly content to have you three share the spotlight. I'll stay here and watch your performance on television."

"Before we go meet the media," said Marilyn, "I have one question for you, Beth. How did you subdue Carlos? I know you used the bear spray to spray Carlos in the face, but how did you trick him in the first place into allowing you the freedom to get the bear spray from under the driver's seat in Jessica's Explorer?"

With a huge smile and winking at Parker, Beth responded in a laughing voice, "We all know Medina was, using politically correct language, over-sexed and wanting to dominate women. So, I used a pair of assets, which we woman have, to momentarily distract him. If you're wondering what I'm referring to, I bet Parker can clue you in. Now, let's go meet the media."

Lightning Source UK Ltd.
Milton Keynes UK
UKHW010147071220
374696UK00001B/53